# BEYOND THE PALE

*'Beyond the Pale' is a reference to the other side of the
boundary fence between the dominion of the civilized British
and the uncivilized Irish in the 14th Century.*

This is book one in the 'Robyn's Cage Trilogy'.

E. McLean

# Front Matter

Edited by

Lin White
Coinlea Services
www.coinlea.co.uk

Illustration

Rossario Rizzo @ fotolia

# Dedication

For Sarah McLean who weaved magic with her own stories.

Special thanks to Arpy, Melek, Kerry and Brian for excellent feedback and comments.

# Table of Contents

Map

# Partial Map of Wellorsland (Not to scale)

Dintropolis

Shuttle

Outlands are all areas outside cities and the Causeways

Transport Causeways

Transport Causeway

OUTLANDS

Lontropolis

Cartropolis

This map shows only three of the cities where the story takes place. Cities are linked by high speed causeways and inner city stations and class boundaries.

# Class Structure

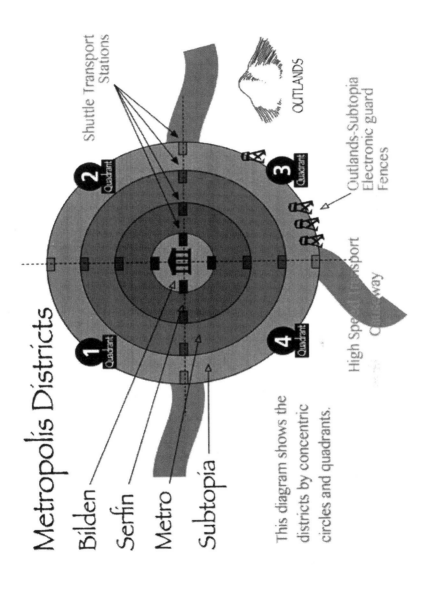

**Metropolis Districts**

Bilden

Serfin

Metro

Subtopia

This diagram shows the districts by concentric circles and quadrants.

Shuttle Transport Stations

OUTLANDS

Outlands-Subtopia Electronic guard Fences

High Speed Transport Causeway

1 Quadrant

2 Quadrant

3 Quadrant

4 Quadrant

# CHAPTER ONE

## Teenage Kicks

There is an old sepia movie running of myself in Church, watching my Mother's coffin slip silently away behind heavy velvet drapes. The Minister is frowning down at me; I feel exposed in the front pew and a bead of sweat runs down my nose. A bell rings close by and I fidget uncomfortably. I want to stay here; the school is too far from Mum. The minister morphs into the headmaster and beckons me forward with beady eyes and a twisted finger. There is no escape. I squeeze out of the pew. Once in the nave I cannot decide which way to go.

Everyone turns to look at me and I look down. My feet are covered with a sticky red substance, a solitary colour in the dull flat panacea, and I struggle to run towards the exit as the bright goo threatens to drag me back. The movie breaks and the torn sequence of pictures flaps and flutters on the spinning reel as the screen is flooded with brilliant white and I burst through the church doors.

The bell is insistent and changes to a shout as I drag myself up from my sleep basement. The sleep basement is a confusing place; mostly it is my sanctuary, warm and comforting, but occasionally it harbours the night terrors. Going there is my Russian roulette of dreams.

I shudder, smack my phone to stop the tenacious bell, and pull the pillow over my head to avoid the slabs of sunlight muscling between my curtains, trying to vaporize me with heat and light. The smells drifting through the window gap tell me it's a warm spring morning. Wet days sound soggy; dry days feel like sandpaper in my eyes. But warm spring mornings smell like heaven, and I stick my nose out from under my pillow and sniff like a rodent, wondering if today is going to be a good day for foraging without being snatched and eaten by an opportunistic eagle.

"Robyn. It's time to wake up. We leave in an hour." My Father is yelling from downstairs. "We have a house to move." The painful, shouted fact jolts the remaining sleepiness from my body and makes me groan aloud. I don't want to go anywhere. I slither onto the floor, push myself up and stumble to the shower, mulling over the sudden change in my future. Most of my life is packed in cardboard boxes, on a lorry headed north, an Artic' heading towards the Arctic. I imagine ice in my blood before I reach the shower.

My close friends were tearful when I told them Dad and I were moving north, some four hundred miles, and to a senior school in Scotland that no one had heard of. All my life, I have been at school in Guildford, Surrey, England; I know nowhere else except cities and schools arising out of descriptions in books.

Some of my friends in the athletic club seemed more worried for the relay team and winning the local running leagues; I was junior track champion last year.

Between the track and the gym I am obsessed with fitness. Martial arts, kick boxing, fencing and an underwater sport called Octopush take up most of my spare time. Octopush involves two teams wearing mask and snorkels, fighting for possession of a lead puck on the pool bottom in order to score goals at either end. A bit like ice hockey without long sticks or air.

My astronomy club doesn't seem bothered I am leaving. We are all losers and loners there anyway, more interested in the size of our telescopes than the length of our friendships.

My best girlfriend, Carmen, keeps repeating, 'Why?' as if there must be an answer to the madness of me going away. I told her we have to move, although I don't believe it myself. Almost as much as I don't really believe she is my best friend; it's what I call image friendship. These superficial friendships that people build around themselves to complete their image.

The fencing club is the thing that I will miss most. I practice every second day, and aside from my dislike of my fencing arm getting stronger and more muscled, I love the way fencing hones my senses; it makes me sharp and quick. Fencing is probably my biggest passion. It's my only real passion. I am a sucker for the technique and the tactics that make a good swords-person great.

Until I watched a master swordsman put flight to eight opponents, I imagined that beating overwhelming odds in a sword fight was the swashbuckling fantasy of Hollywood film directors. But it's not so. With the right techniques and tactics, a master swordsman will literally run rings around a group of less experienced fighters.

As at the majority of fencing clubs, we fight one-on-one. So, it is mostly technique and much less about tactic. Touches on your opponent are scored automatically through the electronic kit we use. Our club has an excellent reputation and I am near the top of the rankings for my age.

To be good you have to appreciate that fencing is an art as well as a historic method of fighting. There is a beauty in remaining calm and in control, defending yourself, until you have the opportunity to strike. There is precision and eloquence in one-to-one fencing. And there is something fair in this type of duel. Both opponents enter the competition understanding that it is about their ability and technique more than luck or opportunity. Fencing is a big part of my life because these elements reflect my personality.

I have fenced at the Royal Guildford since I was six years old and will miss my club too much.

Partially out of diffidence and partially out of dissonance, I have not looked to see if there is a club near my new home and school. I admit there is a stubborn streak running through me.

It's difficult to understand why my Father has done this. He said, 'we need to move on', 'it's a fresh start'. Not for me. He says it will help us forget. Frustration bubbles up behind my grief. How can a new life and a new school be good for any seventeen year old, in the middle of her studies and a quarter of the way through my preparation for my qualifications? I lost count of the times a teacher questioned me on the sanity of moving when I was part way through. They stopped short of criticizing my Dad, and I guessed that was a little bit due to respect and a lot due to their knowledge of my parental circumstances.

I don't want to forget. I told my Father. He told me he didn't mean 'forget-forget'. I shouted at him, told him I want to 'remember-remember' and I called him a moron.

We lost Mum almost a year ago. Well, to be exact, three hundred and three days. Dad cannot pass the bridge where her car went off the road without getting upset. But the long way round to the city is no less painful. When you avoid grief, somehow you remember it more. Trying to forget is a dead end. You cannot avoid grief by memory detour. It's why we build memorials out of rock and marble.

Mum was my best friend and my sister, my rock in an ocean of teenage angst, my guiding light as I prepared myself for maiden voyage into the world. The saddest thing is, I only realize this now and all the things I never told her are stuck like a lump in my chest. Mum wasn't there to see me turn seventeen; she missed my birthday by two weeks. Dad gave me the gold bracelet that she had bought me a few weeks before she left us. The inscription was typical Mum and very apt, 'To the moon and back'. Memories from years ago, of her sitting with me in the garden, pointing out the man on the moon, flooded my senses like it was yesterday.

The moon seems so far away now and I no longer see his smile.

The other irreverent reason for my detour prejudice is my lousy sense of direction. Like my Mum, my preference is for doing things in straight lines. I am a 'shortest distance between two lines' sort of girl. Somehow life feels so much better when things are simple.

Mum originally trained as a Nurse, then as a Prosthetics Engineer, combining the mechanics of false limbs with the medical aspects of recovery. Technology meets physiology, she called it. She fitted limbs on toddlers and retirees with an equal level of compassion and empathy. Mum often had years of regular contact with one patient as limbs had to be replaced; people got older and grew bigger. Her regulars loved her. Mum is, I mean was, special.

Mum and Dad had an incredible relationship. Although they often disagreed, it was with good nature. When Dad came up with a hare-brained or eccentric idea, he'd test it on her. She would say 'Forget-about-it bozo' and Dad would laugh out loud until his sides hurt. They had each found their soul mate and best friend and maintained it in marriage. Mum was a master planner: details, timing, sequence, and preparation. In contrast Dad was master disaster: clumsy, forgetful, ill prepared and badly timed.

The relationship between Dad and me has mostly been good, but we are not as close as I was with Mum. Dad tries too hard. And when my Father irritates me, I have to remind myself that he is trying to please me; often his actions make me want to scream instead.

It doesn't help that he has a stupid nickname for me, 'couscous'. Dad claims couscous was my first word, when everyone else was saying DaDa. Mum tried to tell me he was just teasing. But I can get mega moody with him when he winds me up.

When he teased me in my early teens I'd tell Mum I hated him. Hate is a bit harsh, she'd say; it's 'love-hating'. So 'love-hating' became my fealty to childhood and a bridge between adolescence and maturity. It reminds me that we love each other and I have to be more tolerant, especially now. But it makes me sad to think that Mum has gone without knowing that my relationship with Dad is okay. I look back on my petulant early teens and I don't like what I see. Although I can be hypercritical with myself, it's hard to know if my self-perception is fair and balanced. Others often tell me that I am exceptionally mature for my age; I wish I felt it. Life can be so confusing. I wonder if it's only me who often feels out of kilter with things going on around me.

There was a quote I read, the source being argued on a blog, and dubiously credited to Mark Twain. 'When I was a boy of fourteen, my father was so ignorant I could hardly stand to have the old man around. But when I got to be twenty-one, I was astonished at how much he had learned in seven years.' There were a number of different versions with different ages being discussed, but it didn't matter. The message was synchronistic and it eased my hackles, just a little.

I have a huge amount of sympathy for Dad. He has lost his soul mate. I am sure he and my mum had been destined to be together. There were secrets between them that ran like an undercurrent in our small family, something that caused my Dad to worship my mother. He took her death hard.

Somehow Dad pulled himself together last week; he cooked me the first decent dinner we'd eaten for months. When he looked me straight in the eye, serving my plate, I realized everything was going to change.

Jonathan, my closest male friend and fencing partner, was sad when I told him I was leaving. But then dismissed the distance as 'just around the corner' and denied any difficulty. I recognize it as a brave face; we've known each other since first school. He hated football and I hated girl stuff, so somehow we met in the middle. Jonathan Liberio is eighteen and an orphan from Milan, without other family. He likes being around my family, and Mum and Dad always made him welcome, and organized trips and activities specifically around him. In truth they treated him more like a son.

We'd climbed trees, watched bonfires, and done Halloweens when we were younger. Later we'd gone to parties together. Or if we'd gone out with our respective male and female friends, he and I would end up chatting and thereby responsible for the two groups mingling.

My girlfriends are marshmallow in Jonathan's presence. Predictable and soppy in their cooing, they say his dark eyes are beautiful. My response is to proclaim often, and loudly, that Jonathan doesn't affect me like that. But he and I do have a private joke. I call him 'happy eyes', because his irises blaze when he is anything 'north-of-enthusiastic' about a particular cause.

Jonathan is the archetypical teenage rebel, a cliché, but 'my' cliché and personal hero. Our friendship crosses the common young adult boy-girl divide. There is nothing intimate between us, but we are physical; we hug, tickle, laugh, wrestle and rub noses as brother and sister.

Now that I am leaving him behind, will I miss something? We've never kissed. Am I leaving him to someone else? The thought makes me queasy inside. But contrarily, I don't know if I could kiss him or even if I want to.

I do know I am going to miss him at my new school.

To make matters worse, Dad's new job is Physics Teacher at the school. Dad says it doesn't matter since I don't do physics. But inside, I cringe at the thought of bumping into him at lunch, or in the common room. It will be tough, being on my best behavior because my father is a teacher, while trying to fit in, and make some new friends.

I am downstairs after forty minutes with two bags of personal items that I want to keep close. After a tea and plain croissant, eaten quickly off the side of the kitchen sink since the table has been dismantled, Dad and I get in the car and set off.

As soon as we are on the highway, I pretend to sleep. Even with my eyes closed, I sense that my Dad has turned to look at me. I feel the tension around my mouth, and I am sure he can see it. I snooze to avoid conversation.

After an hour or so, I open my eyes. Dad looks, smiles, but says nothing. I stare out of the window. The motorway miles ticking past are steadily taking me away from my roots. Somewhere up ahead is a new world, and it gets closer with each blank field or anonymous truck stop that sweeps by.

Maybe I should be excited, thinking ahead to our destination in a few hours' time; instead I see an image of my life in chaos. My past is in flames and my future is a black hole. There is no question, if I could return to the past I would. Mum would understand. Neither of us liked change very much. Like fencing, life should be familiar, comfortable and under control.

□□□□□□□□

Despite my determination to dislike it, the house is a pleasant surprise. Dad almost decided on the house over the Internet. He drove up to see it a week ago and clinched the deal in minutes. Dad told me we got it cheap, a quick sale, after the previous owner had gone abroad suddenly. My imagination ran away with me, as I thought of the possible scenarios for the man's hasty flight. I made a mental list of the best reasons for running off, from eloping to running from an assassin, before I got bored and returned to reality.

The estate agent, who greets us with the keys, ignores me. In turn, I ignore her and she writes me off as a moody teenager. So while she concentrates on Dad, I get to explore on my own. The place has been 'deep cleaned and redecorated, to walk-in condition, as agreed', I hear her say as I go ahead of them. I think for a second that she is flirting with him, but it might be sales talk; who knows these days? I had a couple of boyfriends, between fifteen and seventeen, but nothing more serious than dates and movies. The exotic fragrance of young love is still a figment of my fertile imagination and something that only blooms perfectly and timely in romantic books.

The lounge and kitchen overlook a spacious garden stretching out back into some trees and a summery looking meadow bordered by patchy carpets of wild blue flowers. I think they might be bluebells, but I am only guessing based on general knowledge. I decide I like the look and must go check them out later.

On the grass, close to the patio, sit five large ugly gnomes that the previous owner left. They are crying out for rude names and I promise myself to christen them. But perhaps they were from the original famous seven and Snow-White had left, taking Happy and Bashful with her.

The house has two bedrooms, which makes it sound small; it isn't. My bedroom stretches across a half of the top floor, with windows to the front and back, walk in wardrobe and a luxurious private bathroom. Dad seems to be trying to make things as easy as possible for me. I suspect he picked the house for my bedroom, not for the gnomes.

Downstairs Dad has his own study, cum small library, alongside the lounge. In the basement, I find a games room, laundry room and a small gym with all my favourite gym machines and a judo mat. I look. They are brand-new. I shake my head and almost smile at Dad's determination.

The back garden has an ancient gnarled oak with a beautiful tree house quite high up in the boughs. Too bad, there is no way up at the moment; it is without steps. I make a mental note to look for a ladder later.

The first shippers arrive about an hour after us in the much slower lorries and we'd probably overtaken one during one of their numerous tea stops. They had packed most of our old house, I suspect because Dad couldn't face it; almost every item would have a memory of Mum attached somehow. The other lorry would be close behind with the beds and wardrobes.

Of course, to the shippers it's a simple unemotional process. Everything packed safely in boxes and decamped to the correct rooms on arrival. For the first couple of hours, four men carry in the furniture and reassemble beds and tables. Then they unpack all the boxes and replace the books on the bookcases, food in the fridge and medicines in the medicine cabinets, much as they had been in the old house. Dad guides them and generally gets in the way.

Once my curtains are up and my ridiculous super-king-sized bed is assembled, I insist on being left alone to finish my room. Making my bed and placing my books and trophies on the shelf brings a measure of familiarity. As I open each box, I imagine the memories bursting out into the room and looking for their familiar places. A jewellery box crammed with memorabilia and glitz takes pride of place on my dressing table. My favourite books come next, including a first edition worth over eight thousand pounds that an elderly patient had given my Mum for me. Mum called him the Colonel and he was surprised by my collection of books although I'd never met him. So he gave me this special copy of 'The Adventures of Huckleberry Finn', which goes into a special glass case on my dresser.

I arrange my other collections back on my small bookcase near my bed: Dahl, Bronte, Austin, Tolstoy and Fitzgerald. The rest go into my tall bookcases on each side of the window: Alistair McLean, Sally Beauman, Anne Rice, Brian Callison, Sebastian Faulks and so many more. Every so often, I dip into a book and delay the completion of my organising by reading a few pages. Reading makes me think; it is my mental gymnastics. I prefer books to TV. Books teach, TVs leach, or is it leech? Perhaps both. And there is a difference between book words and TV words. The difference is in ownership.

Words are my precious stones; they shine and sparkle when I string them into strands of my thoughts. Great words have value, they give me room to breathe; without the right words, my mind would be a garbage dump of broken ideas and confused thoughts. In the right combination and order, a piece of word jewellery, a sentence, can give you a strength, a confidence, a pride, a feeling, that you cannot get from listening to TV.

After a few hours of sporadic hard work, I have everything unpacked and one of the shippers takes the empty boxes away. I pull on some sweats, grab some cleaning stuff and the Hoover from the kitchen and finish my bedroom.

The noise from downstairs gradually dies away as the activity becomes less in each room. They are doing last minute things like hanging pictures and re-cabling speakers. I wander around two or three times, reminding myself that this is my new home.

Overall, the house is pretty good. But aside from a multitude of old family photographs that have re-emerged, the house is missing 'Mumness'. Her smiling at me, from some fairground carousel twenty years ago, is no substitute.

In the gym I stop and do some floor stretches, cracking my neck and back, rotating my joints and putting my slender frame into a few Ashtanga Yoga positions, cycling through the sun salutations and downward facing dog.

Finally, I take a steaming hot shower in my new bathroom, luxuriating in the clean tiled space and soaping the day's dirt and grime off my muscles.

When I finish I wrap my long hair into a towel and pull on my robe. Once in my bedroom I stare at myself in mirror, as if trying to 'place me' in my new home, much as I did my possessions.

My face is plain without make-up; I am not a naturally pretty girl. My eyes are too close together and different colours, one is pure green, and the other has a grey shade. My ears are small and my lips compete with my nose on prominence. But I am sure my body is beautiful. It is strong, muscled, perfectly proportioned and apart from a small birthmark on my tummy, my skin is flawless.

I understand the fuss about beauty being manipulated by fashion but I also understand that a sleek muscled leopard has a natural beauty that a fatter, older and scarred leopard has not. And although they have beauty in their own way, youth and symmetry is important.

That kind of beauty has been part of the survival instinct for animals for millions of years. The fittest and best genes survive. Well most of the time.

I crash back onto my bed and stare at the ceiling, wondering what other people will think of me at school, a skinny moody stranger arriving after the start of term. This is one thing that Dad didn't get right. There is no time to adjust or settle in to the house. Dad's plan was simple: travel, move in, and go to school the following day. It's my worst nightmare, zero planning.

□□□□□□□

Today is my first day at Greenwich Gate Academy. Dad drops me at the entrance and drives around to the Teachers' car park. He gets to start a bit later on his first day, lucky him, but generally he'll start half an hour before me and finish about the same after me. This suits me; I don't want a lift every day.

The building looks medieval, stained glass windows in some parts and deep archways. It's a gloomy H-shaped structure, surrounded by dark wooded gardens and encircled by a formidable black stone wall. The gates are imposing; there must be some history attached to them. It's almost as if the school got built for the gates and not the other way around. Through the gates a gravelled drive, with fountains on either side of rearing granite horses, leads up to the steps at the main entrance and huge immovable oak doors with ornate carvings.

On the other side of the building are modern asphalted playgrounds and a couple of sports fields outside the wall at the back. I don't know why schools still call them playgrounds; there are not many outside games that have survived technology and online entertainment. That thought somehow makes me sad; have we lost something through technology? Do you experience feelings and values the same in a virtual game as you do in a physical game? Something attracts me to old-style, tactile games, like spinning tops, draughts, pik-a-stik and marbles.

It's easy to see my fifth year peers: apart from the height, wisps of beard and better make-up, we are the only year who doesn't have to conform to the dark blue academy uniform. Like different coloured butterflies emerging from the conformity of the uniform cocoon; a mark of coming out. Fifth years are mostly doing 'A' Levels and preparing for University entrance. Some of us will do sixth year studies depending on our results and speed of study.

There are small crowds of pupils, first years most likely, playing marbles, and 'nearest the wall' with picture cards. The person who tosses his card closest to the wall gets to keep all the other cards that have landed face up. There's twenty minutes before the bell and I have to report to the office anyway, so I stop at the marbles. I watch, because my Dad has a unique collection of his own marbles and he taught me how to play. It's a precision game where you can win or lose your precious marbles. Yeah, I know, sad; but the game captivates me.

The concentration on the faces of the boys and the few girls that are playing tells me they are playing 'keepsie' as opposed to 'funsie'. I push into the crowd and crane my neck to watch the action on one of the more interesting games. That's when confident players are using high value marbles.

I'd love to play, but I don't have any marbles with me. Besides, a sure way for a 'fifth year' never to make any friends is to play 'first year' games, beat them and take their precious collectibles. I pretend to be above the whole thing, but my face must have given away my thoughts. A boy around my age, on the other side of the crowd, stares at me. He lifts his hand in a wave intended to be subtle, cool and embarrassment-free. It doesn't quite work on any aspect; he scores zero out of three. I must have looked surprised, his smile fades into an uncomfortable rictus, and his eyes switch back to the game. It's my turn to feel bad.

I go around the crowd and straight up to him, stretching my hand out like a dork.

"Perhaps we are both a bit old for this game?" I say. "My name is Robyn, I'm..."

"You're new?"

"Yes, today." I say. "You enjoy marbles?"

My hand wants to slap my head for such a stupid comment, but he doesn't seem to notice.

"Yeah me too. Yes. I mean, I'm not new, enjoy marbles that is. My name is Scott. People call me Scotty."

"Hi," I say. He looks back to the game, while I study him for a few seconds. Scotty has long dark eyelashes like a girl and a nervous adolescent adam's-apple protruding from his skinny neck. His arms look scrawny, his fingers strong and warm, but his lower body looks muscled. Despite this incongruence there's something solid and honest in him. I learn that he's my age. And even from our limited conversation, I assess he's mature and smart.

"There are senior games tomorrow," Scotty says. "They play near the East wing. The games are closed, restricted to players with the highest value marbles. But they are interesting to watch." He sees my face, and explains further. "Oh, the school has an old tradition. Marbles are part of our... I dunno. Culture?"

The coincidence struck me. Imagine, I have just moved to a school where they play a game that I have loved as long as I remember.

The colours, spectrums, variety and kaleidoscope of a full tin of marbles have always fascinated me. The marbles' spherical smoothness and chirpy noise, as I mix them around the tin with covetous fingers, arouses something primordial in me.

The muffled rumble when the tin is closed is equally joyous, in a secure acquisitive way. But the most interesting aspect of marbles for me is that they hold a universal, recognisable value. When you see a marble that is unique or special, you know its worth.

"Are you okay? You seemed to drift off. That's the bell."

"Yes. Fine," I say.

"Okay, gotta keep moving." With that, Scotty goes off towards a side entrance, swerving through a melee of pupils hoisting bags onto backs and barging their way to their first classes of the day.

It is automatic; I cannot help myself. I have this habit of analysing people. I don't always get it right, but in my controlled world it is better to have categorised someone and been wrong, than to leave them floating around in my life without definition. Scotty, I decide, is a little soft, unsure of himself. I imagine he spends a lot of time alone playing PC games. It must have taken him great effort to say hello to me in the first place. So I label him sensitive, smart, trustworthy, regular, dependable and friendly. I give him kudos for being the first person to say hello.

My first day induction is giraffine. An efficient, if somewhat tall, ancient and angular, lady registrar, appropriately called Miss Gilly, whistles me through the corridors on a guided tour. I don't want to ask if Gilly is her first or second name. She reminds me of a cross between a great aunt from my childhood and my favourite African giant. She navigates me through a maze of teacher introductions, whose classes I'll attend, and facilities that I need to use. Her looking across the busy corridors, reminds me that smaller herbivores graze beside the giraffe. It sees predators earlier from its high vantage point. A few seconds' grace is invaluable in a life and death sprint.

In contrast, I keep my head down, trying to forget that my Dad's induction happened earlier this morning; Ms. Gilly has other ideas.

"You have arrived at a strange term time. I hope you will manage to settle in quickly. Your Father is starting with us today as well, of course. Sadly, Mr Ferris, previous science teacher, passed on rather suddenly. Luckily, your Dad came along just in time. It's usually impossible to find replacement teachers midway. Anyway, we got your Dad, so that's that. Science labs are where he will be mostly. So I don't expect you will see each other too much." She smiled. "And that's it, Robyn. You have seen most of the school. This is your first class. Mr. Wright is expecting you." She indicates the door, before turning around to head off down the opposite corridor. "Good luck Robyn. Your Dad was such a lovely young man, before the trouble. You are quite similar to him. I am sure you will settle in well at Greenwich Gate." With that she goes and I turn the handle to my first English class.

The door springs open and hurls me into the room, as I cling to the handle. I must have looked startled, for a suppressed giggle simmers in a room of twenty or so pupils my age.

"Come in. Come in. Robyn. We were expecting you." Mr. Wright peers at me, hands me a textbook, and points to a seat halfway back, near the window. A veritable gauntlet of eyes rake me as I stumble between rows of desks to the empty seat, clutching my bag, worrying on my floppy hair and my skirt riding up. My mind stalls like the Windows revolving hourglass, somewhere between the unwelcome attention and the Miss Gilly's last words. She must be confused, I decide. The hard seat squeaks like a ferret as I sit down, much to the delight of my new classmates. They chortle. The boy dressed in black, on the seat closest to me, stays quiet. He stares fixedly at his desk, as much aware of me as I am of him. I'm the new guy, yet he looks as if he's the one who's out of place. At least, I doubt he actually wants to be there.

I glance around the room and spot Scotty, through the sea of unfamiliar faces, on the far side.

Mr. Wright waits until I settle before starting. "This is Robyn's first day at Greenwich Gate. Please try to remember how you were on your first day."

"Hung-over!" a voice shouted from the class.

"I am sure you were, Alexander Thompson," Wright says and the class laughs. "Nothing to be proud of." He looked around. "As I was saying, it would be good if a couple of you acted as guides and mentors for Robyn, for a few days, until she finds her feet."

"Try her shoes," a wag whispers and Wright, hard of hearing due to age, puzzles for a moment at what has tickled the class this time.

"I might as well mention it, since people will find out soon enough. Robyn's father, 'Mr. Donald Gentle', started at the school today. Some of you 'would-be rocket scientists' will get to meet Mr. Gentle in your physics classes." Another murmur of laughter around the room, the group no doubt thinking whom the class rocket scientists are.

I'm not sure if I heard the correct words, as they were low and quick, 'mental gentle'. I go to turn around, when the boy in black, with his head down, speaks from the corner of his mouth.

"Ignore him. Class moron."

"Settle down" says Wright. "Chapter 22." And with that the focus leaves me. Everyone engages with the textbook they had been studying before I came in. It's 'Down and Out in Paris and London', by George Orwell. I'd read it years ago, but don't own a copy.

"Let's see, before we read again. Who's ready to share another impression around the Paris half of the book, so far?" Wright asks. The class goes silent. "How did we feel when the author went back to sleep again after a murder took place just outside his window? Sheldon?"

The boy in black exhales and slumps a little. "It didn't bother me, sir." The class jeers.

"Quiet. Why not, Sheldon?"

"I empathised with him. The author suffered from exhaustion and needed to save energy."

"Goth exhaustion," a back-room wag murmurs.

"Okay, what other message, if any, did you get?"

"That rich people's food gets tossed around and messed with, much more than a poor peoples' stew, Sir."

The class roars its derision and I watch Sheldon shrug and twitch his eyebrows as if he can't give a Monkeys. I decide then, I could warm to this boy. And his feedback on the book is accurate. I'm surprised that the teacher didn't remark on such an astute observation. It had left an impression on me a few years before. The poor got their stew slopped into a bowl; next door, the rich patrons got the same stew aesthetically presented, which occasioned the chefs to wipe the gravy from the edges of the plate with a licked finger.

I look around; despite the class clowns, the pupils in this school tend to be smart or from well-off families. Damn, my Father has placed me in a private fee-paying school without mentioning it.

At the end of the double period, the class gets up and almost runs out of the door before the bell has stopped. All except the petite blonde girl, called Alison, sitting behind me, who creeps up and asks if she could help me get around today, and perhaps tomorrow. I get the slight impression that she might not have too many friends. But hey, neither do I. She chatters as we leave the class and I look across the hall to see where Sheldon has gone.

" ...Thompson is the class athlete and clown. Sheldon is a kind of moody freak with some sort of death wish and a high IQ, Sonia Sorenson is wealthy, well her mother is, and shows it. Mark Davis might be gay but doesn't know for sure. Scotty is just..." I tune out; I don't care to hear her criticisms. Alison is giving me the rundown of most of the people in the class who had spoken at one time or another. A mean thought crosses my mind; I can't remember whom she is talking about, nor do I care.

"What about the guy who whispered something about my Father?" I ask.

"Oh that. Nothing. Just ignore that, him. Barker. Don't bother with it. The boy is just a loud mouth." And then she backs off, looking as if I had slapped her. She says 'sorry' and rushes off in the other direction.

Off balance from this weirdness, I spin around on my heel to walk the other way and manage to slam into Sheldon, who appeared from nowhere holding a small camera.

"You lost?" he says, matter of fact, fiddling with the camera and nodding at Alison disappearing.

"Just making friends." I reply. "Or scaring the natives."

"Yes, I can see."

"Maths next. Mrs. Sinclair." I read the name from my timetable.

"Yup. Let's go."

"You too?" I ask.

"Yup."

"You don't say much," I say, as I hurry after him.

"Words are energy. I use them if needed."

"You spoke to me in class. Said to ignore the moron. Was it a good use of energy? You heard what he said?"

"Did you ask Alison?"

"Do you think that's why she ran off?"

"I guess."

"I'm not getting it." I look at him and he looks away.

"There are some rumours... Look, we are here now. This is our class here. I don't normally repeat rumours, but I will tell you what I heard later."

"Okay" I say. My head spins with impatience and I don't find it easy to concentrate on the Maths. As soon as the period ends, I pack my books into my bag on the floor. As I look up, Sheldon, who'd been sitting on the other side of the room, is fiddling with his camera as he exits with the crowd without looking back. I curse silently.

I don't see anyone familiar the rest of the day. As I sit alone in the canteen, munching an apple and reading, I sense a few people looking at me.

First day over, and I mentally celebrate when the final bell rings. I don't want to wait for Dad; he'll be another hour or so. The weather is clear. Walking might help me get to know the neighbourhood; besides, I have no idea which bus to catch or the district it would drop me. It's pretty much a straight road, with a couple of left and right turns at the end. I had looked on the map a few times last night, and despite my lack of internal compass, my memory is good.

The walk starts to relax me. I've almost forgotten the imperfect day, when a car buzzes past me. I don't see the occupants, but I am sure they shout 'your father is a child killer' in imperfect unison. Damn freaks.

□ □ □ □ □ □ □ □

"How was your day?" Dad says from his study as soon as I come through the door. He must have finished earlier after all.

"Fine." I drop my bag in the hall and push the door. He has a whisky in one hand and two large marbles in the other. He rotates them fast, baoding ball style, without touching. The effect is a mesmerising amber and rainbow meld that appears to rotate in an infinity shape. Surprisingly, his collection cabinet lies open and I realise he is playing with some of his 'untouchables' and reading physics notes at the same time. The marbles, which Dad rarely handles, have been collected over years and are pieces of art in their own right.

"And your first day? Dad?"

One of the large marbles jumps from his hand, as if I have broken his concentration. The marble bounces on the carpet and I pick it up as it rolls towards me. It is the universe in a bubble, whorls and gases from which the light seems to explode as the marble turns. Dad watches me closely as I hand the glass boule back to him.

"My day could be described as..." he searches for the word. "Memorable and inconsequential."

I love-hate Dad when he speaks like that, and drinks this early, as if he has too many secrets or problems. It doesn't make much sense to me. I love him of course. We are all each other has now. But he infuriates me with this inability to talk straight, so I clench my teeth and try to ignore it.

"Did you know the school has marble tournaments?" I say. "A bit weird."

"Weird in what way... good weird or bad weird?"

"Just coincidence weird." He looked up at me. "Don't you think it's weird?" I say.

"Not really."

"Dad, you have the craziest collection of marbles and you have imbued a marble passion in your only daughter since childhood, which is, unfortunately and embarrassingly, undiminished today." I recall my wire spiral earrings that hold a green agate marble inside the wire of each earring. I had bought them for a few pounds in Accessorize years ago, but I still treasure them.

"I guess," he replies, noncommittal.

He returns to concentrating on his notes and a few hand marble tricks that I remembered as a kid. I watch for a few minutes as he makes the marbles disappear and reappear, before going to the kitchen to find something to eat. Why do I think he might be holding out on me?

Around ten thirty, before I go to bed, I look in on him. He has conked out on his Chesterfield in the lounge. The light in the study burns brightly and his cabinet lies unlocked. I pull out one of the long slim flat drawers that house his marble collection. Rows of individual marbles all nestle in their own felt-lined indentations in the wood. There are Oriental marbles, German marbles, and glass marbles with silver snowflakes and animals inside. I pick up a marble with a perfect prism in the centre, another with a blue glass skull, and finally one with a double helix that changes colour as it moves. Without thinking, I slip them into my pocket, and then ponder the reason why. I really have no idea why I took them. But I don't have any guilt or mischievous intent. He won't miss them for weeks anyway and it's only borrowing. Somewhere inside I have a vague idea they'll help me make some friends.

Dad snores lightly and looks peaceful. I close and lock the cabinet and return the keys to the drawer before heading upstairs. I texted Jonathan until I feel sleepy; mostly I complain about the school, my

Dad and the stupid gnomes. He says he misses me and I hug the phone under my pillow as I drift off.

The school doesn't look any less foreboding on my second day. If anything it looks worse; I notice details that I haven't seen before. An earlier downpour makes the woods seem darker and more ancient, rain drips off the moss on the faces of a few ancient gargoyles on the sides of the building. Damp students congregate under the bicycle sheds and in doorways, reluctant to go inside until the last minute. Despite the weather, outside there is space and a degree of freedom; inside the dry dusty academy are cobwebs of rules and control.

A kind of doom has afflicted me since I stumbled into the shower this morning. I imagine my own personal weather forecast. Warning, there is a bad day sweeping in from the direction of 'life sucks'.

So I enter school, cocooned in the music of my earphones, my own personal acoustic bubble. It is a good way of moving through crowds of people that you don't know. They become actors in one big silent movie and I can look at them without feeling out of place. Had it been full blown summer, I'd have completed my psychological camouflage with sunglasses. Instead, I compromise with a slight scowl and frowning concentration, as the music floods my inner spaces keeping the gloom at bay. My favourite list I'm playing, I call 'Sombre Rebel Mood', and includes Happy Mondays' Hallelujah; Radiohead's Street-Spirit; Green Day's Boulevard of Broken

Dreams; Gravity by Embrace; Can't Stop Now by Keane and Do I Wanna Know by the Arctic Monkeys; real mood disrupters. Funny thing is I never can decide if they make my mood better or worse.

Inside my pocket, I caress the three marbles released from their sterile prison last night. I'm still not sure why I took them, but now feel a little wrong-footed bringing these pieces of art into a valueless teenage world of avarice and envy. Then again, marbles belong in the game. They live in the mud and dirt. The marble's heart only beats when it feels danger in a game of taws.

Some people believe that glass is a slow moving liquid; that if you leave a marble on a concrete floor for thousands of years, it will become a glass puddle. I love the idea, but it is not true; it's a myth. Although the atoms of glass are not arranged in regular order like a solid. They are in a form of solid chaos, held together by chemical bonds. I learned this in Chemistry and it's how I see my thoughts on days like this, neither solid nor liquid. Thoughts that should be fluid, trapped inside some impenetrable solid. Like the colours frozen inside the clear glass of the marble.

Mum comes to mind for a few seconds. She would be telling me, right now, to stop being so morose. She preferred to see my smile. Maybe her happy gene has passed me by and I've gotten Dad's 'ogre in a disaster movie' gene. Although, I don't like to admit any similarity to Dad, or to admit that he might have been like me at his age. How could he ever understand? Mum would shake her head. The apple doesn't fall far from the tree. I shiver and hug the scarf

Mum had got me, tighter around my neck, another poor substitute for a real Mum hug.

I realise that Mum speaks as much to me now as she did when she was alive. It seems she is always in my head. She understood me and calmed me; suddenly I know that she did the same for Dad.

As I head to the main entrance, Scotty appears in front of me and mouths a soundless 'Hi' along with his trademark wave. I unplug my music bubble from one ear and cock it towards him.

"Hi. How is your second day going?"

"I don't know, it's only started," I say. Then immediately feel mean for blurting out a sarcastic sounding response.

"Oh" As usual, he looks away, but not before his crestfallen expression stabs me in the conscience.

"Sorry, I didn't mean that. I am a little messed up today."

He understands.

"I thought I'd remind you that there are some senior games on at lunchtime. We could watch if you like."

"Sure. Okay."

"I am off for Sciences this morning. New teacher."

"My Father?"

"Yes." He grins. "I'm looking forward to it."

"Weirdo. I hate physics and I see enough of my Dad."

"He is just another teacher to me," Scotty says.

I roll my eyes, secretly pleased he's said that.

"Anyway, gotta keep moving. Do you want to meet at lunchtime? Watch the games? East entrance?"

"Sure. See you then," I say. Bewilderment might have flitted over my face. The boy never seems to stop. He flaps his hand and goes.

Mr. Wright and English is my first double lesson period again today. It means a marginally more familiar start. At least I know where I have to go. Walking along the busy corridor, I become aware of comments and whispers from boys behind me. One boy out of three says something that gets my attention. I turn around; two boys are looking at a third. Barker from yesterday's English class is right at my back.

"What did you say?" Maybe my single ear has misheard him. He'd spoken thinking that my phones were in both ears. He scowls at me and pushes past. I have a suspicion he'd said 'mental gentle' again.

"Do you mind telling me what you meant? Or are you being a dick-head?" I say.

"You know!" he shoots back and keeps going.

I don't know. I shake and my face must be red. More because I don't understand what he said and what it has to do with me. I hate not having control.

"Ignore him." Sheldon appeared at my shoulder like some dark moody apparition. On any other day, I might have admired his black clothes and a hint of eye shadow.

"Tell you what. I am going to ignore all of you. Why don't you leave me alone too."

He deserved it; he bailed on me yesterday and Barker has wound me up. I turn into the class, go straight to my desk and start getting my books out. After English, where I studiously ignore everyone, I find my way to History. By lunchtime I can breathe more easily. By the time I get outside, the fire-snorting dragon has gone. Scotty waits for me at the East door as promised.

"The big games are over there," he says, pointing and leading me to a crowd of students on the sand at the fringe of the trees. My heart sinks when I notice Barker and Sheldon at the front of the game. Both look up when they see me. Barker scowls and Sheldon looks embarrassed. I ignore both and go to the boy who seems to be organising the players. He takes one look at me and shakes his head side to side.

"You're looking for a game? Eh. It's a closed game here, for seniors." I hear someone guffaw.

"Male seniors, with sane parents, only," Barker says.

"Cool it, Barker," Sheldon says.

"She isn't looking for a game. We came to watch," Scotty answers and defends me.

And suddenly, I know for sure that I'm outside some circle of knowledge, as a few others stare at me.

"I am a senior," I say. I ignore the others and speak directly to the boy with the notepad. "Can I play?" I take out the three marbles and show them in the palm of my hand.

"Whoa. What are they?" His exclamation focuses everyone's attention. "Can I look?"

I nod and he picks them up one by one and holds them to the light. His eyes are wide and crazy as the marbles and for a moment I see a glint of lust.

"You'd be crazy to play them," he says. And he waits with bated breath to hear my reply.

"I'm playing."

The boy punches the air. "Okay. We have our fourth player for this game. I will remind you of the rules of Ringer Game." He looks at me directly.

"It's keepsie. Lag determines order of play. Toss or shoot to lag line, okay. Knuckle down on every shot. Shooters can be won. No hunching or histing. Three high value marbles on the cross from each player." He looks at the circle of faces including mine. "Same shooter all the way through unless it gets taken. Let's see what you have got."

Barker leans forward. He has a blue steelie for his shooter. Two Lutz and a stunning German swirl for the centre. I show them my agate shooter and give him the three others to put in the ring. Another pretty-looking boy with foppish hair and colourful jacket, Jan, shows a fairly standard shooter, but three exceptional Chinese Tigereyes. The fourth competitor, Roy, has an older chipped Sunburst as his favourite shooter and Miller and Oxblood swirls and a gorgeous Black Panther. They are all good items, but I know they are going to come after me. I need to win the lag and get a good run.

Soft ground means I toss in for the lag. Roy lands behind me and Barker shoots too far and gives an angry grunt. Jan lands the same distance away as me. But our Ref calls it in his favour. I watch Jan frown in concentration as he steps towards the edge of the ring; something in his expression advertises that he is relaxed or even amused by his surroundings. Perhaps a boy who doesn't take life very seriously, I think. Jan knuckles down and fires his lucky shooter into the cross, as hard as he can. The double crack draws a growl from the crowd and his shooter manages to shift my Skull and Prism away from the centre and towards the perimeter of the ring. But he is disappointed; nothing leaves the ring and his go is over. Serves him right for being greedy, but he just grins at me as he turns away from the ring. And I hear Barker express his appreciation that my boules are sitting targets for him. This guy has no class or sportsmanship, only a big mouth.

I knuckle down and take out a single marble, the Oxblood. It blasts out of the ring and my shooter remains in the middle. I walk around and pocket the Oxblood, looking for my next target. I am allowed to enter the ring as my shooter is in. I take out Barker's Lutz, one after the other. The crowd cannot believe it and I don't look at Barker as I pocket both Lutz. He is appealing for 'histing' but it seems it's standard play for him to claim opponents are cheating if he is getting beaten. Histing is where the player cheats by slightly lifting their hand off the ground. My knuckles were firmly pressed into the dirt every time. The judge ignores him. I take out another two marbles in quick succession without missing, denying anyone else a turn. Jan is looking surprised when I take two of his Chinese boules out in one hit. They fly from the ring. Jan is out. The shot moves Barker's German Swirl right to the edge of the ring. He is safer there, further away and nowhere for my shooter to go after the shot except outside the ring. It's a risky shot. I look around and notice Sheldon taking photographs. I close him out and concentrate. Barker is watching me and when I finally decide to ignore his marble and go for the last remaining marble, he cannot keep his mouth shut. It sounds like 'mental bitch'. It makes me flinch. In an instant, I change the direction of my aim and strike his marble out so fast it bounces off the shins of one of the guys watching the match. My shooter stops right on the ring edge. There is laughter in the crowd. Barker is out before he fired a shot. Sheldon picks up the marble and hands it to me. "Sorry, for earlier. It seems you can look after yourself."

There is only the Black Panther left and my heavier jade shooter launches it right out of the ring. The game is over and the crowd is applauding and whistling. Barker and Miller never fired a shot. Despite my sharpshooting, there are plenty of others ready to play the next game, hoping they might get lucky and take away my marbles as easily as I took Barker's. Mental? I think to myself. It's Barker who has lost his marbles. I decide not to play again. It's a little unsporting, but I cannot risk Dad's boules a second time. Plenty of people are coming up and patting me on the back and saying well done, and I may have made a few friends as well as a couple of enemies.

Jan is cool about everything; he comes and tells me that he will expect the opportunity for revenge another day, but he is smiling and gracious. I tell him sure. He hands me a red draw-bag to carry the marbles.

"I don't need it today." He is still laughing and he touches my arm and hugs me without the typical self-consciousness of other boys my age.

Scotty hovers a short distance away and gives a smile and the usual wave but he seems to steer clear when there are others around.

"I hate marbles, but you just made them interesting. Sorry for earlier," Sheldon says, falling in beside me. "Everyone is going to talk about you now."

"Weren't they already?"

"I guess."

I cannot bring myself to ask what they were saying and he doesn't expand.

"It's strange to find a school where the students are still into marbles."

"Not all of us. And those who are, still enjoy normal stuff."

"Like what?"

"Soccer, internet," Sheldon says, "parties."

"So in your world, we are nerds? Marble players?"

"Maybe a little," he grins. "Come on, let me show you something real quick."

He leads me back inside the building and up the stairs into the library where he pulls a few yearbooks off the shelves.

"1945. The end of the second world war?" I say.

"Yes, the school was built way before, but see this."

He turns the pages and shows me marble competitions and pictures of boys in short pants displaying collections of marbles.

"So, I guess this is simply one school where Xbox or puberty didn't kill the marble?" I say.

"It's a game like any other game. The world championships were held in a Surrey pub last year. There is no shame in it unless it leads to the exclusion of other healthy interests." And he grins stupidly at me for the first time.

"I guess." I don't mention I come from Surrey, as I try to analyse his expression.

"I have an idea. Why don't you come across to my house tonight? Have dinner with my folks. It would help you settle into the neighbourhood." He cocks his head. "I am only two blocks away."

I open my mouth to dismiss the idea but something in his expression makes me change my mind. "Why not. What time?"

"Come over at seven or so?"

I don't speak to him again after lunch finishes. The afternoon periods go by pretty fast. A few people come up to me and ask about the game. Word spreads fast. I play it down a little. No one likes a smart ass, especially a smart ass who knows she is a smart ass.

'I got lucky' becomes my stock reply of the day. When the closing bell finishes I can't wait to get out and go home but I have to wait a little longer until the French teacher picks up a text book for me from the stock room. She insists. By the time she comes back, almost everyone else has left the school, apart from a few stragglers.

Going out of the front door towards the gate, I reflect on the day. Best not to tell Dad about the marbles, I think. I take the red pouch out of my pocket to see my spoils. Guilt washes over me like a warm current, as I open the drawstring and peer into the bag. Halfway down the drive I'm not watching where I'm going.

A blur flashes in the corner of my left eye. As I turn around, a hooded boy barrels into me. I start to topple and realise the marbles are being snatched from my grasp. The robber doesn't stop, he runs for the trees. And through my shock, I realise that he is still inside the school walls with nowhere to go. So I drop my bags and fly after him. This is another pupil that is going to get a surprise; I stretch out into a full sprint across the grass. He slows up as he reaches the trees. He darts around. I am more reckless and charge straight in until the undergrowth slows me. The small guy twists and turns through the bushes and I imagine we must reach the wall any second. He gets out of sight and I continue to barrel down the path. He runs straight out in front of me just as the wall looms up and the path turns off at ninety degrees. We both slip and my feet trip his. By sheer luck his hood twists around my hand as we slide and tumble to a stop at the wall. I look up and the most extraordinary face is gazing at me. It has something frightening and cunning, yet laughing. I get a split second warning of danger. My impression is a young wizened face with flawless eyes and longish dark hair.

"As slow as your Dad, Missie," he says. With that the material dissolves in my fingers and he seems to slip through the wall. I pick myself up slowly. Shaken. What happened? I check around and touch the lichen-covered wall. It is solid brick, no gaps or spaces in either direction. It doesn't make sense. A boy, but not a boy, has taken the marbles. I saw something amiss in that microsecond I had looked at him. I try to remember what. All I know is he made me shiver.

My instinct is telling me that this is not something I have encountered before and my logic is telling me that my imagination had played cruel tricks on me. How? Day two in a new school and I've lost the plot? But I still can't equate what I thought happened with the physical evidence. The marbles are gone and I had been knocked over.

As I walk home, I make my mind up. I'd bumped my head in the tumble and the boy had vanished while I lay stunned.

How am I going to explain to Dad what happened to his marbles? Although I reckon I have at least a few weeks before he discovers them missing. Enough time to try to figure out who the boy is and get them back.

In any case, Dad is out when I get in and I don't see him. I scribble a note before I set off for dinner at Sheldon's home, still shivering every time I think of the strange attack.

Sheldon's enormous house sits back from the road behind three straight poplars.

His family are immediately warm and friendly. My suspicions, that Sheldon has told them I had recently lost my mother, are confirmed when his five-year-old baby brother brings me a teddy to hug. Its pinafore and necklace give it away as a Mummy bear. I decide not to share the details of today's 'mugging' with anyone; I don't need any additional sympathy.

Sheldon's Mum and Dad, Elsie and Steve, are a team, even more than my Mum and Dad were. Everything they do flows together. It's pure Zen, from setting the table to taking the pie out of the oven and making me feel at home.

Meanwhile, I watch Sheldon play with his brother and sister. He joins in their ditties and fantasies. He teases them with role-play, entertains them with delightful facial expressions full of meaning and enters their play worlds on his hands and knees. The twins' infectious laugh delights me. Sheldon becomes a beautiful man in front of my eyes. The black-garbed, silent crow and gothic wizard vanished outside school. In his place, stands a lion heart and poet. I didn't see that coming; it snuck up on me, a cat on a sparrow.

It's at this point that my 'insignificant self' appears, determined to torture me by tying a knot in my tongue. Sheldon's well-rounded character makes me feel like some sort of immature teenage failure fumbling in panic in the dark for the switch to light up my personality.

"Are you okay?" Sheldon says. He dusts imaginary fluff off his black jeans as he gets up off the floor. I notice a gold locket swing out from under his shirt.

"Sure." I want to ask about the locket, but to be honest, I hardly say much else the rest of the evening. My brain is crammed with too many thoughts, and me frightened to open my mouth, in case they all come tumbling out. Besides, the hustle and bustle of the family at the dinner table makes it easy to participate with nods and smiles.

We take the twins up to bed together. They like Sheldon to read them a story and check for monsters in their closet. I watch as Sheldon settles them both in and they go to bed with shy tired smiles as they look at me.

When Sheldon walks me home I become self-conscious. It doesn't help that his mother had told me he is nearly eighteen, a year older than me. My feet become too large. My cheeks are too 'roundy' and my stomach isn't flat anymore after a large helping of pie and mash. Straight line walking becomes impossible; I even bump into him a few times as we wander across the road.

"This is me," I say. My house looms up and I automatically check to see if Dad is standing at the window.

Sheldon smiles. "See you at school tomorrow. Perhaps then you will tell me what's been on your mind all evening."

I nod hurriedly, mortified, "Goodnight", and dash in before he sees into my mind completely. What I was thinking is marked 'top secret' and filed in my brain under teenage kicks.

# CHAPTER TWO

## The Glass House

Dad knocks my bedroom door at seven in the morning.

"Dad, it's too early."

"Robyn. I need to know if you took marbles from my cabinet." My glum expression answers him. "What have you done with them?" He looks more fearful than angry.

"Dad, I..."

"Please tell me you didn't take them to school!" he interrupts.

"They were stolen, by one of the boys, I'll get them back. Honest." He stares at me as if thinking what to say. "I'm really sorry." Inside I think, 'they are only stupid marbles', but keep quiet when I see the upset on his face.

"Forget them. Don't try to get them back. Just forget they existed," he says. He kneels down beside the bed. "Promise me, you'll forget them."

"Dad, you are scaring me."

"Just promise that you will forget them. They are not important anymore. Promise?"

"Okay, okay, I promise." My fingers cross under the duvet. "Just tell me what is going on?"

"Nothing's going on," he replies. He leaves and minutes later I hear him reverse out the drive and head off to school.

I drag my sorry ass into the shower, feeling chagrin and developing a super reluctance to face day three at the gloom school; but I have no choice. Anyway, I need to get the marbles back. Someone will know who took them. They are going to be sorry to have messed with the new guy.

As soon as I reach the school grounds I search out Scotty and explain what happened.

"Unlucky. There have been a few incidents over the years, but nobody has owned up to them."

"What do you mean, incidents?"

"Thefts," Scotty says.

"And no one has been caught?"

"No."

"Or under suspicion?"

"Not as far as I know." Scotty says. "But you could ask Old Turner, see if anything got handed in."

"And he is?"

"The janitor, who, of course, looks after lost property."

"There is nothing going to get turned in. It was a deliberate theft; he grabbed the bag and left me dazed."

"Well, lucky you didn't get hurt."

"I imagined he said something about my Father, and called me 'Missie'. But I could have been mistaken."

"Strange word. Kind of old fashioned?" Scotty muses. "You could try asking Barker what happened to him."

"How come?"

"He was robbed last year. Come to think of it, he said he couldn't keep a grip of the guy. Everyone ribbed him because he said that he felt the attacker was on a piece of elastic. There were lots of jokes going around."

"Huh. He is more likely to be behind the theft."

"Doubt it, but if you want I will ask around, see if anyone has heard anything," he says. "Off to see your Dad. Got double physics again today."

"Lucky you," I reply, completely distracted. Sheldon is stood a distance away talking to a couple of students and watching me intently. For a second, his stare looks sort of familiar. The more often you look at someone, the more his or her face changes. Yet his face is expressionless, unsmiling.

Sheldon watches everyone and anything; I realise that I have caught him studying me. People surround him, yet he stands apart, invisible almost. He reminds me of someone who films wildlife; he's close to his subjects, but they don't notice him after a time. And all the while Sheldon gains an understanding way above everyone else's. The boy is a natural anthropologist; the thought makes me giggle. His camera palmed in his hand as always, he scans around for unusual behaviour.

The bell rings and everyone rushes to classes. Sheldon comes alongside like a lifeboat in the swell of students. "I need to talk to you later. It's about what happened last night. Important. Take my phone." He scribbles his number on the back on one of the folders I carry.

"Call me either at lunch or after School," he says.

"Sure," I say, now ready to skip classes for the second time that morning, but Sheldon turns away and I curse and growl inside. What is wrong with people around here? Important, he said? I hate being left hanging, blowing in the wind and eaten by curiosity. I kick an imaginary object on the ground. It might have been Sheldon's good-looking head. How does he know what happened anyway?

Morning classes pass uneventfully except for a couple of comments from students who express regret that I'd been attacked. I start to think I'd made a mistake to tell Scotty and encourage him to get involved. It might get to a teacher and from the teacher to Dad of course. He'll know I've broken my promise.

I almost run out of my Economics class at 1200. I dig my phone out of my bag and dial. Sheldon doesn't pick up any time I try. Damn him.

The canteen is busy. One table of teachers is animated about something. Students overcrowd a few tables and leave others empty. People seem to be hyper and the noise makes me think a headache will come. The clanging and plating, banging and scraping of canteens always irritate me; makes me want to diet.

I notice the blonde Alison change direction when she sees me converging on her path. Sod her. I join the shortest queue and pay for a yogurt juice and look around. Scotty gives his usual effete hand signal from across the restaurant and I head over.

There is a loud but dull bang somewhere in the building and before I can reach Scotty's table the fire alarm goes off. It sounds very wrong. The teachers push back their chairs and are up and out of the door in an instant. It's a little strange that they head immediately to the source of the noise without exiting the students. Perhaps they are confused by the direction of the noise. The canteen doesn't seem to be in danger, but people are looking at each other like zombies in an end of the world movie. The canteen supervisor stands at the end of the counter, hands on her hips, and looks across the canteen as if too deciding what to do. Students start to scrape back their chairs and reluctantly push themselves off their tables. A slow chaos of noise and disorder rises up. Students are moving aimlessly. A large man, a teacher I have not seen previously, comes into the canteen and shouts "Everybody into the grounds in an orderly fashion. Smartly please." He repeats it twice before all students are moving in a broadly similar direction. "Michaels, no running." The first-year pulls up and we all spill out the exits into the grounds for a roll call.

I catch up with Scotty in the line. "What's the Hamden?"

"Eh?"

"Hamden Roar, Score. What's happening?" My little bit of cool cockney rhyme completely wasted on private education.

"My lunch is getting cold and I got roasties today. Didn't get the chance to eat one. That's what's happening." Scotty says, clearly grieving over his hot crispy potatoes.

"What made the bang?" Arguably a stupid question, but I voice it because no one else seems interested.

"It seemed to come from the Science block," a girl with Scotty answers.

Dad's safety crosses my mind, but as it does, I see him hurrying with two other teachers into the side entrance. The science block looks normal, no smoke or damage, serene almost.

For a while nothing happens and everyone complains about boredom and the cold. Then someone whispers the first rumour: 'There's been a weird explosion'. 'You're kidding Einstein.'

A few minutes later, the second rumours, murmurs, unsure questions: 'Two boys are missing?'. 'How do you know?', 'That's what they say?', 'Who says?', 'Someone overheard?', 'How can boys go missing?', 'That's ridiculous?', 'Pupils don't go missing, Einstein. They bunk off.'

Then the third rumour emerges: 'Sheldon Dunn and Jan Smith were in the Lab when the explosion happened. They cannot be found.' I realised the rumours are confirmed this time and tell Einstein to shut up.

□□□□□□□□

We are informed that school may be closed for the rest of the week or longer. A whole week? I can only imagine that this is some head-teacher's guess.

They send everyone home amidst rumours and counter-rumours. The teaching staff look drawn and haggard; pupils seem to relish the excitement. An unofficial search is carried out. Have the boys bunked off? All the usual haunts and possibilities are considered and checked. Then the official search is launched. The police, rescue units and local communities turn out to search parks, hills and the coast.

The school is completely turned over by the police when it becomes clear that no one has seen the two boys outside of the school. Staff and some pupils are questioned; it's known from the register that the boys had come to school, and it's thought that both had reached the science labs. The loud bang was heard by almost everyone in the school but nobody seems to know what it was. There is no trace of an explosion; nothing was disturbed or burned.

I pass by Sheldon's house on the way home, but there are too many people and cars. I watch for a minute from the road and decide they don't need me right now.

The evening newspapers carry pictures and profiles of the boys and speculate incessantly. It is enough for me to see the headlines; I don't read the details.

The police come to my house and ask to speak to me the next day. Someone had told them Sheldon had been seen talking to me in the morning.

"Did he seem upset?" a female detective asks. "Was there anything out of the ordinary?"

"I have only been at the school a few days," I say. "I don't really know anyone yet."

"You were getting to know him? Was there anything between you? Someone said you had snapped at him before going into class the day before he vanished?"

"It was nothing important. He was being an idiot." I don't want to get into the whole story of me expecting some information and him letting me down. It doesn't seem relevant now. Some idiot was calling me a name, that's all, two boys missing is more important.

"Okay, and you just moved here with your Dad?" she says. "Why?"

"Mum died, Dad got a new job. We moved." I say. "Not much of a story."

"Sorry to hear that. How were you and your Dad settling in? Was he behaving normally?"

I frown, first because I don't like her repeated double questions. You never really know what she is asking or which to answer. Secondly, what's my Dad's behaviour got to do with this? We barely arrived in this stupid town.

"He is great, it's me that doesn't like it here," I say defensively.

"I am sure you will settle in once we get to the bottom of where the boys are. And everything is back to normal."

I know right then that she didn't believe it for a minute.

"If you think of anything useful let me know," she says and hands me a card.

I don't care about the police. I'm worried about Sheldon and I pass by his house a second time. Inside, the mood is funereal. There are a few relatives staying, maybe the grandmother, I think. Both mother and father have the same worry lines etched on their faces. I say how sorry I am, but nothing I can say is going to help. The twins look confused and as if they have been crying but stop when I arrive as if expecting to see Sheldon behind me like a couple of nights ago.

Back home I shed a few tears for the first time. Not for Sheldon. I hardly knew him, I tell myself. My upset is for his brother and sister and the screwed up school I've come to.

The unctuous detective comes to our house two days later, with a smile that is stuck on a setting between suspicious and grim apologetic. She has a warrant and a load of people with her, equipped to search every corner of the house and grounds. I resent my new room being tossed, my peace disturbed and my privacy violated. My anger must have been evident.

"Sorry, Robyn, it's part of procedure. We have to search the places of the people who have last seen the boys."

I didn't understand then if she was talking about my Father or me.

"Am I a suspect?" I say.

"In what?"

"In anything."

"No, of course not."

"Is my Father?" I ask, watching her face closely.

"No, not really," she says. "We are just following procedure." Her eyes twitch.

They leave after six or so hours. Dad looks tired as he surveys the mess out of the patio windows. They had lifted paving stones and dug the garden in a couple of places. I go and stand beside him and he hugs me and kisses the top of my forehead. One of the stupid dwarfs is lying on its side grinning at us from across the garden. 'Smartarse', I think.

In the evening, Jonathan calls for an update. Although he is sympathetic, I don't think he quite gets the seriousness of two boys disappearing and the house being searched for bodies. At least that's what I think they were doing. I was afraid of the answer, so I never asked the detective or Dad.

"When does school open again?" Jonathan asks.

"They said, after the weekend, likely Monday or Tuesday."

"And still no hints where the boys went?" he asks. "It doesn't make sense."

"No, it's being called the Greenwich Mystery by the papers." The almost permanent news crews are beginning to disperse, but the papers are trying to find angles to keep the story alive.

"I cleared it with my guardians. They said I could travel up and visit you. I can take a day's holiday and make a long weekend. I wish I could drive, but the train is okay I guess."

"Sure. That's brilliant. I could do with a friend up here."

"Will it be okay with your Dad?"

"Of course. He will be cool about it," I say. My thoughts change to wondering the best way to broach the subject with Dad, given everything that has been going on.

"It will be great to see you again Robyn." I feel the same but nevertheless had to stop myself from saying, 'It's only been a fortnight'. It would have been defensive and totally unnecessary.

"Bring your foil and mask. We might get time to scaramouche," I say and he guffaws.

It is a private joke between Jonathan and me. My fencing tutor called it sparring. But Jonathan insisted that sparring relates to boxing, and that the correct term for fencing practice is assault or 'skirmish', from scaramouche. It doesn't matter to me. Scaramouche makes me laugh and think of a strange Frenchman with a curly moustache, and I only use the word to tease Jonathan.

Dad is in the study when I finally come off the call and go downstairs. He is on the floor surrounded by paper and notebooks. I think he might be talking to himself or doing calculations. He has a whiteboard with a diagram covered in annotations propped up against the sofa. His glasses are on the top of his head and I watch as he looks for them to see another piece of paper. When I cough, he stops and casually covers up whatever he had been studying so intently. He waits for me to come and sit close, but his eyes are glazed. If I were to say, 'Dad, Jonathan is coming up for a visit and we are going to smoke from a bong and sleep naked in the tree house', he wouldn't notice. He is distracted, his mind somewhere far away when I ask. He says 'yes' and nods. I could have asked for anything except what he's working on. I know better than to ask that. As I get up from the floor, his eyes leave mine and return to his papers. The top of one notebook is peeking out. It says, 'March 22nd 1978 - Marble-men.'

To say I am mildly curious would be the understatement of the century. I want to ask him, 'What is 1978 famous for?' My father would be nine or ten back then; around eighteen years before I was born, I calculate. But I don't dare ask. It was probably nothing. In any case, he's back mumbling about the drawing on the whiteboard. I look at the board again as I leave the room; it looks like a coke can with valves, wires and tubes sticking out.

It is a weird weekend. Dad spends his time in his study. He has taken to locking the door when he leaves it, coming out only for coffee and toilet it seems. On the Sunday morning, I have a quick look in his bedroom. It is in the same state as the day after the police had searched. Pillows and cushions perfectly in place on the bed. Dad is now sleeping in the study. Back to school tomorrow. I wonder how Dad is going to manage on minus hours sleep and how I am going to manage on minus friends. How crazy is my life?

They came for Dad at the house, in the afternoon, while I was at school. Three detectives took him away for questioning, I learn later. Ms. Guppy, one of the guidance teachers comes to let me know. She probably should have known that my Mother is dead. She doesn't. And I take advantage. "Yes, nothing to worry about, my Mother will be home soon," I say.

"Strange," she says. "I do wonder the point of the police asking us to talk to you."

"Probably because Dad and I are attending the school together."

"Yes. I expect that's it. Anyway. Nothing to worry about; they said it was just routine questions and he will be home tomorrow. I am sure there is nothing wrong. Your Father is a lovely, lovely man."

"Yes" I say.

School is strange anyway. The pupils seem subdued somehow and a few seem surprised to see me. Barker looks as though he was going to say something and changed his mind. For a second, I don't know if he wants to be friendly or horrid, it is hard to tell from his expression. Other pupils studiously avoid me and I notice a few teachers studying me. This is before the rumour of Dad's arrest spreads like a bushfire.

As I walked out of the gate heading for home, I notice a few comments and stares from various homeward bound groups. The community jungle drums have well and truly beat. I put my head down and concentrate on the walk home while thinking of Dad. Why are they persecuting him? How must he feel in all this?

At the end of my street, I stop. There are a dozen vans and cars, film crews, cameramen and a crowd of reporters. I hesitate and it's enough to draw attention to myself. They move towards me as a herd. The path to my house is blocked. I panic, turn around and start to run. I hear shouts and car doors slamming; they are coming after me.

The first car reaches me in seconds. So fast, I think.

"Quick, get in," a voice says.

It takes me a split second to register Sheldon's Mum and Dad. I squeeze in the back of their car. The twins greet me happily from their car seats.

"We heard your Dad had been arrested and we thought you'd be alone," Elsie says.

"Lucky we came when we did," Steve says. He accelerates and turns the corner before the news crews have seen where we have gone.

I feel numbed and humbled. These people, so worried about their own son, are taking time to see if I am okay. I feel slightly guilty for not missing Sheldon enough. I've thought about him but I have my hands full worrying about Dad, I guess.

"You can stay with us honey, until your Dad comes back." Elsie touches my hand through the car seats.

"Sure she can. We don't think for a minute that your Dad should be held responsible," Steve says.

"Thanks. He will be out tomorrow." I think of asking them what they know about my Dad.

But I notice Elsie and Steve exchange glances in the front seat. I decide it might be easier not to say anything. I concentrate on playing with the twins for the few minutes to their home.

They put me in Sheldon's bedroom immediately we arrive at the house.

"He won't mind. He will be pleased that you used his room, when he comes back," Elsie says. Then she sits on the bed and starts to cry.

"Sorry, Mrs. Dunn."

"No. I am sorry dear. I shouldn't be upsetting you. Let me get you a spare toothbrush and something for you to wear. We cannot go back to your house with those silly pressmen there. I will wash your blouse and things and you will just make do until tomorrow."

"Thanks," I sniff.

"Sheldon is everything to his Dad. He is so proud of him. Steve has built a great business, he is a great locksmith and has lots of common sense, but he believes he is not very smart, so he is thrilled to have a son who is academically..." She tails off.

"Sheldon is a smart guy; even though I only knew him a few days, I could see that. I am sure he will take care of himself and come back. I mean he will hate being away from his family. I wish we knew where he was." And I finally tail off by getting upset.

"Dearie me, look at the two of us, sniffing away like a couple of old biddies. It's confusing at the moment since no one has any idea of what happened. But I am sure there will be an explanation and everything will work out for the best. You'll see."

With that, Elsie busies herself organising a tracksuit for me to wear and some fresh towels for the shower. Her big smile as she leaves the bedroom is the saddest thing I've ever seen.

Sheldon's bedroom is a telescope into the landscape of his thoughts. There are geology and gemstone books to support a collection of rocks and crystals. Photographs of otters, swans and dolphins hang on the wall above a desk full of camera equipment. He has a black Mac Pro hooked up to a couple of monitors, and I wonder if it is for games until I see the music keyboard and CDs of digital music and graphics software. I want to know more and to switch on his PC and prowl around his mind. But I don't.

Sheldon is artistic. He takes photographs and composes PC music at least. I look at his desk and inside his wardrobe. He has some fun clothes and shoes. Why does he dress so drab at school? I pick up his photo and look at him smiling. Where are you? What are you doing now? Are you coming back?

Elsie returns with some dinner and nightclothes. "I hope this is okay for you, Honey. Sheldon's Dad isn't really up to eating much these days. Neither am I, to be honest."

"Thanks, Mrs. Dunn."

"If you need anything, juice, anything at all, you know where the kitchen is," she says. "The control for the TV is in the drawer here. Or play some music. Don't worry, you won't disturb us, we cannot hear anything from the other side of the house."

I go and squeeze her hand. She is such a kind woman.

"Goodnight dear. We will see you in the morning."

I climb into bed an hour later, exhausted from the day's events. I imagine I can smell a faint smell of cologne from nearby cushions. My mind whirrs as I try to make sense of the past few days. I have a sense of a surreal landscape and environment all around me. It's all about nature and hunters. I feel out of place. My body jerks with tiredness and nerves and I keep telling myself it's all going to be sorted tomorrow. And when I finally feel asleep I'm thinking about Dad, Sheldon and wondering what an old biddy is.

"Why did they arrest you Dad?" I said. My father has just returned looking tired and dishevelled after 24 hours at the police station and I came home immediately. He slumps in a chair in our lounge.

"They didn't arrest me. I was taken in for questioning," he replies.

"Why?" I sounded like my mother for a second. Sometimes to get the truth out of Dad, she persisted, much like I'm doing now.

"I was one of the last to see the boys," my father says. "They think I might have a clue to their whereabouts."

"Why?"

"Because it's not the first time I have been through this." He frowns. "Now please let's drop it." As he looks away I catch his sadness and I feel bad. He must feel that even his own daughter is against him.

"Dad, I just want to know what is going on. I want to help and I am worried."

"There is nothing to worry about."

"Well wait until you go back into school. My last few days have been hell. People are looking at me as if I am guilty of something."

"I won't be going back to school," he states.

"Why?"

"Because someone thought it was a good idea to suspend me."

"What?" I say. "That's crazy isn't it?"

"I guess."

"What do I do?"

"You have to continue as normal," he says. "In any case, I need you to bring some things from the lab for me."

"Dad, I..."

He looks at me. "It's important. I wouldn't ask you if I didn't need help." He gets up. I notice he has the notebook with him again. I realise he is going back to his study; to his papers and his whisky.

Much later, I hear him talking to himself. 'Is it a revolving door?'. 'It doesn't open both ways'. 'I returned because... why?' 'What is stopping the boys from coming back?' 'I am sure they will be safe for another few days.'

My mind spins. What is Dad talking about? Back from where? Which boys? Jan and Sheldon? Is he just drunk and mixing up his words? It doesn't make sense.

There's no point in challenging him when he has been drinking. I make up my mind. Tomorrow after school, I will catch him in the afternoon and ask him what is going on. If he doesn't tell me, then I am not going to help him with the school. His words spin around in my head as I go to bed. *Safe for another few days.*

□□□□□□□

Scotty stops me at the school gate in the morning. He has a red mark above his eye.

"Robyn, I don't think you should come in today," he says. "Take the day off."

"What?" I look at him not understanding.

"People are stupid. They heard about your Dad and now everyone is talking." He looks uncomfortable. "They are not being very nice about you."

"And your eye?"

"Nothing. A disagreement with one of Barker's mates."

"Thanks Scotty, but I cannot run away from this. I need to face up to the situation."

"I thought you might say that," he says. "But whatever happens I am on your side. So if there is anything I can do to help..."

"Sure, thanks." I kiss him on the cheek and smile. Inside, my stomach is in knots as we walk through the gate together.

The morning is fine. People stare at me from time to time, but that's nothing new. My study subjects don't cross with Barker or anyone else who might want to say something to my face. Surprisingly though, there are pupils whom I don't know who say hello with something sounding like empathy. Empathy is honest and empowering, relative to sympathy and its superficiality. But perhaps I am just being unfair and overly misanthrope as usual.

At lunch, I think I see Dad through the window. He seems to be carrying something to the science wing. He has a straw hat on and sunglasses, with his head down as he hurries along, but I'd recognise that old blue cord jacket and red trousers anywhere. He is suspended and sneaking into the school? What the heck? I need to talk to him and find out what is going on. I can't take this anymore. It's nuts. My Dad is walking brazenly onto the school premises disguised as a saxophone player in a Belgian Jazz Band. My world is slowly becoming more insane. I grab my bag, leave my cup of tea and rush out down the corridor towards the science block. I decide to catch up with him there and then. I can't imagine any plausible explanation for his behaviour.

Being indoors too much is discouraged at lunchtime but most of the teachers, except those unfortunate enough to be on lunchtime supervision, are in the staff rooms or canteen and the corridors are reasonably quiet. I've never been inside the Science wing properly since my induction the previous week and had no idea which classrooms are Dad's. I look through the small door windows into each room I pass. If the room is empty, I try the door. If the door opens, I go in and look around, check the cupboards and see if there is anything to tell me whose class it is. Bunsen burners and a locked chemicals cabinet suggest chemistry classes. One class has a periodic table, space charts and a diagram of the human body all on the same wall; no idea. It's anyone's guess, perhaps a biology teacher with an interest in aliens? Most of the classes are empty; a few have one or two students reading or prefects laying out equipment for some experiment.

Towards the end of the corridor there are four big labs. They are all locked. Looking in through the door windows I can see huge pipes and wires, machines and monitors, computers and something that might be a laser. The last room has an extra tall ceiling. I figure the room must go up to the second floor. Sure enough, I spot stairs and a gantry running around the middle of the wall. In the centre is a huge steel can, mounted on some sort of machine table. It is revolving slowly, and through the door I can just hear the noise. Wires and pipes flow out of the top and aerials and short tubes stick out the side. It hits me like a brick. And just as I realise that it is the coke can from Dad's drawing a few nights ago, Dad comes into view. He is still carrying his boxes as he switches a number of switches and walks into a cupboard and closes it behind him. The machine speeds up to a rotating blur and the noise grows.

I bang the window, although I doubt he will be able to hear me. Since I have no idea how long he'll be in there I decide to stick to my original plan and see him at home. As I turn to walk away from the door, there is a flash of what can only be described as black light, followed by a bang that shakes the building and sounds like a thunder crack; it leaves me disorientated for a second. I rattle the door handle and peer inside. The machine is slowing down. Nothing else stirs. I am still looking in when Mr. Turner, the old janitor, arrives at my side. He's evidently been working close by.

"My Dad's in there," I tell him.

Turner nods and unlocks the door. I am close behind him as he goes in. He looks at me and I point to the cupboard, just as four or five other teachers arrive. Turner pulls open the door.

"Robyn, what are you doing here?" Mr. Wright asks. "The alarm has gone off. You need to join... go outside."

I look at Wright then back to the cupboard. It is empty. Mr. Turner gives me a slight shake of his head that the others would miss.

"Mr. Wright. I just..." I say, before I catch Mr. Turner's second warning expression. "I just got lost. I am going now." It's weak, but it's all I can think of. My mind is in meltdown and I am doing everything to prevent panic taking over. I look again as I leave. There is no exit from the chamber. Dad has definitely not come out. The teachers are looking around. It seems they know where the bang came from this time. But they don't know Dad had been around. And what I don't understand is why Mr. Turner is not telling them what I told him. Dad had been in somewhere in the chamber. He's vanished.

I feel a rising hysteria as I join other students outside. My instinct tells me I need to stay calm and think. All questions have answers, and all problems have solutions. Order eventually arises out of chaos if you encourage it.

I take my 'scrunchie' from my jacket pocket, sweep my hair from around my face, gather it tightly in a tail and bite my lip as I determine to remain calm and controlled and keep any signs of panic off my face.

# CHAPTER THREE

## Irrational Pursuit

We are counted and sent home like before. The story going around is that there was another bang. Coincidence. Everyone is accounted for. But they need to close up the labs and do an investigation into what had caused the bang. But apart from the two boys, everyone is safe; life would go on as normal. Except that I know differently and struggle to keep down my rising panic.

Back home, the journalists have gone, given up. I imagine how many there would be if it gets out that my Dad has disappeared. I decide to keep this secret as long as necessary. I get changed in my bedroom then wait downstairs, half expecting Dad to walk in. But I am not surprised when he doesn't. It isn't until I go into the kitchen that I discover the note propped up against the kettle.

'Robyn, I decided to take a few days off, go see an old friend. I know you are perfectly capable of looking after yourself. There is plenty of cash in the jar if you need anything. If you have any problems call the Dunns. Be back soon. Love Dad. x'

What a liar, I think angrily; he knew where he was going. Had I not seen him sneaking into the school, I'd have thought he was just taking some time out. I'd have been worried, but not half as worried as when I saw him enter the cupboard area and not come out. Now my worry has been replaced by frustration, because I know there is an explanation.

I go through to the study. My subconscious directs me to check the cabinets. As I remove the keys from the drawer, I notice the small notebook of comments has gone. As soon as I slide out the first drawer I know the answer to my unconscious question. All the drawers are empty. He has taken most of his marbles with him. I open the cupboards where his physics books are, jammed with papers and charts. I pull everything onto the floor and start to look through for anything that might help me understand. Of course physics is not my strong suit and I am trying hard not to break down in my frustration of not understanding anything.

By 0200 in the morning, I only know three things for sure. Dad isn't coming home tonight, I am exhausted and hungry, and I am not going to school tomorrow.

The next day, Thursday, I get a call from Scotty saying they missed me at school and wanting to know if I am okay. I say 'not really' and he suggests that he come over right after school finishes. Then Jonathan messages to say 'Enjoy school. Tell your Dad I am coming tomorrow night. Did they find the guys yet?' I text back. 'No. All cool with Dad. See you tomorrow. But don't think we can pick you up at the station. Can you get a cab?'

The rest of the day I immerse myself in the papers; nothing really helps me. I happen to look out of the patio and notice that 'Smartarse' is standing up grinning at me. I was sure he was still on his side yesterday when I came home. Of course, the state I was in, I probably didn't notice.

Scotty arrives after school and once we've made some sandwiches and cokes, he asks me where Dad is and how he is doing, being expelled and all.

"Suspended," I say.

"Sure. I couldn't think of the word."

"He is gone," I tell him. I watch for a reaction. None.

"What do you mean gone?" He munches his sandwich.

"Disappeared in the school yesterday like Sheldon and Jan."

"What?" A mouthful of sandwich nearly exits his mouth with his splutter. "What are you saying?"

"I am saying that my father has vanished and so far you, me, oh and Mr. Turner, are the only ones who know."

"You have lost me. What has Turner got to do with this?" Scotty says.

I start from the beginning and tell him everything. I show him the pile of papers in the study and the empty marble drawers.

"You are taking it very well."

"So far," I say. "Something is telling me that I need to stay calm. So I am holding on and trying to work out what is happening."

"Why did Turner keep schtum?"

"What?"

"Schtum. Quiet. Mouth closed."

"Oh," I say. "Schtum. Good point. Don't know."

"Which lab room did you see your Dad in?"

"The one with the giant silver coke can."

Scotty knows the room, but it is a lab for physics majors. He is the class below. "I don't know much about it, but the machine is an old vacuum. It's just an antique as far as I know. It would probably cost them more to dismantle and scrap than to leave it there as a curiosity," he says. "Of course, Sheldon is in that class and could tell us more. If he was here." And he looks a bit sheepish when he realises what he said.

I catch the flash of movement from the patio at the same time as Scotty. It is the hooded boy who stole the marbles. He is staring through the window. When he sees us, he moves quickly.

"It's him. The boy!" I shout. In my surprise I forget how he frightened me last time.

Scotty speeds through the kitchen and out the back door. I bolt out the front and around the corner. The boy is running towards me, sees me, and about-turns. He runs straight into Scotty and they land on the ground with Scotty on top. I recall how I wrestled with Jonathan, and pile on. Together we pin the boy down and there is no slipping away this time. I pull his hood off and gasp. His face is a mixture of malevolence and mischief. Shivers tingle down my spine. The only way to describe the feeling is if you imagined an old dead kindly aunt, appearing suddenly at the end of your bed and saying nothing, just staring at you. Somehow, incongruence adds to the horror.

"Where are you from?" Scotty asks. The boy stops struggling but Scotty doesn't let go. Nor do I get off his other arm.

"Give me marbles."

"You stole the others," I say.

He grins. "More."

"You stink," I tell him. "Where do you live? What do you want? Where are you from?"

"From Rubicon. Least that's what Donal called it today. I am Huptoou," he replies.

"You mean Donald, my Dad? You saw my Dad today? Where?" I ask.

"Donal from Class 11, many years ago."

"Donald was at the school years ago?"

"Give me marbles."

I ask Scotty if he is sure he can hold him and he says yes. I run back inside and find a few marbles and bring them out. Huptoou's eyes glow like furnaces.

"Where is my Dad?" I say. I hold the marbles out of reach.

He looks from my face to Scotty's and back again. "Sheldon, Jan, Donal all be dead soon if they don't get out."

"Out from where?" Scotty asks. "Why can't they get out?"

"The alternate. The dark matter. Rubicon. The madness," he says. "No one gets out, unless someone gets in." He chuckles. "That's what Donal calls it."

"Huptoou, will you help us? Can you take us there?" I say.

He motions with his arm and I let go. From his pocket he produces Dad's notebook. I snatch it. And with that he dissolves to nothing in front of our eyes and out of our grasp, like a will-o'-the-wisp.

"It's getting cold," I say. Scotty and I sit in the garden without speaking for a good five minutes. Perhaps it is a type of shock. We look at each other and there is nothing to say, yet. We get up and go inside. He gratefully accepts a beer. And it makes us both feel a little bit more grown up.

"What are we going to do?" he says. "Do we tell someone?"

"Nobody is going to believe us," I say. "Try this on for size. The guy was underneath us in the garden and he evaporated like a puff of steam."

"I get you," Scotty says.

I haven't finished. "And people just keep disappearing in the school, including my Dad. And they might all have gone to Madness Town."

Scotty corrects me. "I think he said, 'The Madness'."

"Okay, Okay. Pedant. What the heck difference is it going to make?" I say. He looks at me ruefully. "Okay. I am sorry. I shouldn't have said that." I hug him with one arm.

"No worries," Scotty says. "What's in the notebook?"

There are mostly pages of indecipherable equations. Symbols that neither Scotty nor myself have seen before.

"The maths is meaningless to me." He purses his lips and shakes his head.

The parts of the notebook in English don't make much more sense. I read it out.

'Following this formalism, I have measured the dark matter equation of state for the first time using a number of improved techniques. I have found that the value of the equation-of-state quantum parameter is consistent with vacant dark matter well within the expected tolerance. However, the measured value is lower than expected. I don't know why I didn't see it. The actual masses determined with lens are larger than those obtained through kinematic methods. I have checked our techniques using various simulations. Everything seems to check out. I wish I had someone I could bounce this off. I have analysed possible sources of error that could invalidate or mimic the results. It's close. In light of this result, I can now suggest that understanding the nature of the paradigm breakdown requires a complete general relativistic analysis. Cold dark matter makes up around a quarter of the universe.'

"Ouch. It's a bit of a brain freeze. Cold dark matter?"

"It's my Dad's writing."

"I don't think it's important. Is it?" Scotty asks.

"No idea," I say. "But this might mean something." I point to a list with scribbles, dates, annotations and mind-maps.

*1978 - I exited as Barrow (if I recall correctly) came in.*

*1978 - Turner hid involvement.*

*Vacuum still functional?*

*Stronger magnets?*

*Exit problem? Revolving door? Can get in now, but possibly not out.*

*Vacuum in space-time breaches alternates at speed? Why? How?*

*Turner refusal a minor problem. The key is the speed.*

*What's the next stage after cold dark matter? Is there an alternative exit?*

*Is it a stasis or self-determining life forms? Help or hinder?*

*1978 - Suggests life forms - but astrophysics community would disagree.*

*Schrodinger?*

*Can marbles help us? How? Seems ridiculous.*

*Tomorrow Rubicon. There is no choice.*

We read lots of this type of stuff. Nothing makes much sense, except that we are on the trail of something, the odd word here or there, that we've heard elsewhere. The dots are beginning to appear. If only we could start to join some of them and see a picture emerge. By the time we have gone through the notebook, we are exhausted and it's late.

"My folks will be wondering where I am; I gotta go," Scotty says. "They keep special tabs on me ever since the guys disappeared."

"Sure. Thanks for coming."

"You gonna be okay on your own?" Scotty asks. "I cannot get our hooded friend out of my mind."

For a second, I am creeped out; what if he appears in the house? What else could I do, but lock all my doors and windows?

"It will be fine," I say. "Don't worry. I will be at school tomorrow. I don't want them getting nosey and turning up at the house to find I am alone. Don't tell anyone; I don't want anyone to know what my Dad is doing until I figure it out myself."

"Of course I won't."

"Jonathan is coming up tomorrow evening. He will be staying over for a few days."

"Jonathan?" Scotty looks puzzled.

"My boy friend from back home."

"You have a boyfriend?" He looks slightly downcast, but it may have been my imagination. It has already been a weird day.

"No, yes. I mean, I have a friend who is a boy," I explain.

"What's he like?" Scotty asks.

My first instinct is to say how fantastic Jonathan is, but when I see Scotty's face, I say, "He is okay. Down to earth. I am sure you will like him."

We agree to catch up at school in the morning and to continue our research tomorrow immediately after school. Scotty stands at the door for a few seconds as if he is going to say something else. Then I realise he is about to kiss me. When he recognises that I know what he was about to do he puts his hand on my shoulder instead and gives it a manly squeeze. "Don't worry, everything will work out." I imagine it's something his Dad might have said. I watch him walk down the path and road until he disappears around the corner. I don't know whether to laugh or cry. Scotty is okay, but just not my type, and not right now when my world is collapsing around me.

I wake up just after three in the morning with the name in my head. Turner. I grab my phone to text Scotty. As I key in my text, my phone bleeps and startles me in my dark quiet bedroom. It was a text. 'We need to go see Turner'. It was Scotty. Smiling I text him back, 'Thanks Genius'. I'll tell him tomorrow that I had been in the middle of typing him almost the exact same thing. Turner was mentioned in the notes. Is he the same Old Man Turner? Maybe. I have a good feeling as I go back to sleep wondering what happened in 1978.

□□□□□□□□

At the lunch break, Scotty and I go straight to where we would find Turner. It is a large plant and maintenance room that provides the heating and electrics. It also has access to the swimming pool. Pupils are forbidden. It is down some steps under the main building.

"We cannot just wander in," Scotty says. "It's out of bounds."

"Watch me." I enter the door marked unauthorised and into the noisy plant room. Scotty follows reluctantly.

"What are we going to ask?" Scotty says as he trailed me through a network of pipes and cables around the basement.

"We will start with what he knows about my, Dad, I guess." I haven't really thought it through. "Well, it doesn't look like there is anyone in here." We arrive at a dark passage leading away from the main plant. I push open the double swing doors and go into the gloom.

"What age do you think he is?" Scotty asks.

"It's a good question. He might have been around in 1978. He looks about seventy. Probably should have retired years ago."

"You shouldn't be in here." Turner appears in front of me, wiping his hands on a rag, and I jump.

"Sorry. We wanted to talk you," I reply. He nods and leads the way to a small office. He turns off the radio and pulls out a couple of chairs.

"What do you want to know?" Turner asks, sounding cautious. I sense he is trying to decide what to tell us.

"You know my Dad was in the classroom yesterday. You didn't want me to say anything?"

"I am hoping your Dad will find his own way home."

"From where?"

"From wherever that accursed machine has taken them." Turner reaches into the drawer and takes out a quarter bottle of some kind of alcohol, which he swigs.

"The machine in the physics lab? The vacuum?" Scotty asks.

"Yep."

"What is it?" I ask.

"It's a very old vacuum mounted on a centrifugal table. It used to work years ago. Your Dad switched it on and got it working again. He tricked me into powering it up."

"What does it do?"

"It sucks everything out until it's a vacuum, like space, then it spins that vacuum around at high speed with magnets."

"And?"

"It affects space-time."

"That's it?"

"That's it."

"How did my Dad disappear?" I ask.

"Your Dad and others," he agrees. "Your Dad wanted me to help him. He was going to explain something to me. I said no. I didn't want to play with that machine again."

"It's kind of hard to believe," I say. Turner shrugs.

"Were you the Janitor back in 1978?"

"No" he says. He swigs from the bottle. "I was your Dad's physics teacher back then."

I look at Scotty. We didn't see that one coming. If I were a detective, I'd know what question to ask next. I'm not and I don't.

"So how did the guys disappear?" Scotty asks.

"I don't know."

"Have you told the police about the machine?" I ask.

"Tell them what? Where is the evidence? I am not sure myself if the machine is really responsible for anything," Turner says, looking at his bottle.

"Can you help us get Dad back?"

"No. I cannot. Sorry. I have not done any physics for decades. I have no idea how to get them back. I became a janitor to escape physics. Now if you excuse me, I need to go put chemicals in the pool and you two shouldn't be in here." He motions to the door and guides us both into the corridor.

"Mr. Turner?" I say. He turns and looks. "Does the name Barrow mean anything to you?"

"Sure. He was my sister's boy." He gives a sad look and with that goes off down the corridor.

"That was pretty useless," I tell Scotty as we exit the plant back into the main building, being careful no one sees us coming out.

"We learned something. Turner was your Dad's physics teacher. Your Dad was at the school as a boy," Scotty says. "Why didn't he tell you?"

"Do you believe his story about the machine?"

"You saw your Dad disappear," Scotty replies. "He knew you did. I think he was just trying to avoid answering you properly."

"Let's go to the library." I have an idea.

We're lucky. It only takes us twenty minutes to find the relevant information in a newspaper archive on an ancient microfiche. We only knew the year, 1978. We had to look at each month. But it had made front-page headlines on April 22nd 1978 in a number of newspapers.

'Four children disappear, only one returns'

'What happened to boy's school friends?'

'Boy invents incredible story'

Scotty and I read or rather devour each headline and news article, our heads jammed together on the viewer.

It seems that four children had gone missing from the school. Gentle, Barrow, Banks and Hamilton. After forty-eight hours, Gentle reappeared. He told the most incredible story of being transported to another world. He was suspected of doing something to his three classmates.

"Poor Dad," I say. "He was getting the blame. Nobody believed him."

"Poor journalism and police work," Scotty says. "They didn't think to connect recent disappearances with those in 1978?"

"Maybe they did. But kept it quiet?"

"Possibly why they were questioning your Dad. He was the original suspect and now he comes back it happens again?"

We continue to read the details, looking for some idea of how they disappeared in the first place and how Dad came back.

"I think your Dad had some idea what happened. Look, this article. Your Dad had a period in an institution. It looks like they were determined to cure him and find out what happened to the other kids."

"It's crazy." I'm shaking my head as I wonder how it's possible I knew none of this.

"There is one thing missing." Scotty looks at me.

"What's that?"

"Turner is never mentioned. It's as if no one realised he was involved."

We look at each other.

"Only your Dad mentions him in his notes. Otherwise Turner kept himself out of it?"

"Come with me. We don't have much time." I jump up and run out the library with Scotty following again. We find Barker a few minutes before lunch finishes.

"Barker. Tell me why you called my Dad 'Mental'?" I ask. Barker flinches and makes as if to go around me. I grab him so hard he freezes. "Look, I am not angry. It's important to know where you got your information."

He hesitates for a second. "Okay. My Mom and Dad. They were in the school. They say that everyone thought your Dad had murdered his friends. Everyone knows the story."

"I didn't," Scotty tells him and looks at me in case I thought he did.

"Nor me of course," I add.

"Your Dad was in hospital for a long time. Everyone said he was mad." Barker half shrugs.

"And?" Scotty asks.

"I don't know. I only know what my parents told. I think your Dad must have moved away eventually. It was a surprise to the community when he came back." Barker looks at me.

"When did your marbles get stolen?" I ask.

He looks surprised that I knew this, and then looks pleased to be able to help. "Last year. A boy, who was not from around here, jumped me in the toilets. He was fast. He grabbed the marbles and simply vanished," he says. "No one believed me."

We walk away leaving Barker wondering what's going on. But I actually say 'thanks' to him. Well at least the dots are appearing now. The trouble is, how do I know that I have enough dots to make the picture, never mind solve the problem?

Scotty and I spend the rest of the afternoon passing notes to each other in our classes. Our minds are not on lessons but on figuring out what's going on. We agree we need to investigate more deeply. Turner has to know more than he's telling.

Mr. Wright spots one of my notes to Scotty and reads it aloud to the class. 'You can come over to my place tonight and we can decide how to do it.' It was an innocent reply to Scotty's suggestion that we should question Turner and discuss starting up the machine to see if we could follow my Father. Of course this was not the way Mr. Wright, or the rest of the class, took it.

In the evening, Scotty and I are at the door to greet Jonathan from his cab. He has a few bags with him, probably his fencing gear. But he throws them effortlessly over his shoulder and marches up the path sporting a big confident smile. He looks larger than life next to Scotty, and while he isn't challenged by Scotty's presence, Scotty looks uncomfortable next to Jonathan. Jonathan drops his bags, grabs me and hugs me. When he finally lets me go, I introduce him to Scotty as my favourite rebel from my old school. He does the obligatory bear-hug with Scotty. I can't help laughing at the pair of them trying to portray relaxed manhood.

"Your Dad?" Jonathan says. He catches my expression, frowns and tilts his head waiting for me to explain.

"Let's get inside and we will explain everything," I say.

Scotty and I take Jonathan through the whole story from start to finish, leaving nothing out. The bit he has the most difficulty with is the disappearing boy. He insists on going out to the garden to see where it happened. I think he is convincing himself that we haven't simply missed a plausible explanation.

"You don't believe us?" I say.

"No, I was just trying to imagine. I wondered if there was a logical solution." He is scratching his head. "And you are convinced your Dad vanished the same way?"

"In the Physics lab, yes."

"Then the answer is there," Jonathan says matter-of-factly. "I am a Physics major, maybe I will find a clue in the notes."

Scotty goes out for a second and Jonathan tries to hug me; I won't let him.

"Are you okay?" he asks. I nod.

"Robyn, I know you. You are worrying me."

"I am seriously doing okay."

"You look older, scared," he says. "I just want to give you a giant hug."

"It's just a little bit of stress, tiredness and worry. You know I hate not to be in control."

"Your Dad is missing."

"Yes, I know," I snap.

"You know I love your Dad too," Jonathan says.

Then I blubber and fall into his arms.

"It's going to be okay. Let it out," he says.

My whole body shakes with the release of the pent up emotion. I can't speak, so I drool on his shoulder instead.

"We are a team, you and I. Your Dad will be back, that's for sure. I promise."

I nod and dry my eyes with my sleeve, and pat my saliva into his shirt.

"So we are going to figure things out together. Okay?" I nod again.

Scotty returns with all the physics papers for Jonathan to look at. He looks at my eyes and to Jonathan and back to me again. "Everything okay?"

"Sure," I say. "Just missing my stupid Dad." The pair of them stare at me silently.

We spend the next few hours going through Dad's papers again, Scotty and I handing bits we thought might be relevant to Jonathan to read, and Jonathan laying aside the bits we give him and finding other more interesting stuff and pretending to understand it better than he does. I know he is doing this for my benefit.

But it is midnight when Jonathan finally puts a few more pieces together.

"Here is what I think. Turner is telling the truth. The machine is some sort of vacuum, dark matter manipulator. The physics is way too complicated for me but I have read some papers recently that suggest we don't have all the answers to what's in a vacuum. From what I can understand, the machine was used years ago and some kids were lost. Your Dad managed to get out only as the kid called Barrow went in. The revolving door scenario. Someone goes in, someone gets out. Turner was the physics teacher at the time and knows more than he is saying." He pauses. "But they knew a lot less about physics back then. Perhaps he got a fright. He certainly didn't expect your Dad to come back to the school and turn on the machine again."

"Why did my Dad return now?"

"Your Dad spent his life trying to work out what happened. He probably hated being blamed for the disappearance of his school friends, even though he was never formally charged. Think about it. He would be a young boy with little understanding of what happened, trying to convince adults that he gone somewhere and returned but he didn't know how or where."

"But if this is true where are they, trapped in limbo or something?" I replied. "It's hardly sensible."

"No, but I think the answer to their destination still lies with Turner. Your Dad went back because he knows where it goes. If your Dad knows, then Turner knows."

"So we go ask him again?" I ask.

"Yes, then we need him to get us into the room and turn on the machine. If we can do that, I will go and see if I can find your Dad."

"No. If you go, I go," I say.

"And me," says Scotty.

"But we don't even know where it goes. We don't know if we can come back."

"Exactly. You go, we all go."

"We don't even know for sure if the machine is the key," Scotty says.

"No. But we know it's all Robyn's Dad talks about in his notes and he has gone as if it's a journey and believed he would come back."

"Then should we wait for a few more days to see if my Dad comes back?"

"We should go immediately, if we believe they are in danger," Jonathan says.

"Let's get more info from Turner before we decide," Scotty suggests.

Scotty is right; I have a feeling that Jonathan is being a little foolhardy to show off to me. But then he does love my Dad and would do anything to help even if there is risk for himself.

"I guess the school is now closed for the weekend," I say.

"No. There are always sports and extra curriculum on a Saturday," Scotty replies. "Turner usually works the morning at least and he locks up when everything is finished."

"So it's agreed. Tomorrow we talk to Turner again. If he confirms we could travel, then after school closes, whether he helps or not, we will try to get into the classroom and get the machine going," I say.

Everyone agrees and Jonathan yawns.

"We should sleep. I guess you need to be getting home, Scotty," I say; the speed of his response shocks me.

"No. I cleared it with my folks. It's late. I will stay here tonight, if that's okay?"

"Okay," I say. "Sure." I had planned to sleep in Dad's room and put Jonathan in my bed. Now what?

I take the guys to the bathroom and give them towels. "There is plenty of hot water, decide who goes first. Who needs shorts or toothbrush?" Jonathan shakes his head and Scotty looks sheepish as he takes the towel. I get him a toothbrush and a pair of shorts from my Dad's cupboard. I can't put these guys together in my bed. The lounge sofa is not a great option. There is only one fair solution.

"Guys, when you are done, we are all sleeping in here." I open the door to my room. They both look out the bathroom at each other and me. Jonathan shrugs and smiles. "Give me a few minutes to shower and change and you can both come in," I say.

Ten minutes later, I am in the middle of my super-king. Jonathan jumps in one side and Scotty tentatively slides under the duvet on the other. So what? We are all friends. We kiss and hug good night, laughing at the situation. As I drift off, well before either of them, I am thinking, 'Dad could return even now, I wouldn't mind. I could stand the embarrassment and lecture. I just want him back.'

When I awake, I am surprised to see Scotty sleeping on my left until I remember last night. I hear Jonathan banging in the kitchen. The smell of toast and egg swirls up the stairs, and I get a craving for fresh orange. Feeling a bit mischievous, I give Scotty a 'kissing-alarm' like my Dad used to do when I was little, to get me up for school. Kissing his forehead repeatedly, I make 'muwah' noises for each kiss. In theory, a beautiful way to be wakened up; in practice, the most irritating, annoying and grump inducing way to start the morning. I love-hated Dad for that. For a second I think it is a little bit extrovert, over the top, silly behaviour. Am I bipolar? I hope he doesn't take it the wrong way. Scotty just looks confused, smiles then yawns, blowing morning breath, right in my face.

"Lovely. Thanks for that," I say. "Time to get up."

"Sorry." He looks abashed.

I laugh. I feel normal again.

Downstairs Jonathan has made fresh coffee, although I don't know where he got the coffee; neither Dad nor I drink it. The scrambled eggs look fluffy the way I like it and he has buttered enough hot toast for an army. Scotty and I join him, me in my dressing gown and Scotty in a big old sweatshirt I had thrown at him upstairs.

"I have been for a run," Jonathan says.

"I'm impressed, happy eyes." I reach for a slice of toast. "Scotty and I had other exercise while you were running. Didn't we, Scotty?"

"Sure," Scotty replies. He half smiles, maybe remembering the previous night's aborted kiss.

Jonathan just hoots. Anyone could see from Scotty's bashful expression that I am joking.

The three of us burst out laughing, as we look at each other again.

I catch the 'Smartarse' falling over again, out the corner of my eye. All three of us turn to look as the window bangs. Huptoou is looking through the patio and making no attempt to hide from us. He is holding a piece of paper. He doesn't look as whacky as before.

"That's the guy," Scotty tells Jonathan, as I go to open the kitchen patio door.

Huptoou doesn't run and he doesn't ask for marbles. He hands the paper to me and then goes and lifts 'Smartarse' back up. He comes back and sits on the ground outside the patio doors. The note is from Sheldon; I read it aloud.

'Robyn, if you get this it means that Huptoou is telling us the truth and has found you. He can get out and in a few times, for a few minutes only. We cannot do that. He can do it because he is from here, I think. He told me that he had spoken to Donald's daughter already. That means you and everyone else are trying to find out what happened? Tell your Dad that it wasn't his fault. Jan touched the machine after he left. For the moment, we are alive and well, but not sure for how long. It's a mad, dangerous place; everyone is against us. Tell your Dad if he is coming with a rescue party that he needs to bring details of how to exit. And tell my parents not to worry.'

Jonathan takes the paper and starts to read it again.

I jump up and rush to a kitchen drawer and scrabble frantically for a paper and pen. I find the pen. No paper. I don't want to waste time. I grab the note back from Jonathan and scribble on the other side.

'Shel,

Dad is already there, inside, wherever it is you are. Didn't you see him?

We are coming for you.

Love Robyn x'

I shove the paper into Huptoou's hands. He stands and looks at me.

"What's going on?" Jonathan asks.

"Well he disappeared very quickly before," Scotty explains.

"Best we keep the original note," Jonathan says.

"Why?" I say.

"It's at least some sort of proof of what's going on," Jonathan says, just as Huptoou disappears again in front of the three of us.

"Shoot, shoot, shoot" is all I can think of saying, so I just bite my lip instead.

"What did you say?" asks Scotty.

"I told him not to worry, we are coming to get them," and I do a face palm for a full two minutes. I don't feel hungry anymore.

I can hear Scotty and Jonathan talking and discussing but it is just a buzz in my ears and I can't focus on what they are arguing about.

Finally I tune in when Jonathan says, "We need to write the note down, word for word. What does it tell us? Now we know that the machine is definitely the entry point, and we know they have not seen your Dad; or was the note written previously? We know the place is dangerous and time is running out. Do we try to tell someone, or will that just cost us time and cause them to lock us away from the machine?"

"We don't know what the danger is," I say, "or where they are, or why Dad hasn't returned."

"But whatever we decide, we have to move fast," Jonathan insists. Scotty and I agree.

There are fewer pupils and teachers around on the Saturday as expected, but we have to sneak around with Jonathan, Scotty passing him off as a cousin when anyone got too nosey, and we steer clear of the few on-duty teachers as best we can.

Turner almost groans when he sees us coming. We insist we talk in a corner.

"We want to go in," I say.

"You can't," he says. "It's dangerous. You'll never come back."

"You let your nephew go in? Is that why you didn't tell the police of your involvement?" Scotty asks. "After all, you were the physics teacher."

"It wasn't like that." He rubs his hands through his hair.

"Tell us how it was then," Jonathan says. Turner looks at him as if only seeing him for the first time.

"The machine was designed and built by a local physicist and school benefactor. His name was Jack Wills. He and I were friends. In exchange for donations to the school, the board allowed him to build and use the research lab. It was going to be used to teach pupils as well. No one expected any danger."

"And?" I say.

"People expect a vacuum to be empty. Suck everything out and there is nothing, right? Wrong. There is still gravity in there, and space-time. There is an element of dark matter. We didn't know that then. The idea was to spin the vacuum at extremely high speed, disrupt the fields with magnets and to heat it, then photograph the particles that appear seemingly out of nowhere.

"The day the boys disappeared, I was helping Jack with the chamber. The school didn't know he was there. We had agreed not to run these kinds of experiments during normal class hours."

"What kind of experiments exactly?" Jonathan asks.

"Relativity and quantum mechanics exactly." Turner sounds slightly irritated.

"Anyway, Jack fired up the machine this particular day. Four boys had come to the room. I was a few doors down and came back when I heard the bang. I realised immediately that Jack and the boys had gone. I switched the machine off and kept the key."

"You didn't tell anyone?" I say.

"I let them search. I thought that was the best way. Let them convince themselves that the explanation lay in the room. Then I might sound credible when I said I thought it was the machine."

"What happened?" I ask.

"Your Dad returned. His story was so crazy that I didn't sleep for weeks."

"How did you hear his story?" I ask.

"I heard the rumours; I had a friend in the local police get a transcript of the interviews." He pauses for a second. "I also wanted to know if he mentioned me or the machine. I had been in the room previously and Donald knew me."

"So you let them blame my Dad?" I feel angry.

"Sorry, I didn't know what would happen and by the time he was in hospital it was too late. My sister was angry with me. Families had lost their sons."

"And Jack?" I say.

"He was a loner. Nobody missed him. They thought he'd upped sticks and gone."

"Do you still have the transcript?" Jonathan asks.

"Yes, in my files here somewhere," he nods.

"We want to go," I tell him. "You have to help us."

"You are crazy, nobody came out. They must have all died in there."

"I know you don't believe that. My dad came out. He told people what it was like. Nobody believed him, but you at least must have thought it was strange. A ten year-old was talking about another world. A parallel universe, that's what the paper called it."

"Wait until you read the transcript. It was never released to the newspapers, or the inquest. People preferred a normal explanation."

"Have you seen my Dad's notes?"

"Some. Your Dad was here trying to convince me that he had a solution. He wanted me to look at how it all worked. He wanted me to switch on the machine for him. I saw some of his ideas, the revolving door. As someone goes in someone gets out. He thinks that's how he got out. As the last boy went in, your Dad came out."

"The boys all went in at the same time, or seconds between them." Jonathan says. 'Mr. Gentle came out forty eight hours later."

"That's true, in this side. But it's highly likely the time is different on the other side," Turner says. "Your Dad was convinced he was only in there for a few minutes. That's partly why his story was so ridiculed."

"Did you know that there is a boy who comes here from there every so often?" Scotty asks. "He doesn't use any machine."

"Yes. There are a few that have been doing this for years. They come and steal marbles."

"Why?"

"I have puzzled over that. Somehow there is a door that is open to him."

"He brought us a note out from Sheldon and we promised we would help," I say. He seemed surprised at that.

"So will you help us? Please," I beg.

"Yes," he says finally. He does the biggest face-palm I've ever seen and I feel sorry for him.

□□□□□□□□

We don't do any classes, and instead spend the time with Turner, deep in the bowels of the school, studying the transcript of my father's interviews all these years ago.

There are pages and pages of it, all very similar. They ask the same questions and get the same answers, but one extract has a few interesting points.

'Continue Interview with Donald Gentle. Restart time 1600. Same people present as before. Detective Inspector Giles Thompson (GT) and Detective Sergeant Hillary Dobson (HD) interviewing.

GT: Donald can you tell us again where you were after your class? Where was it? How did you get there? How long did you stay and what did you do?

DG: I told it all already. You have asked me three times now. Why doesn't anyone believe me?

GT: We need to ask you again. We want to find out what happened to your friends, Donald.

DG: We went to a place where people are angry. They tried to catch us as soon as we came in.

GT: What was it called, Donald?

DG: I told you already. I don't know.

GT: How did you get in?

DG: I don't know.

GT: Tell us more about the people.

DG: They were like us, but not like us.

GT: What do you mean?

DG: Their eyes were different.

GT: How were they different?

DG: I don't know. Just different.

GT: What else?

DG: They scared me. They scared all of us.

GT: How did they scare you?

DG: They screamed at us and chased us.

GT: And what happened?

DG: I don't want to tell you again.

GT: We need to hear it again, Donald. What happened when they chased you?

DG: They caught Colin.

GT: Colin Hamilton. Was he your friend?

GT: Yes.

DG: What happened to Colin?

Interviewee upset and given handkerchief.

DG: They bit his head off.

GT: What happened after that? What happened to your other friends?

DG: I ran. I don't know. I ran and ran.

GT: Did you like Colin?

DG: Yes.

GT: Didn't you want to help him?

Interviewee crying - pause

DG: I couldn't help him.

GT: Why not?

DG: He was dead.

GT: I see. Do you ever have dreams, Donald?

DG: Yes.

GT: Maybe you just dreamed everything? Maybe Colin is still alive somewhere? Did you all go somewhere? The forest? The old quarry? The reservoir?

DG: No. I know the difference between a dream and something real.

GT: Okay, okay, relax a little bit.

DG: Okay.

GT: Is there anything else you want to tell us about what happened that day? Anything else you can think of that might help? Anything at all that you have not told us.

DG: Yes. I know none of you believe me. If you did you wouldn't keep asking and asking me the same thing. After the first time you asked me, I knew you didn't believe me. So I didn't tell you something. Now it doesn't matter. I am going to tell you and I don't care if you believe me or not. I don't care.

GT: Okay, Donald, try to stay calm. We are trying to help. Tell us what else you remember.

DM: It was a factory where they killed boys and hung them up. They took the skin off with hot steam. I saw it all when I hid before the door opened again and I was able to leave. They hung all my friends up by the feet. Colin was dead. Stewart and Iain were screaming, but so were all the other people. There was big animals, metal machine people and people working in chains.

GT: Do you like movies or books Donald?

Note: Interviewee is shaking head and ignoring the question.

"Poor guy," Scotty says.

"What kind of boy was Donald Gentle?" Jonathan asks Turner.

"He was a stable, helpful, kind boy. Not the kind to exaggerate or lie. I always figured there had to be some truth in what he was saying. They never got him to change a single piece of his story. My, they pushed him and pushed him. Tried to catch him out. But he never changed one bit. When I met your Dad again, I saw the boy in his eyes. I knew what he was saying was true," Turner says. "Are you sure you still want to try to go there?"

"There is no choice, is there?" I say. "We cannot leave them there."

"My heart rate is going up just thinking about it," Scotty says. "Part of me doesn't believe it and part of me is scared."

We are all pretty much thinking the same thing; Scotty merely articulated it honestly.

"We know Sheldon is in there and still alive. And Jan," says Jonathan.

"Take us to the machine, Mr. Turner. You promised. I am going in," I say. "Even if we don't have a route out. I cannot leave my Dad in there, or Sheldon. Or Jan."

"I don't know. I cannot help you there. Maybe there is no easy way out." Mr. Turner shakes his head. "Even if running the machine this side was what was required, there is no way we can time it. Your time will be different. I have no idea what you will find or even if you land in the same place."

"Let's go before I change my mind," says Scotty, speaking for all of us again.

# CHAPTER FOUR

## Dark Madness

Scotty disagrees, but might be secretly relieved when Jonathan and I argue that he should stay out this time. The idea is that if we can, we'll send word to him to come with anything we need. Mr. Turner agrees and says he will organise a place for Scotty to sleep in the school over the weekend. Turner says he'll stay with him and they will form the 'base camp' together.

More to give us a feeling of confidence than anything, we leave the school, go home and pack two rucksacks with anything that might be useful. From bottled water to extra waterproofs, from torches to a radio, a piece of rope, a padlock, we take as much as we can carry. I pack any remaining marbles I can find, thinking that Dad had taken most until I discover a huge supply at the bottom of his wardrobe. I don't know why we would want them, but I know that Huptoou is keen. I put a few ordinary marbles in my pack, and I pack my agate earrings along with the rest in a money belt under my clothes. It's fairly heavy and it does give me a slight bulk, but nobody else notices.

We return after the school has closed and the last pupils and teachers have gone home for the weekend. Turner signals it's okay; he is about to start closing up properly. He goes around and locks everything as normal, including the big gate at the front, while we wait in the lab.

As soon as Turner returns he starts the machine.

"Take care," Scotty says. We hug crazy tight, nearly squashing my air out. I kiss him once on the cheek and look deep in his eyes. "It will be fine. We will see you soon."

"Good luck bro!" Scotty man-hugs Jonathan, but nobody is laughing this time.

The giant silver vacuum towers above us like some shuttlecraft to the unknown. After five minutes we can hear the machine labouring as it sucks the remaining air out. A large gauge measures the vacuum, but I don't understand what the numbers mean. Sounds like the loud crackling of bacon bounces off the high ceiling at the top of the machine. The cylinder starts to rotate; I have to look away or risk getting dizzy.

Turner opens a leather case and takes out two metal objects about ten inches in diameter. They look like some sort of gyroscope cum electric motor with handles on each side. Burnished blue wire is wrapped around glass and metal that looks like magnets. He gives one each to Jonathan and me.

"Surfing coils. Your dad made these ones. I don't know what they do, exactly," Turner admits.

It is only after I grip the handles of the object that I start to really feel scared.

"Don't we need to go in the cupboard?" I say.

Turner looks surprised. "No. It's only those close to the coils that disappear. It doesn't matter where you start from."

"Okay. Let's just make sure we are all ready," Jonathan says. "Bags, Camera, Flashlight, Water. Do we have everything?"

"Yes" I say. It's pointless going through the list now. It's way too late. I can feel the hum in my body and from Jonathan's expression he can feel it too.

Turner moves far back and motions Scotty to do the same. I hear the machine tone change as Turner operates the control panel. The speed and the noise continue to increase. I look at Jonathan and he's mouthing something to the two mad scientists lit up behind the control panel. I almost have to lip read to get what Jonathan is saying.

"Beam us up, Scotty!"

I don't know if Scotty got the joke, but he waves his trademark wave and looks at the floor for a second. I don't know if he saw us go. There is a flash of blue darkness and I feel myself fly into the centre of the machine. I scream. Something has gone wrong and I am about to be dashed to pieces on this huge burnished rotating drum.

Silence. Darkness. Cold.

'Phutt', a noise, I am alive, sitting on round slippery rocks and other light rubble. It's pitch black and I can hear noises like people breathing or shuffling in the distance. There is a strange unpleasant smell. Cat urine? Unwashed tripe? I want to call out to Jonathan or go into my rucksack for the torch, but a deep primal instinct tells me to hold. I wait, trying to quiet my breath; my heart pounds in my ears and for a moment it takes me back to my childhood when I lay in bed frightened, not understanding that it was my own heart I could hear thudding in my chest and head.

I reach out and feel around, straight ahead; there is nothing. Beneath me, all around are these greasy rocks. I stare at the dark hoping my eyes will adjust, but only purple blackness dances before me. My instinct screams that there is a void surrounding me. Am I correct? I move with caution, terrified I'll fall over the edge of this blackness.

When I ease my rucksack off, the rocks shift beneath me, and one or two small ones tumble down the slope, making a light rattling sound. As I shuffle my body around, my fingers disappear inside holes in one of the rocks my hand touches. Curious, I trace around the sticky holes and slimy contours. The rocks are only spherical on one side. The other side has a design. The little ridges and breaks remind me of the corrugated ridges on a cockleshell. When the jaw moves and my fingers slip inside, I realise the ridges are teeth.

The mass shifts under me when I jump to my feet with a scream. My breath catches in my throat as I scrabble in my bag for a torch. Please, where is it? A couple of sweaters slip from my pack onto the ground. As I rummage, I become aware of noises. Crying. Moaning. Painful noises. Things shift in the dark but don't seem to come any closer to me. My desperate search for the torch continues. Then I cry in frustration and fear when the lights start to come on, in huge fluorescent rows, across what turns out to be a giant warehouse.

The pit is full of bones, hundreds of partially clean skulls in a giant's pile. Huge pulleys, gantries and shovels run overhead, silent and unmoving for the moment. Large band saws and chisel-like machines run along a number of lines below.

The source of the increasing noise becomes obvious: naked boys, crammed in dark cages and cells. Steel legs keep the cages raised off the ground and channels run underneath. Silver boxes with pipes at one end run the length of the cells.

These unfortunates blink in the bright lights, reaching out through the bars and calling something I don't understand. Some have scratches and bald patches where they have torn themselves or been scratched by others. To my horror, I realise that the silver hoppers running the lengths of the cages could be for feeding and the long open sewers underneath the cages take their common waste.

'Oh my God what horror have I come to? Can my Father really be here?' I throw up a little bile on my shoes, as I grab my bag and start to slip down the hill of bones towards the darkest area and away from the cells. The clamour rises as a few catch sight of me. The noise has alerted someone and the lights are now full brightness. I slide off the pile and push myself under the machinery; it looks like a manufacturing line. I drag my bag in as quickly and as quietly as I can. The light is still too bright, so I crawl slowly inside the line, to a giant machine almost at the end that looks like an oven or shrink-wrapping machine. Its bulk creates shadows, and I find the deepest shadow and crawl in, shivering with fear.

When I shift around I can see the end of the cells. The occupants are still restless and noisy, wailing almost and reaching out between the bars as if clawing for freedom. The sight makes me shake and my teeth chatter.

I flinch when the first man comes into sight. He is huge and carries a metal stick with an orange tip. He shouts, it might have been 'shut-up', as he runs the stick across the outstretched arms. I can hear the zaps of electricity and the squeals. The arms retract like so many underwater coral, withdrawing for protection.

The second man appears at the side of the machine I'm under; I could have touched his shoes. I hold my breath; clench my teeth while he wanders back and forth. Finally, he goes towards the other man and after a brief exchange they walk away together. Both of them were at least eight or nine foot tall with barrel chests and muscular biceps. A few minutes later the huge rows of lights starts to go off and I'm soon in the dark again. This time, I prefer the dark. I wait for a long time before I move. Finally, there is silence.

I try to remember what I'd seen from the top; there are only two walls that are free of cells, and the other corner is the direction the men came from. I think about Dad being in these cells, I really do, but I am terrified and can't imagine how I can search cages with hundreds of people without getting caught.

The second 'phutt' makes me start; it sounded from the top of the pile that I just scrambled down. Maybe it's my heightened alertness, the adrenaline, but I take it all in, in a split second. Jonathan! I hurry along in the dark, feeling my way back to the pit. There is slight movement from above; he is rustling in his pack. A couple of skulls roll down the hill and the cages stir a little. Sickened, but out of necessity, I pull myself into the pit and slowly crawl up the gradual incline of skulls and bones.

"Jonathan," I whisper. "Don't move. Be quiet."

I listen. I sense the urgency in my voice has frozen him on the top. I move cautiously towards where I think he'll be and whisper again.

"Psst." He is close, but over to my left.

We bump together. "Really quiet," I warn. I'm sure he can feel me shaking. He starts to turn; I grab his arm and squeeze twice. He freezes again and I put my lip right into his ear in the dark.

"Listen. We cannot use the light or make a noise. There are people all around us. We are sitting in a sort of pit raised above the floor. We are on the top of a pile of... light rocks, which will move and tumble if we disturb them. I arrived here ten or fifteen minutes before you. There must be a time difference. But I am so glad you are here."

Jonathan reaches up and takes my face in his hands, finds my ear and whispers. "Don't worry. I'm here. Why don't we just get up and go out?"

"No. No. You don't understand," I say. I clench my teeth as I reach down for a skull. I take his fingers and trace the eye sockets, nose and finally the teeth. He flinches. "They are all around us. This is not a good place." He gets my message. I hear his breathing change from his mouth to his nose.

"It's pitch black. Do you know where to go?" Jonathan says.

"I think so. We have to move real slowly."

"What's that noise?" he says. I can imagine his expression and head cocked in the dark as he strains to understand the whimpering noise.

"Let's just move," I whisper. "Hold onto me and move slowly. I left my bag down there."

It takes us an hour to find my bag and reach the wall. We are creeping and shuffling while fighting an enormous instinct telling us to run. My skin tingles with static and tension. Both of us bump our heads more than once. And my knees are wet, where I crawled through some cold foul-smelling sludge; I don't want to think what it was. My focus is to get out.

Each time I turn to Jonathan hoping to see some level of comfort and confidence in his eyes, I am disappointed. He is as close to panic as me.

After we crawl across a clear space and feel the flat surface in front, I'm confident we have reached the riveted green wall that I had seared in my memory when the lights went out.

Using the wall as a guide we are able to move a bit faster around the perimeter. The air is a little fresher and we leave the noise of the cells behind. Jonathan takes the lead and I can sense from the noise of his jacket he is sweeping in front of him with his arm. Finally he stops. "We don't know where we are headed. We need to see something."

I hear him put his rucksack down and unzip the fastening. A moment later a faint light appears; a torch covered with a thick woolly sock shines enough light for us to see the paint lines on the floor.

Ten minutes later we are at a huge bay shutter set in shadows. There is an almost invisible grey chain on both sides for pulling it up manually.

"It will be noisy," Jonathan considers. "And we don't know where it leads."

By this time I don't care, as long as it opens and there is freedom on the other side, I would run like the wind. I've had enough of this place. We agree not to go any further; this is our escape route whatever happens.

Jonathan shows me how to pull the chain and starts to go across to the chain on the other side.

"Don't leave me," I say, close to panic now my adrenalin has gone. He ties the torch to my belt, places both my hands on the chain.

"Wait until I say pull. We only need to get it up high enough to roll under," he whispers before kissing me hard on the lips. "Go as soon as you get a gap, okay?"

He melts into the dark across the huge bay.

"Okay, pull!"

The noise is terrible. But it doesn't matter anyway; an alarm comes on.

"Pull. Harder!" he shouts over the noise of a siren filling the giant shed.

It is heavy, the door moves slowly up and I am straining with every fibre. The roof lights start to come on again. We are soon lit up; I can see Jonathan breaking himself under the weight. Shouts from across the building lend strength to my arms. I pull with everything but the shutter hardly budges. A two-inch gap is all we have; I look at Jonathan. He stops pulling and is looking up, desperately searching the wall. He comes to my side. I should have seen it; a power box with a big button is on the wall above my head. He bangs it and runs back for his sack. I see the first guard appear on the other side of the processing line, attracted by the noise of the door motor. He looks straight at me; I stare at his bulk. The door starts to go up. I get down and throw myself through, dragging my rucksack through behind me. A split second later Jonathan's sack is kicked out. I hear the door start to go back down again. No! It's closing and he's inside. I scramble back towards the door, terrified. Then Jonathan rolls out the narrowing gap; he's pressed the close button deliberately to give us time.

Moonlight reveals we are in a huge compound filled with containers and what might be vehicles but I can't be sure. Now lights are coming on in the yard. Voices shout from around the corner and echo inside the door as we run to the containers.

"Go, go!" Jonathan pushes me down between two containers. He doesn't have to tell me twice. The bag stops me sprinting flat out, but I am putting everything I have into my run. The shouts are coming from behind us; somewhere an engine starts up. Jonathan takes the lead, checking every now and then to see if I am keeping up. We duck through rows of containers, turn and change direction so many times, I can't be sure we are still running away.

Jonathan stops dead and I run into him. He backs up and I try to see around him. Some sort of unmanned hovercraft has come around the corner. It hangs in the air directly ahead, blocking our way.

"Other way. Down here!" Jonathan shouts. We start to run and I feel the first electrical charge sear my arm as it just misses me. "Right again. This way!" Jonathan wants us to turn again and again, out of the line of fire. We emerge from between the containers and run along the side of a culvert. The machine is fast. It follows us and fires again. I duck instinctively. Jonathan yells and goes down. I see the charge zap him on the thigh. He tumbles into the ditch and lies still. I jump in beside him, on top of him; he is breathing, but unconscious. The machine flies past, searching; we have seconds until it locates us. Jonathan is still out when the machine comes back and hovers menacingly.

I watch it as it comes in close. It stays just out of arms' reach while it scans me and I fully expect to get zapped too. In the distance, I can hear men coming and see lights of other machines sweeping towards us. I am just about to turn back to Jonathan when I see the movement. Hooded figures appear on the embankment above the machine, three boys. Huptoou. He signals me with finger to his lips and at once the other two jump on the machine. They net the saucer with a black cloth, thick with oil. And they struggle with it while Huptoou comes down and grabs my arm.

"Come," he says. "Quick."

"No. Jonathan." I point at the prone figure.

"No! Okay!" He pulls me.

I look again and two other hooded figures have appeared and started moving Jonathan. I run with Huptoou while the nearby machine goes crazy trying to burn its way out of the oily trap with the boys still hanging on. We don't have far to go. The culvert leads to a drain. Inside we twist and turn, heads low, still running. I hear gates and doors clang behind us and I hope Jonathan is still following. Finally, we enter another tunnel that leads into a large man-made cavern. There are around ten boys waiting for us. I turn around. The others are coming with Jonathan. I learn a few of their names and make eye contact. Gull, Briss, Slav and Coin. They seem friendly enough.

"We walk now," Huptoou says. And I can't be sure, but I feel he is eyeing my rucksack. His face still makes me shiver and I decide not to trust him completely, even though he's saved us.

My mind is whirring with questions, fears, worries and an overwhelming sense of bewilderment and lack of control. Jonathan is still out cold and I cannot have a proper conversation with Huptoou as we march deeper into what I hope is the safety of the cavern.

Finally, I realise that we are safe and stopping. The boys strip Jonathan on a camp bed, and clean and dress his wounds before covering him in thin blanket. Gull gives me some water for him but when I try to make him drink he is shivering and remains unconscious.

Without hesitation I strip off and climb in beside him to try to warm him.

It's not until the middle of the night when he wakes up for water and seems to have stopped shivering. He barely recognises me but pulls me tight against his body as if he is scared I would leave him. We burrow into each other the rest of the night seeking solace in the familiar and turning our backs on the strange world beyond our blanket.

□□□□□□□□

"Where are we?" Jonathan asks. "How did we get here?" He wakes up on the makeshift bed rubbing his head and his leg at the same time. He sounds woozy as he looks around.

The place is huge. Beds and tables are dotted around. Some cut into the walls. Perfectly round dark tunnels lead off in all directions. Dozens of boys go back and forward. I wonder what they are doing. They are like ants scurrying around carrying things. There is a strange smell everywhere, but I can't place it. Last night's experience has placed frightening ideas in my head that so far I have not fully accepted. So, I realise that I don't have complete answers for Jonathan. But I recognise death and organisation when I see them together.

"I don't know exactly, some kind of underground bunker," I say. "Huptoou brought us here after the security machine shot you with some kind of electric stun gun. We are safe."

"It hurts," he says. "How long have I been out?"

"Overnight. But you wakened up to drink water and hug me."

"We slept together?" he asked. "On this tiny bed?"

"You were delirious."

"Hmmm, maybe. But my dreams were nice."

"It's just lucky it was not a deadly weapon that shot you and these guys saved us."

"How did he just happen to be around when we arrived?"

"That's what I asked. He said he was watching for Donald, my Dad. But that doesn't make sense."

"No." Jonathan gets up and looks around and quickly sits down. "Whoa, a little wobbly. Where is Huptoou now?"

"He has gone to get something. Told me to wait. But the communication is not easy."

"What was that place last night? Some kind of factory?"

I hesitate to tell him anything else. He'd not seen as much of it as me. Perhaps my twisted thoughts are simply my imagination affected by the travel. If it is some kind of factory, perhaps the people in cages were slaves. In my heart I knew it was too close to what my Father had described as a boy.

"Where is my pack?" Jonathan asks and I was happy to change the subject.

I point to where it's tied onto mine and both locked with a padlock I found in one of the pockets.

"Trouble?"

"Maybe they think we have something valuable. I didn't get much sleep. One or two of them have been sniffing around from time to time," I nod. "It may just be curiosity, but they still frighten me. Some of them are like boys who never became men, yet lived for fifty years."

"It's a funny description, but I know exactly what you mean."

He stands again and watches the activity. I can see him thinking, trying to figure something out.

"Do you think we are below a city? And these are the lost boys?"

"Why are there no girls?"

"The lost gay boys then?" Jonathan laughs.

"How can you joke?" I look at him. "We are underground. It's not safe to go out. We have no idea how to get home. And we are surrounded by strange-looking boys." I start to laugh nervously and it turns into tears. "I keep thinking of all these people in cages and wondering if Dad could be in there."

Jonathan comes to me and I can just about see his face through the blurry tears. It feels great when he hugs me, but after a few seconds I realise that I have to harden up a little. I am no use to Dad, or anyone, as an emotional wreck. I chose to come here, I remind myself. Buck up.

"Okay, we had no choice last night. We couldn't search the cages. We will figure out what's best to do. Don't worry."

Huptoou arrives just as Jonathan and I are breaking apart. He looks surprised as he hands me a thick envelope.

I tear it open. "It's from Dad," I realise; I read frantically with Jon and Huptoou standing and looking over my shoulder.

'To whoever is reading this,

Welcome to hell. Since you are reading, I must assume that you escaped the factory. For that I am thankful. I hope you have some marbles, for that is what I promised the geldings for any visitor that came through safely. Give him no more than three ordinary marbles. If you have others, keep them safe. If you don't have marbles, I hope you can convince Huptoou to let you continue on your journey and we pay later.

I left here on Wednesday the 16th of May 2048 under the cover of night. The dangers at night are marginally better than those faced during the day. I am going after two boys, Sheldon and Jan, who are in here. They are headed to the fourth quarter where they are hoping to cross into the metropolis. I am not sure what they are trying to do. My intention is to catch up with them and try to bring us all home safely.

I would tell you to turn back. The way forward is not an easy one. Unfortunately, the 'way out' is not the way you came in. We have reason to believe that the exit is equipoise of the entry and as such situated in both geography and time at the polar opposite of this dimension. It would take too long to explain in this letter. Just make sure you note the exact time you arrived. You may need it to exit, if you get that far.

You should go with all haste to the house of Zohar Keshet on the other side of the market. You can trust the geldings to take you there, but trust them no more than that. Limit also your trust in Keshet. Learn what you need to know, but move on quickly. Do not sleep there or you will find yourself back at the factory. I will leave a sealed package there for you. Check that it has not been tampered with. If it has, do not believe the contents. And then I am sorry to say: you are on your own.

Good luck and God bless.

Donald Gentle.'

I put my hand to my mouth. Huptoou is watching closely. I realise that he can't read and is waiting to see what I say and do.

"Marbles?"

"Later," I snap and he doesn't look too pleased, but he backs off a bit. I am shaking my head.

"What's wrong?" Jonathan says. "And what's all this stuff about marbles?"

"It's definitely Dad's handwriting. So, Huptoou wasn't waiting for Dad. Dad had them waiting in case anyone came through. He knew that Huptoou had been going back and forward. He might even have been told or seen Sheldon's note?"

"No. Sheldon was looking for your Dad when he sent the note. He'd have to have seen our reply to Sheldon?"

"In which case he'd suspect that I would put the pieces together and try to come," I say. "And it means that Sheldon didn't get the reply."

"Doesn't make sense. He'd have left a message for you, his daughter, if he thought you might come through."

"The other thing that scares me... Dad is an atheist."

"So?" Jonathan looks askance.

"He says 'God bless' at the end. That can only mean that things are bad."

Jonathan doesn't agree, but I know Dad like I know myself; he is scared.

I write our entry time on the letter; I remembered looking at my watch in the first few seconds. But I'm not exactly sure what time Jonathan arrived. He doesn't know, so I estimate ten minutes after me. I'm not too happy with that.

"Huptoou. We go at night to Zohar Keshet, okay? You take us?"

"Eight marbles," he says.

"No." I do my best to look mean and angry. "One marble."

He smiles and looks pleased with himself. Immediately, I get the feeling he'd have done it for free, included in the three marbles we already owe him.

"Damn. You might at least have the decency not to smile. I ought to kick your butt!" I almost shout it.

Huptoou laughs, although I don't think he fully understood.

"We need him in one piece," Jonathan says, smiling a great big chicken smile directly at the face full of impish malevolence.

"Eat, food and shower. Rest," Huptoou says. "We leave at dusk. Market-a-go-go."

"Jonathan, you go eat and shower. I need to rest here. Catch up a little sleep," I say. I speak slowly so that Huptoou understands that I am not leaving my bags alone.

Jonathan catches on as well. "I will not be long." He takes a towel out of his rucksack and carefully closes it again. He disappears across the hall with Huptoou and a couple of others, while I lie on the bed and lightly close my eyes, with one hand and arm resting on the rucksacks.

When Jonathan returns he has to wake me. I had dozed off and have no idea how long he'd been away.

"Hi. Everything okay?" I ask.

"Sure. I feel better. Not sure what I ate, but it tasted okay."

"What are the showers like?"

"They are okay actually. I was expecting a tin drum or somebody throwing water on me."

"I don't feel like food, but I will go shower now," I say. "Where are they?"

"They are over there and round to the right, easy to find. I was the only one there, but I don't think there are ladies. It's just a big communal area."

"Okay." I grab a towel and change of jeans and set off. I still feel grubby after last night's crawl through the factory muck.

The showers are empty; must be the time of day. There are around thirty showers in a large rocky area with a wooden slatted floor. Hot water flows immediately and I wonder where it is coming from. I decide to move quickly and jump out of my clothes and under the steaming water. I make sure the money belt is as close to me as possible.

It is the noise of other showers squeaking on that alerts me. I quickly wash the shampoo and soap off, open my eyes and look over my shoulder. There is a group of ten boys in various stages of undress and preparing to shower. They all stare at me as if fascinated. I grab my towel, wrap it around me and exit the shower. They continue to watch me as they start their own showers. I didn't see it right away. Well you wouldn't. The sheer horror hits me as I rush back to Jonathan in only a towel.

"You forgot something?" Jonathan asks.

"No. I am finished. I just got some company that's all."

"Oh. Are you okay?"

"Jonathan, did you wonder what my dad's letter meant by geldings?" He nods. "All the boys are castrated," I say.

He is speechless, his eyes wide. "Ouch. Sick!"

"All of them," I repeat for emphasis. "Can you hold the towel around me until I get dressed?"

"Sure," Jonathan agrees. And I watch him; his eyes are completely closed as I dress. "Well, at least there is one gentleman around here," I say.

He grimaces. "Yes, I'd rather keep my bits, thanks. Besides I imagine I saw more last night."

I scowl at him but he can't see me with his eyes still closed and continue grinning at his own joke, until I pull my sweatshirt on and lightly slap him on the ear.

The rest of the day passes slowly. On one hand we want to get moving. On the other hand we are safe for the moment while we learn as much as we can.

It's late afternoon when I see Huptoou coming quickly towards us.

"Hound Dogs are coming. Must you have to go." He touches my jacket, and makes a sniffing sound with his nose and points outside, in the direction of where I imagine our arrival point.

"No!" I cry.

"What?" Jonathan asks.

"When I searched my pack, I took out a couple of sweaters and left them on the top..."

"We go!" Huptoou is nodding vigorously.

"We are being tracked by dogs?" Jonathan queries. "How can they come in here?"

A siren sounds, a long eerie noise in the echoes. The boys scamper like so many rats, fleeing into the various tunnels.

Huptoou shouts "come" and starts running. The underground cave is emptying fast.

For a second, I struggle with the padlock holding the rucksacks together. Then Jonathan picks up his sack and I shoulder mine and we run after Huptoou across the now empty cavern. Two boys join us from the side and we run into a dark tunnel and settle into a slow jog in the dim light. I look at Jonathan but he is watching where he is putting his feet. I do the same. The rucksacks are heavy and the straps pull on my shoulders as we run.

Huptoou has a wiry frame that looks almost ill, but I'm surprised by his stamina and energy. We keep a steady pace for thirty minutes passing a number of cross tunnels and I wonder where they lead. It appears to be a vast underground network.

When we finally slow at a multiple junction, Huptoou signals quiet. All three put their ears to the wall then point to a few directions and make a few hand gestures. I can't hear anything at first, and then I become aware of a noise in one of the tunnels. Running. A few moments later, three boys rush onto the junction. One boy points behind them, nods and holds up his fist twice. Huptoou and the others nod and start down another tunnel with Jonathan and me following. It looks like we have turned ninety degrees. I feel we are going up a slight incline; the running gets harder. For a split second the noise of the dogs reaches my ears for the first time and for the first time in my life I understand the expression, 'blood ran cold'. The feeling of being chased and hunted must sit deep in our primal brain; my senses are on teenage overdrive.

We reach another junction and I am completely disorientated. The boys hesitate; I can see there is something wrong. One boy shakes his head furiously as he points down the tunnel. The others listen then they whisper together. Huptoou comes to me and points to my sweatshirt, under my jacket. "Give quickly." I'm fast. I remove my rucksack and jacket and pull the sweat over my head. The boy called Gull takes it, puts it on and runs down an opposite tunnel rubbing the sweatshirt along the wall as he does.

"Trapped," Huptoou says and he illustrates with both hands, people closing on us from all sides. "Come fast."

The howls are much louder and coming from more than one place.

"That's not echoes; they are all around us," Jonathan says, voice wavering, as he realises.

The feeling of helplessness, relying on someone else, frightens both of us. It is mirrored on our faces.

The next junction is a disaster. Boys appear out of a number of tunnels simultaneously. It is clear from their expressions they are panicking. I look at Huptoou and notice him signalling one of the others. He points up and shrugs. I can see individuals trying to decide which tunnels to take. A scream pierces the air and a boy flies from a tunnel, his neck in the jaws of a large muscular four-legged creature that is neither dog nor cat. The powerful beast skids to a halt and savages the boy.

"WolfCat. Too many," Huptoou says as he grabs me and points up the wall. There is a small metal ladder that goes straight up. I run for it. The end is about three feet above me and the ladder looks broken.

"Leave the rucksack!" Jonathan shouts.

"No. Help me!"

Jonathan crouches and I climb on his back and pull myself up. I climb up enough to allow space on the ladder before I look back. Jonathan is fumbling in his pack. Another WolfCat arrives and starts to prowl towards one of the groups of boys backing up in the corner.

"Jonathan," I call and climb some more. Huptoou joins me on the ladder and climbs, blocking some of my view. I see Gull, still with my sweatshirt on, rush from another tunnel with a WolfCat close behind, but it stops chasing him, pads about with its neck stretched up, sniffing the air. It looks directly up at me.

"Don't stop. No matter what happens!" Huptoou shouts in panic. He has seen it too and unlike me, maybe he knows how high these creatures can jump.

I climb again; we are about forty feet up. My hands start to sweat as I grip the rungs too tightly. My rucksack threatens to pull me back off the ladder. But I need to look down; I have to see what is happening.

Jonathan has taken his sabre out of his rucksack and is running towards the animal that had trapped the boys in the corner. I scream 'No!' inside myself and for a second I am dizzy. When I see him prod the animal then jump back when it tries to swipe him, I nearly fall. Below me the other animal jumps up at the ladder. It can easily jump twenty feet but it can't grip and climb the metal. It pulls a portion of the ladder off the wall just under Huptoou's feet and I feel everything shake.

"Jon!" I hear myself wail.

"Up!" Huptoou commands. I have no choice. My strength is going. I pray as I climb, wondering if there is a God in this place, making sure each rung is solid and each grip is secure before I release the previous one. It is easier to do it with my eyes closed. Ignoring the screams and the roars below I climb one step after another, maintaining a steady rhythm, until I can feel the sweat breaking out on my back. The ladder shakes and I realise that it is not fixed to the wall in places. And I start to worry about the exit, if there is one.

The platform is a surprise. It isn't the top of the ladder. It's cut into the rock about twenty feet square. I need to rest. I struggle to keep my balance as I reach onto the platform with one foot. The weight of the rucksack prevents me from swinging myself around safely. I shriek when a hand pulls me in.

"Robyn? Is that you? I don't believe it!"

Sheldon and Jan are in the shadows. I collapse on the floor at their feet, shaking from exhaustion and fear. It is surreal. Sheldon gives me some water and takes my rucksack off, while Jan helps Huptoou off the ladder.

"How did you get here?" Sheldon repeats. "Is there someone with you?"

I sit up. "Jonathan is down there!" I choke on the water. I don't know what I'm expecting anyone to do.

"You have someone else down there?" Sheldon says. He lies down and looks over the edge.

"My friend. Can you see him?" I crawl weakly to the edge and lie down on my belly beside him. The ground is probably over three hundred feet beneath us. The rocky overhang stops me seeing the whole junction below, but at one point I see Jonathan keeping an animal at bay with his sabre. But it looks hopeless; another animal is slinking around the wall behind him. I turn my face away.

"The guy with the sword?" Sheldon asks.

I keep my face down, bite my lip and nod miserably.

Sheldon watches for a bit longer before he turns away.

"I'm sorry," he says as the screams and roars continue to echo from below. "There is nothing we can do"

He is right of course. Even if the ladder had been intact, it wouldn't make sense to go back down.

I hadn't known Jonathan had brought a sabre along. He and I normally skirmish with foils and the thought brings tears to my eyes. Perhaps he'd just intended to show it to me and decided to take it along without telling me. I curse him for being so brave and foolish, instead of getting on the ladder.

"I think he bought you time to get away," Sheldon says, rubbing my back as I weep.

□□□□□□□□

I am in shock as I hold Sheldon's hand and stumble behind. I don't remember getting out of the tunnel. Jan carries my rucksack. When we stop we are outside in the dimming light among a few trees under an enormous flyover bridge. The park around us smells of fresh leaves and flowers but my nostrils detect occasional greasy-sweet food smells that suggest there are houses or a built up area close by. We walk down a slope towards what looks like a river in the dusk. It's silver grey and moves silently but quickly past the banks. I sense its depth and power, and we turn into an open maintenance bunker around one of the massive concrete legs. There are two or three steps down into the shadows but no roof overhead.

"We are staying here; this is the Great Park," Jan says as he puts the rucksack in the corner. "We can only stay one night." I nod and look at him. He still has an air of mastery but it has diminished. I try to remember the boy who had given me the red velvet bag. Where has he gone? Jan looks ten years older, haggard and exhausted, stressed or both. Sheldon looks better. They lead me to some cardboard and we all crash on the ground except Huptoou.

"I go and come. I have to see my friends," he says. His face has lost some of its energy. "I come back to take you to Market-a-go-go."

"Okay."

"Need marbles."

I nod, open my rucksack and find one small pouch of five ordinary marbles. It seems ungenerous to take one away after everything we've been through. I give him all five and am surprised when he insists I take one back.

"I'll be back," he says and disappears into the gloom.

Sheldon, Jan and I look at each other. There is so much to explain but perhaps no one feels like talking right now. Perhaps they are being sensitive to my mood. All I can think about is Jonathan still down in the hole with those beasts. They leave me to sit quietly for half an hour before Jan speaks to me gently, coaxing me to talk.

"I cannot believe you are here. I wish you weren't. It's not a good place. We thought your Dad might come."

"Didn't you see the reply to your note?"

He shakes his head. "We were just on our way back to Huptoou tonight."

"Dad was already here before you sent your note; he travelled without telling me," I say. "But I saw him go into the class and disappear. And we figured out how to follow."

"Where is he?" Sheldon asks.

"I don't know. We were hoping to catch up with him."

"This place is not easy to survive. We have been stealing to eat. We twice made the mistake of asking for help," Sheldon says.

"What's with the marbles?" I ask.

"Huptoou asks for them constantly. We don't know why he wants them. Of course, we didn't have any to give.'

"Are you hungry?" I ask. They look up. I go into my rucksack and bring out large bars of chocolate and glucose tablets. They both jump on the chocolate, ripping off the paper and stuffing it in their mouths. Sheldon realises I am watching and feeling slightly abashed offers me a piece.

"No, I don't feel like eating. I feel a bit sick. Do you have any water?"

"I will go get some more." Jan breaks off another piece of chocolate, stuffs it in his mouth, jumps up and runs off.

"Be careful!" Sheldon shouts after him.

"Yup."

"The place is full of robbers and muggers, gangs, prostitutes and crazies," Sheldon says. "And I know where he is going for the water."

"How did you find me?" I ask him. "Were you trying to?"

"No, sheer luck. Coincidence due to being forced back here again. We have been staying in the Great Park every few nights. We move around. We heard the noise. It led us to the tunnel that comes out in the trees. We thought it was a way back to the boys. They brought us here originally and we tried to get across the suburbs to the fourth quarter. This area is a ghetto, a slum, there are few cars, nothing works here, everyone is on the take, crime seems to be a constant threat and we are giant magnets for trouble. You cannot get a vehicle; transport is impossible. The infrastructure is completely broken. Walking is dangerous and we stand out as foreigners. We thought we might find the Metropolis an easier place to fit in."

"What happened?"

"We didn't get far. We have been chased, attacked and threatened. Each time we have ended up back in this area. It's the place we know best and can be the safest. 'Unknown territory, full of nasty surprises.' That's our motto."

"How did you arrive in the first place?"

"Your Dad was working on the machine. He went to the basement to put the power on, told us not to touch anything. Jan lifted the coil thing and I was standing next to him. Bang. The next thing we were here. No travel documents or toothbrush. We just kept staring at each other. We had no idea what happened."

"You came in via the Factory?" I ask.

Sheldon shook his head, puzzled. "No, straight to the place with all the boys. Huptoou knew where we were from. It took me a while to work it out, but I realised that this was your disappearing thief. We stayed there for a week trying to get as much information as possible. It took us a while to piece it all together. But I already knew the story of the boys disappearing many years ago, that's what

I was going to tell you. It was lucky we landed with Huptoou. We'd have been dead by this time. We've learned survival from them."

Jan appears back, out of breath, carrying bottles of water. "Yes, but we didn't trust them, did we? So we decided to make out on our own."

There is noise in the distance. Sheldon immediately looks alarmed. "Was everything okay? Nobody followed?"

"All good. Nobody followed. Just the usual fighting on the other side of the ponds," Jan says settling down beside me.

"Where were you going?" Sheldon asks.

I tell him the story from start to finish including staying in his room. He is sad about his folks and the twins. But pleased his Mum and Dad had been kind.

It gets cold so we all bed down for the night. Someone has to stay on guard; Jan takes the first watch and sits close to us while Sheldon and I cuddle tight under some blankets they have. We agree to rest and wait until tomorrow to give Huptoou a chance to come back.

"Do you think we..." We both start at the same time and tail off.

"You first," he says.

"No," I say. "We both know what we were going to say."

He nods in agreement.

"Do you think we will ever get home?" Jan says finishing it for us.

We don't reply. Sheldon pulls me close into his chest and I forgive him for his unwashed smell. For the moment I am warm and safe and although I can see Jonathan's face when I close my eyes, I do start to fall asleep, my body jerking with exhaustion and silent tears drying on my face.

Bright morning light and the sounds of birds bring me around. My neck is sore and my bones are cold. At first my night was full of dreams of Jonathan and me, the times we spent laughing, wrestling, running and fencing together. Then the dreams went dark; I had only sockets where my eyes should be. Animals with no teeth chased us. Dad was always ahead somewhere and we couldn't find him, couldn't reach him. We let the animals catch us and tried to befriend them. We knew we had to settle down and live with them. But the worst part was, I could no longer see Jonathan. I tried so hard to focus, but my eyes were gone, and when I reached out to touch his face, I felt only thousands of maggots squirming in his mouth.

The sunlight has come over the wall of our hideaway. It's early, but very bright. I look up when I catch movement. Jan is up a nearby tree scanning the horizons. I doubt he can see much through the thick foliage, but we'll gain a few moments advantage if people come from the bridge or the river direction. Sheldon tends a small fire, boiling something in a pan. They had let me sleep through the night. They had not wakened me for a watch and that upsets me. I like to pull my weight; it is only fair. Besides I know the guys are exhausted.

Yesterday floods back like a basement filling with cold water, within seconds of wakening from my troubled sleep. I grieve quietly in the corner for a few moments. 'Jonathan, I miss you. I'm sorry. I'd do anything to change what has happened. It's my fault for taking you here. I'm really sorry.' I talk to myself.

"It wasn't your fault. Besides, maybe he is okay." Sheldon appears next to me and reads my mind. He looks tired but fresh. "I hope you don't mind. Jan and I borrowed your towel. We had a swim in the river."

I must have looked aghast.

"No. Not together. We didn't leave you alone for a second," he says.

I relax.

"We have some black bread and a boiled egg each." He indicates the boiling pot.

"Not really hungry."

"Look, I know you are upset. But you have to keep your strength up. Whatever we have, we share and we always eat. That's the rules that Jan and I follow, now you too."

I smile wanly.

We eat quickly. I realise that the guys are always on alert; I wonder how it could be that bad. Jan goes back on watch after stuffing his food into his mouth.

It's another hour before Huptoou turns up. I run to him with the question on my lips and he shakes his head. He watches me carefully; I feel the big fat tears roll down my face and he reaches out and touches my cheek.

"We lost many, many Euny yesterday," he says. "Jon was a good man also."

"Oh, I am sorry, I am so selfish. It's all my fault." I start to cry properly when I realise that these boys that I hadn't thought twice about died because of me. Especially Gull who had taken my sweatshirt to lead the WolfCat off the scent. I feel ashamed. I know only few of their names; now I know they are called Euny. I walk away into the trees a little and turn my back on the guys. I hear Sheldon ask Huptoou many questions but I can't hear what.

Huptoou has brought us some local clothes to wear to help us blend in. Males and females wear the same style of cloaks, but two different colours. I don't understand the point, but I think anonymity is good.

"We had cloaks already," Jan says. "We were robbed."

"They left us with our jeans and sweats," Sheldon adds. "Too distinctive."

My robe is an ample dark green habit with drawstrings around the hood and wrists. The hood flops over my face and when I try to fold it back Huptoou wags a finger at me. He points to the many inside pockets and then to my rucksack. "No take."

"It's about being part of the pack here; at least not standing out," Sheldon explains. He and Jan have similar garments in grey. "I think we have to take what we can in our pockets and leave the rest." He puts his precious camera in an inside pocket and buttons the flap.

It doesn't take us long to split the pack. Huptoou watches closely as we empty everything. I'm happy I have the money belt under my clothes. I look at him and he smiles. Perhaps I'm getting used to him; he doesn't scare me quite as much as before. I give Huptoou one of the torches, a bag of barley sugar and the only pack of playing cards, which I have no idea what he'd make of. I feel stupid and angry at myself for bringing them; like some silly girl guide thinking I was going on a camping trip; a trip that has maybe cost me my best friend.

For a few moments, Huptoou taps the front of the torch and switches the light on and off, more fascinated by the glass than the light itself. He goes off and hides the lot somewhere and comes back a moment later.

Finally, Huptoou leads us out of the park. I notice he checks overhead a lot. I look up nervously; the low grey skies are empty.

"Cloud is good," Huptoou says.

It might be my imagination but we seem to stay in side streets and close to the darker buildings. Despite my poor instinct for directions, I feel we could have cut through the blocks quicker. We see few people; those we do see tend to scurry away as if four people walking together is a bad sign and none of their business. I notice an absence of children and of any signs of wealth. We cross an old railway crossing and pass what I take to be a church. Huptoou makes a sign when he passes but it isn't a sign I recognise, nor does it look respectful.

A few minutes later, we are entering a busy outdoor market where the vast majority wear the same clothes as us. Hundreds of people crowded into the space examine stalls and their range of goods. We move through the crowds slowly. I don't know what kind of market it is, but I don't like the sounds or smells. Before I can push through the crowd and look, Sheldon taps me on the shoulder.

Huptoou gathers us together and pointed all the way through the market to a large house with impenetrable yellow gates and high walls with barbed wire on top.

"Zohar," he says.

"You are not coming?" Sheldon asks what I was thinking.

"I kill him or he kill me," Huptoou says, as if we should understand. He shakes hands with us, says 'goodbye for now', and goes into the crowd.

We start to drift down between the people and stalls in the general direction of the house at the other side. Most people are hidden under their cloaks or habits. They move about the stalls with an air of desperation, searching, avoiding eye contact, and few talk to each other. I catch a glimpse of some faces; they are haggard and pockmarked. Weirdly, I notice a number have silver whistles dangling around scrawny necks.

The few that don't wear the same dull garment include three obese women. I can't take my eyes away. They are heavily made up with fat red lipstick and purple eye shadow around piggy eyes. They don't wobble, they look like they ooze along and the crowd parts to make way. The contrast between the mass of wastrels and these huge blobs makes me feel physically sick.

I get a glimpse of my first stall after these human battleships swept past, leaving a gap in their wake, which quickly fills with eager buyers. The stall is selling some kind of monkey. The seller behind the counter has thick gloves up to his elbows; he takes a timid looking creature out of the cage by the neck and holds it loosely on the weighing scales. He doesn't let it go; I should have turned away then, but I was hardly expecting what happens next. He holds it tighter and slams it down onto a wooden table. The small monkey starts biting, scratching and shrieking. The caged monkeys wail and rattle, until the butcher's cleaver takes the top of the monkey's head. The animal shrieking stops and the crowd clamours instead.

"No!" I groan. "Sick animals." Sheldon comes and holds me and tries to turn me away. Nobody takes any notice of me.

The man scoops the brain from the monkey's head and wraps it in paper. His assistant takes it and I don't see who the buyer is. The crowd surges forward as the butcher splits, guts and quarters the monkey and offers up the various bits for sale.

"Let's go." Sheldon puts his arm around me and we move as fast as we can through the crowd.

We see dogs being brought in. Cats. Some sort of weasel. A cage of moles. Large fat spiders. And trays of giant creamy maggots. If this is a sick meat market, I can't look anymore. Squeezing past these people feels different, now I have seen what they are buying and carrying under their clothes.

We pass another couple of gargantuan lip-sticked women buying something at a stall. One slithers something, which could pass for live slugs, down her throat. We try to get around the obese beauties; the crowd has the same idea and the surge pushes me off balance and in a new direction; I find myself up against the counter. The women are buying large wrapped parcels; small obsequious men come from behind to carry, while the women pay. I watch horrified, then fascinated, as one woman brings out a purse, takes out a single small glass bead and hands it to the salesman. I thought she was kidding, but the deference from behind the counter is obvious. The salesman takes the bead and weighs it. He then returns a pile of other smaller beads in change.

Sheldon looks at me quizzically. "Tiny marbles? Doesn't make sense."

I want to see more transactions. I'm no longer looking at the goods; I'm watching how they pay. I have an idea. I know it's stupid. Inside my cloak, I take the smallest plainest marble from my belt. I knuckle down on one of the counters and shoot the marble into a group of people, quickly enough so that there is little chance of anyone seeing where it came from. I might as well have thrown a grenade. The people who see the marble dive first, others hearing the exclamations dive in as well. They fight bitterly. When one man or woman gets the marble the others pounce and batter and strangle each other in a bid to wrest it from someone else's grasp and manage to hold it in their own. One man tries to swallow it. I think it's as well his arm was wrenched from his mouth in time. They would have slit his gullet to get the boule. A woman grabs the bead and tries to hide it, then holds up both hands to show that she doesn't have it. The crowd tears her apart until she releases it and someone else gets the marble again.

I tear my eyes away from the deadly chaos.

"That was you?" Sheldon asks.

"What does it mean?" I say.

"It means that if you have any more on you we better be extremely careful."

"Yes" I agree stupidly.

"We should walk," Jan tells us. "I see one or two watching us."

We have walked around a little in a circle away from the melee, still keeping our eye on the yellow gates. 'How valuable are marbles?' I'm asking myself. Surely if Dad had known, he'd have warned us. I'm in shock as we wander.

The first whistle is close by me, and then another and another, echoing around the square. Huptoou returns suddenly, which frightens me. He comes to me pushes my hands inside the drawstrings, pulls my hood down and says, "Don't move. Stay still, no matter what happens."

How he found us again, I don't know; I suspect he'd not been far away. I wonder if he had witnessed my dumb marble trick.

My hands, feet and face are now completely covered. Huptoou shows me how to pull the habit tightly around my body. Through the thick cloth I can see him do the same with Sheldon, and Jan copies. I shift my eyes. Everyone in the Market has done the same. Five, maybe six hundred people all freezing and hiding in their clothes? For what? You can tell the sex from the colour. What can't you tell from the baggy shapes? I want to ask Sheldon what's going on, but I suspect he doesn't know. I notice that Huptoou has distanced himself from us a little.

My instinct is to run when I see the men arrive across the other side. They are big, like the men from the factory. I think I can see six, but I'm not aware of what is happening to my left or behind me.

They move through the crowd as if they are looking for someone. They pull up hoods and open cloaks as they search randomly. I see one person unhooded a few feet away; the men seem to look down his throat. If the person isn't what they want, they push them aside like a worthless piece of meat. The whistle blows and immediately the crowd shuffles about twenty feet in different directions.

"Move," I hear Huptoou whisper. I begin to understand; it is the crowd protecting itself, like a large moving shoal confusing the hunters. While the men search, the crowd mixes themselves up. People who have been searched already mix with those who have not; they make it hard for the men who are looking. I realise I need to behave the same and as the whistle blows I move through the crowd. I worry about losing Sheldon and Jan.

The men approach a grey-cloaked figure in front of me. It takes me a second to notice the figure is below the average height. They pull off his hood; it's Huptoou. They look at him and one grabs him and hits him. He is less than a quarter of their size and weight. I am about to lift my hood and scream my anger, until I hear Huptoou shout "No matter what happens" and I realise as I watch them beat him into unconsciousness, he was shouting directly to me. The whistle goes and we move again. I change direction; I've lost the boys; I hope they are tracking me. We move another five times and I see the men take a few more people. You can feel the panic in the crowd.

Nevertheless, this collaborative protection system seems to work. No system or government can beat ordinary people when they stick together. I realise that the system is altruistic in the short-term, but protects the whole group over the longer term.

Finally, a loud, long whistle sounds the all clear. People come out of cover and start searching the stalls again. I look around for Sheldon and Jan. It's impossible in the hundreds of people.

'No problem,' I tell myself; we all know to go to the house. Nevertheless, my nerves are frayed.

# CHAPTER FIVE

## Zohar Keshet

Beyond the yellow gates lies a vast comfortable looking house, the first sign of real wealth we have seen since our arrival. The house has three storeys and what appears to be a massive round chimney or tower rising into the sky. The building overlooks cultivated gardens and a number of outhouses. It could have been any house back home, but it lacks something. It takes me a few moments to work it out; the house doesn't have proper windows. You can only distinguish the number of stories from the open terraces.

Otherwise, the house stands out as an oasis in a desolate war zone. There is a physical difference between the fading warm summer evening in these gardens and the dry cold wind outside the gate. I don't have long to puzzle on this before the door opens and interior lights sweep the steps down to where I stand.

Zohar Keshet has a shrewd expression; he wears pinnacles, a long sleeved cardigan and a colourful cravat. Despite the eccentricity, almost the first sign of normality since we arrived here. The house smells sharply of rose water and smoky cinnamon. For a second, Jelly Bellys came to mind and I nearly smirk. But then it makes me worry how I must smell; I had gotten used to the stench on the streets. Keshet's rheumy eyes, loose jowls and veined nose tell me his age. I estimate one hundred and twenty years old, minus forty years for my own teenage bias. So I settle for eighty and notice how sprightly he moves.

Keshet ushers me in, locking the door behind us and pocketing the key. The hall is a mix of old and new furnishings; wood panelling and slate floors with ornate rugs lead to corridors and grand staircases on both sides. Heavy solid-looking doors with heavy cast iron handles and locks lead to a multitude of rooms.

The lounge has a huge fireplace with three coats of arms hanging above a painting of an unknown herbivore grazing on a vast plain. Two ornate right-angled fireguards with cushions on top, fashioned as both a guard and a seat, sit on a large hearth.

A burnished silver shield above the mantelpiece, with two crossed rapiers behind, doesn't make sense. The artefacts had been mixed up or perhaps the historians themselves had gotten confused. Rapiers are duelling weapons, never used with shields.

A large chandelier, made from a bright hard silvery looking metal, hangs in the middle of the lounge. A tasteful jade statue of a naked couple stands in the corner. Numerous candles in ornate holders flicker around the room, adding to an overall manor house effect.

"Your friends are already here," Keshet says ushering me into a large side lounge. Sheldon and Jan sit at the table eating a bowl of soup.

"You will have a little broth?" he asks. My stomach rumbles and I look at Sheldon.

"It's good," Sheldon says waving a large piece of fresh bread. Saliva floods my mouth and I have to swallow before I answer.

"No thank you," I say trying to hide the sheer hunger that's making my mouth water each time Jan dips his bread in the hot soup. I almost open and close my mouth in synch with Jan as he chews the soggy mass.

"Really my dear? It's already prepared and no trouble. My housekeeper is an excellent cook," he smiles and nod at me.

"No thank you. The market extinguished my appetite for the moment," I say. "The package Donald Gentle left would be fine." For a second, a cloud passes over his face and eyes, before he recovers.

"Certainly my dear." And he leaves the room.

"What's wrong?" Sheldon says.

"I don't know. Nothing, a little paranoia. I don't trust him."

"It's fine. You should relax. He said we can have a shower and stay the night," Jan says. "He is a harmless old man."

I shake my head furiously. "No."

"No what?" Keshet asks when he comes back in the room and hands me the package.

"Oh. Nothing. The boys are saying how great the soup is and I should try a bowl."

"It really is the most delicious soup. You should. You should," he says.

I ignore him and sit at the table with the package and Keshet follows and sits across from me.

"I am glad you made it, my dear. Now who did you say you were?"

"Donald is my Dad," I say.

"Yes, I see." He drums his fingers on the table. "He knew you would come?"

"Yes," I lie. Sheldon looks at me again.

"How long have you been here?" Keshet asks.

"Forever," I say.

He smiles.

"You are not from here. There is a lot I can tell you to help you. Your Dad paid me to help him."

"Thanks. Please tell us about this place. That would be useful, and anything my Dad did."

"Don't you want to open the parcel that I have been keeping so safe? You should. You should," he says.

"Where are we?"

"Country? The country is Wellorsland. We are in Subtopia of course, approximately 260 miles outside Cartropolis, one of our Capitals."

"And the date?" I ask.

He leans forward starting to look interested, and I wonder how much my Dad has told him.

"It's the 28th June 2048," he says and I see Sheldon and Jan both look up this time.

My mind turns this over. I don't recognise anything significant in the date, except that we have jumped forward in time. I didn't see any mention of this in Dad's notes. It makes me feel more apprehensive, like being out of my depth.

"What do they sell at the market?" I already know the answer of course.

"A range of meats for the 'Lower Downcasts'."

"How much does it cost?" I ask. He destroys my attempt at guile with a snorting laugh.

"Let me show you." He takes a large key from a chain around his neck, goes behind a cupboard and unlocks something big, by the sound of the metal clunk. He reappears with a flat closed box about 10 inches square and sits back down. He opens the lid towards me, hiding the contents from my view. Sheldon stares inside the box and I can see his puzzlement.

"This, my dear, will buy three houses like the one you are in now." He holds up an ordinary normal sized marble between his finger and thumb. The most common marble for kids. "It's a Centurion." He studies my reaction closely.

"Your Dad didn't understand the value either," he says.

"Interesting," I say. Sweat breaks out on my lower back, between my skin and the money belt full of marbles.

"This one?" He holds up a slightly bigger tigers-eye. "It's a Legion. Worth ten times the amount."

"You must be an extremely wealthy man," I say.

He laughs again. "Not as wealthy as your Dad. And in any case, I hold these for others as well as myself."

"Do you have other money currency here?" I ask.

"Why my child, this is our currency of course." He looks genuinely puzzled. He shows us smaller glass balls. Three different sizes.

Three different values. "These are Citizens. These are Plebes. And these, Rodents."

"Oh." I can't think of anything else to say. I stare at him. Zone out. I try to calculate the value of what I carry.

"Anyone who has a few Centurions is considerably wealthy, my dear."

No wonder they tried to kill each other at the market for a single marble. I have the equivalent of around millions or billions of dollars on my waist and nobody knows. My tummy lurches in warning. For a moment I imagine what they would do to me in the market if they knew what I was carrying.

"Can you tell us a bit more about the place? As you surmised, we are not from here. Now what do we need to know to stay safe?" Sheldon says.

Keshet looks thoughtful. "You wouldn't rather wait until morning, until after you rested?"

"No," I say pointedly. "Thank you."

"Very well, let me give you some of the history and politics of Wellorsland and Subtopia." He takes what looks like an atlas from the shelf and opens it. He starts to talk but doesn't take his eyes off me, as I begin to examine the package.

"Whoa," Sheldon says, suddenly banging his arm off the table. "I nearly nodded off there... feel incredibly sleepy all of a sudden, I should sleep." His voice has a droning quality.

"You should. You should." Keshet says.

"Do I take it I start from the beginning?" Keshet says.

"Yes," I say, as I examine the package in my hands.

"You really don't know anything about Wellorsland? Or indeed the world?"

How wise is it to admit our total ignorance, I wonder; he bristles with curiosity and yet tries to hide it.

"Pretend we don't. Start from the beginning."

"I heard some rumours about..." he hesitates, "foreigners, in the past. They didn't understand our ways. Nobody knew where they came from."

I stare back at him, trying to give nothing away. Then I look down and rotate the parcel from my Dad, trying to learn if it has been opened and resealed. I recognise Dad's signature across the various paper joins; it would be hard, if not impossible, to open and rewrap without disturbing the alignment of a half dozen signatures.

"Our country, Wellorsland, is one of twenty remaining countries around the globe. They say that in the past there were nearly two hundred countries, but that might be fantasy, since officially history doesn't exist here. History is a word on the forbidden list. Relics from the past are forbidden. But I will come to that in a minute. There are six major capitals."

"How can there be more than one capital?" I tear open the parcel; a small blue bag nestles beside a note.

"Capitals are our political and economic centres. One only would be unconstitutional and inefficient. One would hoard all the power to the detriment of the rest of the country." Keshet continues, "We are in Cartropolis. In addition, there is Mantropolis, Birtropolis, Lontropolis, Dintropolis and Portropolis; large transport corridors called Causeways connect them. The generic name for the inner cities is the Metro-Politic. All the luxury is there." He turns his head and eyes up for a second as he reminisces.

"The capitals are built in concentric circles, inner and outer rings. From the centre to the sub-lands, these regions are Bildenland, Serfin, Metro, Subtopia and Outlands. They are occupied by different citizen groups: Supreme, Establishment, Artisans, Low-Downcast and the Nobeni Class," Keshet explains.

"So the cities and populations are arranged in great rings according to these...?" I trail off. I put the small blue bag in my pocket and read the first sentence of the note. 'Keep the bag safe, do not open it in front of him.'

"Classifications."

"How do you get your classification?" I ask. I suddenly become aware of the silence. No one else is asking questions. When I look at Jan and Sheldon, both appear to be slumped unnaturally, lolling, eyes closed in deep sleep.

"They are given to you when you are born and if you are fortunate the Establishment might raise you to the next classification."

"And you? We are in the Subtopia region, does that make you a Low-Downcast?" I glance down again at the note. 'Do not stay there overnight. He is a trafficker.'

He laughs what seems like an honest laugh. "You are fast on the uptake."

I assume he means smart; he knows that I noticed the boys' unusual sleep, and he knows that I know he knows.

"I am from a higher classification, but I choose to live out here because business is better," he tells me. "Higher classifications can move outwards; lower classifications cannot move inwards unless accorded by the Establishment."

He gets up suddenly. "Let me show you. Follow me." We go into the hall and enter a small wooden door. Stone spiral stairs go up inside the minaret I saw from the outside. The air becomes fresher as we climb, until suddenly we arrive on a small round open balcony with a conical roof, thirty feet above the roof of the house. The height, plus being alone with this man, makes me nervous, so I take care not to turn my back on him or go too close to the edge. He points across a darkening landscape to a horizon, bright with neon light, and a sky a different colour.

"That's the Metro boundary. It houses the Artisan class. The start of privilege and wealth. You cannot see the Serfin or Establishment boundary from here. It is too far, but from time to time you will see their Ion-Health machines rise up to clean the air. In the other direction you can sometimes see the smog and the gas flames of the Outlands."

'The further away from the power, the more miserable your life is', I form the thoughts but don't speak them, 'Effectively a streamlined apartheid, by class and controlled by a concentric geography? Surely not?'

"And people understand their place in these rings?" I ask.

"They accept. There is no choice, the system is tightly controlled," Keshet says.

In the other direction, a substantial building mocks the skyline with serrated turrets and buttresses. Were it closer, next to us, it would loom above like a threatening giant from a Brother Grimms work.

"What is that building?" I ask.

"That is the family who own most of the factories. Didn't you see a few of them, large ladies, passing their time, amusing themselves in the market?"

"Ah yes," I say.

"The Beane dynasty."

Somehow, I feel the shadow and weight of the castle take on greater significance. It dwarfs everything around, like the ladies in the market and the men in the factories.

Otherwise, Keshet's house is the biggest in the area, surrounded by small buildings, crammed close together; shoe boxes that seem functional, rather than comfortable or decorative. Below us, in the now quiet market stalls, a sea of green canvas flaps in the dusty breeze. But the air around the house and rising from the gardens feels light and sweet and smells of oranges and honeysuckle, the kind of air I love to wake up to in the summer.

Finally, he leads me back down the stairs to the table where the boys remain in the same position as when we left.

"So we cannot travel through the next boundary to 'Metro' or further? What stops us?" I say.

"The society is different in each of these circles. They cannot mix. You cannot enter without credentials. It's a fence and robo-guards that guard the boundary between Low-Downcasts and Artisans. It's the iTrust Surveillance band, sometimes called 'the punishment and reward band' that protects the boundary between Metro and Serfin."

I must look perturbed as I listen to Keshet and read at the same time. I glance down at the next line of the note. 'He has been paid to get you to the Metro area in Dintropolis. Only he can do that.'

"Perhaps I am going too fast. Let me show you." Keshet starts to draw a diagram of concentric circles.

First ring.

"The Supreme in the centre are in charge and hold most of the wealth. They are the only classification who can travel outside Wellorsland and don't do much of anything except enjoy life."

"What are the other countries?"

He continues as though he didn't hear my question. "Their lifestyle is luxurious, I am told. I have never been there, but I meet some of them on occasion, when we hunt. The old style Monarchs and Lords are there along with the billionaires."

Second ring.

"The next ring out is the Establishment. They make the rules and run the country. Each Capital's Commissar is there along with

Security Force Commanders and Hegemonic Tzars. They coordinate with the Commissars and counterparts in the other Capitals."

Third ring.

"The Artisans are a much greater population. They are kept at optimum health, wealth and happiness. They are the educated professionals. They control the computers, communication systems, transport systems, broadcasting, weather generators, food production systems, water machines, weapons systems and satellites. They are the collective machine that maintains the system. Their internal security division also controls the iTrust band that they themselves wear. They cannot remove it; it monitors all aspects of their life, including speech, affiliations and movements."

"Like a watch on the wrist?"

"It's a cuff on the wrist and a thin collar around the neck," he says. "They are the only communication devices allowed, and no communicators are allowed at all below Artisan level."

I couldn't imagine what it would be like and say so, while I glance at the note one last time. 'You should find a man called Iain Banks. They say he is somewhere in the Metro third quadrant, Dintropolis. That's what I have learned and where I am headed.'

"It's the price they are willing to pay for food, weather, education and comfort. Of course they have a slim chance to progress to the Establishment; although few ever do. There is not much chance to progress from where you are born," he says.

"What did you mean by optimum health, wealth and happiness?" I am puzzling over his previous point.

"Goodness, you really are sharp. If people are too unhappy or too happy, the system breaks. The premise of the Metro class is to maintain them at a comfortable stasis where they don't need anything but don't have surplus. Metro is the flywheel, the gyroscope of the rest."

"And around here?"

Fourth ring. He points with his pencil.

"Ah, the Low-Downcast in sunny Subtopia. They are paid by the government to produce. Food mostly. They work in factories, batteries, incubators and greenhouses. There are no guns, communicators, motorcycles or computers here. It is all about agriculture, manufacturing, mining, textiles, some forestry, not much, and a lot of metal fabrication."

"And then the last ring," I say. "Everywhere else?"

"Well in a manner of speaking, outside this group we are in, are the Outlands, vast tracts of land that serve little purpose. The Nobeni class survive there. They are diseased and dysfunctional. They exist off the rubbish and sewers from the city. They bring nothing to the country and they get nothing from anyone. Their life expectancy is minimal. There are vast tracks of land that are unusable. The Outlands are contaminated by nuclear reactors, waste and land-gas extraction. The Nobeni children are sick at birth. Nothing can be done for these people. They don't want to help themselves."

It sounds like a contradiction to me, but I don't say.

"What about the Boys we met, I think they are called Euny?" I say.

"The Euny. Ach, they are nothing. They escaped the farm and the factory. They cost me a lot of money." He coughs. "The sooner they are eradicated the better."

"And the Causeways that connect the cities?"

"Giant transport corridors that allow swift travel from centre to centre. Anyone can use them. But of course you cannot enter past your own zone. Transports between the Capitals are heavily armed and patrolled through the Outlands."

"The whole country sounds complicated."

"Not really. It works. It's a system and a network specifically designed to control our limited natural resources. It does it through control of people," he says. "Of course the weather generators serve only the three inner rings. We don't get the benefit here."

"I noticed the cloud, but not much greenery, except for you?"

"Some of us run our own small independent weather generator, my dear. I couldn't live here without that one luxury at least." He points with a gnarled finger. "Ah look, the boys are asleep. You will just need to stay. You should. You should."

First I try to wake the boys. They moan but don't stir. They must be really tired, he tells me, and I pretend to agree. He calls the housekeeper, a pleasant looking woman called Sara; from the slight disapproval evident in her manner, I get the feeling she doesn't care for her master's ways. Keshet wishes me a goodnight and blows out the set of candles on the table as he goes out the lounge, and through the door I see him go upstairs, putting lights off as he goes.

The housekeeper looks at me but says nothing as she and I manhandle the lads one by one to a bedroom, halfway down a corridor that seems to lead into a black infinity, and push them onto two single beds. Sara directs me to the bedroom next door, points to towels and the bathroom and goes out without a word. I kick off my shoes, pick them up and listen at the door for her going off down the hall. As soon as I think she has gone I come out again quietly and cross the hall into a large half lit alcove; I don't want to be trapped in either room. I want time to think. Then I want to see what else is around in this house. There is enough light in the corner to read the final part of my message. And I read the whole note again.

'Keep the bag safe; do not open it in front of him. Do not stay there overnight. He is a trafficker. He has been paid to get you to the Artisan area in Dintropolis. Only he can do that.

You should find a man called Iain Banks. They say he is somewhere in the Artisan third quadrant, Dintropolis. That's what I have learned and where I am headed.

The marbles I have given you are of huge value. Think of the smallest as $1000 and the rest go up from there. They should be enough to get a few people safely to the next zone.

So far I have no news of the boys. I lost track of them and I am hoping Banks can help us. I cannot imagine how they are faring without funds. I left here on the 26th May. I hope our paths cross soon. Be safe.

Donald Gentle'

I sit quietly in the dark, thinking about trying to wake the boys again, when I hear the sporadic shuffling. I squeeze deeper in the corner and watch. Keshet comes along the corridor like a ghost. He goes to one bedroom after the other, listens for a few seconds and then quietly turns the key in each lock with a soft click, leaving the keys in place.

My heart is beating so loudly I think he might hear it, as he turns back down the hall. I can feel the blood rush in my ears as I realise my narrow escape and the danger we might be in. In my mind, I hug my instinct close and give her a big kiss.

For a short time, I can't make up my mind what to do. Going back into the bedroom isn't an option. The boys likely can't be wakened. Decision. I leave my shoes under a chair and run on tiptoe down the hall, keeping close to the wall and stopping every few feet to listen. Most of the house is in darkness; I only see a soft glow from upstairs. I dart into the shadows of the study, the library, the kitchen and the lounge, one after the other. They are dark and barely lit by some sort of luminescent paint. I look around. I check a few drawers: matches, ink, an empty ledger, and an old compass. There is nothing interesting. I decide not to open cupboards; they tend to squeak or something falls out. Reluctantly, I run back to the hall and pad quickly and quietly up the dark carpeted stairs, keeping my back to the wall and looking up the winding bannister towards the light in case of any movement.

The first landing is a black corridor to the left. Nothing stirs; I need to go one more up.

On the next landing, I am more cautious. There is a dull flickering light from the door; I can hear voices inside. I sidle up to the door and look through the crack. Keshet has taken his cardigan and cravat off. There is a thin metal collar around his neck and a large cuff on his scrawny left arm. He is talking to someone on the collar and a huge guy that stands beside him. Keshet's protection, I think; he'd need some living in this area.

"We will check tonight and move them tomorrow. We think the Father is headed to the Commissar. We don't have to worry any longer."

"Sure Mr. Keshet. Everything is under control of course," the big guy answers from the corner of his mouth. "They can go for processing in the morning. No need to keep them."

His jowls wobble when he turns around and my heart sinks; I recognise him from the Factory when I was hiding under the machine. Twice in so many nights I am spying on a giant that causes me real fear.

I don't know how they didn't hear me fly down the stairs; I don't stop or look back until I have crossed over the main hall into the shadows, down a dark corridor. Which way? Take your time, think, get this right; I try to calm my breathing through my nose. I am lost.

When I hear the moan, I think the big guy is behind me in the dark and about to grab me. I spin around. Nothing but dark and a draught; a faint unpleasant smell reminds me of something. I stumble forward listening. The wind, I think, moaning through the house, but it doesn't make sense. The house has no windows and the weather is calm. I trip over the step on the floor and go down on my knees trying to silence my fall by landing gently.

There is a trapdoor-type hatch low down on the wall. My father always says I am impetuous, I recall as I open it. The stench is overpowering and the noise increases slightly. I look down into the dark; it might be a way out. But my father never said I was a fool; I run into the lounge and carefully take one of the rapiers from behind the shield. I check the point; it's real enough and splits the velvet cushion on the chair causing it to emit a puff of grey fur. I stick the rapier through my cloak, piercing the folds to keep it in place, while being careful not to stick my side or leg with the sharp point.

I take matches from the drawer and light two candles, hold both in one hand and, using the other hand as a wind-shield, pad back to the trap door. A few steps become visible from the glow of the candle; ultra-cautious, I step down. Wind and my movement cause shadows to flit and flicker around the halo of light; indistinct shapes loom on the walls as I move. On the ground, a stool bangs my shins and scrapes along the floor. Something rough and hairy touches the back of my hand as I reach into the darkness; a thick hemp rope dangles from the ceiling.

Some kind of store room, I decide. Concrete flagstones disappear across the floor into deeper darkness. Large barrels damp with liquid, shelves laden with pots and sacks that might be grain or potatoes, bulge on the ground. The draught and damp threatens to extinguish my candles and leave me lost in the black. It would be foolhardy to continue; I turn around.

A low faint sucking and blowing of air makes me jump; it sounds like a sigh. My skin crawls as I back up and move the candle far to my left, almost behind me, and peer into the corner.

Faces black with dried blood and dirt appear in the dim light. Boys huddled together for warmth. One watches me with vacant eyes. The others appear to be sleeping. Biting my hand to stifle my sobs, I fall onto my knees at the cage. Jonathan, Huptoou and four other younger boys lie naked and trussed.

I put my hand through the bars.

"Jon."

Huptoou starts first, and shakes Jonathan.

"Jon." I try to touch his cheek but he is lying too far away. I notice his face has been scratched and he has a large bandage on his right thigh. Jonathan jumps towards me, grabs my arm through the bars and hugs it to him; tears flow through the dirt. He doesn't speak.

"Are you okay?" I say stupidly, so stupidly, because I've already seen the dried blood around his swollen mouth. Jon shakes his head. More tears flow and he looks away.

"Tongue," Huptoou says. "Took tongue."

"Nooooo!" I cry as I swoon and fall to the floor.

I wake up; it must be a dream, a horrible nightmare. My head throbs like I had banged it on something. But as tepid dirty water splashes my face from between the bars, the horrors return.

I realise I have been out for a while and they've been trying to wake me. Jonathan is stroking my arm with filthy fingers. He looks at me and I stare. He doesn't hide his nakedness; there is nothing to cover him anyway, but it is as if it doesn't matter anymore. I don't know what he is thinking, but in my head I hear my own words going around and around, 'What have they done to you my love, my brave brother?'

My legs are stiff and cold; I push myself off the floor and one of the boys hands me the remains of a candle through the bars. He must have grabbed it when I keeled over. The other candle was extinguished in the fall. I look at the lock. It is a solid cast iron dead-lock. It needs a large key, I figure. The walls are bare. It's only in movies that keys hang on walls. I look on the shelves and in the drawers.

"Pocket," Huptoou says and he makes a gesture of a hand going in the pocket and points upstairs. I'd thought as much, but I had to look. I nod.

"Take the sword and cut the bonds, I will be back." I hand the rapier to Jonathan, through the bars. Our hands touch as he puts his fingers around the guard and he looks at me with soulful eyes. For a moment I hesitate. A dark thought crosses my mind that he might do something silly. I reach in through the bars and put my hands up around his head and pull him to the bar. I press my lips hard against his until the pain is unbearable. Then I let him go, suck in a huge breath of air and climb the dark stairs feeling with my hands and feet.

All is quiet in the corridor; I run on tiptoe back to the lounge and free the second weapon. Before I can catch it, the shield slips slowly to the ground. It crashes on the mantelpiece, knocking over a few vases, before clanging to rest on the stone hearth.

My heart stops. I hear noises from upstairs; someone is getting up. I pray the big guy has left but it doesn't seem likely. I run to the hall and although my heart is sick, I close the trap door, locking the boys in the dark again. I don't waste time worrying about it. I find the long hall to Jan and Sheldon's bedroom. I stop when I get to the alcove, grab my shoes and recognise the correct bedroom. I turn the lock and push the door. As I put the light on, both boys jump me, knocking me to the floor.

"Robyn!" Sheldon says. "What's going on?"

"We were drugged," Jan says. "Who locked the door?" Both still sound a bit groggy.

"I know you were. Keshet," I say. "But there is no time to explain. We have to go."

We clatter out into the hall. I push the boys into the alcove. I lock both bedroom doors and swap the two door keys over. There is a slight chance it would confuse someone for a few minutes. There is a faint light now at the other end of the hall.

"This way," I say, making sure they take their shoes off before we run along the hall away from the lounge and into the darkness. I can feel the boys close behind me as I pad along in the dark, staying in the middle of the hall in case we trip over a table or chair. I start involuntarily when a large shadow looms to my right, but it is the silhouette of the bannister and stairs leading up. I don't hesitate; I run straight up into the dark. It is the mirror image of the other end; I have the feeling it would take us along the middle floor. I am right. I glance behind me in the gloom. Sheldon and Jan still look bewildered, but the short burst of exercise has helped clear their fuzziness. Sheldon nods for me to lead on. We run back the way we had come on the floor above.

It is a desperate gamble, but that is all we have. I peek out from the middle corridor up to the top landing. No movement or sound. I move to the balcony and look down. All clear for the moment. I signal to the boys behind me and run down the stairs as quietly as possible. I am correct; lights are now on down the other end of the hall at the ground floor bedrooms we have just left. It will be seconds before they realise that we are not in either room.

With forked first and second finger, I point to both my eyes and with my first finger I point down the corridor. Sheldon and Jan nod. They understand there are men looking for us now. We slip across the great hall and around the corner to where the trapdoor is. It's the biggest gamble I've ever taken in the whole of my seventeen years and everything I love is depending on me being right.

I open the door and lead the two into the cellar storeroom and close the door quickly and quietly behind us.

The last of the candles is burning away in the cage and lights the occupants sufficiently for Jan and Sheldon to see. They are struck dumb by the sight before them.

Jonathan stands proud and naked, one hand holding the bars, the other the rapier.

Huptoou seems agitated. Perhaps he knows the gaolers might return. The shadows from the candle hide, but at the same time highlight, his lack of genitals. Four other young boys huddle naked, their manhood intact but shaking in unison with their body's fear, as they watch to see what the older ones are going to do.

"Huptoou," Jan says in greeting. He looks at me and back to Jonathan.

"Your swordsman?" Sheldon assumes then before I answer he immediately studies the lock. "I need some wire, maybe a screwdriver or piece of metal." He lifts the candle and stares into the keyhole.

I scrabble around the shelf in the dark. I find string, something vegetable, sealing wax, what looks like a chess piece and a long rusty nail.

I bring them to the light and Sheldon takes the nail and gives me the candle. "See what else there is." As I turn away to search I see him close his eyes and probe the lock with the nail.

Moments later I bring him a piece of thin metal and corkscrew off of one of the barrels. "You star." He kisses me on the forehead and bends back to his task. From the corner of my eye, I see Jonathan's head go down, but not before I caught his expression of hurt.

I hear the voices upstairs just as Sheldon's lock clunks and he grunts in satisfaction. His Dad has taught him well.

We open the cage just as the trap door opens above and the large factory man backs down the steps, bent over to avoid striking the ceiling, clutching a lamp to his chest. When he turns, he struggles to see beyond the glare of his own light.

I see the naked Jonathan present his rapier; I do the same on the man's far left. He hasn't seen me yet. Sheldon and Jan are somewhere behind. The man is still trying to see the cage where only four boys now remain. Huptoou skirts out to the barrels, climbs up onto the beam and crawls along like a monkey, his back rubbing the low ceiling. The man holds up his lamp and peers up to the source of the scraping noise.

Jonathan strikes first and sticks his weapon deep in the man's abdomen, retreating quickly. The man drops his lamp and roars, jowls wobbling, holding his stomach. The noise is deafening. I immediately worry about the trapdoor being closed and locked until reinforcements come. I try to get to the stairs as the man flails out, trying to punch or grab someone in the dark. Jonathan must have wondered why I have not attacked. He lets loose again and I can see the anger in his moves. The sharp rapier penetrates the big man and although he is losing blood and in pain, he is still dangerous. He catches Jonathan with a glancing blow and moves towards him. The brave Huptoou seizes his moment and leaps onto the man's shoulders. I fear for Huptoou, so I stick hard from behind and below. I don't like sticking a real person in the liver, but this is no time to be squeamish. He falls to his knees. Jonathan slashes and parries, slashes and a quick jab, first through one eye, which pops instantly, and then, with equal speed and precision, a thrust through his other eye; this time he runs the sword deep into the brain and smoothly back out.

I don't wait to see the giant fall; I run upstairs just in time to stop Keshet reaching the trapdoor to slam it closed. I slash his arm and quickly bring point to his neck just above his collar. He tries to back off and push the blade away from his neck. So I slash his other arm, and return the point to his scrawny throat.

For a second I catch sight of the housekeeper in one of the doorways. But I can tell from her dispassionate expression that she isn't coming to his aid or calling anyone.

"Kneel!" I shout.

He collapses onto his knees, blood dripping from both arms on to the Arabian rug.

"Please. Please. I am an old man," he pleads. "I don't want to die!"

"You should, you should," I say.

# CHAPTER SIX

## Artisan Circle

There are two hours left until sunrise. The Factory guy bleeds to death in the cellar. It is the first time I have seen death up close; the smell of blood, urine and faeces makes me heave. I stay out of the basement after that.

We leave Keshet down there, bound, blindfolded and gagged, but I explain to Sheldon that the collar and cuff have some communication and surveillance ability that we don't understand. Perhaps everything has already been communicated to some security service somewhere and they are already on their way. But it is a risk we have to take; leaving without preparation would be worse.

In any case, I am exhausted; I've had no sleep other than my uncomfortable faint in the cellar. I gather everyone together and explain what the note from my Dad said, and everything I had learned from Keshet. Once I have passed on the information, I sit in a chair for an hour and close my eyes; the images of the last twenty-four hours flit across my brain, behind my eyes, like grotesque shadow monsters in a dark stage play. My body spasms.

Sheldon goes off exploring the house upstairs looking for answers. Jan connects with the housekeeper, Sara; she is a real sweetheart. She cries when she understands for the first time what they have done with Jonathan's tongue. She organises food for everyone and medicines and poultices for the injured. I see her prepare some salve for Jonathan, and painkiller, she says, but I have an inkling that Jonathan's anger and renewed adrenalin are keeping him pain-free for the moment. Moments later, I hear her unlock the front door and leave, but in the time it takes me to curse my stupidity, she returns with fresh garments for everyone. Most of us have blood somewhere on our clothes, I realise then.

Huptoou gives instructions to two of the boys, sending them out after they've eaten. He has his own plans and is communicating with his people; perhaps they thought he was dead already. One boy arrives back quickly with a nervous-looking man in tow. Huptoou brings him to Jonathan and me, and explains that this man had once been on the other side of the boundary and had been expelled for some nefarious reason, left unspoken.

"Ask him questions," Huptoou says. "Fallen Artisan."

The man nervously explains some of the process for crossing over between Subtopia and Metro. There are a huge number of checks and scans; we find out that you have to bribe the guards to be allowed to pass easily. He tells us to make sure we have 'A' status on our collars. It would also make things easier. He tells us to purchase Auto Lawyer programmes for the cuff in case we run into trouble; you could buy these at the Gate Services. He explains that when you buy the ticket using the cuff, it includes clothes. When I look puzzled, he says, "You'll see."

He coaches Jonathan, Jan and me what to expect at the ticket gate.

"Border Control and Ticketing are combined," he explains. "You need to understand the sequence."

"Where do we pass Border Control?" I ask.

"Once you have your ticket and have passed into the boarding lounge, you are effectively in Metro territory. It simply means all the checks are done at point of travel and you can now travel freely, on the shuttles through the gates."

He brings two small alloy boxes out of his sack and explains these are the only way to bring in money. He tells me they are locked by Quantum Cryptography. "Put in as much as you like. They go through a machine that sanitises them with radiation, including the inside, through these valves," he says. "They are clear of radiation by the time you get them back. They don't care how much money you take in," he told us, "going out can be different."

He wants one thousand Plebes for each machine. I look at the size and ask for three. Huptoou steps in and pays the guy; he apparently wants to give him a clear message that he didn't see anything and doesn't know anything. The man is nodding his head repeatedly as Huptoou ushers him out the door. Huptoou has intentionally frightened him, it seems; trust is a rarer commodity than glass marbles in Low Downcast land, fear is more reliable currency.

I keep close to Jonathan when I can; he looks miserable and his eyes almost vacant. I want to know what happened after the WolfCats, and I want to exchange what we both have learned about the structure of our new world. But I know I have to wait until he is ready to find a way to communicate. It doesn't stop me sitting with him, holding his hand for a few seconds when he will allow, and wondering what the communication will be like. We used to laugh and joke so much before; how can it ever be that way again? I wonder if he will learn to talk again, but it's a ridiculous desperate thought.

When the old housekeeper brings him a pad and pen, I could hug her. She reminds me of my Grandmother: always one step ahead of the crowd. Sara is a mind reader; at least it seems that way.

"There is an electronics workshop upstairs with Collars and Cuffs and I assume machines to program them," Sheldon tells me, showing me two he has brought.

"The problem is, we could force Keshet to help us, but we can't trust what he will program into these machines. Or if he will deprogram them and turn us in, if we let him live, and we leave here," I say.

"We cannot take him with us," Sheldon says.

Jonathan shakes his head and wags his finger. He takes his pad and writes. 'Leave him with Huptoou?'

"It's a good solution," Sheldon says. "Probably our best chance." He then goes off to have a crack at Keshet's safe.

The boys leave it to me to organise. They drag Keshet from the cellar and I make it clear what he is going to do if he is to save his worthless skin. At first he tries to deny he could arrange collars, but changes his mind when I tell the boys to stick him back in the cellar. He is making me angry. He had thought because we were teenagers he could be clever. He lost. Now he thinks he can play games and stall for time. What he underestimates is how angry this seventeen year old is with what has been done to Jonathan. Even if Keshet didn't physically carry out the cruel deed, he is wholly culpable in my eyes; I have hardened up considerably in the last twelve hours. What have I become? I'd feel little guilt in killing this animal.

While Keshet programs the counterfeit cuffs and collars, Jonathan and one of the boys stand over him. I tell Keshet that Jonathan is looking for any excuse to 'run him through' with his blade, and if he as much as sneezes without covering his mouth, Jonathan will stick him like a pig. And I tell him that if we imagine for one second that the privileges accorded to these cuffs are less than expected, he'd better be prepared to dance with the devil. I have no idea what I mean, but I imagine it scares him.

The cuffs and collars are programmed and Jonathan thinks there has been no funny business. He'd even insisted that Keshet use our own names. Keshet is locked back up, bound and gagged so that he can't communicate with anyone.

"Bingo!" Sheldon calls from the corner; I realise he has cracked the safe. We have additional funds although I am not sure we need them.

Meanwhile, I talk to Huptoou and tell him what we want to do and he agrees. They are to keep Keshet and kill him if there is no contact from us in a few weeks. He is to be locked up permanently, without access to people or facilities; I warn Huptoou that this man would try to bribe people.

Huptoou smiles. "You think Huptoou just a gelding."

I snort. "You do read." He had pretended not to understand previously. Fly monkey.

"Soon I take you Causeway Transports," he says. "And we take Keshet to dungeon."

"Yes," I say, and I know that I can trust him.

"But listen, is much you do not know," he says. "Four people travelling together not allowed by the state. You will need to split; they clever at catching people who pretend to be separate. Don't make mistake."

"Thank-you Huptoou," I say.

"No. Don't thanks me. I never been to the Artisan region. I only say what I hear. It's not much."

"You could come," I say.

He laughs. "They would catch me in seconds. My types don't fit there. You will see," he says. "Besides, I am happy here and someone need to watch bastard Keshet until you safe."

"I really appreciate that," I say.

"The other thing I might say. There one guy I heard about in Artisan area. He's a computer systems guy who will do anything for money. I don't know if he is true, maybe a myth, or if you can find him. They say his name is Contagion."

I look at him. "I will keep that in mind."

Something else has been bothering me. "Huptoou. One thing I don't know. How do you visit the other side? My world? Where is your door? Why can't we use it?"

"You might be able to use it. But it give you only a minute or three on the other side, before it return you back here."

"Might be useful."

"You ready to trade ten years in age, exchange for few minutes at home?" he says.

That's when I realise why he looks like an old man in a small-wizened body. If anyone travels two times, it costs him twenty years in life terms. Huptoou realises what I was thinking.

"Seven times since age of twelve," he says. "But Donal didn't age."

Final preparation before we leave the house includes wearing the collar and cuff. Both make me feel 'tagged' like an animal or criminal, but it's the only way to enter Metro as Artisans, and it is what Dad had advised. Of course, he hadn't known that things were going to turn so nasty with Keshet. But to be fair, we have done everything we can; we have money, information, directions and hopefully the collars and cuffs give us identities and will cause no surprises.

Four of Huptoou's boys turn up and take Keshet off in what sounds like an old garbage truck. I watch as they drag him off. He might be playing a beaten old man, but hatred and anger flash in his eyes as he looks back at me.

"What are you thinking?" Sheldon asks.

"The old man. I don't like the idea that he is still alive. I am angry at him, partly because of Jonathan, but also because he scares me; I just hope we don't see him again."

"Probably not; forget him. We just need to focus on staying safe now and continuing the journey that takes us to your Dad and out of here."

"Yep, you are right."

In the privacy of one of the bedrooms, I put all the marbles that fit into the three Quantum safes. There is one each for Jan, Jonathan and I to carry and a small bag left over. I hand them over to Huptoou when I see him in the corridor.

"I will keep them for you. Until you return," he says.

"No. Use them. Do not travel again. Save what years you have left," I say. He just smiles.

"Last minute checks everyone?" Sheldon calls and I notice Jonathan strap on his blade under his cloak, so I do the same.

I take a few seconds to thank Sara the housekeeper and give her enough small marbles to ensure her comfort. "God speed," she says, pats my arm and puts a piece of paper in my hand as we exit the door.

As agreed, we split up; Huptoou, Jonathan and I leave the house first, with Sheldon and Jan following at a very respectable distance. Sky patrols will become more numerous nearer the Transport Station. We have enough money for a vehicle, but vehicles are a last resort they are a sign of wealth, and an invitation to vicious street gangs near the centre apparently. It is safer to walk and try to blend in and avoid trouble. We have over an hour's walk ahead of us. It gives me time to think.

My main thoughts are for Jonathan. I can't get his injury out of my head. I feel anger and, I am ashamed to say, disgust. I feel sadness and at the same time a strong sense of wanting to protect him. He walks with his head down, letting Huptoou watch out for us, perhaps also thinking about his loss of speech. I've never seen Jonathan look so down, so lethargic and miserable. What can I do to help him?

Am I changing? Would my Mum think I am growing up? The last few days have been traumatic, yet, apart from occasional hysteria, I have coped okay, I decide.

The world that Keshet described frightens me. It seems that the rich are protected in the centres of the cities and the poor are left to a desperate struggle in the outskirts. The metro, where we are headed, sounds middle-class by Keshet's description, yet the people who populate Metro, the Artisans, are controlled by technology.

There is nothing for the youth here. There is no hope. I suspect crime is the fastest growing industry in the outer rings. I wonder how the people are educated. It seems they can read and write. For what though? Why bother?

I touch my collar around my neck as I turn to look back at Sheldon and Jan, who are casually following. Sheldon reaches his hand up and touches his own collar in unconscious acknowledgment. When I turn back around Jonathan is watching. He half smiles, before moving closer to Huptoou, as we arrive at a busy part of the city. Jonathan seems to perk up. He straightens, instantly taller. He is watching and listening now, as if he'd just resolved to stand-up to the world again. It is impressive to see the old Jonathan start to return after such a short time. He is a fighter. And I am happy; we are going to be okay.

□□□□□□□□

The walk had been nerve-wracking and exhausting; it was only thanks to Huptoou's street smarts that we arrived at the Transport Station unscathed. On our own we'd have been attacked and robbed, no doubt. A couple of times I thought we were going to have to draw our blades to discourage unwanted interest, but the criminals were wary and were on the lookout for easier prey.

I can't help thinking if this region is like this, what must the Outlands be like? How can you get any more lawless? Pity to be sick, old or young in this place.

The huge Transport Station looms into view across town. Outside it has the same run down look as the whole area; inside, huge shuttlecraft with perspex windows levitate above magnetised rails. We watch a few of these unmanned craft glide in and out. It reminds me of ski lifts back home, the way it comes in one door and goes out the other, stopping briefly to take passengers who have already qualified to enter the transit areas. Jonathan points at the weapons on the weapons ports; the crafts are heavily armed. I remind him that some of these craft would go from the centre, right out into the Outlands and beyond to other capitals.

Sheldon and Jan are a short distance away pretending not to know us. Sheldon is looking around at the numerous surveillance drones and I guess, like me, he is wondering their exact purpose.

A few sky patrols slide by overhead, but they are not too interested in us. The Transport Station has its own security arrangements. Numerous hovering saucers patrol the crowds; the occasional scanning, zapping and screams of the unfortunates as they are physically ejected from the station keep most people orderly and law abiding.

Huptoou leads us into the Travel Office; he'd already warned us to make no fuss over his departure.

"Good bye and good luck," he says. "I hope you catch up with Donal soon."

An imperceptible nod to Sheldon and Jan as they enter behind us, and Huptoou exits and goes down the steps without looking back; we are truly on our own now.

Jonathan and I ignore the other two as we queue at Gate Services to charge our cuffs from the bank machines. Our 'fallen Artisan' had recommended we put a minimum of three Centurions and to purchase Auto Lawyer; I hope the other two remember. There are a number of options additional to deposit and charge. There is Auto Lawyer, Insurance, Health Assistance, and Additional Security protection. I select all of them. Why? Because it makes me feel more confident, going into a strange region, loaded up with maximum options. I see Jonathan look at me and smile.

"Why not?" I tell him. And I guess about now he wishes he could talk and make a quick harmless joke at my expense.

I take my loose marbles from my pocket and drop them into the machine. My cuff vibrates and a small display flashes briefly with the total value.

We then join a separate queue for tickets. I turn my attention to how tickets and entry permits are acquired. The queues lead to large cabinet machines that double as entry barriers. Beyond the barriers there are thirty or fifty doors with large numbers on. We watch as people ahead of us place their cuffs into the machine. The machine asks them to choose the destination option, scans their cuffs, debits their cuff or accounts, gives them a number and allows them through.

The machine calls me forward. It pulls my cuff tightly into the slot, a magnet I think, and rotates it slightly. I'm hoping the coaching by 'Fallen Artisan' is accurate.

"Citizen Class A. Zone 3 Permit. Indefinite Stay." It reads the cuff.

"Confirm Destination?"

"Dintropolis, Zone 3, Artisan Class." My mind whirrs. It is supposed to be push button choice, not ask questions. How is Jonathan going to go through? I try to turn to look. He has already gone into another machine.

"Visit Reason?"

"Returning home."

"Valuables?"

"One box."

"Clothing and Security choice?"

I hesitated. "I'm not sure."

"Basic, Business, Premium, Supreme."

"Premium," I say. Supreme just sounds a step too far and my mind is on Jonathan.

"9500 debited. Please pass. Door 43."

"Wait please. I have a friend travelling. He cannot speak, he needs my help," I say.

"Jonathan will be looked after. Please continue."

The gate opens, the machine nudges me through and I pass under the arch towards Door 43.

'They knew his name? What the heck?' I try to turn around, but it's like being on a production line. Moving plates take me to door 43. After my cuff is confirmed, door 43 opens and I am alone inside the first of three connecting pods.

"Place valuables box in chute."

I have no choice; I send the box full of the highest value marbles through the machine.

"Weapon detected. Place in incinerator."

They mean the blade, so I take it from under my cloak and watch as it is sucked away to the waste.

"Empty pockets."

There is nothing in my pockets except the piece of paper from the old housekeeper, which I haven't read. It says, 'The Manse, Gubrath, Outlands'. I have no idea what it is but I memorise it before I bin it.

"Disrobe. Place all personal items in the basket."

Initially, I hesitate, and then strip to underwear.

"Disrobe completely."

"I don't believe this," I say.

"Compliance failure. Traveller will be ejected in 30 seconds."

"No. No, it's fine." I quickly unfasten my bra and step out of my knickers, discarding everything including my watch. I am naked apart from the damn iTrust, cuff and collar. I don't feel very trusting right at the moment.

"Step forward onto the boards."

In an instant, soft machine arms on both sides gently hold me by the wrists and ankles. An angled pillar rises from the floor to support my spine, as I am gently spread-eagled.

"Close eyes, hold breath for 10 seconds starting in 3 - 2 – 1."

Warm sprays soap and rinse my body. Machines shave my head and laser the hair under my arms and between my legs.

"Close eyes, hold breath for 10 seconds starting in 3 - 2 – 1."

A second rinsing, then drying. It happened so fast; I am in shock, my beautiful hair. I've forgotten the indignity, and would weep in rage at my hair, but I am being nudged into the next pod.

This room smells of medicine. The door closes behind me. Machines hold me again, take my blood pressure, temperature and blood sample, and scan me head-to-toe three times. An individual robotic arm looks into my eyes and ears and listens to my heart.

"Injection in 3 - 2 – 1."

I am furious. But there is nothing to do; the needles pierce my arm and my butt and I have no idea what has been injected. They are sanitising me inside and outside before I am allowed in Metropolis; they don't want any bugs or virus.

The final pod is, to my surprise, make-up and clothes. A machine offers me blue, brown, purple or green make-up. I haven't worn make-up for weeks. I choose green and the machine scans my face, checks my skin, holds my head firmly and applies foundation, eye shadow, eyeliner, blusher and lipstick all in under two minutes. There is no choice in the deodorant and perfume that are applied. It seems your hormones determine what is suitable.

Finally, the machine offers a choice of designs for semi-permanent skull tattoo. I have seconds to choose. Keep my chicken-skin head or allow this crazy machine to draw on my head like an Easter egg. I choose 'Modern Celt' and hope for the best.

The machine sets to work with laser beam measured coloured drawings. Transforming my scalp into an egg Faberge would have been proud of.

After it blows me dry, I am offered an onscreen choice of three colours and two styles of underwear. Followed by a choice of six similar 'Fashionable Travel Suits' to 'take you home in comfort'. There are three pairs of comfortable shoes, physically presented, while the screen choices are delivered immediately. Everything cross-matched and exactly my size. Back home, I'd have taken hours to choose and combine clothes. Here I have no idea what is stylish. I am just relieved to be getting back into clothes. The machine recommends a plain blue cloak and matching bag, which I accept.

Moments later my valuables case is returned to me; I hope it's clear of radiation.

A plate of shiny silver metal shows me a reflection. The image is okay; make-up is a bit strange, almost garish, but beautifully applied. Something strikes me at this moment. Where is the glass and the mirrors? Windows everywhere are perspex and I haven't seen any mirrors.

Finally, the door opens and I am ejected into the lounge. A travel area for people destined for Artisan Class. Something doesn't make sense. I feel I have stepped into a Tardis. There is a size mismatch between the door I had entered and the one I now exit; they don't connect. It dawns on me that the Pod was travelling, while it was abusing my rights and bringing me up to Artisan standard of cleanliness.

The shops and cafes of the lounge are bustling with people.

"Welcome to ProTelCom. Do you wish to place a call?" A voice says close to my ear. "You are now permitted to use communication devices." It's the collar; it had switched on when I entered the lounge. "Call Donald Gentle," I say as I sit down outside a large fancy cafe with marble counters full of pastries. I'm not expecting a reply; I was half joking.

"Donald Gentle ID 576-398-228 Unavailable." Interesting, does that mean he might normally be connected? Or did that mean they know who he is but he doesn't have a communicator? It might even be another Donald Gentle.

"All okay?" Sheldon and Jan appear. There is no sign of Jonathan; I start to worry properly.

"We didn't expect to speak to the machine," I say. "It's my fault, I should have let him go first. Hopefully he will be through shortly." I look over to the exit gates.

"What happened to your hair?" Jan asks. "Crazy make-up."

I'd forgotten about my appearance. And Jan and Sheldon both still have some of their hair, although they have been shaved to skinheads, and their relaxed garb is fairly low key compared to my travel suit.

"They didn't shave you completely?" I say.

"Everywhere but the head," Sheldon replies.

"And your choice of clothes?" I say. I continue to glare at the gates.

"This is what they gave us. No choice." Jan says. Neither of the boys is worried.

"You'll see; he will come through," Sheldon says.

"Sheldon, he cannot speak. How will he pass the machines?"

We walk to the gates and try to find an office, an official, or some sort of enquiry desk staffed by people. There is nowhere to look through, nobody around and no way to get back. I begin to get frantic.

"I shouldn't have left him. He cannot survive on his own."

"It isn't your fault," Jan says. "You were not to know."

"Robyn, look!" Sheldon points to the viewing platform.

I look up and Jonathan waves. I shake my head. What is he doing outside of the departure lounge?

The three of us hurry over and face him through the thick perspex window. I spread my arms and turn up my palms in an alarmed questioning gesture. "What happened?"

Jonathan looks directly at me, smiles sadly and shakes his head.

"Nooooo. What happened?" I am becoming distraught.

"We'll fix it," Sheldon says trying to calm me. He steps back and starts to look for a way to the viewing gallery.

Jonathan takes out his pad and pen and scribbles for a few minutes, then holds the paper on the glass for everyone to read. 'They wouldn't let me pass. I am "handicapped".

You have to continue the journey, find your Dad and find a way out of this place.

Don't come after me.

I will find my way back to Huptoou.'

This isn't happening. I'm not losing him again. I signal, point and mouth to him. 'No. We will come out and figure it out.' I am shaking my head furiously. He writes again.

'I need you to calm down and think. Take a deep breath. What I am saying makes sense. You can do nothing for any of us here in this place. You three need to get to a safe place. Find your Dad. Figure out what to do then. Coming back here is NOT an option.'

I start crying and I no longer care who is watching. Maybe it is a combination of everything we'd been through and a lack of sleep. Sheldon comes and holds me and I shrug him off. I don't want anyone else; I don't want Jonathan to think I want anyone else. When I look up, Jonathan is motioning me to come close. He places his hand on the perspex and smiles at me, but I can see the tears in his eyes. I put my hand on his and rest my forehead on the plastic, where his chest is.

"Do you want to write something to him?" Jan says. He had gone and found me a piece of paper and pen. Such a kind thoughtful boy, my Mum would have called him; his quiet calmness hides his ability for deep thinking and mega awareness of all situations.

"Thanks Jan," I say. I notice Sheldon watching and for a second I feel bad for pushing him away.

I write on the paper. 'It's all my fault. I led you into this and let you down.'

Jonathan replies. 'No Robyn, we came here together. It was my choice. All the times that you have been leading this group, you made good decisions. Your Mum would be proud of you. Do not blame yourself.'

I write, 'I want to come out and be with you. I'd rather be in no man's land with you than the Metro-politic without you.'

'No. You are not thinking straight. We have to think of everyone. We came out to help the boys and your Dad. You need to go forward, not back.'

I nod solemnly.

I write. 'Okay. I will take the Shuttle, find my Dad, but I won't leave you here.'

He writes. 'You look beautiful. Your head tattoo would start a trend back home. You will do well in the Metro-politic region.'

It hits me what he must be feeling, looking at us three, safe on the other side, all cleaned up and dressed in nice clothes. He has stayed strong of course, as always, while I have been selfishly thinking of how I felt. I start crying again.

I write through a blur of tears. 'I will miss you. Stay safe. Promise?'

He replies. 'My brave Robyn, you are my heart. I will miss you more than home. x.'

With that he raises a hand to each of the boys in turn, gives a last sad smile and turns and walks swiftly down the gantry leading him away from us. In a few seconds he is gone.

Jan and Sheldon keep quiet as we walk back to the middle of the lounge. Our cuffs buzz to advise us on the departure of the next shuttle to South Station in Artisan Class.

The boys follow the signs and guide me as I stumble along.

The shuttlecraft has different compartments depending on your final destination. Huge gating mechanisms and moving corridors direct us along with other boarders to the sealed compartments appropriate to our tickets. There is no open connection between compartments. And we understand that once you are 'immigration' cleared, you can't get out until you arrive at your authorised destination. It means we couldn't have gotten out to regroup with Jonathan anyway, but it doesn't make me feel any better.

We find seats quickly, in a large comfortable cabin with a few other travellers. A table for four with one empty space twists the knife immediately. I watch from the windows as we slide out of the Transport station. I pretend I'm not, but I look for Jonathan, scanning lone walkers outside the station to try to catch a last glimpse.

"He will be okay," Jan says. Sheldon sits very quiet.

My heart constricts with pain and regret and I squeeze Sheldon's hand and murmur, "Sorry."

□□□□□□□□

It takes a while for the emotional pain to subside to something manageable. Jan and Sheldon order and eat a nice meal at our table while I recline and doze fitfully. When I look at them I realise that although on the surface they are sad for Jonathan, underneath they are both positive; it is the first time they have been properly safe, secure and comfortable since they arrived. They are animated as they watch other passengers and families sitting around us, and study the passing landscape and other craft outside in the Causeway.

It is obvious when we leave the border of Subtopia and enter the Outlands, although at first it doesn't look too bad. We see factories in the distance, some lakes and waterways, a small town on the top of a hill filled with dark orange houses. The shuttle enters a dark green forest with lush conifers; I wish I could smell them as they rush past but nothing penetrates the shuttle's controlled air conditioning. After the pines, a long functional tunnel through the mountains, through the other side, we are joined by eight sky patrols who position themselves like convoy protection around the shuttle.

"Look at this!" Sheldon points to the approaching battle-scarred landscape; blackened craters and vehicles pockmark the face of the land for miles.

"It looks like they are at war," Jan says.

But if there is fighting we don't see any of it. The sky patrols peel off and the landscape returns to a more normal view again, although it is dry and barren looking.

Sheldon estimates a total of three hours to reach the outskirts of Subtopia in Dintropolis. A giant grey wall made of sections of framed metal panels and wires stretches up and out left and right into the distance as far as we can see.

Our cuffs buzz as we cross the border. Twenty minutes later we glide to a stop inside a large Transit Station in Dintropolis's LowDowncast area, third quadrant. We don't see the people get on or get off. But there is plenty of activity around the shuttle. I think of Jonathan and wonder what kind of place we are going that doesn't accept handicaps.

Someone at the end of the compartment, apparently talking to himself, reminds me that I have a communication device.

"Call Donald Gentle," I say. Jan and Sheldon look at me in puzzlement.

"Hello?" A voice answers. It is Dad. I look at Sheldon and realise that they can't hear it. The voice is being transmitted through my collarbone to my ear.

"Dad!"

"Who is this?"

"Dad. It's me. Robyn," I say.

"Sorry, you have the wrong person. I am warning you. Don't call me again."

The phone disconnects.

"Call Donald Gentle," I say immediately.

"Sorry, number unavailable."

"What is it?" Sheldon asks.

"I got my Dad on the line. He didn't know who I was..." I say. "I recognised his voice. It was him all right. But he hung up."

"Are you absolutely sure?" Sheldon asks. "What did he say exactly?"

I tell them.

"Perhaps he didn't believe you could possibly be here. Or perhaps he was giving you a warning? It sounded very specific, warning you not to call again," Jan suggests.

I brood for a moment or two.

"Call Iain Banks."

"Hello. This is Iain."

I am a bit surprised and a little lost for words.

"Iain, my name is Robyn, my Dad says we needed to contact you for assistance."

"Hold on," he replies.

"Scramble Activated," the machine says. "1 minute."

"Sorry, who did you say you were? And who is your Dad?"

"Robyn, my Dad is Donald Gentle. He says..."

"Okay Robyn. It's only secure on here for less than a minute. Where are you now?"

"We are on the Shuttle, arriving Artisan Dintropolis in around thirty minutes," I reply.

"Who is 'we'?"

"Friends."

"From the other side?"

"From my home. Yes."

"Okay. Don't use this communicator again."

"Okay," I say.

"You will be picked up at your destination. Go to the Fat Cat Cafe outside the station."

Sheldon and Jan stare at me until I repeat the conversation.

"I guess we have somewhere to go when we arrive after all," says Jan.

# CHAPTER SEVEN

## The Antichrist's Cookbook

We look out as the shuttle slows at the border between Subtopia and Artisan; there is no great wall this time. Instead there is a tower, bristling with aerials, lights and other electronics, set every two hundred feet, forming a guard-line into the distance.

Our cuffs and collars light up and vibrate. "Welcome to Metro Region, Dintropolis. You are now fully connected to the Reward and Punishment network system. iTrust welcomes compliant, responsible and productive citizens returning home. iTrust welcomes new citizens who recognise the benefits and privilege of becoming an Artisan and living in the Metro region. iTrust welcomes authorised visitors correctly permitted and inoculated for your visit."

I take a piece of paper, scribble and pass to Sheldon. 'Everything we say now is monitored.'

"Citizen Robyn. Written communication is forbidden in this zone. Please confirm understanding and future compliance." A woman's voice, slightly stern.

I hesitate for a second.

"Confirm and comply."

"Yes, understand," I say.

Sheldon, Jan and I exchange glances and say nothing else until we arrive at the terminal; I hope the system can't read raised eyebrows or wide opened eyes, as Sheldon signals me to look at the numbers of guards and weapons.

The Transport Station is in the middle of the most incredible towers I have ever seen in my life. The spiralling structures gleam a burnished red from the setting sun. The city is built on planes or levels, the difference in their functions not immediately obvious to me, like a giant layer cake. There is an incredible order and a perfection of hierarchy that would have OCD sufferers cheering. Every structure has its place and integrates seamlessly with every building around it. The city reminds me of the most perfect English garden on a sunny day; elegance and order, but not easy to replicate.

The Transport Stations give way to offices, shops, buildings that look like government, to octagonal buildings on different levels that look more like accommodation for hundreds of families in spacious self-contained units.

There is a glut of laser, hologram and screen advertisements, flashing from every angle. Otherwise, the place was built with people in mind. Cable cars and big wheels blended with hover cars and shuttles. Perspex walkways, tunnels, moving pavements, garden cafes, sculpture, art shops and markets. Despite my need for order, everything is frighteningly congruent, simply too perfect, nothing out of place.

Seeing such a well-maintained comfortable place, after the hardships of Subtopia, is breathtaking. I look at Jan and Sheldon; like me, they are in awe.

Although traffic and pedestrians crowd the centre, calm and conflict-free movement happens smoothly. There is an absence of obstruction; people and objects don't frustrate one another. A clockwork city, I think, everything in harmony and precision. I wonder how it all moves so fluidly. There has to be a regulator; there is no other explanation. There has to be a control system fluent in the language of movement.

The people around us, going about their business, are mostly beautiful or attractive, or at least well-dressed and healthy looking if not perfect. Some men and women have shaved coloured heads and similar jumpsuits to mine; a certain fashion trend maybe. At least I fit in and won't be taken for a foreigner by my attire, although we must look like lost tourists as we gawk and stumble into the streets.

There are many more adverts. Flashing repeatedly on huge screens. 'Unity is peace' , 'Monsters roam Outlands' , 'Our Nation Works' , 'Everyone succeeds in Metro' , 'Outlands is fair game' , 'Subtopia equals survival' , 'Big Society', 'Order is progress' , 'Control is freedom'. It is a blur. You can read the messages, they are so short, but they come so fast that the latest dozen seem to push the first ones you read out of your conscious mind.

It is about now that I notice an advert on one of the giant screens that stands out from all the rest. It says, 'I miss Couscous." It flashes for a second before being replaced by a fizzy energy drink.

"That's... might be a message from my Dad..." I blurt.

"I'd love a coffee. We should get one," Jan says. Smart. I get the message.

"Sure. Me too. I believe there is a good cafe close by called Fat Cat," Sheldon says.

"Straight on. Third block on your right. Fifth shop down on other side of the road." I hear my collar speak and realised that it says exactly the same to each of the guys. We raise eyebrows at each other and walk to the cafe in silence watching all the adverts as we walk. We enter the Cafe and look around. It is busy. My cuff buzzes and syncs with a nearby machine. A waiter directs us to an empty booth.

"This is the last A-List booth Madame. I hope it's okay."

"Sure," I say. "Thanks."

A holographic menu pops up on the table and Jan twirls it with his finger, then flicks open a page.

"Impressive," says Sheldon lifting his eyebrows again.

"What would you like to order?" Our collars speak to all of us again.

"Chocolate," I say. I look at the guys.

"Same."

"White coffee with," Sheldon says then shrugs self-consciously.

Moments later the order appears at the table. Foaming hot cups of coffee and chocolate delivered by our smiling waiter. I am surprised for a moment that it hadn't been a robot, but perhaps this is the personal touch.

"Order debited," the collar says. Sheldon's eyebrows rise again; I begin to think he is connected to the cuff and suppress a snigger, to avoid having to explain. And cuffs and collars do everything, it seems. I realise they are part of the efficiency and collaboration necessary to keep this densely packed city running effectively; but because of the machine, I don't feel I could share my thoughts out loud with the guys.

Our waiter leads a guy to the table next to ours. He looks around sixty, bespectacled, wearing a hat and already carrying a drink. "Is this a quieter table, sir?" the waiter asks.

"Thanks," he says. He sits down, lifts his cup to me, nods and gives a slight smile through a thick red beard. I can see he is still watching me as he swallows his drink. He looks directly at me as he innocently scratches his neck; he doesn't have a collar on.

"I am going to the toilet," I tell the guys.

"Right corner, past the bar, second door," machine voice says.

As I pass the guy's table, he gets up and bumps me, nearly knocking me over.

"Terribly sorry. I am awfully clumsy. Are you okay?" For a second he touches my elbow and squeezes. I look into his eyes and I see comprehension, then a message, but I have no idea what.

"I am great, thanks," I say.

His eyes flick a second onto my cloak pocket. "For a second I thought I'd spilt coffee over your beautiful cloak. I am so glad you are okay."

"Honestly, I am."

"Okay. Off to the bank now. Toodle-pip." He smiles again, places his cup down and turns and leaves the cafe.

In the toilet cubicle, I check my pocket and discover a small plastic box with two buttons on. I keep it out of direct view of my collar or cuff as I turn it in my hand. A small label on the plastic says 'Green Button - use outside'. I pocket it and return to the guys.

"Let's go," I say. I see the 'Where to?' start to form on Jan's lips, but he stops himself. It is hard to get used to being monitored.

"Sure. Time to go," Jan agrees and we all pile out of the booth and out of the cafe onto the sidewalk.

I produce the small unit and press the green button. Sheldon looks at me, puzzled.

"TaxiCab called," machine voice says.

A few moments later, a car hovers to a stop in front of us and the door opens. I climb in and the guys don't hesitate. The door closes and the car moves forward a little to clear the buildings then flies directly up. It is exhilarating if slightly scary; there is no driver. I look out of the window until I get slight vertigo. The view of the city is incredible; buildings, a smorgasbord of architectural elegance and ingenuity, rise from every point, some at inconceivable angles. Architects competing or secret messages to the gods; the buildings have a language of their own. I cannot read them yet. But they have secrets. We travel in and out of highways through skyscrapers and across huge indoor shopping malls before swooping down towards what looks like docks. We fly into a large building on the quayside and down a dizzying vertical shaft.

All three of us are gripping the handles and each other as the car comes to a swift stop on a platform near a huge elevator door.

"Area out of bounds," machine voice says. "Please return to unrestricted areas."

The car doors open at the same time as the lift door. Standing inside is the guy from the cafe. He motions us to hurry.

"Return to authorised areas immediately. Confirm and comply," machine voice says.

I am already out of the car and running to the lift.

The man closes the doors and we are in pitch black.

"Stand still," he says.

He grabs my shoulders and turns me around. I feel something get fastened on my neck and wrist. He leaves me and I suspect he has done the same thing to Jan and Sheldon. The lights go back on. I have a contraption around my wrist and collar.

"Hello. I am Iain," he says. "Let's go where we can fix your bands." He presses a button on the huge cargo lift taking us down further to a sophisticated workshop.

"The cuff and collar are jammed at the moment. It stops them hearing, seeing or tracking. We do that initially to stop them punishing you and raising an infraction."

"What's the difference?" I ask.

"One is painful, the other goes on your record and gradually makes life painful if you get too many," Iain says.

While he talks, he plugs each of us into a machine for a few moments.

"There, they have a virtual, well behaved, copy of each of you to follow for a while," he says. "It's a program that takes your details, creates a standard and somewhat boring activity, but enough to convince them you are going around like a model citizen."

He removes the contraptions from our bodies and leaves the collars and cuffs.

"No point in taking them off, you will want them again when you travel or shop. For now you are connected to BankNet, my own network."

He leads us upstairs into a stunning open plan lounge with a view through a panoramic window of a broad river and across to the other side of the city. Through to the right I can see a massive luxury library, and on the other side, a stunning dining area with tall marble art and bronze sculptures, and kitchen with tall stainless steel units and thick wooden worktops.

"Welcome to my dock house," Iain says. "It's secure and your iTrust is off, so we can speak freely. Frankly, there are not many places that you can."

"My father told me to come to you. Was he here?"

"Yes, quite a few weeks ago. It was a hell of a reunion."

"You know him?" Sheldon asks.

"Okay, hold on. I expect you have lots of questions, and I have a few for you too. Also, I need to help you understand this place if you are to survive for much longer; you have done remarkably well to get this far. This place is deadly if you don't know what you are doing. But first let me get you some drinks and snacks, then we will start."

We all sit on the sofas looking out over the river and docks, eating a selection of antipasti and drinking a pleasant light ale. Modern art and sculpture grace the room and balconies. I notice that most of the artwork is the same shiny silver metal that I've seen everywhere. I ask Iain what it is and he gets up and hands me a large ingot off the coffee table.

"Keep it," he says. "It's almost the most common metal on Wellorsland, but a little more rare back home."

Iain asks us to tell him everything that has happened so far, and what we have learned about the place. I do that, with Sheldon and Jan chipping in and reminding me of something or explaining their own experience. Iain listens intently. When I talk about Jonathan I choke up, and Jan takes over in parts. Finally, I explain that my Dad told us in a message to contact him and to trust him.

"Your Dad wasn't expecting you though?"

"No," I agree, "His note was addressed to 'Whoever', but I called him and told him I was here."

"First mistake. Never call or email anyone here unless you know for sure your cuffs are off and also your phone line is scrambled. You can only scramble for a minute. After that they pick you up."

"Okay."

"Let me paint the picture for you," he says. "This country is completely controlled by the Supreme and the Establishment. There is no freedom. History has been erased. In fact, 'History' is one of the words you are not permitted to say. Nor can you own antiques or old books from the past." He pointed to some around the room, illegal and punishable by a long sentence.

I gawked. Books? My lifeblood.

"You will need a list of all the words to avoid. I will arrange that. You will probably need a list of citizen regulations as well. You already learned you couldn't walk in more than three people max, or pass paper communications between you. I will get the citizens' handbook for you.

"The capitals are like giant roses, more sweet smelling in the centre, and as you move out to concentric rings life becomes less rose tinted until you reach the thorns. Life in the Artisan or Metro Zone isn't bad; everything is catered for, in return for compliance and hard work. Fine, if you don't get tired of smelling rose all the time. But no good for people who want to smell the seaweed occasionally."

"Why is it built in rings?" I ask.

"Circles, the natural shape for power and controlling the ebb and flow of change. Think of the old medieval castles, the traditional large cities. The closer to the centre, the closer to power and privilege."

"Most cities have a mix of rich and poor," Jon says.

"Not here. There are many reasons not to mix rich and poor: avoid dissent, keep control, define the hierarchy or class easier, manage the technology and borders."

"Great geographical circles of social status apartheid," I say.

"Something like that. But as I remember, such things as language, status, education and culture have always maintained the boundaries between the rich and poor. This is probably a progression, a refinement of something that's always existed."

"The difference between the regions is stark," Jon says. "We stayed with boys who hardly had any money or belongings."

"The boys that saved you are geldings who escaped the Farms and Factories. Huptoou is a modest and unassuming leader, but it was he who organised the mass breakouts."

"What did the boys do on the farm?" I ask.

"You don't know?" Iain said, "Ah okay. They don't do anything. They are raised specially to provide meat for the inner cities. They geld them and feed them hormones to fatten them."

I feel sick. My factory suspicions completely confirmed. These poor people. I still tried to push the thoughts from my mind. I recalled their helplessness and the overwhelming smell of lost hope. Can you smell lost hope? Does it have a worse odour than despair?

"People? You are kidding. Why not cows, pigs and sheep?"

"They poisoned them over years of genetic modification and intensive farming. Livestock has not been used here for hundreds of years. Then there is radiation from war and disused power stations that pollutes most of the land. The cities and the causeways are the only clean areas. So you couldn't put cattle out to grass even if we had them now. In effect there are three types of vegetables: synthetic, chemical or real. Real are only in the black market here, extremely expensive. Perhaps grown in tiny quantities in the

Supreme Class. Meat is standard; it's purified human protein. Many people have forgotten its origins or have chosen to forget.

"In the Subtopia, people eat anything," I say.

"Yes, they do," he agrees. "Perhaps it's more healthy."

I look at Sheldon and Jan. Both look a little bit sick. I realise they are both wondering what they had eaten on the train.

"There are two interesting things for you to know about the meat trade. A nationwide mafia called Beane runs it. You may well have already upset them, if they know it was you who kidnapped Keshet."

"We took his money," I say. I want to be up front with this guy, I am confident that we can trust him and he will guide us.

Iain roars with hearty laughter, and then becomes serious. "Oops. Then for sure you have a big enemy. Keshet would be holding money for them."

"I guess," I say. "I'm not worried for me, but now think about Jonathan still back there."

"The second thing about the meat trade is they plan to get some of their supplies from where you came from, thanks to Mr., or should I say Dr., Jack Wills."

"I know the name," I say.

"The School benefactor that built the vacuum machine? He is still here?" It is Sheldon who remembers and speaks after being quiet for so long.

"Yes. He is seventy plus now, I think. His machine provides a gateway, a portal through which the Beane dynasty has experimented with 'importing' a limited amount of fresh meat. They are looking for a way to expand it. It's also the means by which Huptoou crosses over for a few minutes."

"You mean they have taken people from our world? To use as food here?"

"Children. That's about the gist of it. But so far no more than a few maybe," Iain says. He rubs his beard reflectively. "I think your Dad may have plans to change that.

"The thing is, I suspect your arrival may have thrown a spanner in his plans. He'd wanted to get the boys, exit and destroy the machine at the same time. Unfortunately, the Establishment must know you are here. Keshet probably advised them that more foreigners arrived. He was aware of the first times we came through."

"I don't understand," I say.

"When your Dad and I came through the first time all these years ago, we landed in the factory. One boy was killed almost immediately. I forget his name."

"Hamilton," I say.

"That's right. There were four of us, inseparable back then. Hamilton, Barrow, Gentle and Banks. We were the best marble team in the school.

"And while we think by some technical aberration your Dad was catapulted back home to safety, Wills landed inside Serfin, captured and questioned. In the meantime, Barrow and myself were hung up for processing. I guess I should be thankful to Keshet, because he realised he had something unusual and stopped the line. I think he may have suspected we were from somewhere else. Luckily he thought we were worth more than meat and his curiosity probably saved us.

"He kept us to himself for years, trying to figure out how to get more from us. He wanted to know where we were from. Where we got the marbles we had in our pocket. How to make glass; we didn't know back then, and even if we did, there is virtually no silicon or sand in this world. It's more rare than hen's teeth. That's why the few windows that you see are perspex. And why marbles are currency. But I suspect there is something to do with the quantum physics that I don't understand. It was not a coincidence that we arrived in a dimension that valued what we did, marbles."

"It's a still a madness, but it starts to make more sense now," I say.

"Back to the Establishment for the moment. If I really am correct they will be hunting you already."

"Why?"

"Because you are a massive threat to the status quo for a start. They have been waiting for the machine to throw others through for years. In their eyes, an army could come through. Anything that doesn't fit their ways is eradicated or at best ejected to the Outlands. The Establishment run tourist trips to the Outlands, where people pay to go on human safari. They take regular ships in and shoot up anyone they find. They consider it sport."

"Can they find us here?" I ask.

"It's a shame that you forced Keshet to use your real names. He must have been delighted to do that. He'd have known it could make you visible," he says. "But don't worry, I will fix that. You need to have secure identities as soon as possible. It takes a few days, your Dad wouldn't wait for his."

"Keshet is a nasty piece of work," Jan says.

"He played on the Establishment's fears for years. A real politician is Keshet, deceitful, treacherous, self-serving and duplicitous. It made matters worse when Barrow and I escaped. You see, I helped Keshet in the workshop in the early days, before the bracelet systems were as sophisticated as they are now. One of Beane's security killed Barrow during the escape, but I made it here and have lived here hidden ever since. They consider me a contagion; I make it my duty to spread choice and freedom whenever I can."

"How did my Dad find you? He thought you were dead," I say.

"He is a smart man, your Dad. He got the information out of Keshet, without telling Keshet who he was. He paid Keshet to help him get here. Your Dad booked into a hotel in the centre and advertised on billboards. He mentioned things that only we would know from childhood. I met him in the exact same coffee shop as I met you."

"Why did you never try to go home?" Jan asks.

"I did once. It cost me about ten years in age and sent me straight back here," Iain says. "Your Dad thinks he has a way out. Maybe he has. I am no physicist. But there is nothing for me back there anymore. My folks are most likely dead and I have a life here. And before you ask, I am no cannibal; I don't eat their disgusting protein. In fact, I hate the people who govern this place and allow this

travesty." He laughs. "Hell. It's good to meet some sane people."
And with that he comes and gives us all a big hug each.

I wake up in the middle of the night shouting out for someone,
don't know who. I am sweating and for a few minutes confused as I
try to recall the dream and figure out where I am. Then I remember.
We had talked with Iain through until evening, and until I couldn't
keep my eyes open any longer. I'd fallen asleep on the couch and
wakened up just as Sheldon was carrying me upstairs. He wanted to
stay with me in the bedroom, but I told him I was fine and needed to
get a good night's sleep alone. The truth is, I had wanted him to stay,
but I felt it would have been unfair to all three of us, Jonathan,
Sheldon and myself.

I lie in the dark, mind spinning, and think over some of the
hundreds of words that we can't use, 'History, Democracy,
Constitution, Socialism, Anarchy, Fairness, Equality, Justice,
Fraternity, Freedom,' and many more. There are too many to
remember. I decide to avoid anything other than day-to-day
conversation. Iain said there were bonuses for using words like
contented, happy or relaxed.

Some of the rules he showed us were designed to stop people
collaborating, questioning, thinking and reasoning. 'No asking
questions about government policy', 'no-unauthorised meetings', 'no
collaborations on non-work projects', 'no hidden communication' and
'no questioning lack of government transparency'.

Despite the machines' constant surveillance it is required that you report anyone who you suspected of breaking rules, no matter how small. You get bonuses for that too; bonuses buy additional luxuries for your family.

The state 'newspapers' and online news channels are called Daily Cascade, Concentric News and The Ripple. Iain tells us that the contents and headlines change as the publications cross the boundaries. In other words, the headline and content emphasis would be different between Artisan Class and Subtopia. When Sheldon asked why, Iain told us it was 'to manage perception in each class'. Communication is one direction; there is no feedback. Back home, poor people could read a rich man's news. Here they cannot.

This country oppresses me like a dark room; I am a seventeen year old girl who loves to be free and in the sunlight. I just want to go home and run the annual half marathon, through the forest near my home, with my Mum waiting at the finish to hug me. I shrug off the crushing political thoughts and I pull the blankets around me and doze through until daylight and the call for breakfast.

"Good morning all," Iain says. "I trust you all had a well needed rest." He is looking at me. I nod sleepily while sipping a mug of tea.

He continues, "Today will be a practice day. I will show you around the city and we will do normal things. Although we do have to be careful; we will be plugged back into iTrust. We will find somewhere for you to stay; it is too risky for everyone to stay here, eggs in one basket and all that. And we will arrange bank accounts so that it is easy for you to spend without attracting attention. The other thing I want to do is get you a weapon. They are illegal of course, but it is better to be caught with an illegal weapon than shot by one."

"And my Dad?"

"That's the very next thing I will be doing. I need to find out where he went and what he is up to. My suspicion tells me he has tried to see Dr. Jack Wills, but by this time he must be wondering where you guys are. If I can find him, perhaps we can meet here."

"That is what I want," I say.

"Then finally, finally, finally, we will agree a strategy to get you all out of here," he says. "Easy as that."

It's like one big game to Mr. Banks; it wouldn't surprise me if he leaves his tag or mark behind every time he outsmarts the Establishment. I don't ask.

"What about Jonathan?" Jan asks and I silently thank him.

"Hmm, that is going to be much harder. Getting him passed by the physical system is almost impossible," he says. "I need to think about it. But there may be no choice, you might have to leave him."

"That is not an option," I say firmly and everyone becomes silent for a few moments.

"I have been thinking, before we go, I need to reprogram the cuffs. It doesn't make sense leaving any trail in your old names. If you are signing for bank accounts and apartments, best we don't advertise," Iain says.

"Okay," I agree.

"I won't make up a complete new identity, just do enough this time to disguise you."

"What is the difference?" I ask.

"Until I can give you a completely fresh identity, rebuilt from scratch, there is still a fair chance that you will get found by Beane or the Establishment. It could happen tomorrow, it could take them a fortnight. We will just need to be on our guard until it's fixed. Meanwhile, I will give you some electronic camouflage that will allow us to confuse and hopefully delay them."

"How does that work exactly?" Jan asks.

"Well everything in Metro is copied and stored online. Think of a system that's a massive electronic reflection of life. It's a huge data set. That means that inconstancies are easily spotted, aberrations, changes from the norm, outliers, anyone doing anything extreme. There is no tolerance in Metro for people who live outside the established society norms. Consistency means control. Inconsistency is the beginning of rebellion. You three are potential blips in the data. I need to try to hide you and most of the things you do."

Jan is deep in thought and Sheldon raises his eyebrows.

With that Iain goes off to the workshop while I return my thoughts to Jonathan.

Two sleek hover cars belonging to Iain come up from somewhere in the basement. Four of us can't travel together so Iain goes in the front vehicle with Jan. They seem to have hit it off; Jan likes listening to Iain's stories, of which there are many. Sheldon and I follow at a respectable distance in the second vehicle, reconnecting our collars and cuffs as we head downtown. Iain has explained that as soon as we are in the air we have to say, 'Detach BankNet' and we'll automatically be returned to the iTrust network. I immediately feel 'on my guard' when I know our collars can monitor us again.

We swoop through the levels, buildings and towers. Sheldon looks as though he is beginning to relax and getting used to the car. He presses his face to the window and his eyes soak up every bit of detail. We can't say much to each other under surveillance, but it occurs to me that he hasn't said much since I pushed him away. It makes me feel bad, I like him; he is a great guy, it is just a screwed up situation.

Our first stop is a large downtown bank, known as the 'Bilden Bank'. It is one of the most impressive buildings I have ever seen. We fly through automatic portals into the vast multileveled corridors that make up the banking hall and I wonder if the bank is ever robbed, since you could actually take your getaway car inside. I want to share the funny thought with Sheldon, but I'm not sure, maybe 'robbery' and 'getaway' are banned words or at least likely to draw attention to us. The cars let us out in the middle of one of the halls and we walk to the tellers sitting at large purpose-built desks.

We sit on comfortable chairs that immediately connect with our cuffs and collars. They give the bank our details so that the Bank Officer can see them up on a screen. Our Bank Officer is a smart, intelligent-looking woman about thirty. She radiates a confident and pyroclastic persona; hot, smooth and potentially dangerous. She is dressed in a tight suit that makes me think of Star Trek for some reason; there isn't a hair or ounce of fat out of place, like she'd been airbrushed to perfection. Sheldon is staring at her with his mouth hanging open until I nudge him.

"You'll catch flies," I say.

At another desk close by, an equally attractive lady is attending to Iain and Jan.

"Uh. Oh. Right," Sheldon replies. A grin breaks out on his face.

"Pervert," I mumble under my breath.

"Restricted word. Please do not use. Confirm," machine voice says.

"Understood," I say.

The Bank Officer smiles. "Welcome. How can Bilden Bank help you today?"

"We'd like to open an account and make a deposit."

She asks all the details about account access, credit facilities and if we are married. Then she asks how much we want to deposit.

"A substantial amount." This is what Iain told us to say. I hold up the travel safe. "We want full confidentiality and access by code." Iain explained that large sums of money are the only area of semi-confidentiality. And that's for the convenience of the wealthy. The less money you have, the more the system knows about you.

"Please come with me," she says and leads us through a number of secure doors behind her desk, into a large private vault room. "The account auditor will join us on screen and we will get your money out of the case and booked in. It's quantum cryptography I believe? Our machine cannot unlock it. You will need to do it manually."

"Okay. Thank you."

I unlock the box and place it in the machine. A number of screens light up and the Auditor appears on one and says 'good morning', just as the machine starts to scan and deposit the marbles.

When the number quickly turns into millions I'm pleased to see an almost imperceptible expression of surprise flit across the girl's face. It must have counted the easy marbles first. Towards the end a number of the more unusual marbles appear on screen and it takes a few seconds before each is valued and the Auditor presses a button to confirm.

"The total amount is □601,560,341.22." I recognise their currency symbol from Mathematics, but can't recall its function; something to do with contours and integration. I make a mental note to ask Dad or Iain.

'And that's not the full amount,' I think. I didn't tell anyone, but I have saved a number of marbles in the belt for a rainy day.

I know from the final expression of the Bank Officer that I am an extremely wealthy young lady. As we thank her and leave, I can still feel her looking at me in astonishment. We must have been the richest teenagers she'd ever seen.

Going back to the car, we find Jan is finished too and appears to be walking ten feet tall, like he thought he owned the world; I nudge Sheldon and we laugh at the sight. Jan the multi-millionaire.

The next stop is an expensive department store with over forty floors. Iain told us that we needed a range of clothes to fit in, and suggested that we wander around alone, shop, then meet back at the cars in a couple of hours. 'It is okay to allow the Store Assistants to recommend styles for you, they will make sure you don't look out of place,' he told us. I'm not surprised to realise that all my sizes are already in the cuff and everything fits perfectly. I wonder what would happen if you put on a few extra pounds, and promise myself to ask Iain that later. There is a certain style that I begin to like the more I browse. Some would say it is slightly tomboyish, slightly masculine. But they are real high quality comfort clothes; not too dressy, but chunky and chic at the same time. High collars seem to suit my shaved head. I match boots and belts with jumpsuits. And buy contrasting hats and modern soft wool jackets with silk lining. I find a cool range of berets. I also buy some very functional sports clothing, boots and combat trousers, reminding myself that we are still in danger.

Back at the cars, Sheldon and I burst out laughing at each other. I have to get help to carry all my parcels; he has four bags.

"Did you actually buy anything?" I look askance at him.

"Everything I need for the next week or so." He smiles. "You look like you had a shopping frenzy."

"We don't know how long we will be here," I say. He understands.

Jan and Iain are already waiting to go. Sheldon helps me load up and we are immediately off again. I lose sight of the first car as we arrive on a platform on top of a group of residential towers close to where we had shopped.

A smartly dressed woman is waiting for us at the entrance to a large penthouse apartment and leads us inside. Iain had said we didn't have time to choose, so he'd order two new apartments close to each other. All we had to do was sign the contracts once we looked around.

"Welcome to Tahoe Suites. Would you like to have a wander around, and then I can answer any questions you may have. All furniture, facilities and upgrades are already fitted; full security systems, integrated automotive options with Lexsun executive vehicles, weather control, all robotic cleaning and waste management and a corridor to Penthouse B next door, as requested," she tells us.

"How high up are we?"

"This is the top of this building, there are ninety floors and the building is around fifteen hundred feet high, excluding the spires," she answers.

It's like being on top of the world. Our luxury lounge is on the bottom floor of three floors, with panoramic windows all round and an enormous terrace that could be opened or closed.

"Is the building swaying?" I ask Sheldon.

"Either that or I have been drinking," he says smiling.

One half of the middle floor is an enormous kitchen and separate dining room and behind a solid stone wall the other half is a huge garage-hangar, storage and workshop.

The bedrooms, luxury bathrooms and dressing rooms, along with a swimming pool, gym, sun terrace and sauna, are on the top floor. The views are exhilarating in the perfect weather and Sheldon points out the large smog machines cleaning the skies.

"What makes the smog?" I wonder aloud. "The city looks like it is run on clean energy." No one answers.

We sign for the house and the estate agent authorises the security systems and doors to work with our cuffs.

"Do you want all the facilities fully integrated?" she asks.

"Sure," Sheldon and I say together, both blagging.

"Okay, you are all done. The apartment will adapt to you automatically. Enjoy your new home."

Five minutes after the estate agent left, the entry buzzer sounds. Jan's face appears on the screen. "Hello, this is your neighbours Jan and Iain. We'd like to invite you for coffee. Please come along the corridor. Be careful; it's dark, there are no lights installed yet."

The door opens automatically and closes behind us as we step into the dim connecting corridor. The lights die completely and I take Sheldon's hand as we continue down the corridor feeling with our hands.

"Stand still." Iain's voice.

He puts the jamming machines on our collar and cuffs again and shouts for Jan to switch the lights.

"We can talk freely again," Iain says once we are inside Jan's apartment.

"I hate the bands," I say. "It's like having the government in your head; little dictators talking to you if you do something wrong."

"I will bring a machine here to both apartments. It is an extension of BankNet, so you will be able to log on and off. In the meantime, they are jammed to allow me to remove them."

"Why? I mean why can't we remove them all the time?" Sheldon asks.

"Because there are sensors all over the city that alert the authorities if there is someone not wearing."

"You don't always wear them," I say.

"That's because I know where most of the sensors are. I can just about get away with it unless the security drones come past scanning," Iain explains.

"Then why are we taking them off now?" I ask.

He laughs. "Because where we are going, we go together and it's highly illegal."

The armoury is a huge modern well-lit bunker somewhere outside of the downtown area. It is hard to find and heavily guarded. It seems they know Iain and even expected him. One of the armourers, a heavily tattooed fellow with an eye patch and a paunch that sticks through a black ammunition harness and hangs over his belt, looks ex-military, aware but untrusting. He puffs out thick grey smoke from a dirty looking stogie. He is the first person I've seen smoking since we arrived here.

"Still smoking that shit?" Iain asks him.

"You want one?"

"Why do you ask that every time?" Iain says.

"Because I am polite," he laughs loudly.

"Irritating and stubborn like a donkey more like." Iain gives him a hug. And they smile at each other for a few seconds.

"What's news?" the man asks looking at us.

"Mo, these are friends of mine. They need some self-protection weapons."

"They don't look old enough to shoot anything."

"Sure they are; they can shoot just fine. They just need something easy."

"Really, and my granny is a fighter pilot in the UNATO forces."

"What have you got?" Iain asks. "The Beane Mob might be looking for them."

"Shit, guys. I wouldn't like to be in your pants if they catch up with you. In fact that's what will be in your pants if they do. Shit." He laughs again, snorting loudly, at his own joke.

"I need your help," Iain tells him.

"Sure you do. It's not enough that I sell illegal weapons. You got me supplying to underage kids now?" he says. "You know how deep they will bury me in the Outlands if I get caught now."

"Yeah, you tell me every time I give you business and spend money with you," Iain counters.

Mo laughs heartily. "Come on, let's see what these guys can do." He leads us through double doors to a gun range and shows us a choice of hand-held weapons that could easily be concealed, and could stun or kill someone. The guys are eager to try a few guns but my eye has been drawn by something else, a female hologram explaining some kind of metal tube. It was the word lunge that caught my attention. While the guys practise on a load of virtual targets I ask about the tube.

"Nah, it's no good for you. It is a type of laser sword. No use without training."

"A sword. Like Star Wars?" I ask.

"Star Wars. It's not a weapon I know," he says. "What's a Star War?" He turns to Iain who shrugs.

"May I see it?" I ask.

He scowls, but goes across to the display and brings a package out of a drawer. He unwraps it and switches it on. It's a silver tube with a variety of buttons and lights. He hands it to me.

"Okay, hold it out in front. Point away from us and press the 'en garde' button."

The light sword buzzes out in front of me and feels similar in weight to a metal rapier.

"See, impressive. But no good without entering training," he says and motions for me to switch it off and return it.

"I will take two," I say.

"Look, there is no point in taking your money. You'd be dead as soon as you got in a fight with this; I would lose a customer. And your Uncle Iain here would be pissed at me." He sees my determined face. "Seriously? Okay. Let me introduce you to Marlene."

He marches us to the ring on the other side of the hall and switches a number of controls on a console.

"I have set it to gentle stun. It will sting a bit but at least you might learn a lesson. Marlene is our virtual trainer."

A woman appears in the middle of the ring brandishing a laser sword.

I look at Iain who just smiles and shrugs. It is obvious this is the first time he's seen it. The guys join just as I switch my sword back on and enter the ring. Marlene reacts and presents, as I circle towards her.

"Can she fence?" I hear Iain ask behind me. I imagine Sheldon must have nodded or shrugged, he'd not really seen me use the sword properly at Keshet's house. I can't take my eyes off of this virtual fencing master who is smiling as she circles closer.

Her attack is swift and I parry, let her come, and draw her in as she attacks again, block her and return a lightening attack. She counter parries, and then surprises me by a light riposte as if she is testing something in my defences. When her real attack comes I'm ready. I cede parry and allow her to come. She comes too far forward down my left flank and I am able to step left and turn quickly, forcing her to turn out. As she does, I advance, once, twice and gain on the lunge. My full lunge takes her by surprise and strikes her in the chest. The buzzer sounds a hit and Marlene resets back to on guard. We fence for 15 minutes and I know the point at which Mo turns up the proficiency; Marlene's fighting style changes and I am hit twice in the arm. It feels like static electricity and smarts a little. The pain sharpens me up and I manage to hold Marlene off and hit her back twice in the rest of the session.

"Bravo," Mo calls. "I give you special price now. I have never seen anything so gauche." He is pretending. I know he was impressed.

"You should watch Star Wars," I tell him, wiping a little perspiration from the bridge of my nose.

I twirl the silver tube in my hand and caress it. "It should have a name. It is Yuenu from now on."

"Sounds foreign," Mo grunts.

"Yuenu or Lady of Yue was a great warrior from another place and time, who taught the sword," I say. How could I tell him she was Chinese?

"Come, I have something else for you. This is a present." He gives me a watchband that produces a light shield when held in front. They didn't have this in Star Wars. And despite never using a shield with a rapier, I can see that a lightweight electronic shield could be very useful.

"May I have two?" I ask. He looks surprised, but I have to ask, Jonathan is never far from my thoughts.

Mo then helps the guys pick out two of the most expensive, easiest to use guns, plenty of ammunition and three protection vests. Sheldon picks a shoulder holster for his and Jan decides to keep his in an ankle strap.

We leave, Mo bemoaning that even high school students are killing people these days.

When we arrive back at the apartment, there is someone in the kitchen. I look at Sheldon in alarm; so much for security. Neither of us has our weapons out of the packaging or boxes. How stupid. We move cautiously to the door to look in. Jan and Iain have gone through to the other apartment. I don't want to shout. A man is standing by the sink, looking out over the cityscape. When he hears us he turns around. It takes me a few seconds to speak. Sheldon's mouth is hanging open as I run to my father and hug him until he prises me off a little to look at me.

"Nice skull top," he says.

"It's fashion, Dad," I say. "Is that what they call it?"

"Just kidding. You'd look gorgeous in anything. I am just so glad to see you. I was so happy when Iain told me the boys and you were safe and well here."

"Surprise!" Iain says from behind. "Sorry, I wanted to be sure he was going to arrive here. I couldn't tell you while we were connected to iTrust, and after that we were busy at the armoury."

"It's fine. If you'd told me, I'd have worried every second," I say. I hold tight to Dad's arm.

"Can we sit?" Dad asks. "It's been a tough trip, worth it when I see you are all safe." We move to the lounge and sit on the sofas positioned to take advantage of the skyline view.

Iain coughs and Dad looks up.

"We are not all safe, Dad. Jonathan..."

"Jonathan? He is here?" he asks. "Of course, I should have realised; you'd not come alone."

"Subtopia, Cartropolis. Near the factory. We had to leave him," I say.

I quickly explain everything from the moment we set off to the sadness of leaving the injured Jonathan behind at the shuttle station. The colour drains from Dad's face when I tell him of Jonathan's injury.

"Is he somewhere safe?" Dad says.

"We don't know. We hope he found his way back to Huptoou."

"Well, we will be going back there of course. That's where the machine is that is going to return us all home once it has a few adaptations."

"Why did you tell us to come here?"

"First, I was hoping to learn a bit more from Iain; I knew I'd need his help if I was going to track down the guys, Jan and Sheldon. I didn't even know what they looked like. Huptoou had told me they were going into the Metro. I now know you didn't make it." He paused. "Secondly, this is the safest place to be. Despite the surveillance, you don't have the same unexpected danger. It is hard for anyone to reach you here without you being warned. You can hide here with the help of money and electronics. Of course, the Establishment can find you anywhere."

"What would they do with us?" I ask.

"They would take you to detention centres in the Outlands to torture you for information," Iain says.

"And when we leave here, Dad?"

"They are already trying to track us; once Keshet realised you were not local, he knew that I was from outside as well. He raised the alarm before you caught on to him."

"Sorry, Dad."

"When we leave here, they will be waiting for us. Beane Mob, the Establishment Authorities and unfortunately, maybe Jack Wills' people. He has a lot of influence here now. He spends his time between his laboratory in Serfin and a house in Subtopia where he has built another quantum vacuum. I talked with him."

"He must have been surprised," I say.

"Kind of. He tried to have me captured. They don't want us to leave and he doesn't want us to use the machine, but he wants other information from me. I have a plan."

# CHAPTER EIGHT

## Warrior's Rite of Passage

Iain brings the machine as promised; it's a secure router that allows us to switch to BankNet while inside our new apartments.

"Donald, they got your virtual identities," he pants when he arrives. "They found them and stormed a building downtown before they realised they were virtual."

"How did you find out?" Dad asks.

"I monitor your electronic shadows. I saw all the activity online and hooked into the store's cameras. It was a real heavy operation they launched to get you."

"At least that shows they work; lucky you guys were offline," Dad says.

"Can you explain to me what it is again?" I ask.

"Sure, it's simple. When you go off the iTrust network and onto BankNet, we cannot just allow your activity to cease on iTrust, so we use programs that register as you. They go shopping and generally keep busy. Virtual Robyn, Sheldon and Jans that don't leave an obvious hole when you are not there," Iain says. "They found you and physically turned up to catch you."

"Got it this time," I say.

We lie low for a few weeks, jumping every time sky patrols pass the apartment. Sheldon and I use the gym and sauna.

Jan spends the time complaining that the TV is full of subliminal adverts that are designed to control you. He decides that this world is about instant gratification. There is no history and people are discouraged from thinking into the future; everything is about the now, Jan says. He talks about bread and circuses and I make a mental note to ask him what he means.

Iain gives Jan an interactive hologram PC. He wears a helmet and facemask, and seems to talk with the machine and point into the air. There is no keyboard. From the little I understand, Jan can delve into the net database and learn a lot about this world. Some of the stuff has legal access; other stuff he is in a sort of underground net with access to places that few people could roam. Iain is spending a lot of time teaching him how to move around safely.

"Where do you go to, Jan?" I ask him one evening when he comes off the machine looking tired.

"It's a bit hard to explain."

"Try me," I say.

"Okay. Back home, people are beginning to collaborate across boundaries, across barriers. When people collaborate, they cannot be controlled. You cannot cage an idea."

"So?"


"This world is about preventing collaboration, establishing control and boundaries, and maintaining an imbalance of power."

"And they do this through the iTrust and managing information?"

"Back home we have a vision of robots or computers taking over mankind. It's nonsense. We are inside a giant computing machine. We are human components, connected by wifi, wearable technology and surveillance. We make data, pass data, use data, but just like components inside a giant PC, we all have to operate within certain tolerances for the machine to function."

"You are losing me," I smile.

"This society is what we will become if we continue to lose our humanity."

"Are you being a luddite?" I joke.

"No, I am deadly serious. Mankind is being subsumed inside a giant computer cage."

"Surely it doesn't matter. We are going home soon."

"No, in a sense it doesn't matter; this is a parallel world, a part of the multi-verse, something we don't understand. But I think it is also a glimpse into a potential future."

"Like what? Why wouldn't they want equality here?"

"Prosperity equals longevity. They already live three times longer in Bilden, through stem cell technology."

"Really?"

"Equality is better for the community, not for the oligarchy."

"That's always been true, right? It's luck and hard work that make some people rich."

"Perhaps. But here, everything is manufactured. The state decides on your university education place, your job success, the lottery wins, your medical appointments, your tax audit, and your loan application. I could go on. There is no fate or luck in this world."

"How do you know all this?"

"I meet with a number of Iain's friends online. There is an underground. A resistance of sorts, mostly old professors and academics who do more talking than anything else. They call themselves the Angry Academics."

"And the young people?"

"There are two types. One type is integrated into the establishment in Artisan and is fooled by the system into believing they have choice and potential for progression. The second type of youngster are disenfranchised, disorganised and divided."

"And bread and circuses?" I ask.

"That's a whole other story." he says, smiling. "It's a bit like Iain said. If you only know the intense smell of a rose, you cannot imagine the sweet-salty smell of freedom in seaweed."

With that he kisses me on my cheek, adjusts my scarf and goes off to his room.


Over the weeks, I try to draw Jan out again. He seems to be studying and working at an intense rate. I mention it to Iain.

"Jan is a smart guy. He is doing what comes natural and is the most interesting for him," Iain says.

"Which is?"

"Extrapolating vast amounts of data and knowledge. He is a modern day philosopher." Iain laughs. "Leave him alone, he will be teaching me new stuff soon."

Jan comes into the lounge just in time to hear the end of the conversation. "I am beginning to understand what when and where we have surfed to. The machine has skipped us across a number of grooves in the multiverse and pushed us out a few extra decades."

"So this is our world in the future?"

"Not necessarily, but it could be. Now it is. But back in our own world, it neither is or isn't."

"Lost me again."

"It doesn't really matter, what is important that I am able to study the data and look back in history and see the decision points that might or might not get us here."

"It's important work," Iain encourages.

So Jan has no interest in coming with us to Mo's or lazing on the rooftop, it seems.

"Isn't it wonderful to be so rich and lazy?" Sheldon jokes one day while we are relaxing at the roof pool. "What will I buy today?" We haven't been out at the shops since the first time. I think he is kidding.

I laugh. "Let's buy the most expensive clothes and jewellery, eat at the most expensive restaurant and go to an exclusive club."

"A club? We are probably too young," he says. He lifts up his sunglasses to look at me, maybe to see if I'm serious.

"We will buy our way in. Money talks," I say, affecting a ridiculous pompous voice. "We will tip everyone who gets in our way."

We laugh together.

"Seriously, we should do something out. We will never be here again with all this money. Maybe there is a casino or some sort of show. But the thing I'd like best would be going out to see what the music is like," Sheldon says.

"I love to dance," I tell him.

"I love any kind of music, but I am an embarrassment on the dance floor; two left feet," he explains.

While we relax and chill, Iain programs us new identities, but explains that although they are better than the ones we had, they still only provide limited cover, because the first place they will search is new people. "Always be on your guard," he tells us. And I think about keeping our weapons close. Perhaps we are all a little too blasé about the dangers.

Dad stayed with us in our apartment, and I feel he is happier and more confident now. Although he initially wasn't happy that I'd come through the machine, he seems to trust me more, as if he thinks I've grown up a little. He agreed he shouldn't have lied to me in the first place and we promised each other we'd never do it again. He told me the whole story. He first met Huptoou a few years after the first incident with him and had begged Huptoou to bring him some proof that the boys were caught in Subtopia. Huptoou thought he was doing Dad a favour bringing him the only thing he could find, shoes of the boy who had died. Dad was stopped going home, with the shoes in a bag, by a local patrol. The dried blood on the shoes led to Dad being re-accused at sixteen and although there were no bodies, he ended up in the high security wing of a mental institution. He was there until he was twenty-two.

"So had you looked further in the library you might have found the rest of my story, but you put the pieces together pretty good as it was," Dad says.

"Dad, I am so sorry," I tell him. "They locked you up for killing your best friends when you were only ten, then again when you were sixteen; you were completely innocent and sane. I feel sick."

"It is okay. The institution was where I studied physics and where I met your mother while she was studying psychiatric nursing. She was the only one who ever believed me."

"Wow." I'm thinking of the brilliant confidence my mother had in her own instinct.

"The only thing was she'd never agree to me going back to the school," Dad says. "The community had done a good job of burying the whole story."

"But you wanted to clear your name somehow?"

"That's it. And maybe just be sure that I had been somewhere. It's easy to doubt your own sanity with something like this."

I rub his arm.

"But your Mum was right as always. Look at the mess. We have you and three other boys in here now. I am sorry I have been so selfish."

"It will be fine, Dad," I say. "Won't it? We will get out of here?"

"I am not going to lie to you. It is not going to be easy. But we are going to get home. I promised that to your Mum."

"You talk to her?" I smile.

"Of course, what do you think?"

"Me too," I tell him. "All the time. I feel she is watching out for both of us."

"Probably cursing me for being a bozo," he says miserably and hugs me as I roar with laughter.

☐☐☐☐☐☐☐☐

The following week, I catch my Dad and Iain together; they are reviewing the communication traffic around the city. It is illegal, like monitoring police frequencies, but they wanted to set up an automatic program that scanned for anything that might indicate the authorities were closing in. They both look at me.

"I have been thinking if there is any way to get a message to Jonathan," I say.

Jan and Sheldon come in from the other flat and stand beside us.

"You might. Anything is possible from here. You might send a personal courier for example. But they would have to find the Euny. And even if they did find them, we don't know for sure that Jonathan is there," Iain says. "Him getting a message back to us is pretty impossible. You saw how they sanitise everything coming in."

"The courier could bring back a verbal reply," I suggest.

"Sure he could. We'd need to make sure he wasn't tracked and followed coming back to us. All it would take is for someone to intercept him and he'd lead right back to you," Iain explains.

"We will go soon enough. I promise," Dad says. "I know it's hard, but try to relax."

"How much longer before you know if it's safe?" I ask.

"We need to watch the system for a little while longer. They are watching, waiting for us to move as well. In both cases, we are seeking each other's 'activity trails'. Think on it as changes in the regular data that throws up some discrepancies," Iain explains. "Like a boat's wake through the sea."

"So if we stay still they won't look for us?" I say.

"No, all the time they are searching the data anyway. For sure, they are looking for us. We just make it easier by running and thereby attracting attention to ourselves."

"I see."

"The longer we hide, the greater the chance that they will think they lost us."

"Meantime we are watching the watchers," Jan adds.

"You got it in one, my friend," Iain tells him. "We have so many subversive programs watching the data, a flea's fart out of place will not get past us."

"Sheldon and I were thinking about the chance of going for some regular shooting and fencing practice. I guess that's not an option?" I say expecting a negative answer.

Iain and Dad look at each other. "Sure. It should be safe enough. Mo's of course. It's not de rigueur down the local gym." Iain roars at his own joke.

"Uh, then there would be no harm in us going out for a night sometime. Dinner, a club?" I ask.

"It's not the best idea at the..."

Iain cuts dad off. "It's not the worst idea. We are just as much of a target sitting here inside these apartments," he says. "As long as we are all not together at the same time and everyone stays alert."

Dad shrugs. "Fine, as long as you are careful. But best I come too." He is smiling.

"Forget-about-it, Bozo," I say.

〇〇〇〇〇〇〇〇

Mo, the armourer, is considerably friendlier than last time; he almost seems pleased to see me. When I ask if it is possible to practise in the fencing trainer, he says 'For you Darlin' anything is possible.' He mostly ignores Sheldon, which I find funny. Three times Sheldon has to ask to be set up on the firing range.

"Oh, okay. Let's see if I can get someone to teach you properly," Mo finally tells Sheldon. He goes and talks briefly to a couple of men who are sitting eating behind the counter. One looks over and shakes his head; the other gets up and comes back with Mo. He looks like he'd seen a few battles. His face is scarred and he walks with a slight limp. I notice that his eyes are friendly and smiling, despite his battered face.

"Gristle has agreed to teach you what you need to know. He is the best. The price is six Citzs for an hour. You probably need two hours. How about ten Citizens for two hours?" Mo says.

Sheldon nods and shakes hands with Gristle. I decide to watch for a few moments before I jump into the ring with Marlene.

"Let's cover a few things that will help you protect yourself in any situation. First, there are the physical aspects: your strength and your reactions. Then there is your state of mind: your attitude and your confidence. Finally, there are knowledge and techniques."

Sheldon nods and I can see he is interested now.

"You need all of these three things to be competent to look after yourself in a hostile situation," Gristle says. "So let's demonstrate this a little."

He takes Sheldon over to a table and I follow to watch. They both sit down facing each other and Gristle hands Sheldon a large knife, while he holds a short rubber pipe instead of a knife.

"You're right handed, so left hand palm down on the table. Hold the point of your knife, right hand, in the table about six inches apart. I'm gonna do the same," Gristle says.

"Okay." Sheldon licks his lips.

I notice there are a few scars on the backs of both of Gristle's hands.

"Now, the object is to stab each other's left hand. But neither of us can move our left hand until the point of the other's knife leaves the table. Okay?"

"You want me to try to stick this knife in your hand?"

"Don't worry. Just do your best. I'm gonna stick your hand with this piece of rubber way more times."

"Got it," Sheldon says.

"Okay, anytime you are ready." Gristle smiles.

I watch; Sheldon moves fast. His knifepoint comes down in the centre of where Gristle's hand had been a split second ago, but to the right of where Gristle's pinky is now.

"Again!" Gristle calls and Sheldon tries again to stab the hand. It seems the man has extraordinary reflexes.

Sheldon moves a third time without warning and Gristle moves his hand and stabs Sheldon's hand hard with the rubber tube. Sheldon yelps, so it wasn't as pain free as I imagined.

They play for five minutes, Sheldon fighting hard to avoid the man's lightning reflexes.

"Okay. Stop," Gristle says. "This illustrates the things that I told you. Physically, I am much more practised. Mentally, you are worrying about getting stabbed by the rubber. Once you were hit the first time, you became wary. Finally, there are some techniques. Initially, I am looking at your eyes and your face muscles to see your move, not the knife. Then I watch the eyes and knife to see if you are going to feint, one way or another."

"It's really interesting," Sheldon says.

"Every weapon is like that. Preparation is key," Gristle says. "So let's have some fun on the range and, if we have time, some proper hand to hand."

I leave them to it and go in to meet Marlene. Gristle's philosophy applies equally well to fencing. The art of fencing is really an intricate study of techniques, mental attitude and physical condition.

We spend much of the afternoon exercising and practising. Mo joins in and helps Gristle teach us some hand-to-hand combat and martial arts. Despite his potbelly, Mo can move as fast as a snake. He laughs when he surprises me a few times.

"Never underestimate your opponent, Kiddo," he says, laughing. "My girth is camouflage, not a handicap."

It feels great. Sheldon agrees with me that we would do this every day until we are headed back to Subtopia.

We practise daily for six weeks. I feel the change in my body and improvement in my skills. Fencing had made me fast. Hand-to-hand combat has hardened me up. I am still a little underweight but I manage to hurt Mo and Gristle in a few of our bouts.

Mo and Gristle seem to enjoy teaching us, everything from knots, traps, camouflage, survival, tracking and trapping.

Sheldon isn't a natural warrior according to Mo, but he is brave, competent, steady and reliable, a good man to have at your back. "Bravery and confidence are the father and mother of winning," Mo tells Sheldon. "Focus always on the idea that you cannot lose, if you really want to win." Sheldon is a decent shot with a rifle and pistol, much better than me. He is calm. I tend to shake a little. Sheldon tries fencing but although he learns technique, he never seems to move instinctively or fast enough to beat me. Hardly a day passes when I don't think about Jonathan, but more especially when I am fencing and comparing him to Sheldon.

Mo promises to take Sheldon and me on a trip with another man, to learn extreme climbing, caving and outdoors survival. I said we would ask Iain and Dad, but I really want to do this.

In the meantime, we have planned a night out, after weeks of dreaming about it. But like the weapons training, we couldn't convince Jan to come with us. He really prefers to stay at home with his computer.

"Hey, let's have fun tonight," I tell Sheldon.

"Okay."

"I mean, when we go out, let's try to enjoy everything without worrying about this messed up world."

"Sure." Sheldon is frowning lightly. He didn't get what I meant.

We say thanks and goodbye to Mo and Gristle as we do every day. Mo laughs when I tell him we are going out, but says to be careful, he didn't want to have to come and rescue me from the Beanes.

We head off home and I realise that the threat is never far away and I am relaxing too much. It took a real warrior like Mo to see the need to remind me.

There is no one home when we return, so we shower and change, put our iTrusts back on and get ready to go to the vegetarian restaurant Iain had recommended. Iain explained that while we had to keep the iTrusts on, we were to limit the use of names in our conversations. And he would be tracking us just in case the system started to home in on us.

"Don't worry too much. Just be cautious, keep your wits about you."

Iain changes the subject and promises us the vegetables would mostly be real and healthily flavoured. I am looking forward to it after the exercise, plus I've hardly been eating anything after the stories of the meat source; my weight has gone down a few pounds despite some very hard muscle tone all over.

Sheldon wears a striking checked jacket with a blue grandfather shirt. His locket glints every now and then just at the opening of the collar. He wears unusually high-waisted trousers; it seems to be a style here.

I wear a dark purple jump suit with bare shoulders and triple ruff collar. I choose a broad leather belt, bright with silver studs. The combination pulls my waist in and pushes my breasts out. I deliberately put on my marble beads bracelet and my wire and marble earrings. A silver-cage cap completes my ensemble that I had bought the first time we had shopped, because the assistant said it looked great on me. I never really expected to wear it. It moulds to the contours of the top of my skull and flows into a fine mass of intricate silver tassels at the back of my neck that swing as I move. Some crazy eye shadow completes a slight Nefertiti-dreads look. I wish Mum could have seen it.

Sheldon stares at the new me, out of the corner of his eye, all the way to the restaurant in the back of the hover car. It reminds me of the night I watched him with the twins. I am the one who is shy and clumsy. I have this strong feeling of confidence and think that I know what he is thinking. We travel in silence the whole way.

Socrates, the club restaurant, is overwhelming. Tables float around the walls in a dark cavern. Invisible platforms take diners to and from their tables, like magic. The candle-lit cave resonates with a low sonorous music, which melds visuals, ventilation and smells into a perfect atmosphere. When I look down at my feet it seems we are suspended above a water garden with large fish swimming around a lily pond decorated with lights and fountains. In the centre of the room, a lady floats in the air with a sphere-shaped harp-like instrument. She plays lead, to the bass that seems to come from the belly of the cave.

A flying waitress arrives at the table. I can't help myself staring at her. Her face is proportionally exquisite, like I'd never seen before. What makes someone or something so strikingly beautiful that you catch your breath? It couldn't be simple symmetry or exotica. Her eyes lock on mine for a few seconds and I feel I have been busted for staring when I should have been looking at the menu.

"What's your name?" I ask on impulse.

"Harriet." She cocks her head and smiles quizzically.

"This is Sheldon, I'm Robyn," I tell her as quietly as I can. Sheldon flashes me a warning with his eyes.

"Nice to meet you both," Harriet says. "We are not used to the guests that eat here being quite so friendly." She smiles.

Harriet kindly makes some recommendations, so we just order a selection of the specials and the recommended sparkling wine.

Sipping my wine, I stare at the black ceiling above. It is difficult to tell how far away it is; it's like looking into a constantly changing nebulous galaxy of unusual colours and light. Other diners, older than us, are looking around too. All are dressed and bejewelled with hues and refraction that match these faraway worlds on the ceiling.

"Amazing," I whisper. "Iain never mentioned this. He knew I'd be surprised. He did this deliberately."

"Right. Never seen anything like this either," Sheldon says. "The place is stunning and you look so beautiful. You fit in with all these beautiful people, I feel like a klutz."

"Sheldon," I mouth his name, barely saying it, "I have never seen you as a person who could look awkward or out of place anywhere."

"Thanks. You are being kind."

"No, don't be silly. I admit it took me a couple of days to see what kind of person you were. Sheldon, you are different from the rest and that's what I like about you." I sip my drink.

"I started to think that our friendship might have developed after dinner at my folks. You handled everything so elegantly, made the twins and my Mum and Dad fall in love with you. You were so 'together', I was jealous," he says.

"No way; you are crazy. I watched you at the dinner. You are the one that was so 'together'," I laugh. "When I stayed in your room I realised that you were much more than just 'together'. You have interests and knowledge that make you the person you are."

"What would have happened if things hadn't led us here?" he asks.

I reach over and take his hand. "We are never going to know that. But I do know that I didn't come here for my Dad only. I came looking for you too."

"You couldn't miss me, you hardly knew me."

"No. That's true. And remember it's not so long ago I lost my Mum. I didn't really have a whole lot of room for missing anyone," I say. "It wasn't a case of missing you, but more a case of wondering what I had missed. I don't connect with people easily."

"Me neither. Why do you think I am a Goth at School?"

"I'm not sure."

"It's not because I want attention, it's the opposite. I seek obscurity; to be left alone and think the thoughts that I want. People mistake my dress and expression as some kind of painful depression; it's not."

"Where did I come in?" I ask.

"I invited you past my guard. You are the first person to see beyond my black walls," he says. His face is unsmiling, but kindly.

We eat silently for a few minutes. The food is delicious and I try to focus on the flavours for a minute. But I realise that I have no idea what he is thinking. I am thinking about the future.

"You need to know something," Sheldon says. "I will wait to see where all this takes us. Our priority is to find Jonathan and all get home safely. I know you care for him, that doesn't matter to me. I just wish for all of us to be safe and life to be back to normal. After that, I am going to chase you, pursue you, I will make you mine, my Reine d'Epées. You are everything I ever wanted."

I am a little bit stunned. I want to hug him, kiss him, but that isn't possible right now. My feelings and emotions are all over the place.

"Let's agree not to worry about anything tonight. Let's have fun. It might be the last chance we have before we start our journey back," I say.

He nods and smiles and I grin back. "And you look pretty stunning yourself tonight, Mr. Dunn, especially when you smile," I say.

"I don't take compliments very easily," he says. "I find it difficult."

"Learn. Get used to it," I say, pointing my finger at him.

The time passes quickly as we chat, and open up our dreams and wishes to each other. I admit to him that 'freediving' in the ocean was something I wanted to try. It fascinates me that people could hold their breath for minutes and go deeper than a diver on air. I tell him I will show him pictures of the 'Blue hole' when we go home. I don't want to mention it is in the Bahamas.

He tells me that he wants to play some of his music compositions on stage one day. And we both look at each other realising that we've learned a little more about each other and ourselves.

Our stunning waitress comes by twice to check everything is okay and swap our plates for a hologram menu that floats above our table.

We take our time and argue over the sweet. It seems we like the opposite; Sheldon a fan of traditional heavy chocolate cake, while I am more interested in pastries filled with cream and flavoured liquor.

After the sweet we decide to pass on the coffee that was offered.

"What is the club like, Harriet?" I ask. "What kind of people and music?"

"It's amazing. I go down occasionally when I get off work. But a little too expensive for a student on a waitress salary," she says. "A lot of the people in here will go down. And the music is BeatSex mostly. Although there are different rooms."

"Thank you."

"I love your earrings. They are amazing," she says. "Are they real?"

"Thanks. Yes. Student? What are you studying?" I ask.

"City Lighting and Architecture." She smiles. "It was what my dad did. He designed some of the buildings around here, but not this one."

She takes our plates and leaves.

"I like her," I tell Sheldon.

"I noticed."

"What do you mean by that?" I ask.

"Nothing." He holds up his hands in surrender.

"There are perfectly normal people here," I say. "This world..."

"Careful," Sheldon warns. For a second I'd forgotten we were under constant surveillance. "Let's go dance," he says.

We reach the BNW Club by an elevator that seems to drop forever. I cling on to Sheldon and he snatches the opportunity to plant kisses behind my ear, between the jewellery, sending a nice shiver up my spine.

"Naughty," I admonish. But I don't move away.

When the lift opens, the music and atmosphere overpower my senses and lift my spirit immediately. The club is packed; the vibe is electric.

"Wow." I take Sheldon's hand and push through the crowd to get onto the nearest dance floor. Any tiredness from the fencing leaves me as Sheldon and I get into the music. It's fantastic just to dance and not care about anything. I notice a few men and woman watching me, maybe my dancing is a little bit house or hip-hop, but I don't care, if this is BeatSex it is making me happy.

Around us, couples dance with super high energy, their movements fluid and toned. I notice males dancing together and it surprises me from what I know about this seemingly closed society. I catch one guy sharing something to his friend's hand and a few minutes later, they had both surreptitiously put something in their mouth. Weird holograms dance beside us on the floor, and every now and then would interact with us, copying moves, smiling and dancing to a similar rhythm.

I reckoned the music was loud enough at one point; I pulled Sheldon's head towards me and put my lips to his ear.

"Here's to the revolution," I said. Sheldon threw his head back and roared with laughter. iTrust stayed silent.

"I think people are on something here," I said in his ear.

"Really? I hadn't noticed. But then I'd hardly know what to look for," he said sounding innocent.

"Just watch people long enough and you will see that they are trying to escape reality," I said. "Their faces and dancing change after they take something."

Once we have enough dancing and fooling iTrust, we decide to go get a drink and find a seat; we take the time to look around the place. It's mostly couples, relaxed, happy, excited, drinking little it seems but looking completely chilled. I find myself wondering if this is representative of all the nightlife. Maybe it is because it is upmarket. Are there clubs here where people get stupidly drunk and aggressive? I doubt it. This society has a surface structure and a deep structure, I decide. The surface structure is controlled and reserved. The deep structure is hidden, wild and dangerous. True human nature cannot be caged by systems.

We wander. BNW Club has a few floors and rooms where you could hear a variety of music styles. In some rooms, stunning men and women dance in cages and platforms. In other places, the music is quiet and sweeps over the room in time with vast tidal waves of light.

We discover a couple of quiet corner seats in a room where couples, male and female, are doing a weird sort of head dance. They start with foreheads and noses together and dance in a coordinated flowing motion, sometimes tracing each other's body contours with soft fingertips. I find it strangely erotic and appealing.

"That's too weird for me," Sheldon says.

I want to try, but I don't want to push him; he's done really well already. He's been so kind to push his dancing limits and take me here; I can't punish him by telling him how much I'd like to get up there and dance now.

We continue to watch the people while we relax back in our seat and sip our drinks.

"Hi." Harriet appears beside us. "I didn't expect you to come in here."

"Why not?" I ask her, smiling.

She comes close to my ear and whispers. "Let's just say that it's a particular style of euphoric music and dance that's usually enjoyed with a certain plant extract."

"I see. It looks great."

She pulls me to the floor and I don't resist. I look at Sheldon and smile. "Be back soon."

Harriet leads me into the crowd then turns to face me. She touches my cheek and draws my face to hers and our foreheads and noses touch lightly together as if it is the most natural thing in the world.

"Close your eyes and move with me." Her fingertips trace my neck and bare shoulders and transmit the rhythm of her movement to me at the same time. Her lips touch mine and I am surprised when she presses her tongue lightly between my lips and delivers a small piece of a chewy leaf into my mouth.

She draws back and looks at me to make sure I chew and swallow the juices.

I am lost in an instant; the dance is so fluid and light and I feel I can see her every movement with my eyes closed. My hands move naturally towards hers and we trace each other's fingers in a sort of intimate high five as we move sensually together. When I open my eyes, she is looking straight at me.

"What?" I say.

She smiles and kisses me briefly on the lips. She comes closer and moves with me in a way that is casual, unthreatening, yet charged with erotic confidence. I forget about Sheldon and everyone else around us on the dance floor until she breaks apart.

"You will see that most of the people in here didn't come from the restaurant," she says as she leads me off the floor. "It's mostly exotics who come in here. Young people who enjoy exotic-trance."

'Thank you. I really enjoyed the dance," I say.

"Sure. No problem. I did too. I just thought we'd better get back to your boyfriend before he missed you." She smiles.

"He's not my boyfriend." I feel I want her to know.

Sheldon stands up when we come back to our seats. It is old school polite and the first time I have seen him do something like that.

"You guys are not from around here, right?" Harriet says.

"Not really," I agree.

"I thought not. You don't seem clued up enough. No offence. It's refreshing." Harriet smiles.

She sits with us for another thirty minutes engaging in animated talk. The time passes super-fast and I can see she genuinely doesn't want to leave us. I learn quite a lot about her. Her family are in

Subtopia. She works three jobs in order to study and transfer money home. The metro isn't all easy life, I think. Harriet seems resilient and irrepressible, however.

"I really have to go and catch-up with my friends across town. You can come if you want," she says.

Sheldon thinks we should stay where we promised Dad we would be. Reluctantly I agree with his sensible precaution.

"Next time." I hold her hand.

"Let me give you my Comms." Harriet presses a button on her cuff and types something in. When she holds her wrist close to mine, my cuff vibrates twice.

"I have your number now?" I ask.

"You guys really don't know anything, do you?" She giggles. "Call me."

I can hear my Dad's voice, 'impulsive and a little reckless' as I surreptitiously take two marbles from my zipped pocket, palm then and hold her hands.

"Don't show anyone," I say, pressing both marbles into her fingers.

She automatically goes to open her hand.

"No." I squeeze her hand closed. I see in her eyes that she knows what it is.

"What are you doing? I cannot..."

I silence her with a kiss on the lips. I whisper in her ear. "Trust me. Take them. One day I will explain."

I see confusion and a small tear in her eyes.

"You are so lovely," she tells me as she kisses my cheek, waves cheekily to Sheldon and bounces off in search of her friends. I see her wipe her eyes before she vanishes in the crowd.

Sheldon and I move to another room and sit in a booth overlooking a different dance floor, and just watch for a while. He puts his arm around me and I rest my head on his shoulder.

"You are amazing. I feel humbled," he says.

It has been a magical night. But as soon as it is time to leave, my thoughts start to turn to Jonathan and home again.

'Make it soon please,' I pray as we wait for the car to pick us up and return us to the apartments.

□□□□□□□

Something doesn't look right as we fly past the apartments. Lights are off in one and Jan is sitting on the floor up against the window in the other. My instinct tells me to proceed with caution.

"Don't take us to the garage, take us to the roof," I tell the car.

"What's wrong?" Sheldon says.

"Don't know. Let's just be very quiet going in," I say.

The car has banked around and started its approach to the roof-landing platform.

"There is someone down there. He is not one of us," Sheldon says. He points. I see the silhouette close to the pool. The guy is huge. Factory big. My guts swoop.

"Take us to the other roof. Building B. Without lights," I order.

We swoop into the dark and land quietly on the platform of the opposite building. I instruct the car to wait, and not return to the garage. Sheldon and I move across to the lift.

"Stairs better," he says. I open my handbag and take out Yuenu and ready my thumb over the button.

Sheldon looks, probably surprised that I had carried it to the club. He'd not have gotten away with taking a gun with him; now I wish we'd hidden one somewhere in the car or on the roof.

"Let me go first," I say. I bring up the light shield with a quick tap on the watchband. I can see the faint rectangular glow head to toe, but I have no idea what weapons it would stop. I curse myself for not being properly prepared as I kick off my shoes and go onto the balls of my feet.

Building B, where Jan is staying, seems empty. It is black and nothing stirs. It must have been empty for a few hours. We cross to the other apartment via the unlit corridor. The front door of our apartment is jammed open and Sheldon and I pad into a position where we can see into part of the lounge.

My heart stops. Dad and Iain sit on the floor. It looks as though their hands are bound behind them. Iain has a bloody nose and mouth. A large Factory man is slowly pacing in front of them, holding the large electronic cattle prod that I had seen being used on the people the first night I arrived. Another man sits on the sofa, his hands steepled in front of his mouth, elbows resting on his huge fat knees. He is the only one speaking.

"The boy is unconscious. That's unfortunate. So, back to your story. You say that you don't know where our money is? You didn't take it? And you don't have anything to give us for our trouble."

My mind races.

"You know, if I believed you, we'd simply kill you now and be on our way." He is shaking his head. "But sorry to say, I am not naturally known as a trusting man. My father's teaching, I expect. So, this is not going to be easy, especially for one of you." As the man finishes speaking he nods just once.

I almost cry out as the standing man jabs the electronic prod at Dad who groans long and loud when the stick discharges into his body. Three times they do it, once on his face. I can see he is shaking, dribble running from his mouth, after they stopped.

"Try to get up to your room and get your gun," I whisper to Sheldon.

"Firearms prohibited. Please confirm compliance," machine voice says and I can tell Sheldon hears it too before he pads off to try to get upstairs. I curse again. "Switch to Bank Net," I whisper and I hope Sheldon will do the same.

"What's it to be?" the fat man is saying. "Are you going to tell me what happened to our money?"

I step forward into the room. "Stop. I have your money," I say.

Iain moves his head slightly, in warning, and I catch a brief reflection on the window of someone behind me.

"Ah, who are you? Perhaps the daughter that visited poor Mr. Keshet?" Fat man says. "He said you'd make a good breeder." I know he is trying to distract me, hold my attention. My instinct says to wait, don't look round.

The reflection moves again and suddenly a man with a gun grabs me from behind. I press the button and swing the light-sabre across his gun hand. It takes off his forearm and while he screams and lets me go, the gun clatters to the floor and I swivel and sear off his left limb as well. He falls.

I turn and look; the guy with the cattle prod is almost upon me. The shield takes most of the blow, but I am bowled over by the force of the charge. When I jump up he is a little more cautious than his first attack, now he realises I have a shield and has seen what I can do with the light sword. He circles menacingly, but he has no technique. And while he is physically strong and heavy, he isn't fast. I'm furious, my aggressive onslaught must have scared him, but now I need to be calm and concentrate. He desperately tries to use brute force to hit me with the cattle charge again, but he is wary of my reach under his slightly shorter prod.

He makes a single mistake; he turns his front foot as he lunges at me. He then over extends his second lunge. I move out of his way; he doesn't have time to recover while he regains his balance. I take his left arm off, swipe the tip off the prod and tear open his left knee, taking the patella clean off. He collapses. It is his last mistake.

When I turn, Fat man is off the sofa, holding my Father with a gun pointed at the side of his head.

I retract my sword and switch off the shield.

He stares at me; I imagine he is deciding what to say and wondering where his man on the roof is. I am too.

"You need to drop the light sword and come over here," he says. I drop the sword on the sofa and move to the centre of the room.

He lets go of Dad, sticks his gun in his pocket and bellows as he swipes me with his fist. It's a glancing blow, but enough to knock me down and make my ears ring.

"I am not going to shoot you," he promises. "I am going to give you a good hiding while your Dad watches. Maybe someone will start to remember where the money is."

He towers over me as I lie on the floor, a leg each side of my body. I thrust my hand between his feet and power the shield. He staggers back with a combination of surprise and pain as the shield expands into his groin. I jump up over the sofa, while he struggles to get his gun out. He manages to fire two shots that glance off my shield, when I jump up brandishing my sword again. I leap towards him, he jumps back towards the first body and I land at his feet, slipping on the bloody floor. He points his gun down at my face just as my sword takes both his feet off. He shoots a hole through the sofa as he falls forward. I have to twist and roll in the blood to avoid him crushing me with his bulk. He lands on the lower half of my body and tries to turn to shoot again at close quarters, but I cleave his neck with the blade.

I am close to passing out; bright lights swim before my eyes. The guard from the roof appears in the doorway pointing his gun. I see him kneel down at the other side of the big guy to check him and I almost smile. I want to say he is dead, but I can't speak. His face looms into mine, and for a second our eyes lock as he puts his hand on my throat and squeezes. The last thing I remember is his head exploding and warm blood swamping my face.

□□□□□□□

"She is awake," Sheldon calls, but I can't actually focus. When I finally do, Iain and Dad have come into the room looking concerned and happy at the same time. I watch their faces. I feel like I have just come out of anaesthetic; everything is too bright, confused and unsteady. Dad's mouth is opening and closing.

"You look like a fish," I tell him.

He smiles.

"Sheldon, you look rather sexy today," I hear myself saying without shame.

"Thanks."

"You are still under the effects of the painkillers," Dad says.

"What?" I yell. It's unnaturally loud even to me. "You don't think he is sexy?"

"Do you have any pain?" Iain says.

"Iain. Iain. Iain. Do you know something?" I say.

"What?"

"You are alright for an old guy. And I feel great! Wheeeee!"

I can hear them laughing.

"Whasfunny?" I look from one to the other. "Did you call me Cous Cous, Dad? Is that why you are all laughing?"

After a few minutes of helpless laughter, I start to recover. I take some deep breaths. I have some pain in my hip. I feel a bit sick.

"You okay?" Iain asks as the memories come flooding back to me.

"Dad, your face is cut," I say. "You will have a scar."

I touch it softly with my fingers and he flinches.

"What happened? Where are we?" I say.

"We are safe for the moment. They found us online and set a trap for us. Your Dad and I thought we were meeting a couple of mercenaries who we could pay to help us. It was lucky you and Sheldon had gone out all day and came back when you did; you saved us. What do you remember?" he asks.

"Pretty much everything now, until the last guy was strangling me and his head blew up."

"Thank Sheldon for that and his shooting practice. He shot from the balcony," Iain says.

"I have never been so scared in my life," Sheldon admits. "But there wasn't a choice."

"When the big guy fell on you, he banged your head and cracked your pelvis. It's not severe. But you might find climbing stairs and twisting a bit painful for a while," Dad says. "Plus you have been concussed."

"It might take him longer to climb stairs," I say.

"We had to run from the place. The authorities were listening in all the time and we only managed to avoid their arrival. They are searching everywhere for us at the moment."

"How long was I out for?" I say. "And where is Jan?" I suddenly remember.

"Three days. Jan is okay," Dad says. "But he was shot in the stomach and he is being taken care of by friends of Iain."

"Is he going to be okay?"

"I promise," Dad says.

"Where are we now?" I don't recognise the place. It is a concrete place lit by harsh light.

"This is my bunker. It's a last resort. We couldn't risk my Dock home for the moment." Iain says. "I think they are on to me now."

"We have one bit of good news for you," Sheldon says. "We got a message about Jonathan. He is with Huptoou."

"He sent the message?" I ask.

"No. Our factory friends tonight told us; they are angry at them. Apparently, Jonathan and Huptoou are raiding the farms and processing units. They are probably higher up the Establishment wanted list than we are right now."

"You should continue to rest for a bit. I will give you more painkillers if you need it. See how it goes."

# CHAPTER NINE

## Hunted

We lie low for more weeks; Iain's bunker is well supplied. Jan returns from his nursing and we both start to recover. In some ways, physical recovery is easier than the mental; it's hard to describe how I feel after killing. The guy at Keshet's house didn't count; he'd died when Jonathan justifiably skewered his brain. I've killed two since. One bled to death from horrific injuries, the other I sliced through his head and upper vertebrae nearly taking his neck right off. I try to be angry with these men, so I can hate them, so I can slough off the feeling that I have done something wrong. It's actually difficult to maintain anger against a dead person, I learn.

The blood and gore made me sick. I had no idea the human body could be so disgusting and messy. The smell of blood and guts clung to my senses like a bad cold, heavy and choking in my sinuses. But the worst thing about killing was the screams, the shocked expression and realisation of the dying that they were mortally wounded. It was a look that was accusatory and seemed to say, 'You didn't have to do this. I wouldn't have done this to you. You will get what is coming to you, just wait.' There was a day's worth of negative emotion wrapped into the four minutes it took to bleed to death from the severing of a major artery.

Occasionally, I'll wake up from a bad dream; Mum used to say it was nature's way of tidying up. I doubt any amount of brain tidying is going to let me forget. The only positive point is Sheldon shot one guy in the head to save me. So we are technically murderers together, Bonnie and Clyde. What a sick thought; I think they killed for fun, I must remember to look it up. In the meantime, I wake often in a cold sweat, my heart thudding, after seeing the faces of my victims.

Jan and I get closer during this time. He isn't like either Sheldon or Jonathan. If Sheldon is a poet, Jonathan a rebel, then Jan is the magician. He is more in control of his life than anyone I know. I didn't understand it before. He was in control even when we were in a dangerous place and he'd been injured. I think long on this idea. The other thing that I've been slow to notice is that Jan's flirts never stir any sexual feelings in me. When he compliments me on my style, or looks, it is genuine.

While Jan and I exercise a little, Iain, Dad and Sheldon discuss how we are going to make a break out of the Metro Area. The first stop is to meet Mo in the velvet underground, a dangerous world that exists beneath the surface of Artisan Class.

We face a whole lot of problems; our identities have been blown and we are completely offline. Iain's programming and counterfeiting machines are back at the other place, which he is sure the authorities will be keeping under surveillance hoping that we'll show up. We are not sure to what extent the bank accounts are compromised. But we are not going to know that until we try. We have no way to exit Metro legitimately. The moment we crossed over, they'd be on to 'illegals'. Normally, they have authorisation to shoot people who cross over without authority, but they are intent on trying to capture us. They will be looking out for us at every Transport Station, crossing point or terminal and using the drones and sky patrols to scan for our faces.

Some of the problems are down to me; I ask Iain a lot of questions, trying to come up with ideas that might solve some of the obstacles to getting home. When they decide the time is right to see Mo, I insist that I will go too and nobody objects. I guess I earned my place when I chopped up a few bad guys. Or maybe they are scared of me now; I laugh to myself, and then gag when I recall the carnage. The metallic smell of warm blood haunts my nostrils each time I remember.

Jan stays behind; he isn't fit enough yet. The four of us take our weapons and go out to meet Mo. We descend into the basement and through a number of maintenance chambers and tunnels. Iain leads us through a couple of underground drainage channels and into what looks like a disused subway. It's the only way to avoid the monitors, he says, but we have to watch out for 'Robo-Patrols', automated units that shoot anything that moves down here, including tramps, rats and illegals. We are lucky, the only thing we meet are cockroaches, who seem surprised to see us.

"What the hell have you guys been doing?" Mo asks. "Half the country is out looking for you. Did you know there is a reward on your heads?" He sits at a table in some sort of makeshift bar deep in the underground, cracking nuts from a large fruit bowl that is full of what looks like real melons, grapes, peaches and oranges.

"Well as long as you're not collecting, Mo, I guess we are okay for the moment," Iain says.

"Hi Robyn, I hear you've been slicing and dicing," Mo says to me as I sit down. I smile; I honestly don't have an answer. He shakes hands with Dad, Iain and Sheldon and pushes a bowl of green grapes towards me. I say thanks and gingerly pop one in my mouth. They are real, amazing. Sheldon raises his eyebrows and I return the gesture, smile and push the bowl to him.

"I knew we'd find you here," Iain says.

"Well normally I am here once a week, but until the heat dies down, half the city's crims are down here. The bar has never been so busy. Can I get you a drink?" He calls a man over and orders beers for everyone including me.

"We were just about to get out, when we got busted," Iain says. "The Beanes turned up first to get their money. They must have been tipped off in advance. It probably saved us. We got out before the authorities swarmed the place."

"It sure looks that way," Mo says.

"We need another way out," Iain explains.

"How bad is it?" Mo asks.

"No IDs, Collars, no access to my place," Iain says.

"You still got money?"

"Sure."

"How much money do we need to get us out of here safely?" Dad asks.

"Money makes things possible, I didn't say it made things any less dangerous," Mo replies.

"You have something in mind?" Iain asks.

"If you cannot get reliable IDs, the way I see it, you have only two options. You have to bust your way out, or you have to cheat your way out."

"We're listening," Iain says.

"Well I reckon you could find a pilot willing to risk the crossing on a supply ship. The odds of getting across without being shot down, I'd say less than 10%. The same goes for busting out by road. They are so well organised, sky patrol and the army will be on you like a guided missile."

"That was my reading of the situation," Iain agrees. "What if we hired a load of mercenaries and shot our way out?"

"Risky, and you don't know how many of you guys will end up on the casualty list. Say 30-50%. Besides, how are you going to know whom to trust? These guns-for-hire guys will shoot each other to get your reward." Mo snorts and bangs his beer on the table.

"So that leaves sneaking out," Dad says. "What are the options?"

"Difficult to stow five of you away on a transport ship. But not impossible." Mo hesitates.

"Four people," Iain corrects. "But the same problem with trust, and all our eggs in the one basket so to speak."

"Is there any way to get on a Supreme Safari ship?" I ask.

"Only at point of origin. You'd have to board in BildenLand and travel out with the ship," Mo says. "They are always guarded by sky patrols, so it could be difficult to get away from them once you were there."

"Still, going into Supreme might be easier. They won't be expecting us to go that direction," Iain says.

"I know someone who can get you into Supreme, but his IDs won't let you move around. They are pretty flimsy. Won't stand real scrutiny if you get scanned. You go in as workers. You might make it to the compound of one of the many Safari companies and board a ship to the Outlands," Mo says.

"Any other ideas?" Dad says.

It seems that my idea is the best we have, and Mo promises to make a few enquiries. It means going deeper into the lion's den before coming out again. But at least those who are searching for us wouldn't expect it. We'd go in with the lower workers and come out with the privileged. Once we were free in the Outlands, we'd head back for Jonathan. It is a weak plan, but it is all we have.

I see two hard looking, heavily armed men strolling to the table.

"Here comes trouble," Mo mutters.

I am surprised when they ignore everyone else and address me. "What's your business down here, Kid? Is college out or something?" I grip Yuenu inside my bag.

"You want to come with us?" the other says.

Dad goes to spring up, but Mo grabs his arm and shoves him back down forcefully.

Mo looks relaxed. "Guys, you really don't want to start anything here. But if you do, here is a fair warning. I personally saw to the training of this young warrior. You really don't want to do anything that upsets her, while you are still enjoying life. But if you have a death wish, don't let me stop you."

"Sure Mo, we was just kidding, right." I can see they still have not made up their minds.

"Stand up, Kiddo," Mo tells me. I do what he said.

"Slice and dice this, Kiddo," he says as he throws a whole melon in the air. It is in four pieces before it hits the ground and the air buzzes with the smell of hot melon. I switch off Yuenu but keep her in my hand.

"As we said, Mo, just kiddin'." The men walk away quickly.

Mo stares at their backs until they are around the corner. "They are part of an underground press gang. Probably trawling for people who have fallen off the system. Artisan down-and-outs to be used in the brothels and sweatshops."

"How did you know they'd go, Mo?" I ask.

"I didn't," he says drawing a huge weapon from under the table. "I had you covered, Kiddo."

Everyone laughs and I learn another important life lesson. Good friends are invaluable. And sometimes you never know who the best ones are.

Two weeks later, the plan is set; Mo has got us temporary worker IDs that would get us into Bilden and into the Legend Safari Company. According to Mo, he's been told that this Safari Company runs regular shuttles to various parts of Outland. We'll have to find a way to board a fast ship without getting caught. Hopefully a tourist ship coming straight from the Bilden would be less likely to be searched. It is risky, but it is a plan.

Iain isn't coming with us. His intention is to rebuild his life in the Artisan centre. Dad asks him to come home and he smiles and says 'This is my home'. He's been here too long, I suppose. But in any case, his staying behind doesn't stop him organising things; he is determined to beat the Establishment again.

Sheldon, Jan and I have to get a special makeover that ages us, makes us look like workers. Iain and Mo take us to some illegal place where they make your hands and face ten to fifteen years older. It is weird. Looking at Sheldon is like looking into the future. Not bad, I think, but keep the weird idea to myself. I find a metal surface to check my own transformation and am horrified. "Iain!" I wail. "Promise me that this will return to normal."

Iain just laughs lightly, "You look great," and hands me a uniform and electronics tool box. "Try to look comfortable with these and see if there is a place you can hide Yuenu." Guns would never get through the scanners, so I spend half an hour hiding both swords I have, in the handle of a large torch, and the rest of my high-value marbles in another. It is the best I can do; on a whim, I stick my lucky ingot into the case as well.

We move in the early morning using two cars that drop us behind a building close to an Artisan-Supreme shuttle station on the boundary. We have to board the workers' transport for people who are going into Supreme for work. Since a lot of it is regular maintenance work we have temporary IDs and permits as part of Legend Safari annual systems review. It is nonsense; if someone cross-checks us, we'll be in deep trouble. The workers' transport is a regular shuttle that doesn't need as stringent checks; workers already hold a permit and are counted in and counted back out every day. Similarly to the shuttle transport, the workers' transport separates the travellers destined for Bilden from the travellers destined for Serfin.

Iain is nervous. "Once I leave, you go back online with your collar and new IDs. Remember, don't do anything or say anything that refers to your previous names or lives; the machine picks things up quickly and they are going to be scanning for you," he says. "Once you arrive at the Safari Company, you need to decide the right time to disconnect the collars. Once you do, remember, they cannot go back on again."

He'd warned us of this a few times already; it is clear he is worrying about us being stuck in a situation where we have no way back.

"Goodbye and good luck," Iain says. "Break a leg."

We all hug him and thank him, before he runs back to the vehicle while watching the sky.

"This is it, guys," Dad says. "iTrust online."

I hear a load of reference numbers in my ear and a confirmation of a work permit. I hope others have the same as we four stroll to the workers transport in our uniforms, carrying our toolboxes and equipment. Boarding the transport is easy. Cuffs are synced, IDs and permits checked and toolboxes given a cursory scan for guns, explosives or other illegal contraband.

"Looking forward to work today?" Dad asks me.

"Sure. It will be good to get the job done and get home," I say.

"Let's hope the job goes smoothly and we don't run into any problems," Sheldon adds.

We set off with around forty other workers scheduled for work inside Bilden, well aware that we have to pass Serfin first.

I recall what I have learned about Serfin as we pass their boundary without trouble. They are the glue that holds the country together and maintains order. That is a polite way of saying that they ensure that the country continues to be run for their own benefit. These are not people who want change, but then people on the top of any society rarely do.

We don't see much of Serfin from the air, but I see a marked difference between the regions.

It is clear that there are no businesses or factories here. There are no skyscrapers or towers. Instead, greenhouses, swimming pools, equestrian centres and what looks like tennis courts are spread-eagled across lush countryside, inside huge estates with enormous houses. In the distance, I think I might be able to see cows and sheep on a hillside, but it is hard to tell. There is no overcrowding or deprivation here. I guess the health and life expectancy would be much better as well.

I puzzle how there can be such blatant organised inequality as this; surely there must be an equipoise that causes change. The extremes of hot and cold water will always find a way to an average, unless of course a physical barrier separates them.

I wonder when change happens, if ever. Is it really when the discomfort of the bottom classes exceeds the effort required to overthrow the existing order? In other words, the more unhappy people are, the less they have to lose and the more they feel that any struggle, no matter how dangerous, is worth it? Of course, if people don't see the unfairness and inequality then they will quietly suffer their lot. I promise to discuss this with Jan, when I got a chance.

I am completely lost in my thoughts when the sky patrols come alongside, and our transport slows. A man beside me groans.

"I hope these clowns don't delay us," he says. "We still have to stop in Serfin Transport station."

"Do they come on board?" I ask.

"Sometimes, if they find a discrepancy in the passenger manifesto. They are communicating with the onboard purser right now."

I look at Sheldon and Dad and open my toolbox at my feet. My heart is beating as I make sure Yuenu is accessible. Who would take the other weapon? Dad? Sheldon?

"They are leaving. We will be able to get to work on time," Dad says. Guarded language for the benefit of iTrust.

"Maybe," the man beside me says shaking his head.

I watch as the three sky patrols shoot off and we return to a normal speed.

"Your first time?" The man asks. I nod. I see Dad's warning glance. We'd agreed to speak as little as possible.

"Yes," I say.

"You are going to be surprised by the greed in Serfin. They reckon the Supreme own eighty percent of the wealth..."

"Political Infraction. Desist," machine voice says. The man looks at me with an expression of annoyance and fright.

We descend five minutes later into the Transport Station in Serfin. This is to let workers in the other compartment off, I guess.

I see the four armed-guards hurrying towards our transport as we come to a halt. Dad tenses up as the door opens and the three men and a woman barge on. They produce hand-held devices and start to scan all the passengers. If there is any sort of facial recognition, Dad is in trouble. And I hope our age disguises hold up to scrutiny.

Within minutes the female officer reaches us. She scans us in quick succession, Sheldon, me, Jan, then the guy who had talked with me. The machine must have alerted all four guards at the same time. There was no signal from her, yet the rest of the guards come and grab the man, manhandling him roughly off the transport. The woman gives me a last look and follows behind.

Of course, I am relieved, but I am more shocked that someone could be taken for simply being a little critical of the regime. A little slip of the tongue, I think. A finger of fear pokes me in my stomach as the doors close and we head deeper into the centre of power.

The Bilden entry port is like an impregnable fortress; it could never be taken by force. Our transport slides past heavily armed towers and vehicles to the security station. The whole set-up makes me think of an old castle hundreds of years ago. The trades and the townsfolk lived outside the gates while the serfs worked the land a little further away.

We are marched off the bus by some sort of robot that processes us one by one. Queues of workers in multiple lines, waiting to get through. It is busy, so I have a few seconds to ponder on what to do with Yuenu. Keep her close and risk discovery, or leave her in the toolbox and risk discovery, but without being able to reach her? I plump for leaving her in the toolbox, when I see the way the machine is scanning people ahead of me. Then I see Dad's expression and follow where his eyes are looking. The machines are going through the toolboxes item by item. There are only five people ahead of me, I can't walk out of the queue or leave the box down without being noticed.

"Knuckle down," Sheldon says as he presses something into my hand. "You right, me left."

I take the marble he has given me and fire it up into the air to the right. I think he fired his on the ground to the left.

"Look!" I shout, pointing up. Okay, it's the oldest trick in the book; it even feels lame as I do it, but it worked before. It happens so fast that only a few realise what had gone up in the air, but their shouts are enough. Men scream and run to where a young boy is chasing the marble as it bounces once and rolls. I feel someone take the toolbox off me; I turn, it was Dad. He strolls through a gap while the machines are distracted and while we wait in the queue Dad locates the smaller shuttle that will take us to the Safari Company.

The machine studies me as I go through the scanner. I feel it looking at me, twice, through its wire-gauze eyes. I shudder. Maybe it had seen the marble come from my general direction or was suspicious of my shout, but can detect no misdemeanour to detain me.

Finally, it lets me through and I clamber on the smaller vehicle along with Sheldon and Jan to join Dad. Moments later we are travelling across Bilden. It is a better, more elaborate and ostentatious version of Serfin. We marvel at the land and obvious wealth we can see as we cruise overhead. Luxury yachts moored beside helipads, airfields and enormous white houses with white sandy beaches, lagoons and lush tropical gardens.

But I don't feel this is nirvana as I recall the fear on the man's face as he'd been arrested. This is no free paradise. There is a cost of obscene wealth to the human psyche, unless you are a sociopath.

The Legend Safari Company is a huge park with fancy offices, and a dozen large shuttlecraft being loaded up with supplies and pallets of equipment. Large mobile homes or recreational vehicles are being guided onto each transport. Our smaller vehicle lands close to a hangar and a plush office, where the workers with us head to register or sign in.

"Our work is across at the supply warehouse," Dad says. "We will meet the Chief there and see what we need." I know he is making it up. I can see him looking for the best place to get us on a craft; he leads us between huge metal portable cabins that are either temporary accommodation for the safari or some sort of equipment containers.

"iTrust disconnect," Dad says once we are in sight of a shuttle whose loading looks almost complete. We do the same. There is no way back.

"We have no idea where this is going," Jan says.

"I know. I was thinking that. But what option do we have? We don't even know the names of anywhere in the Outlands," Dad replies.

"Actually, I do," I say. "Wait here for a second." I trot quickly over to another transporter where a man is pressing buttons on a remote winch to operate a pallet lift.

"Hello!" I hail him and he stops the machine for a second and removes his ear defenders. "You'll catch trouble..." he shouts, "...if they see you without these on." He points to his ears.

"Nah, we cannot wear them on acoustics. I got plugs in." I point to my ears. "Listen, we need to check the digital acoustic couplers on the shuttle that's going near Gubrath. Would you know which one that is?"

"I think it's quad three, but I could be wrong. Ask Mike or Harry in the office."

"We don't have time to walk back there. The boss gives us hardly any time as it is."

"Shaun!" The man calls inside the shuttle's fuselage. "Lady needs to know where Gubrath is. I told her quad three."

"Nope." A bald headed man pops out the cargo door. "It is quad one in Outlands." He studies me for a bit before going back inside to whatever he was doing.

"Sorry. Quad one then. There are two shuttles going to quad one today. Do you know which one?" He points to a shuttle taxiing in.

"Yeah, the one that's due to leave first," I claim.

He points to another shuttle. "Leaving shortly. It's a four hour journey, don't get stuck on board."

"We won't. Thanks; I need to get my crew. Have a good day," I say, walking back to the group.

"We need that one," I tell the guys, pointing. They are still trying to figure out how I knew, as we cross the tarmac and hurry up the ramp into the craft. "It's about a four hour trip," I tell them, to add to their curiosity.

Inside there are four of the large camouflaged Legend Safari vehicles. They are RVs, recreational vehicles. Jan tries a door; it's unlocked and he opens it slowly and peers inside. "Lush," he says.

"Quickly. Let's see if it has somewhere to hide. We need to stay together," Dad says.

Jan was right, luxury, with a lounge, kitchen area, toilet and shower facilities. The driver's cab is awash with controls and electronics: radar, weather, satellite positioning, lights, cameras and communications. Above bedrooms at the rear is some sort of viewing gallery for looking out; I climb the ladder.

"Assuming no one comes up here and looks around it has a perfect hiding place for three," I say.

"Okay, you, Jan and Sheldon take it and lie low. I will try the front end," Dad says. "If it's a four hour trip, set your watches." He hurries off.

Sheldon and I climb up and lie down; we can see out the window to the ramp. Something else is being loaded. Some sort of cage made of very close chain link, but we struggle to see what is inside. My age mask is irritating me and I peel it off. Sheldon helps but it hurts as it's stuck on my skin and hair in places. It feels good to massage my face and get a bit of oxygen back in my cheeks. Then I help Sheldon with his.

"Freedom," Sheldon says scratching his eyebrows and nose.

Jan keeps his mask. "I am going to keep the older look for the moment," he says.

Sheldon and I turn back to the window.

Five minutes later a number of Jeeps arrive. Men and women get out laughing and joking, showing each other pieces of equipment as they wander up the ramp to board the aircraft. They are excited, examining everything around them and suggesting friends have a look at whatever interests them.

"If they come in here, they are going to find us."

"Dad will not be able to see them coming. We need to tell him," I say.

"I will go." Jan is nearest the exit and backs out quickly down the ladder.

"Quickly," I warn him. "They may come on here right away."

Sheldon points to a long horizontal cupboard. "Can we squeeze in there?"

There are some cushions and blankets inside. I take them and squeeze them into another space and we slide in and close the door. Sheldon goes first and I back in to his front; I can feel his sweet breath on my neck.

"If they look in here, we are screwed," Sheldon says.

"Then we will be taking over a Safari craft," I whisper as I touch Yuenu in my jacket pocket.

"I hope Jan finds your Dad okay," Sheldon says. "I hope your Dad is okay without a weapon."

"Don't worry," I say, as I start to worry.

We hear voices, a few bangs, more voices and then an indistinct tannoy announcement from the aircraft. There is a loud hum as the ramp comes up, and the metallic clang of the bay door closing.

"We are going," I whisper to Sheldon as the craft starts to shudder slightly. I squirm around to face him, reach my arms around and under his jacket, put my lips on his cheek and squeeze us tightly together. I feel his eyelashes tickle my face.

Nerves make me laugh a little and I can feel him looking at me in the dark. He smells like a pine forest and his back is broad, strong and comforting under his uniform. I am about to suggest we get out and change our clothes when we hear male voices. They are having a look around. We hear them opening the shower and toilet.

"Oh shit. My toolkit is still out there. They're going to see it!"

Sheldon takes my head in his arms and kisses me hard, crushing my lips against my teeth. We both freeze like that. Not a real kiss. Unmoving until silence descends again. The men have gone. My lips feel a bit numb.

We wait for a while then quickly go out and change. I take my lucky ingot and second sword out and stuff the overalls in the toolkit before hiding it in a corner under a seat. On impulse, I strap the second sword around my lower leg using a piece of webbing off the couch. We squeeze back into the cupboard.

"Where are we going?" Sheldon says after a few minutes.

"Nowhere. We are in a cupboard in the dark. And my Dad is next door." I giggle. "I wonder if my Dad and Jan are this close."

He laughs quietly. "Where are we going?"

"We - are - going - home." I kiss his nose in-between each word.

"No, I don't mean that," he says.

"You mean us?" I growl.

"No." Defensive. Silence. "I just wanted to know how you decided which shuttle?"

"Oh. Keshet's landlady gave me an address in the Outlands."

"Butterfly kisses," he says, changing the subject.

"What?"

"Your eyelashes are tickling me."

"And that's what they call it? Butterfly kisses?" I say. "That's nice." And I flutter harder in his face until he surprises me with a real kiss where the butterflies move to my tummy and toes.

The feelings catch me by surprise, but so does the visceral memory and sadness when Sheldon's tongue darts between my lips for a nano-second.

"No" I say. "I cannot. Not yet."

# CHAPTER TEN

## Outland's Safari

Guilt, care, love, desire, friendship, sadness, confusion drum down on my brain, like sheltering under broad banana leaves in a monsoon. Sometimes the large drips get your face and mouth; other times it goes down your collar and back. A single kiss can be an explosion of possibilities and obstacles. Who knew? I wish I had Mum to talk to. In any case, it is focus on business again; we know the transport is due to land. Being focussed helps me wring the wetness out of my brain and get my head screwed on again.

"Robyn?"

It is Dad. I roll out of the cupboard with Sheldon behind me. Dad's head looks over the edge. He is halfway up the ladder. 'Do I look guilty?' I think, and I feel myself blush.

"Everything okay?" Dad says. "A few minutes to land, I think. We are going to have to play it by ear. But I was thinking they might drive these trucks out and we'd have a better chance of sneaking away. What do you think?"

"Or we might end up in the middle of a convoy, with no chance to get out and a few armed men in here," Sheldon says.

"I think Sheldon's right."

"Then let's look for a place to hide in the loading bay," Dad says. "Where is Jan?"

"He was with you!"

"No. Why do you say that?" Dad asks.

"He didn't come and give you a message?"

"No," Dad says. Our minds race with possibilities. "Let's make sure he is not in here, asleep or something."

"You do that," I say. "Sheldon and I will have a look around the loading bay. Maybe they will be concentrating on their landing for a bit yet."

For a second, I think he is about to argue. "Be careful," he says and starts towards the front of the carrier, quietly speaking Jan's name.

Moments later, Sheldon and I are outside the vehicle and sneaking around the perimeter of the metal loading bay. There is no one around. We check a couple of the other vehicles that are open. They are empty and Jan never answers when we whisper his name, loud enough to be heard above the engine noise. There is nowhere else to hide and I am sure he'd never go to the front of the craft, towards the lounge and cockpit. Jan is too smart for that. We reach the cage that we had watched loading. As we get closer, I see the white flash blinking through the slats, eyeballs in the dark; there are people inside. My hand goes to my mouth and I look at Sheldon.

"Jan," he says as he holds my hand and walks around to the other side of the cage where the door is. There are around ten people inside. There is no logic in it, the locked cage had been loaded before we took off, but I still check in case Jan is there. I gasp when I see one face staring; it is the worker that they had dragged out of the shuttle compartment. He recognises me, I see it in his eyes. "Help us," he mouths, before Sheldon drags me away.

"Back to the van. There is no place to hide out here. We don't know how many of the crew will come down here for landing and unloading," he says and I agree, still thinking about the man and wondering where Jan has gone.

"Did you find him?" Dad asks.

"No. And there is no place to hide out there. Your first idea to stay in the vehicle is the only option."

"And Jan?"

"It doesn't make sense. He couldn't just disappear, unless he is in the forward cabin or cockpit. Are you sure you didn't miss anywhere?" I ask.

"Check if you like. But be quick. We need to get back in hiding," he says.

Sheldon and I back into our cupboard again. This time I give Dad one of the light swords and I take the marbles out the toolbox and put them in my belt. The next time we come out of here, it is increasingly likely we will meet someone. In the dark cupboard again, I hold Yuenu in both hands in front of my chest. I need to be out of the cupboard in second ready to defend us if anyone discovers us.

"If I shout 'push,' I want you to push me out the cupboard as hard as you can," I tell Sheldon.

"I don't get it," he says. "Push with both hands?"

"No. With your chin, Bozo. What do you think?"

"Weird," he snorts and we both start sniggering nervously in the dark until the craft bumps onto the ground with a loud thump.

After a few minutes it seems there is activity everywhere; the sound of chains being released, engines starting and stopping, shouts and okays. Then shuttle engines dying down and generators switching on; tannoy announcements and a heated discussion from far away.

It sounds like three men who come into our vehicle. They are loading their gear and some stuff is being stowed in luggage compartments outside. A few boxes are shoved into the lounge and it sounds like they are banging around the kitchen. I strain to hear in case Dad shouts for help; I hope they don't find him. So far none have come into the back cabin.

Sheldon squeezes my arm when the truck starts up and begins to reverse out and down the ramp. Directions are shouted and other engines rev-up, joining ours. I have a sense we are outside now on rough ground, from the bumpy movement as the vehicle parks up.

Fifteen minutes later we set off.

"We don't know what happened to Jan," I say to Sheldon. "What if he is not with us?"

"What can we do?" I hear the tension and frustration in his voice. "Let's be patient."

Patience is not my middle name, my mother used to remind me. We've been driving for an hour. My instinct says time to move, so we do. We roll out of the cupboard, making as little noise as possible. I come down the ladder holding Yuenu and stand by the door. Sheldon lies on his stomach looking out of the window, just as the vehicles roll to a halt.

There is a roar of shuttle engines and Sheldon watches something in the sky. I listen at the door to hear if the men would stir; one minute looking at the door, the next minute looking at Sheldon. His posture is tense as he stares, fixed on a point.

"Shel," I whisper, and he holds up his hand without looking round. Minutes pass.

All of a sudden, Sheldon squirms backwards off the platform and comes down the ladder fast. Biting his lip, he looks at me, as if thinking what to say or what to do.

"What?" I almost cry out in frustration.

"We are up in the hills, in some sort of valley. The shuttle didn't land, it dropped the cage in the centre of the trucks."

"And?"

"The sides opened up and men and woman ran out in different directions, up the valley as far as I can see." Sheldon, afraid to draw the conclusion, hesitates.

"They are going to hunt them?" I ask.

"Worse, I may have seen Jan," he says and starts to shake, his face a grey sick pallor.

The trucks start to move and a shot rings out.

"Are you sure?" I ask. He nods.

I hug him. "Then we have to do something, right?"

Sheldon straightens up, nodding. His face sets in a determined expression as he points to the door. We go through together, trying not to make a sound. I grip Yuenu in both hands.

Two men lie on their stomachs, on the left side of the truck, stationed at a window specially designed to shoot from. A quick glance out of the right window reveals another vehicle on our right; two trucks lead at the front.

Time stands still for me then. It's funny, I know the situation right away; the vehicles move up the valley two abreast. The quarry are all running ahead of a square of four vehicles. Shooters would be pointing outside the trucks to the left and right, covering both sides of the valley. A stark choice for the hunted; try to hide, try to run ahead as fast as possible, to outrun the vehicles, or try to climb up the sides of the valley. Poor Jan, I become afraid for him and angry with myself, although I don't know why. The trucks move at walking speed as the men scan for targets.

Sheldon nods in the direction of the recumbent men and we move forward, as I press Yuenu's button. Neither men hears the noise of the sword, and I realise they have earplugs in. A first shot goes off outside, the ricochet echoing in the valley.

I can't stand it; I stand between the men at their feet and scream, holding the sword between their midriffs.

They look around and one startles. The other shows no surprise or fear; a slight smirk crosses his face while turning around. A long scar crosses his right eye and down his cheek; this man is no stranger to weapons and injuries.

"Slide out," I tell them. "Easy. Onto the floor. Leave the rifles where they are."

"Put the weapon down," the scarred man says.

"You really don't want to mix up my baby face with..." My threat is interrupted.

"Whoever you are or wherever you came from, you better put the weapon down. Tell your boyfriend to back off, or you are going to regret interrupting my holiday." Scarface stretches out his hands for my sword. "Give it to me."

His eyes bore into me, while his companion looks from one to the other.

"My friend is out there and time is running out. If you don't do as I say, and take your hand back, you are going to lose your trigger finger," I say.

He lunges, tries to twist around and grab me around the waist. I step back fast and take his fingers off with a small strike. He gasps for breath, in shock.

"I warned you. Now! Sit. On the floor. Both of you." I shake with adrenaline. "For both your sakes, you better pray my friend is okay."

They both dive onto the floor. Scarface clutches his hand and blood oozes between his fingers.

Sheldon stoops, checking their jackets for weapons. The companion has a pistol in a shoulder holster; Sheldon takes it and places the two rifles well out of reach, and goes off to the front.

"What is happening out there?" I say kicking the companion. "How does it work?"

"It's a warm up, before we hunt in the villages. We drive them up the valley and shoot them as they run."

"So they have no chance?"

"These are criminals, worse than animals," Scarface spits.

"There is not much cover out there. We usually get all of them," Companion says.

Sheldon returns with Dad. "Driver is in his cabin," he says. "It looks as though we will just keep following the vehicle in front for the moment."

"Dad, Jan is out there." He nods, takes a look at the two men, rushes back to the front and returns with two rolls of sticky tape he had seen. Minutes later he has both men bound and gagged. I become impatient and anxious, as Dad wraps a towel around Scarface's hand. Two more shots ring out and time may already have run out for a couple of people.

"Take the rifle," Dad tells Sheldon. "Right, together, shoot the tyres of the forward vehicle across from us. As many times as we need to make it stop. Robyn, watch the driver's cab door in case he stops and comes out to find out what's happening."

Dad and Sheldon fire shot after shot. I cover my ears; the sound is deafening in the cabin. The lead vehicle stops, rear tires shredded. We keep moving and start to pass the stalled vehicle on our right. The second vehicle behind starts to pull around from behind the stationary vehicle. Dad and Sheldon turn the attention to their front tyres; a smaller target, and neither of them are marksmen.

"He's getting around behind us," Sheldon calls out.

"Shoot his window," I cry in frustration. "Shoot the driver."

They do. The front of the vehicle explodes under the hail of the high velocity bullets.

The hunters and the organisers are taken by surprise, confused; what idiot would shoot out their tyres or windscreen? Loud messages come over the radio in our cab, men appear at the windows and doors, jumping out of the two disabled vehicles, rifles in hand and scurrying to find cover. The front vehicle on our side soon realises that something is wrong and stops. We pull up behind them. Our own driver sounds confused through the cabin door, he shouts out the window to ask what has happened.

Two shots ring out and one whines as it passes our vehicle. The third shot comes through the vehicle, through the bathroom door and smashes something inside.

"Get down," Dad says. I lie on the floor watching our prisoners and Sheldon lies down with his rifle pointing at the door, while Dad crouches and pulls open the driver's door.

"Drive. Go around the truck in front. Do it now!" he shouts, pointing his rifle at the driver.

The vehicle lurches to the right as we go around our leading trailer. "Keep your foot down!" Dad threatens. A couple of shots hit the back of our vehicle, around our tyres. Perhaps they're now more worried about hitting their own people. Dad moves warily to the front of the cab, crouching. I scuttle behind him and enter the cab on my haunches. Someone climbs up on the outside of the driver's door, his reflection on the wing mirror. I scream a warning just as he levels a pistol through the window. Dad dives and fires, while the man shoots our driver by accident and then ducks down. Our vehicle starts to slow as our driver clutches his chest and slumps to the side.

I dive to the driver's door just as the man pops up; he clings on to the window ledge and tries to raise his pistol again. I slash and miss when the truck jolts to a complete halt. The man fires as he falls off and the shot sings past my ear.

Dad's expression is one of shock as he wrenches the driver to the floor, jumps in the seat and gets us moving.

When I look, Sheldon stands behind me. "Watch for Jan. I will take the right-side," he says. "We need to hope he knows it's us. He knows we must be here; he will have realised there is too much shooting."

The vehicle bounces around on the rocky ground and we move much faster than before. Leaning out the door, I hang on to the wing-mirror to give Jan the chance to recognise me. It is another stupid mistake. But luckily, the truck bouncing over the rough ground spoils their aim. Someone with a telescopic sight shoots the wing mirror off and I tumble off the vehicle.

"Robyn!" Dad and Sheldon shout together; they thought I'd been shot. The vehicle grinds to a halt and both jump out and run back to me.

"I'm okay." A couple of shots pin us down. Sheldon fires back as we crouch and try to move back to the door of the vehicle.

"They will be waiting for us to climb up," Sheldon says. We have no idea the direction the shots had come from. In the distance, a truck comes steadily towards us.

"Help me!" A shout. We look around. The man we had talked to on the shuttle, crouching and running, towards us, off the hill. "Help!" Dad points to the direction of the other vehicle, making a frantic motion for the man to keep his head down. Too late; as he reaches us, his head explodes like a balloon filled with red paint and porridge.

We three use the opportunity to scramble up into the cabin, Sheldon coming last as a couple of shots ring out again.

"Check our prisoners," Dad says jumping into the driving seat.

The machine lurches forward again and Sheldon goes to fire out the back, while I check that our captives have not managed to break their Sellotape handcuffs. All good.

"Is that him?" Dad shouts from the front, pointing at a figure running towards us, from the direction we are heading.

Minutes later Jan has scrambled on board and lies on the floor gasping for breath. "First time I have ever been used as target practice. It's a real rush; I think I peed my pants and my stomach wound is hurting."

After about another ten minutes, the other vehicle stops following us. It looks like they have turned back to the two disabled vehicles. When Sheldon tells us this, Dad stops the vehicle and we let our prisoners out, un-gag and untie them and tell them to walk.

"You will pay for this!" Scarface spits. "I will remember all of you." Companion says nothing; he starts to walk in the direction we had come.

"Dad, let's go. We should drive." I go back in to see how Jan is. He's fine, looks a little bit winded from running. He promises to keep a lookout at the back, and I return to the cab where Dad and Sheldon are getting rid of the dead driver.

"We cannot take him, but they are going to blame us for his death, that's for sure," Dad says. "If they catch us, there will be no clemency." I nod, thinking about the gravity of the situation, before gritting my teeth and helping Dad and Sheldon wipe up blood and tissue with a load of towels.

I see Dad look at me, thinking, when we wash our hands at the sink.

"What?" I ask.

"For a moment, I saw your Mum. I am proud of you," he says. "You have her strength, like I never imagined." He kisses me on the head and tells me he loves me. I notice Sheldon watching.

Dad tells Sheldon to take the wheel, while he tries to figure out the navigation equipment; we have no idea where we are or which direction we are headed. After a while the valley opens out into a broad plain where we can speed up a little. Sheldon is gripping the wheel and staring at the road with a determined concentration; he's never driven before and it shows.

"I think this is where we are, quite a long way from Subtopia and where the Euny are," Dad says pointing at the screen. I notice he didn't mention Jonathan. "These are the villages around us. Gair, Inver, Gubrath and Curham. Whichever track we take through the hills we pass by one or two of them." "Gubrath I have heard of, but it doesn't mean anything, in terms of geography. It could be close or miles from Subtopia," I say.

"According to the wider map view, Gubrath is before we come to the border, it's the longest route. But it goes into this forest pretty soon. We might get some cover before dark." He sets the coordinates and track for Sheldon to drive. "About a mile up ahead, we are going to turn a ninety degree right turn. I am hoping that this track will also be the one they least expect us to take. It almost doubles back."

Sheldon and I nod, Dad's confident decision somehow making things feel slightly better.

"Are you okay?" I ask Sheldon, switching on the radio.

"Sure. Enjoying my first time," he frowns. "Just getting used to the speed. Is that the fuel gauge? It seems to be going down quickly." Dad comes and looks.

I find the Legend Safari frequency and there is a lot of traffic; they are after us. Sky patrols have helped the vehicles get moving again and the company security has set out from another quadrant to join the chase.

"I think we are popular," I say.

"And I think there is a fuel problem," Dad says looking up from the travel computer. "We may have a leak." He looks at the electronic maps again on the screen. "We'll be lucky if we reach the first village on the other side of the forest. And even if we get there, we have no idea what these people are like. I cannot imagine they will be friendly towards rich city types driving a vehicle like this."

□□□□□□□

The forest is a welcome sight and we all watch the fuel gauge and the sky and road behind us on the last half mile down the hill into the thick dense pines.

"We will stop in the centre of the forest and check the fuel lines," Dad says. "Or as soon as we think we are out of sight of the road and sky."

"Okay," Sheldon responds.

Five minutes later we are off the road under a tall dark canopy. I walk with Jan a little way into the trees.

"If I smoked, I'd have a cigarette now," he jokes.

"Yeah. You must have been so scared," I say. "You were unlucky, twice."

He half laughed. "I couldn't believe it, I walked into them and one poleaxed me right away. I didn't even get the chance to cry out."

"We heard nothing."

"When I woke up, they had me tied up like an animal in the lounge, while they questioned me. It took a few cracks on my head before they believed my story that I had stowed away since the last trip. I didn't want them to start asking how I had gotten into Bilden. They thought I was from Outlands."

"Fair game," I say.

"Yes. I knew as soon as they pushed me into the cage, what the intention was," Jan says.

"Poor thing. You must have been terrified."

"There was a guy in the cage from the shuttle."

"We saw him. He asked for help," I say. "We couldn't save him."

"Robyn, to be honest, I knew if I could be saved, you guys would do it," he says. "But I thought it might take time for you to figure out what was going on. I knew that I couldn't outrun the trucks forever, so I concentrated on outrunning as many of the others as I could. I figured I'd hear a dozen shots before I'd have to really worry about cross hairs on my back."

I shudder.

"When I heard all the multiple shooting, I turned around and waited."

I hug him then, partly for him, but mostly for me; I just want this nightmare to end.

"The guy in the cage gave me this. Got no idea what it is." He hands me a round white stone with an unusual symbol.

"Lucky charm?"

"Keep it. Please. I want you to have it, if it's lucky."

The symbol looks like a backwards 'B' with a curved back and two dots in the upper part. It looks rather like a little foetus.

"I am sorry for getting you into this mess, Jan," I say. "And for taking your best marbles in the game."

He jokes, "Yes, I am still angry about that, seems like years ago. Anyway it's not going to spoil our friendship."

"Thank you. I value your friendship. You, Sheldon and Jonathan, I couldn't have any better friends."

We walk back to the vehicle, arms around each other's shoulders, best friends. Sheldon jumps down from the cab and joins us.

"Group hug," he says, just as Dad comes out from under the vehicle and tells us he thinks he's fixed the fuel tank, and he's found some spare fuel, but doesn't think it is going to get us very far.

We decide to break from the forest as soon as it is dark. We plan to see if we can get to the next village; maybe we could buy more fuel and continue on through the night.

We relax in the dark for a couple of hours before Dad gets us moving. "I estimate about three miles to the edge of the forest. Keep eyes open for any lights in the sky or around us."

Driving out of the forest puts me on edge again; I have a slight pain in my stomach. We keep the main lights off and Dad drives as fast as he dares on the unlit road. For thirty minutes we bounce along looking up at the stars any time there is a gap in the cloud.

We are past a boundary fence and down a narrow track before any of us realise.

"Is this correct?" Dad asks himself out loud. "Feel like we went off the main road, but I didn't turn anywhere."

As we round a bend, we see the lights too late. There are a number of armed men and vehicles blocking the path. Bright spotlights are pointed at our vehicle.

# CHAPTER ELEVEN

## Lodge

"Just take it easy," Dad says. "We can't fight them."

Sheldon cusses and my heart sinks. I don't want to get captured; we've come too far.

Two armed men come to the window.

"Good evening Sir. You are part of the party from Feldham Corporation? Came in on the late evening shuttle from Mantropolis?"

"Yes. Yes. Good evening." I can hear Dad's relief.

"Okay, we are on radio silence here. Please turn off all electronics and navigation equipment. And all vehicle lights," one man says. "We don't want to alert the game. Headlights shine a long way in the dark and they constantly scan for our communications."

Dad reaches over and switches everything off.

"We are not sure how many are turning up tonight. But there is plenty of room. Your host arrives tomorrow at some point. But I expect you will be ready for some supper and to get out at first light tomorrow, Sir?"

"Sure," Dad says.

"How many of you are shooting and how many observing?" the other man asks.

"Two and two."

"Excellent. If you make your way up to the top of the hill and park up, you can take Lodge 6. The door is open. The main house is close by. There will be plenty of people still up and someone will fix you supper if you require. Have a great hunt tomorrow, Sir."

"Thanks."

We drive slowly to the top of the hill.

"We could make a break for it, Dad." I can see he is trying to figure things out.

"Did you see the double fence? Even if we could break through with speed, we have no idea what would be on the other side. We could run smack bang into a bunch of trees," Dad says. "We are trapped."

The lodges appear as shadows in the dark. A dim light indicates number six. We pull up alongside three other vehicles.

"Let's go in while we think what to do," Dad says.

The lodges are enormous luxury cabins with every possible facility. I don't care. I am only interested in continuing. I am tired but completely wired.

"Robyn, we need to just sit down and talk this through," Dad tells me.

The four of us sit around a table and Sheldon brings us juice and soft drinks from the bar.

"Okay. Any guesses where we are and how safe we are?" Dad says.

"It's a hunting lodge," Jan says. "My Dad used to go to one in the mountains."

"We are safe as long as they think we are one of them," Sheldon says. "Did you see the weapons the security guys were carrying?"

"I am surprised they didn't greet us with a shower of bullets," I say.

"This place is out of the way. They are maintaining radio silence," Dad says. "They don't know about us. I think we are fine for the moment. But it's only a matter of time before they find out about us; we need to think how to get out of here. I don't think we can slip away at night, and besides I don't know how far the fuel is going to take us. Unless we can find some."

"They must fuel up here," Jan says.

"One or two of us are going to have to go in there and ask questions," I say.

"Yes, it has to be me," Dad says. "But I will take one of you with me."

"Then it has to be me," I say. "I can conceal Yuenu in case we need to get out of there fast."

"No. It's my turn. You have seen enough danger," Sheldon argues. "I took a pistol off one of our prisoners, remember."

Dad agrees with Sheldon. Argument settled. They go off to see what the situation is; Jan and I go back into the vehicle, ready to make a quick getaway if we hear trouble.

Sheldon pops his head in the RV door after ten minutes. "It's all clear. Your Dad is just talking to a couple of people. Otherwise the place is empty."

"People have gone to bed," I say.

When we join Dad, he is in conversation with three guys. He waves us to a table and excuses himself from the men with a last few words.

"I didn't want to introduce you." Dad sits down. "They are much too curious. Asking who I knew and so on."

"What did you learn?" I whisper.

"This is one of three lodges in this area. They are completely portable. They move them with some kind of silent super ship apparently. This is a huge operation. These guys are guests of a large Bank."

"What about fuel?" I ask.

"There is no access to fuel until 0500 am. They fill everyone up then. We are on a hill with a fairly steep drop on two of the four sides. We are expected to start the safari at 0600. The trip is in two parts. Part 1 is in vehicles. It takes place in Gair, the village just over the next hill. The second event is on foot in the next village. Gubrath."

"A short hop over the border," Jan says.

"Exactly," Dad replies. "But it's a day out with these guys, with a chance the others are on their way here."

"Are they likely to realise we are not with them?"

"The only thing that worries me is there is some sort of sky scanner that tracks kills. That means something is looking down at us."

We get some bread, cheese and ale served by a friendly porter, while Dad informs us of everything he has learned. I hadn't realised how hungry I was until my stomach groaned. I gobble down a few chunks of bread and swill with the beer.

"I think it's our best chance. We stay with these people until we get the chance to break away safely or until we feel we are threatened. That means we have to act normally," Dad says. "Talk to people. Go to breakfast. And generally try to fit in, especially in the morning before we set off."

I turn to a noise outside. Five men and one woman come through the door, bringing cool air with them. They'd obviously just arrived. We must look nervous as we all keep our heads down and yet watch them to see if there is any sign that they know us, or us them. They seem in good spirits, which is a good sign. They all wish us a good evening on their way to the bar. I notice a couple of backwards glances at us; maybe our lack of enthusiasm seems off to them.

After a few minutes one of the men comes over with his beer and greets us again. It seems he just wants chitchat and to impress us with his hunting prowess.

"It's great to see youngsters taking up the sport," he tells us. "I started at twenty-five. Which was young back then. My father taught me."

"I see," says Dad.

"How did you get that bad scar below your eye?" he asks.

"Is your father still around?" Dad changing to a neutral subject.

"Sure. He is eighty-five. Still hunts," the man replies. "He is coming in the morning with a few business associates. You'll get to meet him."

"Well that's fantastic really. Now if you excuse us, I think it's time I got these youngsters to bed," Dad replies. "They have an early start in the morning. Are you going on the morning hunt?"

"Sure, sure. Well maybe not the morning; depends on the bar and how late we sleep." He grins. "Probably just the afternoon hunt in the second village. Much more sporting," he says. "Look, before you go. Let me show you something." He puts his beer down and insists on leading us to a double door at the other end of the bar. "You are going to love this."

We go into a large hall and he switches on the lights. At first I didn't know what I was seeing. I hear Jan draw in a breath.

"Yeah, great, aren't they?" the man says, mistaking shock for wonderment.

Around the walls is a collection of trophies. Men, women and children had been shot and mounted in a variety of poses. The man is already walking around to start the tour.

"Eh thanks, this is really great, but I think these guys need to sleep," Dad says. "Maybe we can look in more detail tomorrow night when we have more time?"

The man's disappointment is replaced by the prospect that he could show us tomorrow. "Sure, sure. But let me show you one." He points to a large angry-looking lady, poised ready to throw something. "My father got this one in 2026 when I was a boy. She ambushed him with a rock, while he was tracking her family."

I look at the woman's face. I'd never seen a combination of fear, anger and surprise, set in a rictus, but then I'm only seventeen and not from this sick place.

Dad thanks him and rushes us out and back to the lodge. I don't make it. I throw up chunks of bitter cheese until I can only retch.

What are we joining tomorrow?

I ask Dad if I can share his room. I really don't want to be alone, and I lie awake the whole night, aware that Dad is lying close by, also staring at the ceiling.

□□□□□□□

We don't go for breakfast as planned. How can we? None of us could be normal with these people. Instead, we take juice, water and biscuits from the room and go to the vehicle to wait for someone to come and tell us where to fuel. Sheldon gives Dad the pistol for under his shirt and Dad returns the other sword to me. "It's better with you. I would probably cut my leg off." I strap it back around my leg. Meanwhile, Sheldon and Jan make sure they are close to the loaded rifles. The waiting is causing all four of us to be nervous. I can't stop shaking.

I go from window to window watching a few more people arrive and others prepare. There is an air of excitement outside that we don't share in our vehicle; people move briskly, shifting bags and rifle cases between vehicles and the lodges. A woman is looking through a telescopic sight at the pale moon and I try to balance this normal act of human curiosity with what we saw last night.

Finally it's our turn to move. It looks like we are the fourth vehicle, out of six, on the narrow track. A man comes to the driver's door and tells us to move up to get fuelled. He reminds us to stay off the radio, to move slowly and not to gun the engine.

"Stay as close as you can to the vehicle in front," he says. "We don't want our quarry to hide in-between or get under the vehicles. It can get dangerous then. But don't worry, security will be keeping an eye on things."

The guy who fuels us says, "Have a good one," and motions us forward when he's done.

A few minutes later the last trailer has been fuelled and we start to move.

I see the man from last night come out and point him out to Dad. He is meeting a car; probably his father.

"I don't think he is joining us this morning." Dad says sounding relieved.

The man opens the car door just as we pass and an elderly man gets out looking around.

I jump back out of the front cab and Dad turns his head while continuing to drive.

It's Zohar Keshet.

# CHAPTER TWELVE

## Genocide

I can't explain how I feel. I sit down, shocked, as we drive at funereal speed down the dark road in this convoy.

"It could mean anything," Sheldon says, but I can see that he doesn't believe it.

The words 'Sheldon, please don't lie to me' form inside my head, but that would not be fair. Instead I say, "I should have killed him when I had the chance."

Both guys are crouched beside my knees on the floor of the vehicle.

"Don't talk like that, Robyn. I promise you, we are going to find Jonathan," Jan says and Sheldon nods as he strokes my arm.

Dad's call from the cab shakes me from my unpleasant reverie; we all crouch behind him.

"I have been thinking. We cannot do anything; we are stuck bumper to bumper between these vehicles. But we have to appear normal at all costs," he says. "Two of you need to be shooting out of the window occasionally. Shoot trees and rocks."

"Yes," Sheldon says. "Jan and I will do it; no need for everyone to look out the window."

They are doing this to protect me, I think.

Dawn is beginning to break as the death convoy enters the outskirts of the village. I stay on the floor beside Dad as he drives, and hold onto his arm. I don't want him to be alone. The village is set on two sides of the main road; small houses festooned with brightly coloured shutters line the terraces, still in shadows in the early morning light. Somewhere in the distance a dog barks and I think our engines are loud in the morning silence. We stop and idle as if waiting for a signal. Washing hangs unmoving, there is no wind. Nothing stirs apart from a few starlings setting off into the fields from wherever they had been roosting.

Suddenly the convoy lurches forward again. I see a few men on the terraces running behind the houses. Dark shapes, not villagers, they are moving with deadly purpose; a couple of trained dogs run with them. Men signal each other as they go up and down a few alleys between buildings. The noise is startling in the silence; loud bangs and explosions echo off the brick. The first family runs out of a building in nightclothes and ducks around the corner. A woman covers her face and rubs her eyes as she shepherds her children.

"What are they doing?" I say but I think I already know the horror of the answer.

"I think they are using gas," Dad says. I look at his face. It's grim.

The first vehicle must be in town. More people run out reluctantly; they are trying to stay in cover. They keep to shadows, run into other buildings. I see one man and a small boy emerge on a roof holding hands.

Two shots ring out from in front and the man tumbles as the boy stands there in shock. One of the front vehicles has their first kill of the morning. I am furious; I have never felt such anger.

"Robyn, remember we cannot do anything. There are too many of them. I understand what you are feeling, but we need to keep control here. Please don't watch anymore, it's breaking my heart to see you." Dad speaks gently but firmly. "I'd rather you go in the back. There is no reason for the two of us to suffer. Just hang in there, we are going to get out of this."

I look up to see a family of four run down a street on the front of the village. They are so close. Multiple shots ring out. The family drop onto the sloping track. The father twitches until another shot causes his body to jump. Seconds later, a dark stain fills the cobbles between the four.

I squeeze Dad's arm and go into the bathroom, close the door, sit down and put my head between my knees and cry.

When Dad knocks on the door, I hadn't even realised that we'd stopped. I have cramp in my legs and I'd stopped flinching and counting bodies every time there was a shot. When I come out Dad and Jan are looking at me and Sheldon is driving. I have a vague sense that hours have passed but I'm not sure.

"Are you okay?"

"I'll be fine," I reply.

"Have you been sleeping?" Dad asks. "We are headed towards Gubrath. They plan to stop some way outside the village and have lunch. They are meeting up with others."

"Sick monsters. I hate them!"

"I know, but you have to try to keep your feelings under control. We need you, Robyn. We need you strong."

I think for a moment.

"Sorry Dad. You are right. It wasn't any easier for you guys," I say.

"No, and the guys have done a great job. Sheldon didn't complain; he just got back on with the driving. You could go and see if he is okay." Dad allows himself a sad smile.

Nodding, I go to the cab; Sheldon looks around quickly then back to his driving.

"Are you okay?" we say at the same time. Sheldon nods and pretends to be staring, eyes fixed on the road ahead.

"I just keep saying to myself, we are going to get out of this. Sometimes I pretend it is all a bad dream and I am going to wake up," Sheldon says. "These people..."

"Don't. No need." I know what he is thinking. The people we had seen gunned down were ordinary people; they were families. He is reminded of his own family. There are no monsters in closets, except those travelling with us in a convoy.

"We will get away, somehow today, tonight, I promise."

"I know."

"I love you."

"I know." I say as I rest my forehead on his shoulder and feel the muscles move as he steers. It doesn't take long to soak his shirt.

"Sorry," I sniff. And a small laugh burbles out.

"We are going to make it," he says. "Just believe it."

The vehicles pull into a large grassy plain for lunch and a briefing on the more difficult hunt coming up. At least that's what the guy who comes to our vehicle says. There are eight large camouflaged vehicles and four well-armed security trucks. Support staff arrives in another couple of wagons to do catering. We are trapped in the mesh of vehicles; there is no way out.

I look out at the people moving around their trucks; they are jubilant. Men stand in small groups talking animatedly, every now and then breaking into laughter. One man raises and sights along an imaginary rifle, fires, and then mimics someone holding their stomach and running. His companions laugh and slap him on his back.

"Okay guys. We need to go out there," Dad says. "We have to go to the briefing and show our faces in the crowd for a few minutes in any case."

Lunch in the large tent turns out to be a good place to hide; it is easy to concentrate on getting our food and avoid conversation. We are still too nervous and sick to eat, but we agree we should force some bread and tea down to keep us going. We eat then wander around until they shout us for the briefing in the now cleared lunch tent. I see a group of guys looking at a scoreboard and pointing in our direction, no doubt indicating that neither of our shooters had scored anything.

Two men move to the front of the tent and people start filling up the canvas seats that are turned to face the speakers.

"Okay folks. In just over half an hour we will be moving off to this location." The first speaker points to a rough hand-drawn map. "We drive to here. We kit up and we split into the six groups listed on the wall over there."

"We have tried to balance the groups by experience, age and shooting ability. Why? Because this is the way we ensure that people are safe and no one gets their head blown off by an inexperienced group," the second man says. "There will be two guides with each party. It is their responsibility to keep all of you safe. Therefore, you do exactly what they say. If they say lie face down in the mud, they will be saying it for a reason. Do not hesitate or argue if they tell you to do something. These are the rules and they are designed for only one thing. That is, to keep you safe."

"What should we expect?" someone asks from the back.

"Well this place has been hunted a few times, but never on foot. The last cull was three years ago. We fully expect to see a good range of stock and don't be surprised if we see a few charges. They will attack with clubs, stones or anything they can lay their hands on," first man says. "Also, they will go to ground, try to hide after the first drive. We will smoke them out and that's when things will become more desperate and therefore dangerous."

"Drivers will move the trucks to the other side of the village through this longer route. It will take them around forty-five minutes. You will meet them here at the end of your march at exactly 16:00," second man said. "If you don't have a spare driver, one of the company will do this for you, just let Lou know. There will be two security cars with the trucks and two will come through the village with the remaining trailers after the last hunters have gone past."

"An' guess what? You newbies need to study your group and know the route that is planned. You might get separated from your group, then you are screwed. Better you know the route by heart so you can get picked up by the truck coming through behind. Them coloured routes on them maps are your lifelines." An older fat man sits at the side, he doesn't look like he's part of the organisers, perhaps only an experienced hunter, but they obviously know him.

"Right. Thanks for that John. Okay, are there any other questions?" first man says. "Right. We move out at 13:30 precisely."

People are getting up to look at their teams. I see Dad and Sheldon exchange glances. We go and look; we are split across three groups. Dad and Jan are in one, Sheldon in another and me in the third.

Dad grabs one of the organisers. "My kids need to be with me," he tells him.

"The inexperienced are split between our staff. It is not possible for one or two of our staff to guarantee the safety of everyone else when they have too many inexperienced to look after in one group. Sorry."

Dad walks back to the truck with us. "We could say we are sitting this one out. But we don't know the circumstances at the other end. They are already wondering about us."

"One of us drives. That takes one out of the equation," Sheldon says.

"Okay. Here is what we are going to do. Robyn and Jan, take the truck. Sheldon and I go with our groups and do our best to fool them. Two of us walking through is enough risk."

"I don't like it," I say. Dad ignores me.

"Now, when you get to the other side, if there is any way of getting on the outside of the other vehicles, that would be good. Ideally, pointed the direction we want to go in case we have to make a fast getaway."

Jan drives and we drop Sheldon and Dad, carrying their rifles, at the rendezvous point. We wait until they join their respective groups and set off into the town. I watch Dad go on one route through the centre and Sheldon go high up on the outskirts of the village. After a couple of minutes the convoy starts to move and we follow the other vehicles down the back road to the other side of town. As I look back I see Keshet, his son and around six armed men jump out of a vehicle; they are in a hurry. They look around as if searching for someone, before hurrying to the man who is marshalling the vehicles and the man who coordinated the groups' departure. My stomach swoops with fright.

"Jan. I think we have a big problem. Keshet is there with his son. I think they are looking for us."

The organisers point in the general direction of the village, then directly at our line of vehicles as we disappear around the corner.

I switch on the vehicle's navigation equipment and curse as it takes a few seconds for the map to come on screen. I look. We are heading away from the village onto a road that curves around. The longer I waited, the further away from the village I would be.

"Jan, keep going!" I shout. "I have to warn Dad and Sheldon."

"Where are you going?" he yells back.

"I am going to try to get across that field into the village."

"Ah shit. This is not a good idea. Robyn!" I hear him call out as I drop off the vehicle and off the side of the road into the field. I hear the convoy stop; one of the security men must have seen me, but I don't look back. Instead, I put my head down and pump my legs and arms as fast as possible to deter anyone from chasing after me. I have Yuenu in my right hand and I can feel the other sword banging clumsily on my leg.

As I reach the village boundaries I hear the first of the 'flushing' activity. It sounds as if there are flash-bangs and gas canisters going off on every street. I aim for the middle of the town. I need to cut through a few yards and alleys, and as long as there are no dead-ends I should be able to find a way through. I run down a street where a few of the villagers are coming out of their houses to see what the noise is. A few are shouting something and already moving up the street. I feel I am only a few streets and blocks away from some of the beaters. I can see smoke rising a few streets down. The shooters will be some distance behind. Dad had gone in close to centre, but I don't know his route, I have no idea where I am and my sense of direction is already letting me down. When I hear shots being fired and a few bullets hitting buildings I realise the danger I am in. These guys will shoot anything that is in front of them.

I have to keep moving; a couple of people watch me, no doubt wondering who I am and why I am running blindly towards the noise. There is a larger building at the end of one alley, an indication that I am nearing the centre. It might be a church or an office.

A man steps out and blocks my way, a villager, and his intent is obvious. He is dangerously scared and angry.

Yuenu comes alive. "Back up," I say. "I need to pass. I am not part of this."

I have no idea if he understood my words. But he understood my face. He steps back and I run on down to the bottom of the street and straight into a stream of villagers fleeing. Men, women and children are in panic as long-distance shots pick off a few of them.

With the shield switched on I try to go against the flow of the crowd by keeping close to the buildings, but there are too many people crouching and running towards me in desperation. I fall. Another couple of shots close by from unseen shooters convince me this is not going to work. I turn and run with the crowd while I try to think what to do.

I see another couple of people fall. Kill shots. Instant. People scream and keep going.

We reach a crossroads and hunters appear at the bottom of another street. They aim and fire and the girl next to me, sprayed red, tumbles and doesn't get up, but lies twitching with her eyes open. The crowd splits in different directions; they merge with others coming from other streets. And I realise that everyone is being driven towards the large square ahead. The chance of me finding Dad or Sheldon in this is impossible. It is more likely to endanger them if they see me and come running.

I only realise how fast I am moving when I pass two young girls, holding hands and frozen in one spot. Their eyes are wild with fear as they look around at everyone running and falling. I stop and backtrack a few feet, grab their hands and pull. They yell, but they move; not fast enough. I try to keep as low as possible. Where to go? People are rushing past us; sometimes I see the same people running back.

I feel sure I am going to die here, without seeing Dad or Sheldon again.

It is a frightening chaos of death and panic.

The sign takes a few minutes to register. 'The Manse' and the symbol from the stone in my pocket on a sign that points across the street and up the lane. I change direction suddenly and the girls squeal again. As we enter the lane, I see men in the distance coming towards us. I can't tell if they are hunters; I think so. There is a wall and a sign on the gate, The Manse. I push the girls through into the grounds. I could weep; it is a bunch of ruins from many years ago. I don't know what I was hoping for, but not a broken building.

"We need to hide!" I shout over the screams and the gunfire. "We need to hide in there." I point to the overgrown ruins.

The older girl nods and pulls me around the thick undergrowth and through a gap. We go behind a wall and inside the shell of a smaller building. There is a place to hide under the window. They grip my hands tightly. I am wondering if I might leave them there and go looking for Dad and Sheldon, when I hear the men at the gate.

"They went in there. Go flush them out," I hear the voice say.

I let go of the girls and point to the hiding place and start to take Yuenu out. Then I black out with a pain and lights inside my head.

□□□□□□□

There is a sharp pain when I move my eyes. I open them and struggle to push myself up.

"You made it. But I wasn't expecting you to arrive like this," Sara, Keshet's old housekeeper, tells me.

There are around forty people in the room as I look around; a few watch me, and others are busy with families.

"What happened? Where am I?" I ask.

"Under the old Manse. A hidden bunker," she says. "One of six in the village."

"Ma, don't tell her," a large boy next to her says.

"And this oaf clobbered you," she says. "Brought you and the girls down here. You have been out for a few minutes."

"He probably saved us. Thanks," I say. "The hunters had just started to search the grounds."

The boy looks pleased.

"Our people searched you and found the stone. They knew you were not one of them. But they couldn't figure out who you were. When they told me, I came over from the other cellar," she said. "Imagine my surprise when I saw you."

"My Dad and friends are out there at the moment." I suddenly realise I don't have my things. "My stuff?"

"Gilby, give her all her stuff back. She is on our side," Sara says. "Your friend is here."

Gilby hands me the swords, watch and stone.

"Thanks." I am happy to have Yuenu back. For a second Sara looks puzzled by my reaction. But I miss the cross communication.

"You cannot go out there at the moment." she says. "How did you arrive anyway?"

"We stowed away on their vehicles." It's true, but it's the short version.

"So you have some good information," she says. "Let's talk to our men who are trying to fight back."

She leads me to the far end of the cellar, through families who look tired and scared, to a table with a group of men standing around a map. I notice they are a rag tag bunch without decent weapons. She explains briefly who I am.

"How many are there?" A bearded guy called Porter asks.

"Probably between thirty and forty," I say. "All extremely well-armed."

They look at each other. It is probably worse than they had hoped for.

"We know all 'bout their high-powered weapons," Porter says.

"How many of you are there?" I ask. "Is there somewhere we can see what's happening?"

"Our village defence force was about eighty men, but we don't know how many survived," the man says. "We are worried they are going to smoke us out of the bunkers. If they find them."

"They are well equipped, it's likely they have something that can locate you." The thought of being smoked underground fills me with horror.

"We have an exit onto the hills at the end of the village and from there into forests. But these men are hunters. They will shoot us as we emerge or pursue us there. The woman and children won't have a chance," Porter says.

"Show me where it comes out," I say.

Another man traces a line from our bunker to another, then out to the North East of the village. "We come out here."

"Then there is no time," I say. "Gather up as many men as you can and let's go. I have an idea."

There is urgency in my voice, which stirs a few, but just as many look hesitant and doubtful. Why should they follow a young girl?

"Listen. I know where their vehicles are waiting. We can try to take them and use them to force our way back into the village. But time is crucial," I say. "They are massacring people out there. Next they will come for the people hiding. We need to run."

The men look at me, measuring me for a few seconds; then, some nodding, they start to grab their stuff and I see a few old shotguns, and a couple of hunting cross bows.

We run along a badly lit tunnel into another bunker and Porter shouts at a few men, sending them running through a passage to the next bunker to get others. He opens a door to a shaft and a rough burrow that goes down into the earth. It isn't paved or shored up like the others and there is a damp smell of earth and decay. We have to crouch.

"Bring lights," Porter shouts and we start to move down into the dark as fast as we can. I think there might be twenty of us by the muffled steps and the panting of breath behind me. Porter and a few others in front of me check to see if I am okay from time to time; they seem grateful for my help. The air is dank, and earth and dirt fall off the tunnel roof and go down my neck as we scurry along. I try to push the thought of a cave-in from my head. I pray quietly that we will find the vehicles okay and that we aren't running out of town while the rest of the townsfolk are massacred. With these thoughts in my heart, fifteen minutes are an eternity.

When Porter stops I am relieved. I push through to the front to where he is opening a door.

"Let me go first. They know me," I say. He nods.

I look out. We are on the side of a hill with a narrow lane about fifty feet below us. There is nothing to be seen. I try to visualise the map and I curse my sense of direction. I have no idea if we have to go up the road towards the village or find the trucks parked further away.

I force myself to be patient and just look and listen. A vehicle door slams, down the hill, away from the village. We'd arrived at the front of the vehicles.

Porter looks at me.

"You and I can walk to the trucks. Some of them know me; so we should have a chance to get close. The men need to follow behind and get ready to run in."

"Sure. Let's go," he says. His jaw is set and his gaze steely; he reminds me a little of Mo.

We run down the grass onto the road and start to file down the road, keeping close to the hedgerow. We almost run into the vehicles as we round the corner.

"Stop," Porter mouths and holds up his hand. "Everyone stay until you hear my shout. Then come as fast as you can. We will be depending on you." He swaps his old shotgun for a pistol with one of the men. "Okay, are you ready?" He looks at me as if weighing me up, pushes the pistol down the back of his pants and takes a deep breath. This man has courage and a sort of presence. I remember what Keshet had said about the Nobeni. 'They are diseased and dysfunctional. They exist off the rubbish and sewers from the city. They bring nothing to the country and they get nothing from anyone.

Their life expectancy is minimal.' How could he be so wrong? It doesn't make sense.

Porter pulls me to the centre of the road and adopts a casual saunter. "Whoever you are. Thank you," he says looking at me.

"You are welcome." My heart thumps in my chest at his deliberate calm and the threat we are about to face.

"This is a beautiful village. You should see it in the autumn." He smiles at me.

"I am sure."

"People help each other here; we are a good community."

"Yes." I believe him, although his words are designed to make us act natural together as we walk around the corner.

The bark startles me. "Hold it right there." We reach the first of the vehicles. Three security men are levelling weapons at us.

"It's me. We're from the Feldham Corporation," I call back.

"It's the girl," I hear one say. "The runner."

They are still wary of Porter. Two keep their guns on him. The other turns back to the cabs. A few drivers come out to see what the noise is. I spot Jan coming through from between two trucks, looking all around, and taking everything in. He is trying to figure out what I'm doing.

The Security focuses on Porter. One keeps a gun trained on him while the other goes to pat him down. I will Porter not to do anything just yet.

"Where have you been and who is this?" the guard asks just at the same time as he finds Porter's gun.

His companion next to me dies silently as Yuenu comes alive and takes out his throat and slashes his arm. Before he hits the ground, I am around behind Porter. The guard looks up from Porter's belt to find himself facing Yuenu. His mistake is to underestimate how fast Yuenu and I could take heads off. I am drenched in his blood as he falls clutching wounds in his neck.

The third guard turns around when one of the drivers shouts. His first shot catches Porter in the shoulder, spinning him around top of the second guard. A quieter shot rings out; Jan shoots the third guard twice in the chest. Drivers run to their vehicles for their weapons or to find cover, as a rush of men wielding old weapons and pitchforks charges around the corner. Porter is up and holding one of the guard's weapons. He shoots. Men follow behind him as he runs at the trucks. The first guard kills one or two men from the ground before the crowd overruns him; I should have killed or disarmed him. But there is no perfection in carnage.

I go to Jan and we run back to our own vehicle. There are a few more men, latecomers, running down the hill. Maybe we have forty or fifty.

"Did you see Sheldon? Dad?" Jan asks.

I shake my head.

"What's the plan?" he asks.

"We are going to drive into the village."

"Wow. That's going to be interesting."

I know what he is thinking. "There is no other way. It's already a massacre up there."

Porter appears at the driver's door with a couple of others, looking as if they are ready to bludgeon us. "No, Jan is with me," I shout. Porter's face is ashen; he has a giant bloodstain on his shoulder.

"We have taken all the vehicles. Six," Porter says. "We have about twenty weapons. The plan is to have five or six men with weapons in the first few vehicles. Collins here is going to come with you, rear guard. He will help you for a bit, then he has to make sure his mother is okay."

"Great thanks. My friends, my dad, are in there. Not everyone is an enemy," I say. "They will have rifles; they will not be shooting anyone. Please. You cannot afford to shoot them. You need all the rifles you can get."

"What do they look like?" he says.

"I dunno. Like good people. Like a Dad." I can't even think what either is wearing or see their faces.

"You will recognise them by their actions," Jan says.

"Pass the word," Porter tells the man next to him, who runs off. "Make sure everyone knows," he calls after him.

"The other thing, which I forgot to tell you. There are vehicles coming through behind the shooters. I don't know how many. But at least four security trucks that will be well armed."

"Thanks." Porter nods and runs off to the lead vehicle.

We are at the back of the convoy. I don't want to be here, but men intent on protecting their families and their villages are eager to take priority positions without thinking of us.

The urgency as men jump between trucks and take up firing positions is palpable. As the vehicles move out, bodies of drivers and security guards become visible all over the ground, between the trucks. We drive and Jan winces as we bump over a corpse.

Collins stands with me behind Jan in the cab, cradling a guard's rifle and holding on as we start to get faster down the lane. He shakes and his breath is ragged.

"Do you shoot much?" I ask.

"First time," he says. "But don't worry. Everyone knows what you did. We are all going to do our best for you, and the village."

His reply surprises me. Humbled, I shut up making teenage small talk.

I reckon the vehicles in front would be in the village a full minute before us. The firing starts before the village is in view.

"We need to break off towards the upper side of the village if it's safe. That's the best chance of finding Sheldon. Dad is going to be at the heart of all the action in the centre," I say. "If we get Sheldon, then we come back to the centre."

"If we get to the Manse we can go right, it will take us one street past the square and up to the higher terrace," Collins explains. "It might be dangerous; that's where a lot of shots were coming from."

We run smack into the middle of a fierce gun battle; one vehicle is on fire and another has lost its wheels. The village men are out and shooting back from behind the vehicles; in the distance hunters are running, trying to take cover. The other RVs have continued up the hill towards the opposite end of the village. I look for Dad as we turn and we have to duck down as a few bullets thud into our vehicle. Collins has gone to the back and is shooting at something on the left side, as we turn right at the Manse.

"Where now?" Jan calls.

"Straight I think." I point. He floors the accelerator and swerves trying to avoid a number of bodies on the ground.

The surprise of the four hunters when we turn the corner is obvious. They are trying to figure out what's going on. I recognise Keshet's son and I see him look at me as Collin's shots make them dive into a nearby shop.

"Head down, Jan, and keep going!" I shout. We roar past and I watch Collins run to the back window and loose off another few shots to keep their head down. The guy is doing fine.

Two streets later we are at the edge of the village. The terrace. Towards the end, I see a figure in the distance, helping a woman and carrying a child. He is obviously not a hunter, but the child hides his face.

"Sheldon?" I hope, although he is coming from the wrong direction.

Jan turns right and heads towards the figures.

It is hard to tell who is the most surprised; I barely register the woman and her child. Shock, I realise, comes in many forms. I jump out of the vehicle before it stops. The shooting from the square stops and time stands still. I hit him; I pummel his chest until he gives the child to the woman and hugs me. I bawl something incomprehensible. To the woman, I must look like some deranged jealous wife, bald and covered in blood.

We push each other away to arms' length and stare. Jonathan takes his thumb and forefinger and gently closes my open mouth and rubs my head. He is smiling and his eyes are the happiest I've ever seen them.

"Happy eyes," I whisper as I kiss him gently on the lips.

"Jonathan, brilliant to see you, man." Jan appears from the side and hugs both of us. "We need to get out of here."

Collins is standing at the door when I look around and he nods to Jonathan. "You know Jon?" he says to me.

I nod. I can't speak. 'Since a whole lifetime ago' I think as I squeeze him again.

A few minutes later we are all on board and Jan is driving us up the last part of the terrace. We see no one else.

"I am going to jump off here," Collins announces. "I want to check on my folks." He offers us the gun.

"You should keep it," I say.

"No. You are going to need it more than me now. I live on the other side of these houses. Everything looks quieter here," he insists.

I take the rifle and pass it to Jonathan, and Collins jumps out while Jan turns the vehicle around.

"Where to?" Jan asks.

"We might as well head back down into the square," I say. "Slowly. Let's go slow and watch for others."

I start to explain to Jonathan what is happening now. There is no time to tell him everything since we last saw each other. He understands that Sheldon and Dad are somewhere in the hunting party and that the villagers are fighting back. He indicates by hand signal that we should join quickly. He's right; I'm stalling for time, greedy for a second lottery win, hoping for Sheldon to appear.

"Yes. We should move quickly," I say. "Jan, the square is back down and to the right. Can you find it?"

The vehicle accelerates down the hill.

"There are about forty hunters around," I tell Jonathan. "They shoot to kill." I look at the woman and child. "The bullets pass straight through the vehicle. Maybe they should lie on the floor?"

Jonathan nods and I watch as he signs something to the woman. Something passes between them; I catch a look. It only clicks when she signs back; the woman can't speak. She is attractive with a surprisingly intelligent face; why hadn't I noticed before? Now I am dumbstruck as they lie down on the floor. But I keep my questions to myself, and my feelings hidden.

At the square, some sort of sick order has emerged. Enemy lines. We can see the battle positions of the two groups of fighters. The hunters have grouped around their trucks that had entered the village behind them. They are keeping up a steady stream of fire, but their targets are no longer fish in a barrel. The villagers are a main static group and five or six small groups, slowly moving through the streets and houses that they know so well, firing sporadically; no doubt fearful of running out of ammunition.

A few shots hit our vehicle as we stop alongside another truck and the main group of villagers. Porter is there looking through binoculars.

"They are retreating," he tells me. "We have someone they want." He points and there on the ground is Keshet's son, tied up.

"Keep him," I say immediately. "Tell them to leave and he will be released."

"That's what we thought; they know we have him and are ready to release him," he says. "But do you know this man? They brought him out for a swap." He hands me the binoculars. Keshet and two of his goons were standing behind a man with a hood on. "That's Keshet, this man's father."

"No I mean..." He doesn't finish. Keshet yanks the hood off and my Father blinks in the light, gasping for air through his nose. He is gagged and bound.

"Dad!" I cry out through pain and shock. Why didn't I see this coming?

"I thought it might be, they didn't take the hood off until now. They were trying to pass him off as one of the villagers," Porter says.

"Keshet must have recognised me," I say. I don't know how; the last time I saw him I had long hair.

"Don't worry. We do the swap," Porter says. "We owe you. We have men posted around. It will be hard for them to do anything."

"Okay," I say. I hand him back the glasses.

I go and explain to Jonathan who nods. He goes straight to Porter, points to himself and then Keshet's son. Porter looks confused for a second. Jonathan pulls the son to his feet, points the rifle between his shoulder blades and marches him to the side of the truck where he can be seen.

I should have guessed. My unselfish Jonathan would do anything for my Dad or me. For a second I feel my Mum standing beside me saying if she had a son, that's how she'd want him to be. Tears flow freely down my face from the tension.

On the other side of the square they push Dad to the front and make it clear they are ready to swap by walking forward a few steps, point at Dad and wave.

"Okay," Porter says. "We are in business. But be careful. We cannot trust them. March slowly towards them. Make sure you time it well; get to the centre of the square at the same time. That's roughly halfway."

Jonathan nods.

"Keep them covered as you return, don't turn your back. My men will be watching, but retreat quickly," Porter says.

After an initial stutter, the two opposite parties walk across the square towards each other. No one else moves. Somewhere a bird calls, complaining about the silence that has descended from so much gunfire before. I try to see the man who is behind Dad, pushing him along.

My heart is in my mouth, I can see Dad's expression as they reach halfway, and his eyes are wide as he is swapped for Keshet's son. Dad is trying to work the gag off by moving his jaw and neck. Jonathan walks backwards as fast as he can. He holds Dad's arm, pulling Dad faster until they are almost jogging. When they get close to the barricade, two of Porter's men jump out and pull Dad and Jon into cover.

I run to Dad, just as one man unties his hands and the other undoes his gag. Dad's face doesn't look like a man grateful for rescue. "They have Sheldon!" he shouts. He knows how much it is going to hurt me. I am stunned for a second.

Jon comes up and Dad hugs him and kisses the top of his head. "Thanks, son." To Jonathan it is the highest accolade. He looks over at me, but I am looking at the other side already.

"They want to swap someone else," Porter says. "We don't have any more of theirs."

I take the glasses; it's Sheldon, with a bloodied face.

"They should have kept me." Dad is at my side. "I'm sorry."

"No, it's fine, Dad. We just have to see what they want," I say.

I turn to Porter. "Could some of your men be holding someone or something?"

He shakes his head. "No. It's not possible. I would know."

I look back to the glasses. It seems they had put Sheldon's hood back on and lined him up with two others.

"They just brought out another two men in hoods. They must be villagers," I say.

"Don't worry, I will go myself, and ask them what they want," Porter says. "Get me a white cloth from one of the vans," he says to a man next to him.

Keshet appears in the glasses. He is standing with his son. Both appear to be smiling.

"What do they want?" I murmur as I watch. "We don't have anything to give them."

Seconds later, the son lifts a pistol and presses it against the hood of one of the men. I am no longer sure who is who. I step forward; I don't put the glasses down. "Okay, take it easy. We will give you whatever you want," I mutter.

I don't hear myself scream as Keshet's son shoots all three men, one after the other, in the sides of their heads. They crumple to the ground like puppets whose strings had been cut.

I start to run but Dad is too quick. He holds me around the waist and we both go down on the ground. And he clings to me until I can't fight anymore.

# CHAPTER THIRTEEN

## Win-lose

The hunters begin to withdraw. I watch through an angry blur of tears as men run to vehicles and they cover each other as they start to move out. I dry my tears and try to stop shaking.

"It's okay. We will go as soon as it's safe." Dad reads my body language and is frightened that I'd run there too soon. Jonathan appears at my side and he signs to Dad to grip me before I realise his intention. They are going to hold me and Jon is going to go instead.

"Let me go. I need to go," I beg.

"Wait. Let Jon go first," Dad says. He grips me and looks desperately into my eyes. "Please."

Jonathan is already running. The last of the hunters' vehicles are disappearing. Jonathan is just over halfway when the bombs start dropping into the square.

"Mortars!" someone screams. "Pull back!"

A direct hit on the vehicle furthest away. Men jump out covered in flame.

Dad pulls me hard by my arm as I turn to watch Jonathan running back, blown over by a blast. He is quickly up again and head down, pumping his arms and legs to get back to us and off the wide open square.

There is something sinister about the regularity and increasing ferocity of the mortars. It is simple revenge, I think through the noise. They just want to destroy as much as they can because they were beaten.

"Aircraft!" Porter shouts as two jets screech overhead firing rockets up the main street and into a building.

"Go! Everyone! To the manse!" Porter screams above the din of high explosive.

Jonathan runs into our trailer; moments later Jan jumps from the cab with the baby and Jonathan has his arm around the woman. The aircraft have turned and are strafing all the way across the square and up the street. Our vehicle explodes as shells rip through it.

Twice, I check to see if the others are behind us, and we run into the ruins of the manse with them following. I am conscious of the whump-whump of mortars ripping up the square and I think of Sheldon lying out there amongst the rubble.

Porter appears at Dad's side and leads us to the hidden entry and down the stone steps into the cellar. The place is full now. Men stand with their families as if guarding them; others stand without family and from their faces you can tell whether they are bachelors or have lost someone. The noise from outside is muffled and contrasts with the acute sound of a child sobbing somewhere. The low fearful explosions in the ground mix with the ache of a sob that came from deep in the chest and barks out in the air.

Some people are watching us; we are the strangers. Maybe they think I had brought this trouble on them by helping them fight.

Perhaps some think the hunters would have left earlier if it hadn't been for me.

After fifteen minutes people start to look up. The sound gets less and then stops.

"Everyone wait. The men will check around the village before anyone moves." Porter sends a few men into the tunnels to connect with the others and check the town. He must feel it is over. I can see the pain etched on his face. He finally sits down and opens his jacket to look at his wound. Sara appears and takes over. I kneel beside him as Sara starts to undo his temporary bandage. "I am sorry if I caused additional problems for your people," I say.

"Don't be silly, girl," he grunts. "The people are looking at you because they know you saved me and allowed us to bring the vehicles into the square."

"Some say the Good Man sent you," Sara says. And I am surprised again. The only person I had ever heard use that expression was an old Scottish woman. She used it often instead of God.

"When do you think we can go up?" I ask.

"Soon. Very soon," Porter says. "But lass." We look straight at each other. "Don't expect too much. For your own sake."

I nod.

"Were you close?" he asks, wincing as Sara prods his wound.

"Like my Prise de tasses," I say. "But I never told him."

Dad and Jonathan are on either side of me when we come to the surface. Jonathan carries the rifle just in case, although Porter told us the hunt has withdrawn completely. The smell of cordite hangs in the air with the silence. Debris scattered from the explosions crunches under our feet. A child cries in the distance and somewhere an animal is yelping in pain.

We go down the lane and across the street to the edge of the square.

"Bloody bastards," Dad says.

Jonathan turns around and around beside me, looking at the devastation.

The square is black and pitted with craters. Buildings are torn and smashed. A few fires burn and smoke plumes spiral silently in aftermath. A butterfly flutters past like a sign from God. I can hardly make out its colours through a flood of tears.

I start to run. They are expecting it and both come close and trot alongside, except when craters make it impossible, they have to go around or behind and I get ahead. I let out one big sob and feel my heart has leapt out. The guys close in and hold my arms to stop me collapsing as we reach the spot where the hunters had last been. There is nothing left; I see Jonathan looking at a child's shoe complete with foot. But he doesn't say anything and I pretend not to see. The ground is pockmarked with multiple shell holes. Why have they done this? There is no reason except a form of revenge. High explosive has decimated everything; nothing bigger than the shoe remains.

Dad drags a dirty gold chain out of a small pile of rubble, and holds it up. He doesn't know whether to keep it or throw it. Somehow doing either is an insult to whoever had owned it.

"Show me where you pulled it out," I say.

He points and I bend down and sift the stones and dirt with my fingers until my nails are black. A gold locket appears. When I hold it I break down completely. All the time I wanted to know what was inside; now I don't want to know.

Crying, I take the chain from Dad; he tries to clean it but I won't let him. I thread the locket and let him fasten the chain around my neck.

"It's his?" Dad asks softly. I nod. "Why don't you let me look inside?" he offers. I shake my head.

Jonathan comes and puts his arm around me.

"Let's go home," I say.

# CHAPTER FOURTEEN

## Grass Roots

We don't stay with the village even one night; we want to get away from this place. We'll take our sorrows with us and they have their own dead to bury. We are strangers again in our own private grief. I walk around doing things pretty much in a daze. Mum is by my side, but stays silently. Sheldon doesn't appear. And I have nothing to say to him yet.

For the sake of all of us, we need to move on.

There are only two serviceable vehicles; we pick the least damaged and siphon fuel from the others to give us a full tank. Jonathan is helping but for a frightening moment I wasn't sure he was coming with us, until I saw him kiss good-bye to the mother and her child. She looked devastated; I looked away when she looked at me. I have seen enough heartache.

Sara comes and gives us food for the journey. Porter shakes hands and hugs me. "I am sorry for you, Robyn, for what you lost here. But I thank you for what you gave us."

He hands me three white stones, each with a different symbol.

"What are they?" I ask.

"Nobody knows. Superstition," he says. "They are banned by the state. People say that when you have all twelve different stones, only then you will know. We pass them between us as tokens of esteem.

These three belong to our village. The men agreed you should have them. It would make me proud if you accepted them."

"Thank you. I don't know what to say."

"You are going back home?"

"Yes."

"It's not here is it?"

"No," I say.

"Well I wish you peace and happiness, Robyn. We will not forget you."

"Nor will I forget you or this village." No matter what, I realise that this village is and always will be part of my story. A chapter that never got finished. Leaving it feels right and wrong at the same time. My saddest moment is realising that I understand what it must be like for soldiers to leave their fallen, so many miles from home; for the second time in my life I see the poor substitute of a granite or marble memorial.

It's dark when we finally are on board and turning the vehicle onto the road. Dad and Jan are going to sleep and drive between them; Dad takes the first stint. A number of villagers come out to wave us off; many do not, but who could blame them?

It isn't far to Subtopia, we have learned. Maybe six hours to where the Factories are. But we have to pass the border between Outland and Subtopia. We haven't figured out how we are going to do that yet.

Dad explains we need to see Huptoou, before we can go to one of the factories and configure the machine. Besides, we are going to need help to get in close to the machine. It will be guarded.

While we drive, Jonathan takes paper and explains what had happened and how he came to be at the village. I read it aloud for Dad and Jan. Jonathan had been working with Huptoou, raiding the farms and sabotaging the factories. The Euny didn't have access to guns, so Jonathan was teaching them how to fence. They had built up a regular schedule of daring raids in the evenings or early mornings. They would rely on stealth to get them close enough to surprise and overrun the guards.

During a raid, when Jonathan, Huptoou and many Euny were away, Keshet had escaped. They had no idea how; Huptoou was convinced there was no traitor in the group. But they couldn't explain how Keshet had killed four Euny guards and disappeared without help.

They had gone immediately to Keshet's home. Because of his promise to me, Huptoou was determined to recapture the evil man and Jonathan was worried Keshet could put the rest of us in danger as we travelled in Metro. They didn't recapture Keshet, but they met Sara who advised them to go out of town for a bit. She heard Keshet was bringing Government troops. Huptoou refused to go and Jonathan accompanied the woman because she wanted to introduce him to someone who would teach him signing. Jonathan had been at the village two weeks and was surprised when we turned up. The story made us feel lucky, as if some things were going right for us.

But Sheldon's death sat like a black apparition reminding us of what we had lost and what was still at stake. We all sat silent at the end of the story.

After a few minutes, Dad returns to concentrating on the driving and Jan goes off to get some sleep.

I should be exhausted. My mind is numb with anguish, and 'what-ifs' and 'regrets' worm through the mess behind my eyes. After a hot shower, a hard scrub and a change of clothes, I sit in the back of the trailer with Jonathan and talk. I tell him about Metro, the sword training, the BNW Club, the apartment and the fight with the factory guys. There are no stories without Sheldon. He is everywhere. When I close my eyes I can see him laughing, somehow mixed in with the men I had killed. Perhaps, if I hadn't killed anyone... I leave the thought unfinished. I need to stop thinking.

"Are you okay?" I ask Jonathan. He nod and takes the pad.

'I am more worried about you. It's been a tough time.'

"Yes. I killed some people," I say.

'It doesn't matter. You had to. When we go back home we will be normal again,' he writes.

"The woman back at Gubrath...?" I ask.

'A friend. A very good friend. I came to like her more and more. And her daughter. But there was nothing in it. She was teaching me signing. The community made me welcome. They told me they had been hunted, but I didn't believe it. I thought maybe they had got mixed up in some sort of conflict.'

"Oh, I completely forgot when I was telling you about Marlene, the training. I got you something." I bring the sword and shield from my bag.

I put the band on his wrist, get him to stand up and switch the shield on. He still looks bemused, so I fire up Yuenu. His eyes light up; then he jumps back when I tap his shield with Yuenu.

"Ha. Now you're interested. I carried this for weeks for you," I say and he looks up, understanding that I fully expected to see him again.

'Does it cut?' he signals with a swipe and a frown.

"Please be extremely careful when you light it up in here. It's not like an ordinary blade; you cannot rest it on your thigh," I tell him as I hand the sword to him and show him where to press.

"Try this." I throw a cushion up in the air and he swipes clean through. We switch the swords off and fall on the sofa. The smell of burning feathers causes Dad to shout through from the cab. But we are too busy laughing in a cloud of white that we just can't answer. It is the first time I have seen Jonathan laugh with his mouth open since they took his tongue. I hug him and blow feathers off my nose with upwards puffs of my lips.

Sleep isn't easy as the vehicle bounces over the roads. Jan is driving now. Dad is in a corner, drinking hot tea and studying a notepad; he looks skinny, wasted. Jonathan is sleeping next to me and I am so tired I can't sleep, but I can see pictures. My memories contain huge sickening chasms of guilt and blame that my dreams bounce over in time to the vehicle.

I remember that I had taken the locket off when I showered. I need to go get it.

As I get up and stretch, Dad looks up and gives a wan smile.

"Can you just check Jan?"

I nod and go straight into the cab.

"I was thinking. This vehicle is going to be very noticeable in Subtopia," Jan says. "Remember, they mostly have old stuff. Everyone is going to see us and remember us."

"You mean if they don't rob us," I say.

"Exactly. Sheldon and I struggled to stay out of trouble from the gangs there," he says. "Sorry. I didn't mean to..."

"No. It's not your fault. We cannot avoid his name," I say, wiping a silent tear. "I just miss him."

"We both do," Jan says. "We got very close in our first days; we relied on each other to survive."

"Lights up ahead," I interrupt.

"It looks like a small town."

"Okay pull over and I will get Dad," I say. "We may be better to go around."

Dad comes and we study the navigation system maps.

"As you thought, it's not showing on the map," Dad says. "And there is no alternative route without backtracking a hundred or so miles."

"And we don't know what we might find on an alternative route," I say.

"Yep, and we are close to the border here. Let's drive." Jan turns the truck back onto the road and heads for the town.

Jonathan joins us, rubbing sleep from his eyes. "A border town," I tell him.

"Okay, let's just be prepared for anything," Dad says as we cross from the dark into the town lights.

It looks like there are only a couple of long streets and a few cross streets. The main drag is packed with shops, cabaret clubs, casinos and bars, everything lit up and full of people. There are plenty of vehicles around, but all private, nothing official looking. I notice a couple of small shuttle types that we'd used in Metro, coming and going behind the buildings. A number of people walking have pistols tucked into the back of their belts and look as if they could use them. A couple talk on some sort of communicator.

"Where do they all come from?" I ask. "Nobody has money around here. Subtopia?"

"It's possible. We are not so far from the border. Maybe people come across to do stuff they cannot do in Subtopia," Jan says. "Guns, gambling, vice and phones."

"Well at least it has a 24hr fuel stop and grocery," Dad says. "And it is the kind of place that will know ways to cross the border."

We fuel up first and buy a few groceries, snacks and juice mostly. Dad asks the shopkeeper which bar we'd get information in. The man lifts his eyebrows and says, "Just about any bar where you are willing to pay." But then he recommends 'Pearls' in the middle of the drag. Dad asks if it is safe and the man just snorts and turns away.

We park the rig outside the door. The disadvantage is everyone could see it; the advantage is we could get away in a hurry if we have to.

I insist that I'm coming; I simply don't want Dad and Jon to go alone. Jan agrees to stay in the trailer and guard it with a rifle, ready to come to our aid if we have any trouble. We have a pistol and our two swords between the three of us.

'Pearls' is a stereotypical cheap strip bar, smoky, dimly lit, sticky floors and men staring up at half-dressed harlots grinding on a dirty stage. The floor is dark wood, scuffed and stained by years of business, and the walls are burnished metal all the way around. The stairs going up at the side with the piano beneath them remind me of some old movie I once watched one lazy Sunday morning.

A few drinkers watch us as we come in, smile lazily in our direction. The barman stops polishing glasses and stares as we come to the bar.

"Beers?" he asks.

Jon nods like a strong silent type and lays down a couple of glass beads. The beers are popped and slide in front of us in seconds.

"What's the town called?" I ask the barman.

"Noname," he replies. And I have no idea if he is serious.

"We are wondering about crossing the border," Dad says.

"Crossing the border is illegal without the proper papers," he answers.

"Is that so?" Dad says. "We were just wondering where people would go who didn't have papers."

"If there were any such people. They'd probably be wise to talk to the man sitting over at that table. He used to be a pilot."

"Thanks," Dad says. "What's his name?"

"Noname," the barman says. Dad purses his lips, frowns and nods and I nearly burst out laughing.

So we don't ask the guy at the table his name, or give him ours. It seems people don't do names here.

"Sit down," he says when Dad mentions the border.

"I got a good nose," he says. "There are so many undercover here, even using the word 'border' can get you arrested. You guys are not border undercover, and yet I cannot place you. That makes me curious."

"You are right. We are not from here," Dad says.

"If you had been you wouldn't have parked that rig out there," he says. "There are one or two checking it already."

We automatically look out the window.

"Oh great, you all look together. Make it obvious," he says. "I guess I better watch myself around you green-casts. Otherwise I get me arrested."

"Sorry," Dad says.

"No problem. Now try again. There are two men sitting in the corner nearest the door. Undercover," he says. "And the guy with the dark orange shirt on behind me. Undercover."

"I see," Dad says.

"Much better. You guys are catching on already," Noname says. "But your lack of street smart tells me I can trust you; so no harm done."

"We need to get into Subtopia," Dad says.

"Well it's easier than getting into Metro, but you ain't going anywhere in that thing."

"The vehicle?"

"Well of course the vehicle," the man says. "Besides, there is a huge activity at the border, seems they are looking for some people. Just like you, come to think about it. Not even the small illegal shuttlecraft are risking the journey. You are the reason the smugglers have to stay at home." He laughs aloud, for the benefit of the whole room. I realise that he's known all along who we are.

Dad wises up fast; I am impressed, he talks the same as the guy.

"What are they promising as a reward for these people?" Dad asks.

"Alive only as it happens," Noname muses. "They must have some knowledge that they cannot get out of them dead."

"How much?"

"Four centurion in total. Can you imagine?"

"And how would people recognise these excessively valuable citizens?" Dad asks.

"Perhaps you should ask the guys who followed you in here. Beards at the bar; or the rather weaselly-looking characters to my left," he says. "Need I go on?"

With a sinking feeling, I realise that nearly everyone is watching us surreptitiously, either while reading their communicators, squinting from under a hat or in the reflection of the metal on the walls.

"And they are not coming over because?" Dad asks.

"Because they'd all have to fight each other. And the prize might be damaged, is my guess," the man says. "Is there anyone in the vehicle?"

Dad nods. "One boy."

"Best bring him in. They will try to take anyone who is separate from the herd," Noname says.

Jonathan stands up. I see him grip the sword in his pocket. He looks at Dad, who nods for him to go.

"Why should we trust you?" Dad continues.

"If you can pay me, you can trust me. If you cannot then you shouldn't. Without a guarantee, then I am just like all the rest, a man dreaming to get his hands on the kind of money that will make me comfortable in Metro or even Serfin, who knows. A man likes to dream." He smiles directly at me.

"We can pay. What can you do?" Dad asks.

Jan and Jon return and sit down. Jon is carrying the rifle. I'm not sure if this is a good thing or a bad thing at this moment.

"Good, good," Noname says. He looks at each of us in turn, thinking. "There are two problems. The first is to get you out of here.

Nobody wants you to leave and I am aware that a couple have called for reinforcements. One is on an illegal communicator even as we speak. The second problem is to get you across the border, where every border guard and his boss are dreaming to be the ones who catch you."

"What do you suggest?" Dad asks.

"Well, whatever we do, we have to be quick, before one of these dimwits gets brave, or worse, gets the bright idea to collaborate with the others and agree to share the money."

"Will they do that?"

"They could have a truce, but I'd be betting it wouldn't last longer than a spit on a griddle," Noname says spitting on the floor.

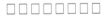

"You get us out of here safely and across the border, we will give you the equivalent of twice the reward; half when we exit here, half when we are safe on the other side. If one of us gets hurt, the fee is reduced."

"Okay, but you understand the journey will be on foot. The best I can do is getting you out of here and into the woods close to the border. Part of area is swamp; I will guide you through that. A friend of mine will disrupt the listening pods and we will cross together."

"When do we move?" Dad asks.

"Do you have anything in the vehicle that you need?" Noname says.

"Like what?" Jan asks.

"Like money to pay me?"

"There are some necessities we'd need to get," Dad says.

"Could one person carry everything?"

"Yes," Dad tells him.

"Okay, in a few minutes, I am going to summon my ship. We will get on," he says.

"And the stuff in the vehicle?"

"Ah that's the good part. While I am bringing the ship, one of you will have exactly two minutes to get into the RV, pick up everything you need and climb out on the roof. I'd advise lying flat at that point."

"Do we know where everything we want is in the vehicle?" Dad asks. "Jon?"

Jonathan our constant volunteer stands up. I tell him where to find my bag. My cuff is in there; I am loath to leave it. Dad wants his notebook and Jan suggests some coats and refreshments if we are going to yomp through swamps in the middle of the night. I have my money belt on; Yuenu is lying snugly in my trouser pocket.

Noname produces a keypad and types.

A man in a long dirty buttoned-up coat stands up and blocks the way as Jonathan crosses the floor. He draws an ugly looking bowie knife and licks it, then wipes it once, twice, on the sleeve of his jacket. Jon doesn't hesitate; he draws his sword and faces the man. I'm not sure if the man had seen a light-sword before, but he doesn't back down. Jon strikes. He could have killed or injured the man;

instead he hits the knife, cutting the blade off, and slashes the man's long coat open from collar to pocket. The man jumps back.

Three men with guns stand in the doorway now. The music stops and girls get off the stage. The place falls deathly silent.

"Jon!" Dad calls. Jonathan walks backwards to the table, switches the sword off and sits down. The men know we have a sting now. We've just lost my personal favourite weapon, the art of surprise.

"Unfortunate," Noname says. He bangs on his keyboard then gives up. "They are not letting you out and the signal to my shuttle isn't working."

"What now?" Dad says, looking around at the increasing menace in the room.

Noname stands up and announces loudly. "Sorry guys. Cannot help you. Things are too hot for me." With that he picks up his bag and leaves via a back door at the side of the bar but not before he winks at me.

□□□□□□□□

Three groups of men have moved to the centre of the bar to talk together. Others are considering their play. Who is going to move first?

Two men with weapons levelled come to our table and one speaks loud enough for the room to hear. "One way or another, you will be coming with some of us." He stares at Jon and Jan, looks at Dad. I am mostly ignored. "It's probably best you give up these weapons you boys have."

If you could imagine the fury of a lioness protecting her cubs, it might partially explain the deadliness of my reaction. There is no way the men I care for are going to be taken to Keshet or the Factory men. I'm not losing anyone else. My leap into the air off my seat, and my downward stroke with Yuenu, are powered by feelings that I have never known before. I take both men's arms off at the elbow before their brains could send a signal to their fingers to pull the trigger.

Dad is up like a shot. Jan levels his rifle. Bottles roll off the table and Jonathan appears beside me. I hear his shield switch on; it's hardly visible in the light. I do the same and we shuffle to the left in front of Dad and Jan.

"You need us alive," I yell. "We know that we are worth nothing dead. So there's your problem." I kick one of the guys lying on the floor. I see a few men look at each other. "You cannot shoot us. So unless you think you can take weapons off of us, back off. We are getting out of here."

Nobody moves. Everyone is waiting for something that they know but we don't.

"They may have called Keshet," Jan surmises.

"Stay together," I say. We step around the table as a group behind the shields.

Suddenly men start leaving. They get up and go through the door quickly. I turn and see the barman exit a bar door at the back. The girls are already gone.

Dad notices as well. "We need to get out of here. Keeping moving. Back to the vehicle."

The first canister comes from behind us and explodes in clouds of smoke. The second comes in the window and lands in front of us.

"They are trying to smoke us out!" yells Dad.

"They have locked the door!" Jan shouts.

"Cover your mouths," Dad says looking for a way out. A whiff of the gas makes me dizzy. They are not trying to smoke us out; the plan is to put us to sleep, incapacitate us, but keep us alive. I look at Jonathan and Jan. Both are struggling, trying to sip a few breaths by holding their shirts to their mouth. I feel myself start to go under.

The crash is deafening in my befuddled mind; it feels like the roof is caving in as wood splinters explode around us. The shuttle has come straight through the window in reverse. The gas swirls about, pushed by clouds of fresh air from outside. I can't see or hear properly. I feel Dad grab me; I look at his face, not understanding. Suddenly Noname is in front of me winking and pulling me on board. I look around dizzily and Jon is helping Dad and Jan up, before climbing up himself. The door closes and the gas that had come in the craft with us is being pumped out and replaced with fresh air. We nudge back through the hole in the window.

"Do we need things from your vehicle?" Noname shouts from the pilot seat.

"No!" shouts Dad.

"Yes. We do!" I argue, head still swimming.

Jonathan springs up, goes to Noname and points to the roof of the vehicle.

"There is no need!" Dad shouts.

"Dad there is," I say.

"What?"

"I cannot remember."

Jonathan and the Noname look at me.

"Trust me," I say and pass out.

I don't know this until much later. Jonathan risked himself again; he entered the vehicle from the roof hatch and fought a couple of men who had broken in and were lying in wait. One managed to stab him in the leg. Jonathan retrieved my bag, and a bag with water and some basic supplies, climbed on the roof again. He threw the bags up and launched himself inside the hovering craft while men below were scrambling to their own vehicles at the back of the bar.

I wake up as we bank around hard; Jonathan is gripping me and holding onto the craft to stop us tumbling. Dad is up front with Noname and Jan is holding on close by.

"What's happening?" I ask as we swoop in an even tighter turn. My head is still spinning.

"Three craft managed to chase us. One crashed somewhere back there," Jan says. "Our pilot is flying for his life, I think. If they manage to force us down, they will kill him, that's for sure."

That explains the flying; he has nothing to lose and everything to gain.

"Lights are going off," shouts Noname. The cabin plunges into darkness. We run with only a few lights showing on the dashboard, for about five minutes. I struggle up to look out. There is enough light from a half-moon shining through the clouds to see the shadows flitting by. We are low. Noname looks as though he is enjoying himself and winks at me again. He turns us suddenly, up in a one hundred and eighty degrees loop and back the way we came. He takes us along a small river, so close to the dark water I can see the disturbance shining on the moonlit surface.

"We have lost them. I am going to try to get us to the trees," Noname says. "We are running on vapour."

Moments later I feel the craft shake.

"Strap in or hold something. We are going in," Noname says.

Dad pulls me to his chair and fastens the straps over two of us. There is no time to check Jon and Jan as we smash through the undergrowth, breaking branches and saplings as we burrow into the forest. I am still praying there are no big trees ahead in the dark when we finally shudder to a bone-breaking halt.

"Everyone okay?" Dad says.

"We need to move very fast. Get away from the craft. They will have registered the crash and be here in minutes," Noname says.

Moments later we are following Noname, wading knee deep in muddy water between silver saplings, heading away from the crash as fast as possible. I carry my precious pack, but still can't remember what I needed, but am glad we have reasonable supplies of fresh water despite the weight. Mo's words echo in my head. The most important thing is water. And the day you will learn that is the day and night that you will go without. On a long hike with people chasing me, I'd choose water over a weapon.

Jon now has his arm around Jan, being helped along. It is only then that I realise he's been injured. I look, Dad is carrying the rifle. I take Jan's pack off him as punishment for getting Jonathan injured. I grit my teeth and push hard through the horrible smelly swamp.

A light flashes in front of us through the trees; everyone freezes, tries to stop splashing. It comes from a clearing just ahead. The light flashes again in a sequence.

"It's our friend who is going to jam the listening pods on the border." Noname rushes forward to meet him. The men hug and exchange a few whispered words, and Noname beckons us forward.

"He will want his first payment now." Dad says.

As I started to reach through my clothes into my money belt, I feel the wind of a small craft rush past. Lights off and silent it swung into the clearing, and a shadow hanging in the door shoots Noname and his associate, one after the other. It happens so fast, but Dad already has the rifle off and is on his knees aiming up. He ignores the man at the door and peppers the cab. The craft rears up as the pilot tries to get away. Dad keeps firing even as the craft plunges into the ground a few hundred feet away and explodes.

Noname and his associate don't move.

Jan goes and looks at the bodies and bends over them. I wonder what he is doing until I see him take an electronics box from the associate.

"This is going to bring people. We need to get away from here," Dad says. "Any idea which direction?"

It is Jonathan who takes the lead and limps quickly across the clearing, leaving us to run in his wake.

As we walk, I think how terrible it is to die for a cause but be without a name.

☐☐☐☐☐☐☐☐

The border is another sapling forest, signposted with skull and cross-bone warning signs. 'Area is Mined.' Noname had not told us this; he had planned to lead us across a live mine-field. I curse him then regret cursing someone who gave his life.

"Okay. We have time. Let's think about this," Dad says.

Jan comes forward with the electronics box. He switches it on and puts the strap around his head. He turns around and the machine whines. He turns another way and it is silent. He plays around for a minute or two, switching a couple of switches and walking towards the border.

"I think I have got it," he says. "It does two things. It can steer us between the mines. And I think it can squelch the listening pods."

"What's the catch?" I say.

"I have no way of knowing if either is working," Jan says. "Kind of like playing a video game for the first time. There is an initial learning."

"In a minefield?" I say waiting for a smart reply.

Jonathan and I both hear the chilling howl at the same time. We know what it is: WolfCats coming from behind us. I stare at Jonathan; I see him tense. He's not yet shared the story of how he escaped them the first time.

"We have no choice, Dad. These sounds you hear are WolfCats. We are dead if we stay here."

Jan says wait and walks in between the trees. He turns, moves in further, changes direction again, goes forward always watching the dials and listening to the sound. He comes back the same way.

"I think I have it. We have to walk in single file. Hold on and try to stay in each other's footprints," he says. "Whoever is on the back will be in most danger as they may deviate most from my footsteps."

Jonathan grabs me and pushes me behind Jan. I look over my shoulder; he is pushing Dad onto me. He holds onto Dad's backpack and deliberately takes the most dangerous position. WolfCats howl from across the forest behind indicating they are getting closer.

"Ready?" Jan says. "Keep looking down at the footsteps of the guy in front."

We set off. I imagine us being blown up and all our body bits hanging from the trees. 'Hey, where are you,' my head would call out to my torso. I start to laugh. Dad thinks I am crying and squeezes my shoulder, which makes me worse. If anyone were listening on the listening pods they'd be wondering what the hysterical sniggering sounds are.

The first WolfCat crashes into the forest about five minutes later. I hear its low growl and imagine I can smell it. I hear Jon's sword go on. There is a rush through the bush, then silence. It is passing us on our left. I think I see its eyes.

"It's through the trees to our left," I tell Jan.

"Okay." He turns us tight right. "Careful. Step exactly as I do. We are passing between some mines."

Again I catch the eyes of the WolfCat as it stalks around with us, before it charges. There are two explosions and hot meat rains in the trees for a few seconds, setting off another couple of mines close by. The sound leaves my ears ringing. After five minutes we come out on the other side. We can hear WolfCats howling at the perimeter. Their handlers must have held the rest back.

□□□□□□□□

Despite Jonathan's poorly leg, we make excellent time to the Great Park just as dawn is breaking. To Jan it must feel like being back at the beginning again, one big circle. Jonathan, like me, would be recalling the underground tunnel, I think.

Luckily there are few people around, I am aware that we are wearing clothes that make us stand out. I fear our luck has to run out eventually. A couple of sky patrols pass high overhead, don't stop and bank around into the distance. Jonathan takes us along the side of the river where I had hidden the first night with Sheldon and Jan. I had slept close to Sheldon that night and I remembered feeling his heart beating as he kept me warm. Two hearts in pieces now.

Jonathan passes the tunnel exit where I had climbed out without him. The day that I had left him down there with the WolfCats. Guilt whispers over my skin and I murmur 'sorry' under my breath. He doesn't notice.

It seems he knows an easier and quicker way to get to the Euny. After twenty minutes he leads us down closer to the edge of the river, a culvert. We stop and listen; only a constant trickle of water echoing in the tunnel breaks the silence. Dad and Jan exchange glances. Nobody speaks.

Jonathan signals and we follow him into the tunnel. After a couple of turns and a few minutes' walk we emerge overlooking the Euny lair. The large cavern where the Euny had first taken Jonathan and me has been destroyed. It is difficult to see in limited light; it looks like tunnels are blocked, the roof and walls are caved in, in most places. Jonathan signs for us to wait, hobbles down a pile of rubble and across the cavern and disappears in the gloom. We hear him try to move something then we see his silhouette limping back across to another doorway where he manages to switch on a few dim lights.

We start to climb down. The place is completely deserted and has been destroyed. A smell of death hangs rotting in the air where the ventilation is bad.

Jonathan's face is infused with anger; I can see the hurt and pain. His friends have been taken. And he can't say what he is thinking.

"They were all here?" I ask.

He nods.

"Were they attacked?"

He gives a slight shrug, and his expression says, 'I think so. Maybe. I feel broken.'

"Do you know where they might have gone or been taken?"

Almost resigned, he nods again; his eyes are dull.

"I think he might," says Dad. "And it's not good news."

# CHAPTER FIFTEEN

## Soylent Process

Nobody wants to rest for long. But I make everyone sit just inside the tunnel where the air is fresh. They all drink water and eat some sweet milk biscuits. I catch Dad laughing at me as he watches me insisting to Jan that he needs to eat and drink. Jonathan refuses to let me look at his wound. I understand that he doesn't want to disturb the bandage. After twenty minutes we are moving again.

Jonathan leads us across the river out of the main suburbs. He walks with the stoic gait of a wounded soldier returning to his regiment; his jaw is set like a steel trap and he is breathing through his teeth. We are all exhausted, but it is him that I worry about most. I give him my share of the water without him being aware.

Further away from the more populated areas, the chance of meeting dangerous people, any people, becomes less. There is still some danger from overhead patrols. There is little cover but then again the patrols don't expect many people to be out here. My tension becomes less the further away from the Euny lair and I guess everyone feels the same.

We pass derelict buildings and streets of empty houses, which give way to a few warehouses and abandoned factories. It is hard to guess the type of industries, but I imagine there would have been whole communities and generations of families working here in the past.

As we walk I try to figure out what industry might have crashed here. Giant cranes, enormous steel doors, gantries and brick factories six stories high and thirty windows wide. Rope works? Sugar mills? Engineering?

"Over this hill?" Dad says in reply to Jonathan's signals. "Okay, not much further."

We crest the brow of the hill after a steep climb up a narrow wind, to look out over a flat land. It looks like acres of reclaimed polder.

Row upon row of long windowless barns sits in dozens of monotonous grey fields stretching into an infinite perspective. It is loosely fenced all the way around as far as the eye can see. We duck under the chain-link fences to the side of the closest buildings. A strange dusty smell wafts on the morning air and makes me want to sneeze.

"It's a type of incubator farm," Dad recalls. "Iain mentioned them." He looks at Jonathan who nods in agreement. "They keep the boys here."

"This is what you and Huptoou have been raiding?" I ask Jonathan, who nods. "And the factories?" He nods again. He stares at me to read my expression; his face is sombre and somehow feral and in that instant I realise that he has some particular empathy for these boys, and a smouldering anger worse than I originally thought.

Jonathan indicates that there are no guards, so we go inside. Each barn holds two hundred boys of similar age, who are chained in rows in long feeding and sleeping stations.

"It looks like the chains are automatic," Dad says. He points to where each chain runs into the wall. "They extend their reach in the morning, letting them get to the troughs. Probably winding back in the night to pull them onto their sleeping place."

The boys are castrated and glossectomised, from what I can see.

Giant wall-mounted TVs spew a constant diet of movies, cartoon, mild pornography and interactive games. The noise inside the large barns is deafening even early in the morning. Any boy that looks at us quickly turns back to the TVs, disinterested. The place smells of a peculiar type of mustiness and disinfectant. Fat flies buzz around and boys eat from troughs, scooping cereal with their hands, grunting loudly, occasionally defecating and urinating while eating. Automatic sprays run back and forward rinsing the boys with what looks like lukewarm water and foamy antiseptic.

Jan goes close to a few of the boys. He clicks his fingers and claps his hands in front of faces. The boys look once then look away.

"How are we going to search all these sheds?" I say to Dad. "There must be sixty to eighty."

"I don't think we have to."

"Eh?"

"They are not here."

"This is sick," I say. "If the Euny are not here, let's get out."

"I think Jonathan wanted us to see this place. We are only stopping here on the way to the castle you told us about," Jan says.

"That was my guess too. Right, Jonathan?" Dad says.

Jonathan turns, blinking and nodding as he looked at all three of us in turn. He makes a fist and bangs it into his chest and points at the boys before drawing his finger across his neck. I try to hug him but he won't let me at that instant. He signals we should go and sets off out the door.

"Leave him," Dad says. "Don't worry; he just needs time."

It is another thirty-minute walk to a village street where the Beane dynasty house towers over us like a vast prison. Dad leads us to an alley between hundreds of small box houses that lie in the shadow of the monster. I am worrying about Jonathan; his leg is increasingly bothering him and I dare not ask him to let me see it. The additional walk has put a strain on all of us.

"If I am right, Jack Wills wants to talk with me. He guessed that I have the answers to take us out of here and probably thinks I can help him adjust his machine to do what he wants," Dad says. "So I am safe until I give him what he wants."

"And he is here?" I ask looking up at the sheer walls towering above us.

"No. I don't know where he is," Dad says. "But if I go in there, they will take me to him."

"And?"

"You need to find a way to follow. See where they go..."

"That's the plan?" I hiss. "You are kidding me. Jonathan can hardly walk. We don't know how, when, or even if, they will take you out of there again. And even if they did, how are we going to guarantee that we are able to follow?"

"We are so close, Robyn," he says.

"Dad, we have not come this far to take such a crazy risk. Didn't you always warn me about being impetuous?"

Jonathan and Jan listen.

"Where did you think they had taken the Euny?" Jan asks.

"I am sure they would be brought here. I thought there might to be a way to get to them. I was wrong. I hadn't realised what kind of place it was. I'd only seen it from Keshet's house, the same as you." Dad looks at me.

"I have an idea," I say. "We'll recruit an army."

We have enormous wealth still spread between us. There must be people in the community who would be willing to help us, to take risk for the right reward. With the others agreeing it is worth a try, Dad knocks the first door. The man opens sleepily; surprise spreads over his face. Perhaps the rest of us should have stayed out of sight.

"Sorry. Good morning, don't worry. We just need a little help. Can you tell us who is in charge of the village?" Dad says.

The man blinks but doesn't reply, just swallows.

"The Headman? The Chief?" Dad tries.

Jonathan catches on before any of us. The man understands exactly what we want. But he isn't sure if he can trust us. He has already decided we are not like him, until Jonathan points to his own mouth and signs. The man's eyes widen and he signs back. The pair communicate for a few minutes, then shake hands. The man is keen now and turns to Dad to repeat by hand signs what he'd obviously told Jonathan. Round the corner. Cross over. Five doors down in the village of mutes.

As we thank him and leave, I am wondering, 'Why the tongues?' Moments later we are sitting in the house of Samuel Baker, his wife and three young daughters. Intelligence and goodness shine from his eyes. When one of the girls brings him a pad and pen I am more confused. They are also without tongues.

"We want to know about the castle," Dad says.

'It's a bad place. Those who go in don't always come out,' he writes.

"Have you been in? Do you know how to get in?"

'Yes, there are ways. But the Beanes are well protected and well-armed. Why would you want to go there?'

"Our friends are in there and it's our only way home," I say.

'That's good reason,' Samuel writes.

"We don't understand your relation with this place. Why live close to the castle? And sorry to ask, but why are the village all mute?" Dad asks.

'The same reason as he?' He nods at Jonathan.

"Unfortunately, he doesn't know what the reason is," Dad explains.

The man looks surprised and a little perturbed.

'Voting,' Samuel writes, 'Verbal voting is an ancient custom in Subtopia. When you are mute you cannot vote.'

"Who gets to vote?"

'Ha real Freemen in Subtopia are few. The authorities try to catch them when they can. If they find them, they lose their voice.'

"No, the Market. If they had caught us under the cloaks," I recall, feeling sick. Madness. Sheer madness. Huptoou called it the Madness. He was right. Dad never asks what they did with the tongues. I have a bad feeling about that; he is right not to ask.

'But it maintains control and the status quo,' he wrote. 'It also stops us from sympathising with the livestock. We are forced to be herdsmen for the boys from the farms. Being mute prevents us responding to their cries for help.'

"How do your people feel about their..." Dad chooses his words carefully, "...overseers?"

'The people here will always be resigned and cowed as long as they hold control over our life and death,' he writes. His face falls. 'We do not have the money to lift ourselves out of the shadow of penury or the collective voice to change things. We are indentured to the Farm owners. Things are what they are.'

People have nothing without a voice, I think.

"Is there anyone here who would be willing to take us into the castle?" Dad asks.

'Possibly. Some of the older men without families. Nothing to lose.'

"Will we be able to trust them?" Dad says.

'We are that monkey that speaks no evil. Our tongues may be lost, but our honour isn't. If they say they will help, then you can trust them. I will find you some men with big heart and soul.'

One hour later we are in a small hall with around five men. Not exactly an army. Simon explains this was all he could get, others are scared. Some of them had worked there in the past. He tells us that they will lead us through underground entrances. But there are guards: big men who kill people without a morsel of regret. I say we know them already; we have met them before.

Dad asks Jan to stay with Samuel, who is going to buy us a vehicle in case we need it. Jan agrees reluctantly but Dad explains we all might need to get out of here fast if things go wrong. Someone needs to keep the bags.

We give the village men the marbles that would have gone to Noname. Simon takes them and says they will benefit the whole village; for some reason I believe him. Dad promises another marble to each of the men who are coming with us.

By mid-morning we are entering a dank tunnel that takes us under the thick stone buttresses, supporting the walls, and down into the castle's foundations. Limping badly now, Jonathan is leading with the group of men, all armed with swords.

It doesn't take long to meet the first guards. They are not used to threat or any form of resistance; the three men are taken completely by surprise. They die quietly and quickly, their weapons taken by us.

Jonathan is signing a lot with the men. They are explaining the different floors, levels and entrances, it seems. I sense Dad is a bit frustrated because we don't really know what's going on. But there is hardly time to write things down. We just follow at the back.

"He is a good leader Dad," I say.

"I know. We just need to be careful. That's all. I don't want to lose either of you."

Jonathan comes to us finally; we are all hiding in the shadows of a small courtyard. I am looking up inside the castle to windows four and five levels up. The second and third levels had a weird balcony running all the way around and no obvious windows.

Jon writes.

'Dungeons. Stock rooms. Down.

Processing factory. Ground.

Guards and armoury. First floor.

Living quarters. Top floor.

Second, third, fourth. Don't know.'

"How many people, guards?" Dad asks.

Jonathan shakes his head. They don't know.

This is a huge place. It is going to be difficult to find anything.

"If the Euny are still here..." I say.

"Yes, we need to start with the dungeons and factory," Dad suggests.

Jonathan looks uncomfortable, perhaps at the memory or idea of being trapped underground. He points to Dad and me, to go down with two men. He and the remaining men would keep the doors open.

I agree, we don't want to be trapped down there. I prefer the idea of Jonathan protecting our way out.

Dad nods and we turn to a steep flight of stairs leading to the dungeons.

□□□□□□□

The familiar smells overpower my senses as Dad and I enter the dungeons closely followed by our three nervous-looking men. My eyes adjust to the gloom. Rows of large cages and barred cells line the walls. I pad silently along, looking in each. They are empty. I stop and listen; silence except a loud drip from a nearby tunnel and the faint sound of the wind. I run down the next tunnel; more empty cages. And the next, getting deeper into the bowels of this mausoleum. I hope Dad and the others are keeping track of the directions as they run behind me. I am leading them in, but I couldn't lead us out again if my life depended on it.

I stop and try to imagine the layout under the castle. These might be ancillary rooms; perhaps there are main rooms we have passed.

"There is nothing here," I say to Dad.

One of the men indicates with his finger, back around to the left, turn right and straight.

"We'll follow you," I say.

The empty chambers make us careless; we are not as silent as before.

"Quietly," I whisper as we run.

The man in front of me turns the corner and runs straight onto a sword. He dies without a cry. The guard withdraws his blade from the man's chest and turns to face me with a smile that hardens when Yuenu lights up. Maybe he's heard of me; I hope so. I see Dad level the rifle.

"No Dad!" I call out. We need as much silence as possible.

The guard is cautious, but I can see he is sizing up my strength. I don't look much. Heavy combat in a confined space is better for him. Slash and cut. I need to counter his strength by keeping him on the point of my blade. I sense the men watching fearfully from the side, wondering if they will have to fight the man next. They needn't worry. The guard is a clumsy oaf. I allow him to think his swipes are forcing me back, until one wild swing takes his sword away from the front of his body. I thrust and stab just above his knee.

Perhaps Dad should have shot him. My mistake; his roar is voluminous in the empty caves.

He lunges at me in desperation, careless, but resulting in a bold attack and his sword tip cutting my sleeve. Close.

I parry his next thrust and, before he recovers, step quickly inside his defence and stick my sword through his neck. It is over; I step back quickly to avoid him falling on me.

Dad touches my shoulder and the men move out of the way as Yuenu and I pass.

We move on into a large cave, the biggest yet. There are cages that would have held hundreds, yet not one soul inside. I can see the men look puzzled. The only thing left in here is a bad smell and thousands of weeping ghosts.

"Let's get out," Dad says.

□□□□□□□□

Jonathan looks at us when we get back.

"Empty. Only one guard for the whole place," I say.

Jon motions to cross the courtyard and leads the way.

The factory is silent except for the sound of a rat scampering across a nearby table. The machines are still wet and dust-free. Pools of blood lie on the floor; I have a sense that a lot of produce has passed through in the last few days and the place is on a break. I jump when one of the men kicks something metal and the clang echoes in the silent chamber.

I shiver. This place is full of new ghosts; people have been recently slaughtered here. I don't like it, my instinct is warning me of danger. The men are watching me as I look around. From their faces, it's obvious that they don't like this place any more than I.

This vision of the boys being crowded into the pens sticks in my head. Fattened boys, queuing to be stunned and hung upside down on the overhead rails that run into the gutting and skinning shop. They would know what was going to happen to them. They would hear the squeals echoing from next door as they shuffled nearer to the butcher's knife, the unfortunate ones coming awake as they were gutted or steamed of their skin.

I suddenly realise that the mute village are complicit in their own way. They bring the boys to this place from the farms; like shepherds delivering sheep to the slaughterhouse. The boys would cry, bleat for mercy, but they'd see only silent grim-face unsympathetic men that couldn't speak to them.

"We need to keep going," Dad says. "Up."

We go back to the stairs again, all glad to leave this bloody place behind.

On the next floor we move cautiously into the guards' quarters. We run into six men who are sitting at a table eating and drinking. They are taken by surprise; no one moves. Dad covers them with the rifle, while our remaining men truss them up like livestock.

"Where is everyone?" Dad asks one of the guards. He doesn't speak.

"Who else is in the castle?"

"Gag them." I point to one of the men's mouth. For a second, the villagers think I meant to take their tongues. They are horrified. What must they think of me? Do they see me as some sort of cruel leader? Perhaps my age and sex adds to what they think of me. Of course they had seen me kill.

Jonathan signs and they understand. I didn't want their tongues removed.

We find no other people on this floor, only empty beds, kitchens, offices, and bathrooms full of absence. Weird. It doesn't feel right. But I shake off the strange idea that they are waiting for us.

Dad leads the way on the next flight of stone steps to the second floor and the third floor. Both large draughty halls are without windows and filled only with the stone pillars that hold up the next floor; they stretch to all edges of the castle. In the centre, a vast square balcony overlooks the courtyards. This is what I had seen when looking up. There doesn't seem to be any function to either floor, except to let the wind run through. Perhaps it takes away the smell from below.

□□□□□□□□

As soon as we step onto the fourth floor, we know it is different. I can feel the presence of others as we push open the large doors to a great hall. There is a cage in the middle of the room, surrounded by other cages and bars. So many bars that it is hard to see the gaps between them or where the joins are. In the centre cage, about one hundred feet away, there is a man on his knees, chained and facing away from us. The wooden doors are at our back and an entrance through the bars ahead of us.

One of the men who are with us comes in front of us and tries to push us back, stop us entering. He signs urgently to Jonathan, who looks doubtful but gets his pad out.

'The man has heard of this place. It is used to trap enemies,' he writes.

"Dad?" I say.

He shakes his head slightly as he looks around, trying to make sense of the structure. It seems like we have a choice, we could go forward amongst the bars, or back out. Dad is thinking the same.

"It's the only way up. You have to go through here to reach the stairs on the other side," he says.

The man in the centre cage calls out weakly but he is too far to make out what he says.

"Ask our friend what happens with the cages. How does it work?" Dad says to Jonathan. A few signs between them and a shaking of the head says he doesn't know. The man signs out a bunch of letters.

'He said it's rumour. It is called Muscipulam,' Jonathan writes.

"Sounds like Latin," Dad says.

The man in the middle cage calls out again. I grab Dad's arm.

"Listen. Is that Iain?" I say. And I know I am right when he calls out, "Donald."

"Okay. I go forward, you guys stay," Dad says.

We nervously agree and Dad moves off between the bars. As we watch, he turns and twists through the passages, sometimes coming back towards us before turning again. Sometimes it looks like he reaches a dead end and has to back-track. It is a maze, I realise. A maze made of bars, probably the same abundant metal that my lucky ingot was made from.

It is difficult to see, but it looks like Dad reached the centre and is in front of Iain. We hear them speak. Jonathan and I step a few steps forward automatically, expecting Dad to call us now.

"Get out of here!" Dad shouts suddenly. But it is too late; a set of bars comes down and separates Jon, myself and one other man from the other three villagers.

We try to lift the bars; it's no use. Jon strikes them with his sword causing only a slight graze. We are in the maze, like Dad, but now we understand someone must have been watching.

"We should go forward," I say.

"Get out!" Dad shouts a second time.

"It's too late," I call back.

Jon and I move through the maze. The lines upon lines of parallel grey bars make it difficult. Gaps are impossible to see, dead ends look like corner turns and corner turns look like dead ends. After a few minutes we have not made the progress that Dad had. Something isn't right. We are moving in another direction, no matter how we try for the centre.

It is a detail that makes me realise someone is playing with us. A deep scratch that had run across three bars changed position. When we passed the first time, they were together. Now there is a gap between them. I can see the scratch continues from the two bars, over to the other side of the entrance onto the third bar.

"The bars are moving. The maze keeps changing behind us," I say to Jonathan.

He nods; he already knew.

Our villager touches my shoulder and points. The other villagers have ended up in the maze, going in the opposite direction. How did that happen? Didn't they see our predicament?

We come to another dead end and about-turn.

The screech makes me jump. Some sort of animal has come into the cage. I can barely see them between the bars as they scurry along the floor. They are too big to squeeze through the bars, but smaller than a man. Whatever they are, I doubt they are going to be good news for us.

We move down a corridor that heads towards the others. We might group up, I think. But it comes to an end and there is a set of bars between the three villagers and us. Our man signs to his colleagues, who look terrified. We can all see and hear the creatures running through the maze in our direction.

I see the first one at the side of me. It stretches through the bars to try to grab one of us. It is a type of monkey, about the size of a six year old. Its wild eyes, sharp claws and mouth full of teeth tell me all I need to know about its intentions. I fire Yuenu and try to slash its arm. It is too quick for me. It runs back the way it came, to join its companions trying to find another way in. I count four of them.

When they get into the adjacent cage where the three villagers are, they launch a ferocious attack on them, underneath their swords, around behind, biting and slashing, legs, necks, so quickly we couldn't do anything. Jon and I try to reach through the bars with our weapons. One bites me hard on the arm and I nearly lose Yuenu. Jon manages to whack it one before it springs off in the other direction.

We watch helplessly as the four beasts kill our friends in a bloody feast. One animal stares me straight in the eyes as it sinks his teeth around a man's throat.

Jonathan pulls me away.

And we run back along the corridor of bars as the animals chase around after us trying to find a way in. They turn, and we turn. Once I think they are in beside us. No, they are running parallel to us, trying to claw and bite between the bars.

It becomes a blur; I no longer know which direction we are running in. I am turning blindly when someone grabs me.

"This way," Dad says. He pulls me into the gap that we were about to run past.

We all go to the centre of the cage.

I look down at Iain over Dad's shoulder as Dad hugs me.

"Sorry, I was trying to warn you," Iain says.

At this point most of the maze disappears, bars drawing up into the ceiling, leaving us in a double cage in the middle of the huge, now empty, room. With another line of cage around us that holds the deadly monkeys.

The bars around Iain lift, leaving us all together. I watch, frightened that the outer bars will lift allowing the creatures in. Nothing happens. The monkeys snarl and run around the cage.

"Well. Well. That was a bit of unexpected fun." A factory man's voice bellows over a loud speaker above us. "Now. What you need to do is throw these lovely swords of yours through the bars. And the rifle of course, but I am much less afraid of that."

"If we don't?" Dad calls up to the roof.

"Then we will open up the cage and let our little pets loose."

"We can, we can," says Keshet's voice.

"If we throw our weapons, what are you going to do with us?" Dad shouts.

"We will talk. Maybe we can come to some sort of deal. Maybe we will take you to see Jack Wills. He is anxious to talk to you. You have one minute to decide; I am not a patient man."

"You cannot trust them!" whispers Iain.

"There is no alternative," Dad says. "Our only chance may be to try to bargain with Jack Wills."

Imagine the feeling of parting with the one thing that has kept me safe and saved us on a few occasions. Part of me thinks Dad should try to shoot a couple of these creatures with the gun, and we should stand and fight the others.

"My brave Robyn, we are in a cage. Whatever happens, we are not going anywhere," Dad says. "They can simply leave us here until we starve if they like."

He is right. Jonathan pushes his sword through the bars first. I kiss Yuenu and slide her through as well. Dad is already sliding the rifle out. The monkeys run around hoping to catch one of us. But I know how fast they are; my hands and body are back inside the cage quickly.

A few seconds later the space the monkeys occupied is reduced by bars dropping; it moves the monkeys to a trap door which they exit.

"They bite indiscriminately," the large factory man says as he walks across the room with two others and old Keshet and his son. "It is not possible to train them."

"No, they are no worse than you," I say, shaking with fury when I look at the man who had killed Sheldon. I glare at him, willing him to read my mind.

"Ah the young Robyn. The girl who killed two of my dear sons and badly disabled another."

The man stood on his left has false limbs, but I don't recognise his face. Hey, I get the blame for everything around here; my fear turns to black humour inside my head. He stares at me though, so perhaps we have met before. I turn back to listen to the older man.

"You surprised us by turning up so soon. We had baited the trap, but we hadn't put the word out yet. We thought you'd come for Iain, but really thought we'd have to wait until the news of his capture reached you."

"What are you planning to do with us?" Dad asks.

"Well that depends. Mr Wills wants to meet you. He is working on a machine for us, and he believes you have the key. You and Mr Banks here will be sent to meet him, while we keep the two young lovebirds in this gilded cage. As a surety against good behaviour, you understand."

"My daughter and her friend stay with me," Dad says.

"I'm afraid that won't be possible. I am sure you will change your mind if we leave you caged here to watch each other starve," he says. "Look, think it over. You can have half an hour to discuss it. We will be back for you then."

The group moves off, but not before Keshet's son comes towards the bars.

"You will look great in my trophy room," he tells me. I am too slow to spit in his face.

□ □ □ □ □ □ □

We talk quietly and quickly. No one trusts them, but we have no choice. Jonathan and I hold each other.

"You guys go. Try to make a deal," I say. "It's our only chance." I feel my body shaking again and Jonathan squeezes me tight.

Thirty minutes later two men come back and lead Dad and Iain away, leaving Jon, myself and the poor villager in the cage.

"Please don't be long Dad," I say, pretending to be brave and sounding terrified.

"I love you both," Dad says. For all the times my Dad says stupid things, sometimes he gets it just right. They go quickly across the hall and out of the double doors.

"How long will we be here?" I say aloud. "There is no toilet or even water."

Jonathan answers by nodding in the direction of Keshet's son and the son of the factory owner coming into the hall.

"We are moving you," Keshet's son says. "Hands through the bars. We will tie you."

"Where?" I say.

"Oh, somewhere there are toilets and somewhere to lie down," he says. The other son laughs.

Our villager puts his hands through first; they tie his wrists together. Jonathan and I look at each other. We hate it, but what can we do? We have to play along for now.

Moments later they are dragging all three of us along the corridors and down the stairs, ropes around our hands and necks bending us forward.

"You miss your boyfriend?" Keshet's son asks.

I ignore him.

"So you don't want the message he left for you? The last words he said," he taunts. "Let me see, he says, tell... nah you don't want to know."

"I will kill you," I say.

"You killed my brother," the factory son says clobbering me across the back of the head. Jonathan struggles and tries to kick out to protect me.

"You touch us and there will be no deal with my Father!" I shout.

"You'll be in a window with a price ticket on, in a grocery shop in Metro, before your Father comes back here," the boy says.

My stomach cartwheels as they lead the three of us down into the factory.

The noise is deafening. The outside gates are open and hundreds of boys, naked geldings, are being pushed into the factory. The crying and wailing of the herd coming in is punctuated by screams and moans on the other side of the factory floor.

Jon and I really start to fight. Three factory men come and grab our ropes and drag us towards the pens. I can see Jon struggling. They pin me on my front at the edge of the pen and I can see boys slowly moving forward beneath me. They cut the rope off my neck and wrist, run a sharp curved blade under my collar all the way to my waist, and split the back of my clothes. Then shoulder to cuff, each arm, opens the sleeves; the back of the cold steel scrapes my flesh. Then down each leg of my trousers, waist to heel; my clothes peel off and they roll me naked into the moving pen below.

The fall winds me a little; I scramble up from between the mass of skinny legs. The village guy falls in front of me. We are in a moving crowd of naked bodies. Sheer walls reach up on either side. I look up; the sons are laughing as they watch. Jonathan is nowhere to be seen. I turn around in the direction of the flow as the pens narrow gradually, squeezing us tighter. The apex narrows from fifteen abreast to three abreast in the space of ten metres. I can't see beyond that, but I can hear the screams. The boys around me are mostly younger. The village guy turns and looks at me as if asking me what to do. Some boys are silent, just shuffling forward. Others seem to bleat like sheep, calling for their ma. I try to fight back against the crowd; it is impossible.

I am struggling to breathe, in panic, as I look around for Jonathan and a way out. Minutes later, I am passing through the narrowing entrance, pushing on the village guy's back. Ahead I can see three lanes of single file. Boys are now being squashed into one or other lane. Men with some kind of commercial air-gun are grabbing each boy by the hair, putting the gun to his head and firing. Stunned. Some kick and scream; others just collapse as the man next in the production line hooks them up by the ankles onto the overhead line regardless of their state of consciousness.

I hear screaming and then I realise it is me, I try to stop going through but the force behind is too much. I am two away from the gun; the villager is in front of me, no longer struggling. I break my nails on the wall trying to climb up.

Moments later, they stun the villager, and up he goes upside down onto the rail, hook through his heels, his eyes wide open looking at me as he screams without a tongue.

I am next. I try to scratch and bite the man; thick leather gloves protect his hands and arms. I feel the muzzle of the gun press into the skin of my head. And I give up too.

# CHAPTER SIXTEEN

## Love and Hate

Grunting, the man lets go of my head and puts a harness around my shoulders. The straps chafe under my arms as I am hoisted up out of the production line and swung back onto the side of the wall. Urine and faeces run down my legs. The sons are standing close by, laughing at my distress. Jonathan is on the side on his knees, now in some sort of harness and collar to stop him going crazy. Through my tears I realise they made him watch all the time I was in there. We both thought I was going to die and be processed. He looks worse than I felt.

There could be no reason for them to pretend to process except a sadistic need to deliver the maximum amount of torture. A simple killing will not satisfy these two.

"Rest. Tomorrow it's his turn and you get to watch. Or maybe both of you. And the one who goes through first saves the other one," Keshet's son says.

"Yes. That will be a spectacle," the factory son agrees.

They take us to a coop with dozens of others, remove Jonathan's harness and throw us in. We both slip in the filth and blood on the floor. Jonathan is the only person in the place with clothes on. He takes his shirt off and puts it on me. I shake and sob when he takes off his jeans, holds them in his teeth and slips out of his boxer shorts.

He makes me put these on as well, trying to help me step into them without messing them with my filthy feet. He jumps back into his jeans and hugs me close.

Everything that is happening is beyond the comprehension of a seventeen-year-old. Then in a weird moment of clarity, I realise that we've been here for eighty-four days; it is my birthday in the real world. I am eighteen. My eyes are already closed as I make a wish.

□□□□□□□

"Missie. Missie." In my dreams someone is calling me to another place. We are jammed up on the side of the cage; Jonathan and I hug for warmth. Once the factory had shut down for the night, they hosed everything down with freezing cold water including us, and then switched off the lights leaving us in the dark. My ears had been pierced by the sounds of the shrieking and the bandsaws cutting through bone. The noise of the mincers and the shredders, the cutters and the ovens had all left their mark. Even in the silence, sounds ring in my head between the tinnitus and earache from the extreme cold.

"Missie, Missie," persistent, like a dog pulling my blanket off. I struggle to come to the surface; it is safe down here in the womb of my subconscious.

I awake with a start, a dark face close to mine, a little light shining in his eyes; Huptoou is staring, his face close to mine between the bars of the cage.

"Don't worry. We are here," he says.

I raise my head with difficulty and look around. There are dozens of Euny in the factory all armed with swords.

"The guards?" I ask as I try to wake Jonathan from his exhausted sleep. I fear he is hypothermic. His lips look blue in the dim light. I shake him hard and he stirs.

"The guards downstairs are dead," Huptoou says. He moves around to where his men are getting the cage opened. "We stopped here. We came to find you. We didn't go up. Euny don't like this place."

"Did you see Jan?" I ask.

"He with some of the boys, following Donal. We find out soon enough where they gone," he says.

Jonathan helps push the cage door open and we climb out shivering and slipping underfoot.

"You stink, Missie," Huptoou tells me, giving us both a warm cloak.

I start to laugh and can't stop myself. I laugh until I cry again.

The angry part of me wants to find Keshet's son and take revenge. But I want Dad more, and both Jon and I are exhausted, so tired we can't count up the hours of sleep we had. We are confused and muddled. So we exit the castle silently in the night leaving behind a few dead guards and the memory of nearly becoming burger meat in the Beane Factory.

Huptoou assures us that we will know early morning where Dad is, as soon as one of his men comes and tells us. We will go immediately, he promises; I don't want Dad to finish his deal and come back to the castle looking for us.

The Euny have a new lair, safer, deeper underground, well protected and luxurious compared to the one that the troops had found and destroyed.

"We knew Government were coming. We got out," Huptoou explains. "Thanks to Sara."

We get cleaned up. Huptoou has told the boys to give me privacy this time. Although Jonathan is in the next shower cubicle, I don't mind. I'd have stood in the hot shower forever; but I want to get out to clean and bandage Jonathan's wound. We come out the bathroom in towels and the boys give us t-shirts and shorts.

"It's much better than I thought," I tell Jonathan. The injury is bright pink around a crusty scab, with no pus and little inflammation. Seeing how well the wound is healing on his thigh makes me feel miles better. I won't let go of him.

We sleep fitfully, huddled up in the same blanket. Some of the boys lie in pallet beds and cubicles a few feet away. Others are across their underground home in small groups. And it feels good to be surrounded by friends as I drift off. Dreams come and go, but some internal alarm makes sure I am awake for the dawn. I actually feel rested and able to eat some bread and jam for breakfast.

"Good news for you. Your Dad is with another man, Iain, at one of the houses of Jack Wills," Huptoou tells us. "It's not too far from here, but you cannot go in your shorts." He hands us both a pile of clothes including the traditional hooded cloak. He opens another bag. "Do we have to take these to your Dad now?" he says. "I have been keeping these safe for him." Inside there are three of Dad's surfing coils.

"We will take them to him now," I say confidently.

As the dawn breaks we are getting ready to move out with all the Euny. Huptoou thinks we need everyone. He makes sure we have cloaks, weapons and a guide. We split up into smaller groups and Huptoou runs between his captains making sure everyone understands the plan. We are to rendezvous with Jan as soon as possible.

We meet Jan outside the house of Jack Wills. He is massively pleased to see us.

"Are you guys okay? I'd have given anything to be with you," Jan says. "Did I miss much? You look like you both had a hell of an experience."

Jonathan and I just look at each other and let out huge sighs.

"We nearly had a homemade burger. Saw a few wild monkeys. That was about it," I say. I give him a hug and a kiss. "It's good to see you too." We smile weakly as we group hug and Huptoou joins in.

"Where are my Dad and Iain?"

"Both inside. No guards, they are not expecting anyone," Jan says. "How many of you are there?"

"We have seventy-three Euny Skirmishers with us," Huptoou says proudly.

"Do you have weapons and a cloak for Jan?" I ask. Huptoou gets one of the guys to bring it. With the hoods up, we all look similar.

"We are going to surround the house and flood in the front door," Huptoou says.

"Are you sure?" I ask. I don't like the idea of not knowing where they are.

"They went in through the gate. They didn't come back out. We have people watching the back," Jan says. "Until someone goes in properly, we won't know."

"Fair enough. I'm ready." I weigh the sword in my hand; it is strange not to see the familiar light and hear the buzz. Simple steel. Nothing more.

The front door is unlocked and we pour in, a silent army of boy swordsmen. Some go upstairs. Others run into the rooms. Jonathan and I stay in the hall waiting until we get a sign where to go.

The house is empty; it feels too much like yesterday for my liking. We wander around looking for signs that anyone has been here. There is something familiar about the house. Then I realise the awful coincidence; this is our house. There are extra rooms but the structure is similar. I run outside and look at the tree. It is much older, heavier. But I can see pieces of wood high in the branches where the tree house should be. This house had been Jack Wills' house before ours.

I look down towards the bottom of the garden behind the trees. There is a large structure at least three stories high.

"Jan, Huptoou," I call quietly and we gather the troops from the house and slink down the garden in two long narrow lines, keeping to the cover of the edges. We reach the giant shed with high sliding double doors, with a serious looking power supply next to it. The door is slightly open and lights shine out; there are indistinct voices arguing. One might be Dad's. I'm not sure. I look around; Jon, Jan and Huptoou are close; dozens of Euny are scattered around the gardens, behind bushes brandishing swords. It might have been comical in any other setting.

It is Jonathan who takes the decision. He waves his sword in circles in the air, a practiced signal, and everyone charges silently as one. A shower of Euny patters to a stop behind Huptoou and Jonathan at the door. They ready themselves. Huptoou looks around at Jan and me, nods to Jonathan. They count silently on Huptoou's fingers, 3-2-1; four Euny pull the doors apart and the rest rush through the doors shrieking. We join the throng and push in. There is one gunshot.

Inside, Beane senior, the old Factory man, is standing with Keshet, surrounded by fifteen Euny, swords pointed at the men's necks. Two guards are pinned against a wall by another crowd. One guard has been stabbed and cut. A Euny lies on the ground, gunshot; two others attend him. Iain kneels to help the boy on the ground. Dad stands with another older man; I don't recognise him, probably Jack

Wills. They are close to a huge machine, similar to the vacuum back at the school. It is on a rotating platform and reaches to the roof.

We stay in the main group of Euny who are waiting for a command.

"Call them off," Old Beane says. "We will keep our deal. You will get your daughter back when you confirm that the machine works. We promise you can go home."

"Even if I trusted you, you plan to use the machine to come to my time and take children," Dad says.

"Call these boys off us," Beane repeats. "We will go bring your daughter, and things will be final."

Both Jonathan and Jan look at me; I shake my head urgently and pull my hood lower. I move beside Huptoou.

"Get one of your men to take the bag to my Father, now." I point to the surfing coils.

A second later a Euny threads through the crowd and gives Dad the bag. He looks inside, surveys the crowd for a few minutes and puts the bag down on a chair close to him.

"Very well. Leave the guard's weapons. You go; I want to see my daughter and son back here," Dad agrees.

I keep my face down, as Keshet and Beane exit the warehouse with the two guards. They have no intention of bringing me back; they are saving their own skins and going for reinforcements.

"Huptoou, can we defend this place?" I say. "They are going to come back heavily armed. In fact, they may already be on their way if the sons have realised we are gone."

"We cannot defend against guns. They may have guns. Many will die," Huptoou says. Jon nods in agreement.

It's as I thought. I run up to Dad and Iain.

"We don't have much time before they come back with reinforcements. The Euny cannot defend against guns!" I shout.

"Slow down!" Dad grabs me and hugs me. "You are all here? I don't believe it." He looks at Jan and Jon.

"Dad, what are we going to do? They are going to come back."

"Don't worry," Dad says. "Have someone tie Dr Wills up. Make sure there is no chance of escape. I don't want him messing with the machine."

Jonathan goes as usual. The old man is furious but he can't resist. Jonathan drags him out into the garden and ties him to a tree out of the way.

"What's the plan, Dad?" I ask.

"We are all getting out of here now. I have shown Iain how to destroy the machine. But I was trying to get him to come back with us."

"If Beane is going to be back here soon with men and guns, the boys will be in danger."

He nods. "Huptoou, send your guys home. It will get too dangerous here soon."

"Yes. But one or two will stay. I will stay," Huptoou says.

Dad runs to the platform and starts the machine. I hear the air going out and the machine starts to rotate.

"Iain, what's your decision?" Dad shouts.

"I stay here, I am not coming with you," he says.

"Then you should go quickly. They will hunt everyone. You need to be far away before they return. Jan has a car outside," I tell Iain.

"Eight minutes," Dad says looking at the dials. "Everyone back up a bit, for the moment." He dashes around the machine clearing away a few bits of rubbish, checking dials and looking up at the revolving drum. He takes the surfing coils out and lays them ten feet from the machine.

"Our bags are in the car. I will go with Iain and pick them up," Jan says.

"You have five minutes until the machine goes. Seriously," Dad tells him, looking at the machine again.

The Euny disappear like mist as Huptoou dismisses them and organises the three that stay. One is on lookout near the house, the other two stationed near the shed door.

Iain hugs us all quickly. "Safe trip, be safe, be happy."

"Thanks for everything," I tell him. He runs up the garden with Jan to the car.

"Four minutes!" Dad calls out. "We have three coils. You, Jan and Jonathan will go first; it takes less than a minute to reset the machine, I will be right behind you." He looks at me.

"No Dad. You are not..." I begin.

Jonathan steps in shaking his head. He points and signs, holding his two fingers side by side; Dad and he will go together. I notice a weird look that passes between them, like they are hiding something.

"He is right, Dad. You need cover while you reset the machine. They could come back." I give them the solution.

"Okay. You and Jan in three minutes. We will come after."

"Huptoou. Goodbye," I say. We hug, everyone solemn.

Two shots ring out. Jonathan grabs a rifle and runs to the window. Huptoou and I run to the door and look out.

Jan and Iain are running with the bags back down the garden, the Euny lookout is shot as he runs behind them. He tumbles over in the grass and doesn't get up. More shots are fired, a couple hitting the shed.

Jonathan fires into the house from his spot at the window. I grab the other rifle and join him shooting into the dark of the windows; I can't actually see anyone.

Jan and Iain come charging in. "There is an army of them up there, gathering on the road. More arriving. It's impossible!" Jan shouts. "They are surrounding the place."

"One minute and counting!" shouts Dad. "Jan, get over here."

Huptoou appears at my side. "You and Jan get ready. I will make sure your Dad gets out of here, okay?"

I grab my bags from Jan and take my money belt from inside. I give it to Huptoou and kiss him. Jan and Huptoou shake hands.

"Thirty seconds!"

"Jan. We are going." I grab his arm and take him to the surfing coils.

The third coil lies empty, but I know the quicker we go, the quicker Jonathan and Dad will be back.

"Iain, take the third coil," Dad shouts. "You cannot get away now. They will catch you. You can always come back."

"What about Jonathan?" Iain asks. Jonathan turns from the window for a second, shakes his head and fires a few more shots. "What about destroying the machine?"

"Don't worry about it. We will do it. Go!" Dad calls frantically, looking at the dials and stepping back. I can already feel the thrum from the coil. "Ten seconds."

Iain decides and jumps beside me, grabs a coil; a bang and the machine sucks us in and spits us out.

□□□□□□□□

When I open my eyes and look around, I am lying on the grass halfway up the garden of the house, our house. To my right, Jan crawls on the ground like a dog, looking dazed. I hear Iain's voice. "That was a rush. I don't remember it feeling like that before."

I start to laugh; we are home, actually home. I kiss the grass and scream. Then stress and relief makes you do strange things; I grab my bag and look inside. The cuff is there, and my ingot. And memories hit you at the most inopportune times. I remember that I'd left my precious locket on the bathroom cabinet when I last showered in the safari trailer, all these days ago. That stings me and steals a little bit of my elation.

We wait for ten minutes for Dad and Jonathan, but I'm not worried because I know there is a time difference. But I am eager to see them safe and share in my joy at being home.

I hear the 'phutt' and Dad appears nearer the house. I get up and run and jump on him. It's nothing to what Jonathan is going to get when he arrives. I whoop and kiss Dad all over his face, a serious face.

"What's wrong?" I say. "Did something go wrong?"

Dad shakes his head sadly and his eyes well. "He is not coming, Honey."

"Did something happen?" I ask.

"No. He never was coming."

"How long did you know?" I shout. "How long did you know?"

"He made me promise not to tell you. I begged him. I told him how important he was to you, to me too. He was like a son." Dad sobs and tries to hug me. "I'm so sorry."

I get up and move away. "Why Dad, why? Why didn't he come? And why didn't you tell me? I could have made him."

"I'm sorry."

"You both tricked me back there. I told him to stay behind." I realise what their exchanged look had meant. "You deceived me."

I collapse on the grass and Iain comes and sits beside me. "He told me too. He felt handicapped after what happened to him. He believed he was no longer good enough for you. He loved you, he told me so. Your Dad and I told him to give it time."

"Did you know?" I accused Jan.

"No. He never told me. But I know he felt some responsibility to the Euny. He was so angry about the hunting in the villages. I always thought he'd come home and end up going back," Jan says.

"I need to be alone," I say, getting up. "I am going in."

"Okay. If you need us, we are here for you, please don't shut us out," Dad says. "Jonathan asked me to give you this. He said I would know when the time is right. I hope it's now." He takes a thick envelope from inside his shirt and passes it to me.

I don't look back as I go inside the house, find my bedroom and close the door. I look at my clock. The date doesn't make sense. I find my iPad inside my desk and key in the passcode; the same time and date show. We've been away a bit over a week.

So many heartbreaks in so few days. I want to scream.

I slump on the floor in the corner of my room and rip open the envelope. Sheldon's locket drops out, along with a letter.

'My Darling Robyn,

There are no words to describe the pain in my heart from losing you.

I never wanted to hurt or deceive you. But I knew if I told you I wasn't coming home, you'd have lost focus. The place was dangerous; I wanted you and your Dad out of there safely.

Don't blame them. I made them promise not to tell.

Once I was injured, I had no right to expect anything from you. The love we shared since childhood would be diluted by sympathy and sorrow and I wouldn't allow that. I couldn't allow my own bitterness at my disability to come between us.

Sheldon was my hope for your happiness. I thought there was a chance that we could still be great friends and I'd be the funny mute uncle to your children, I bled with you when he was lost. I promise you, I'd have given anything to take his place.

There are good people here that deserve my help and there is a fire in me that will be hard to put out. My hate for the men who did this to me is gone, but my rage against their culture that slaughters innocents is tenfold.

Forgive me for seeking happiness with Ellie and her daughter. I feel they need me in their world.

In time you will understand that my decision to stay was the right one for all of us. You of all people know how I think.

Be happy again, that's how I will always think of you. It is enough for me to know that you got home safe and to remember your smile and sense of humour. I didn't open the locket, but I will be there in spirit when you do and when you go to see Sheldon's Mum and Dad. This will be the hardest challenge you will ever face.

Love you, to another world and back.

Jon x'

He was wrong, I think; the hardest challenge is now and losing him, and I hate him for what he's just done.

I feel numb as dark and cold come into my room like twin phantoms. I must have been in the corner for hours. I've lost count of the number of times I read the letter; trying to squeeze one more drop of meaning from the words. What is the expression, go and lick your wounds? My wounds are deep. After Mum, I've lost another two people that I'd started to care about. Why am I saying 'started'? Am I lying to myself, holding back, in denial? I am wounded because I loved them. What is better proof of love than how you feel when you lose someone?

For now, I had made no distinction between brotherly love, parental love or sexual love. It was all one amorphous mass. Sheldon, Dad, Mum, Jonathan, were my life, my love, and most of it has been torn from me. If life is a rose, then petals have been ripped from mine.

Wounds? Something is missing.

I look at my arm. Where is my bite mark from the monkey? There is nothing. I scream and jump up, nearly tripping over the bed in the dark in my haste to get downstairs.

"Dad, Jan!" I shout.

I'd kissed my Dad on the grass; his face had been smooth, unblemished.

"Dad?" I call.

He is sitting in the lounge with Iain when I burst in.

"Are you okay?" he asks.

"I kissed your face, it was smooth. You looked fresh. I wondered why." I am breathless.

He shakes his head, not understanding.

"Your scar is gone, your injury went away when you returned. Look, my bite. Healed. Gone!" I scream.

Jan comes in and I run to him and drag his shirt out of his jeans. His skin is clear. No marks from the wound on his abdomen.

"I don't understand. What's going on?" Dad asks.

"Everything heals when we come back here," I say. "Look, my bite has gone."

As usual, Jan is the first to get it. "The machine was destroyed, Robyn, there is no way back for anyone else. Jonathan was planning to do this himself once we were safe."

# CHAPTER SEVENTEEN

## Life's Compromise

The healing process when you lose a loved one is long. Many elements go into the cure; much needs to be analysed and explained. Tears must be shed, again and again, until they become futile. You need to discover gratitude for the things that you manage to hold onto, and acceptance for the things that you don't. You learn to believe that there is meaning in what happened and hope for the future. You need to see clarity through madness, and rainbows through depression. So many rare ingredients in the tincture of recovery, but the most important is the desire and willingness to swallow the bitter pill of 'what-if'.

Did Dad and I deserve blame for what had happened? Should we feel guilt as well as sadness for the people who have died? Could we have made better choices? Did Sheldon have to become a casualty or Jonathan hurt?

How much influence did we have over life? It is a huge force, a monster. Could one immature girl have done anything to change life? Can anyone change things?

I wallowed in bed for hours that night and the next day, talking with my ghosts. Mum compared it to walking to the Antarctic, the toughest journey. Sheldon told me to listen to music and watch sunsets for him, live on his behalf. Jonathan asked a simple question, 'Is life many skirmishes or a single battle?'

Recovery was a journey and a destination. Finally, I pushed myself out of bed and made a list of the things I needed to do to start my journey.

My recovery began today, the anniversary of Mum's birthday.

Dad, Jan, Iain and I have a long chat; the idea is a gigantic debrief before Jan goes home and Iain returns. The conversation is calm. Jan is looking forward to seeing his family. But we all know his reappearance is going to get a lot of attention. Any mention of involvement of Dad or me is going to open up old wounds and additional suspicions.

The school would know that I have been away for a week. There need be no complex explanation needed there, and Dad's school suspension would get reviewed soon enough.

"My idea is to tell the police that Sheldon and I went onto the firth and took a small boat out," Jan says. "It capsized and we were both swept out to sea."

"How do you explain your nearly three weeks' absence?" Dad asks.

"I woke up under docks somewhere, cold and wet. I couldn't remember who I was or where I'd come from. I spent weeks on the city streets," Jan says. "My memory gradually came back and here I am."

"You are not a good liar, Jan," I warn. "You are too honest."

"I know. But I can be vague. I don't need to remember anything except coming back home," Jan says. "It's better than facing days of pointless questioning that will drag all of you back into the discussions. It will just make controversial headlines that follow us for the rest of our lives."

"Just like Dad's," I suppose.

"Exactly," he says. "My way everyone gets peace, including the Dunn family. I cannot imagine telling them the alternative, the truth. Can you?"

"What about Turner and Scotty?" I ask.

"I will talk to Turner. I am sure he wants to put everything to rest, the best way he can," Dad says.

"I hope Scotty hasn't told anyone," I say. "He must be worried."

"Yes. We should speak to him as soon as possible," Dad says.

"Dad, it's best that Jan and I speak to him, sound him out." Dad agrees.

Iain talks for a few minutes on why he has to return; there is nothing here for him. Dad tells him he can stay with us. He agrees he'll stay for a few months and take a rest before going back. He wants to go around and have a look at his old neighbourhood, to know if his parents are still alive; but as long as they are at peace, he doesn't want to shock them by reappearing and then telling them he is leaving again. They have probably mourned enough.

"We don't want anyone wondering who I am; I can be your handyman for a few months, until I get things together," Iain explains.

"We are going to build an extension to the house and a hangar at the bottom of the garden," Dad says. "You could help me with both."

"Are we? What for?" I ask.

"To be ready for the future," Dad says. And for a split second, he annoys me as usual with his vague answer.

Scotty comes around to the house the next day. Dad agrees that I should speak to him alone. Jan has set off to his home via the city centre. He plans to walk into a police station and tell them who he is.

Scotty simply stares at me when he arrives, looking shell-shocked.

"Come here," I say. I hug him.

"You look different. Older," he says, quickly adding, "I'm pleased to see you."

"You thought we were not coming back?" I ask.

"I stayed at the School both weekends. Turner and I camped out near the machine," he says. "During the week, I tried to be normal at school. It wasn't easy. I kept expecting to see Huptoou or you appearing."

"Sorry. There was no way to get a message out," I say. "Even though our time was different."

"How different?" he asks.

"We were there for nearly three months; I turned eighteen. Here, I still have a few weeks to go," I say.

"What about the others?" he asks.

"Jan is home safe; we came back together."

"Great," he nods and waits as I gulp in a breath.

"Sheldon lost his life... I, sorry," I say. "I'm not really over it yet. We were getting close there."

"It's okay, let it out," he says rubbing my arm.

"Jonathan decided to stay and join some rebels," I laugh through my tears.

"Will you ever go back, Robyn?" Scotty asks.

"No. We were lucky to get out. The place is dangerous. Besides, the machine that brought us back was destroyed," I say. "Nothing will take me back there. It's best forgotten."

"You are going to stay at the school though?"

"Yes, Dad and I agreed that running away from here wouldn't help either of us," I say. "I have you and Jan here, for a start."

"Thanks," he smiles and I hug him again.

I tell him that Dad and I agreed not to tell people and explain the reasons why. He feels bad for Jan having to pretend to have drowned and lost his memory, until I point out the alternative. Eventually he agrees that it is best for everyone, but reminds me about Turner.

"Someone needs to talk to Old Turner. I spent a lot of time with him. He is a good man. He has been worried sick about you guys," he says.

"Dad is going to do that today or tomorrow."

"What was the story about the marbles? I never really got that."

"Somehow the value of marbles crossed over to a world with no silicon or glass with my Dad's original marble team," I say."Which doesn't make sense, where else would they have come from?

Anyway we were millionaires for a few weeks, we could buy almost anything we wanted."

"Seriously. What was that like?"

"There was nothing that it could buy that I wanted."

"Strange contradiction."

"Or perhaps the best things in life really are free." And for a few seconds, Sheldon, Jonathan, Mo, Sara, Harriet and Huptoou appear in my head smiling.

□□□□□□□

After a few days, Jan calls me.

"I don't want to speak much over the phone," he says. "Easier to speak face-to-face."

"Okay. Why don't you come round?" I ask.

"I will, but my folks are still clinging for a bit. They hardly let me move without checking I am not going to lose my memory and disappear," he says. "They are getting me all these medical tests in the meantime."

I laugh out loud.

"Yeah, well." He laughs too. "The other thing is, it's probably best not to complicate things by running around to yours. People talk and the newspapers are still a bit interested at the moment."

"Good thinking, I understand," I say.

"The reason I called is to let you know that I talked with the Dunns. Of course they are sad that Sheldon didn't make it, and I did. But now, at least, they have an explanation."

"Thanks."

"Thing is, you can go around there anytime now. They mentioned you a couple of times."

"Thanks for letting me know. That's exactly what I plan to do. I have something to give them," I say.

"Let's catch up soon?"

"Yes, I'd like that."

"Do you think you changed?"

"In the last few weeks? Because of the experience?"

"Yeah." Cautious.

"Absolutely," I say. "I learned a lot about me, about life. And part of me changed..."

"But?"

"I am mixed up; I feel I left part of me there. And I don't know what to do."

"Me too. Maybe we can try to make sense of the feelings when we meet?"

"Sure. We should do that. Soon."

"Okay, let me know how it goes with Sheldon's folks. Big kiss, see you."

As I close my phone, I think he is about to change his mind and speak and I have a weird feeling from his tone and questioning that he has something important to tell me. But I don't want to push him and he doesn't call back. 'Patience' Mum says at the back of my mind, causing me to smile.

"I brought you something that belonged to your son," I say. Saying his name would cause me to fold. I take the locket out of my pocket.

"That belonged to his grandmother," Sheldon's mother says. She looks old and tired; damaged, I think. And I can't say anything to help her. "How did you get it? Sheldon wouldn't have given it to you."

"He left it in the bathroom, one of the times, at my place," I say.

"Oh, Sheldon never told me he'd been to your house. Isn't that curious," she says. "So strange that he took it off; it was never off, even in bed."

"Yes."

"His grandmother and grandfather, well, Sheldon used to think that they had the found perfect love," she says. "During the war, Gran and Grandad used to experience each other's ailments, even miles apart. This level of connection fascinated Sheldon. Of course, they went through lots of hardship and came out the other side still smiling and holding hands."

I hand the locket over to her.

"You must keep it now dear. He'd want you to have it," she says.

"I cannot. It belongs in your family," I reply.

Her eyes narrow. "You did see what's in it?"

"No, I never looked. I thought it too private."

"My goodness, you are special. I pried, first chance I got." She laughs. "So, not even tempted?"

"Yes, of course... But..."

"Look now." She takes the locket, presses the catch and spreads it open into two hearts. She puts her fingernail in and pulls out a third heart on a hinge. All three hold photographs.

The first is a sepia picture of a man in uniform with a cavalry moustache; next to him, a strikingly beautiful woman wearing a tight crepe bodice, under a parasol. Thirdly, there is a picture of a girl.

"Oh." She puts her hand up to her breast in surprise. "I wasn't expecting that. That's not you."

"No. It's not." I smile.

"I don't know whether to tell you or not now, but I am sure he had a picture of you in there. On the first day at school, I saw him put it in. You were playing marbles. I don't understand."

"Don't worry."

"I don't know who she is, do you?"

"Yes, I think I may have seen her around. Not sure."

"He never mentioned her." She sounds confused and a little disappointed. As if Sheldon had gone and taken secrets with him, and broken the link she had with me by removing my picture.

"He probably intended to. But..."

"Yes, I expect so, my dear; he really left us both too soon, I think."

We sit and cry together for a few minutes.

"You take the locket anyway. I know he'd want you to have it. Do what you like with the picture of the silly girl inside. I expect it's just someone he saw briefly and didn't really know. You know he was always taking pictures of people and animals." She sniffs and wipes her eyes.

"Yes. Okay." I smile. "I know."

She closes the locket again and fastens the chain around my neck as my last remaining tear drips on her hand.

"That's settled then. You'll keep this and I will tell you a little about my Mother and Father, while you stay for dinner. The twins are looking forward to seeing you." She changes the subject completely. "And I want you to promise that you will still come and see us every so often. I am sure Steve would like that as well."

"Sure. Of course I will."

"Okay, how about you help me set the table while I put the dinner on? I've never heard what you plan to do with your life when you finish school."

"Sure," I say.

I can't tell her that the girl in the locket is Harriet from the restaurant and club in Metro. Besides, I need time to think why Sheldon had put her in there. He always had his little camera with him and he understood people better than Freud. The trouble is I don't even understand myself.

Dad tells me that he's spoken to Turner who agreed that things had to move on. There is no point in raking up the past. Best let alternate worlds sit out there somewhere else where they should be. No good would come of the two worlds colliding, Turner said.

I am not sure Dad quite agrees with this philosophy; but I think he is keen to get some closure as well. However, Turner agrees that Dad should have the vacuum machine for a token donation. The school wants rid of it in any case. And Turner convinced the school board that such an old machine should no longer be on the premises, even as a curiosity.

Dad and Iain build a concrete plinth at the bottom of the garden, run electricity to it and build a huge hangar to accommodate the machine. They do this over a period of two months alongside the extensions and extra bedroom for the house. Iain does most of the work, with the help of a local builder. Dad helps in the evenings when he returns from school. When everything is complete, Dad supervises the relocation of the machine, with a specialised haulage company.

The plan is to refurbish everything and to use it for research. Dad is going to do some research and write up his papers on Quantum Theory and Iain decided he'd sign up on a technician course as a mature student and work as Dad's lab assistant and IT specialist. Dad invites him to stay with us in the extra bedroom and I marvel at my Dad's evolution. Has he done this by design, or is it simply order arising from chaos?

A few weeks later there are some technical discussions around the effects of our trip. Had we aged at all? At first they tiptoe around the idea that Jonathan would have come back whole again. Then we flat out discuss it, as I bite back the tears.

"Your hair never returned right away," Iain points out.

"No," I agree. "And it wouldn't be fair to tell Jonathan anything else. It could only hurt him, since there is no machine to come back."

We have a look at the cuff I had brought back; it doesn't power up here, which dad can't explain. He wants to take it apart, but I won't let him. "It is best as a useless souvenir of time when people were handcuffed for their own freedom," I tell him. Dad just looks at me, and smiles.

I make one huge mistake; I allow one of my teachers to take my ingot to a metallurgist. Stupid, because it turns out to be Rhodium; one of the rarest elements on earth is one of the most abundant metals in Wellorsland. The teacher becomes desperate to understand where I had found a large ingot of a metal worth more than gold. I tell him I can't remember; somewhere years ago on a school geology trip is the best I can think of. Dad simply says "Impulsive" and smiles. He is right, I had not thought about it; the consequences could have been worse. What if the metal had not been one that existed at home?

As it was, the last I heard, my teacher is spending every weekend climbing hills, everywhere there had been a field trip.


< < < < < > > > > >

"Dad, I have one thing I have to tell you and one thing I am not going to tell you and I don't want you to ask."

"This sounds ominous."

"When I attended the therapist she referred me to the General Physician."

"Something is wrong?"

"Not exactly, I guess it depends how you look at it."

"Go on?"

"You've guessed already!"

"Don't be ridiculous. You know I am the world's worst guesser, just get on with it."

"The Doctor congratulated me, asked me if I had planned to have a baby, and told me that I was having one anyway."

"Well," he says quietly.

"Well? That's all you are going to say?"

"You are not going to answer my next question. So I guess we will jump to the next stage."

"I am keeping it," I say quickly.

"University?"

"I am still going."

"Then congratulations. You will be a mother. Unexpected but we will be okay. I wish..."

"...Mum could see," I finish for him.

I go up and hug him. Neither of us cries. I am thinking that everything happens for a reason, I sense a special boy growing inside me, and I imagine Dad is still thinking that I am impulsive.

Printed in Poland
by Amazon Fulfillment
Poland Sp. z o.o., Wrocław

61147646R00235